EVE OF DESPAIR

Other Books by D.I. Telbat

Dark Edge: Prequel to The COIL Series

The COIL Series: Christian Suspense (5)

Distant Boundary: Prequel to The COIL Legacy

The COIL Legacy Series: Christian Suspense (3)

COIL Legacy Collection: 3 Books in 1 Volume

The ELM Series: America's Last Days (3+)

The RESOLUTION Series: America's Last Days (4)

The STEADFAST Series: America's Last Days (6)

STEADFAST Collection: 6 Novellas in 1 Volume

Last Dawn Series: America's Last Days (4)

Leeward Set: Where Christians Dare (2)

Never Lost Series: Trafficking Rescue Novels (2)

Arabian Variable

Called To Gobi

God's Colonel

Soldier of Hope

Short Story Collections

EVE OF DESPAIR

America's Last Days

BOOK TWO OF THE ELM SERIES

D.I. TELBAT

Every Life Matters

IN SEASON PUBLICATIONS
USA

Printed in the United States of America

EVE OF DESPAIR: America's Last Days
/ D.I. Telbat -- 1st ed.

Categories: Futuristic Christian Fiction;
Christian Suspense

D.I. Telbat / In Season Publications
https://ditelbat.com
https://books2read.com/DITelbat

ISBN 978-0-9864103-0-7

Cover Design by Streetlight Graphics

To the Despairing:
May they remember their Rock.
Psalm 42

Acknowledgements

The team that works with us to whip every manuscript into shape grows more vast every year. Thank you to everyone who sees the Casperteins as I do and shares the same faith in and for Jesus Christ. Firstly, thank you to the dependable Dee who has remained vigilant toward perfection for every book since the beginning. My thanks to my on-the-ground faithful proofreader, Sharon, for her continued input and encouragement. And thanks to our Beta-Reading Team who has proven themselves many times over by advising, editing, and reviewing. My books wouldn't be as clean of errors as they are without their input. May God greatly bless each of you for your kindness toward me and my mission!

Map of San Diego, California

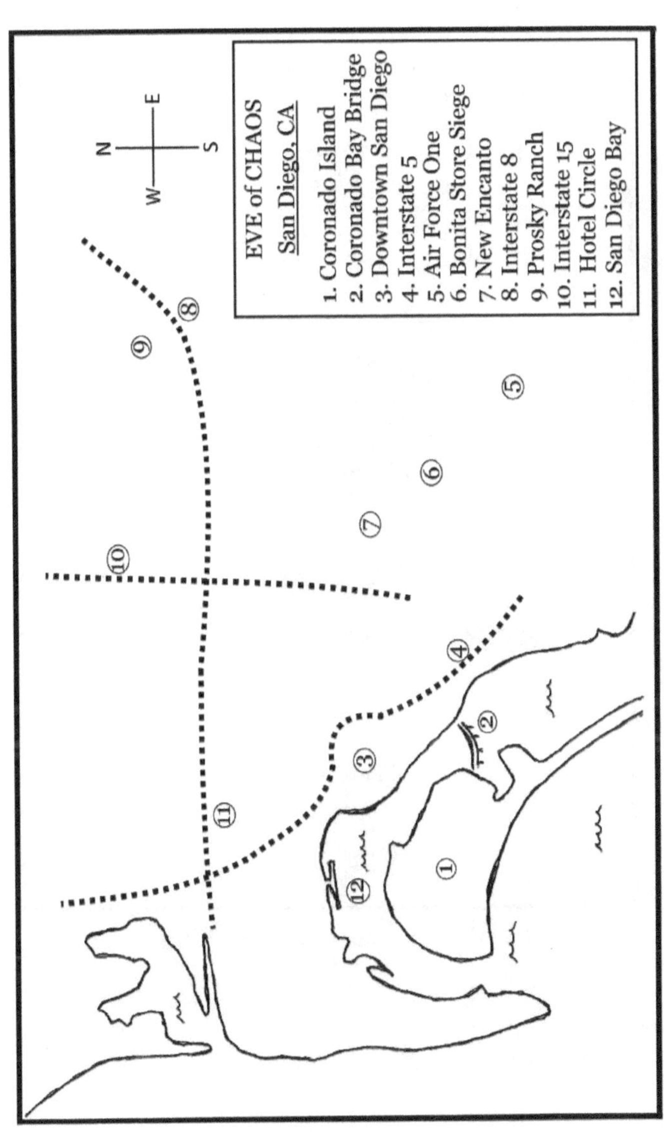

Map of The Garden

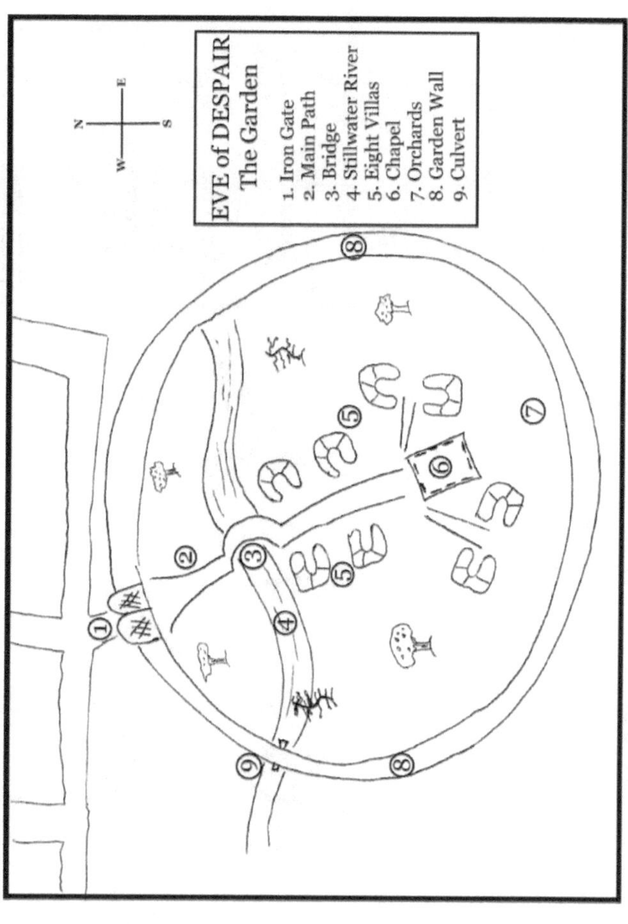

Preface

Previously in *EVE of CHAOS . . .*

Millions have died in America from the Meridia Virus and most communities are ruled by roaming bandits. Panic and starvation have cost even more lives in the days and weeks that followed what is now called Pan-Day. Survivors hide in whatever shelter is nearest to water, cautiously searching for food that scavengers may have overlooked.

But the Caspertein family is not hiding. In downtown San Diego, they investigated the original biological attack, then prepared provisions and security measures long before Pan-Day arrived. Led by Titus Caspertein and his young son, Levi, a small band of followers of Jesus Christ have taken up the ELM motto: *Every Life Matters*. Rather than shrink away from the spreading strife, they insert themselves into the surrounding neighborhoods to offer aid, rescue, and survival skills to liberate those who suffer from fear and famine. Above all, they carry with them a message of living hope and eternal peace because of the good news of Jesus Christ.

Titus is accompanied not only by his twenty-year-old son, but also by his wife, Annette, living in a fortified condominium two blocks from San Diego Bay. They've adopted a Down syndrome child named Gabby, and in Levi's apartment lives an ex-bandit named Dusty, whose lifestyle was disrupted when Levi showed him mercy during a rescue mission.

Also living with the Casperteins is Carla Criswell, who keeps her last name a secret since her father is newly-elected President Criswell of the Pacific States. This government is run from Coronado Island under the ruthlessness of General Brogdon and his cruel sergeant from Canada, Dom Lesage. The Pacific States Defense Forces (PSDF) raid and confiscate provisions far and wide by the might of their five thousand soldiers for the families they support.

COIL operatives from the past have also taken shelter at the ELM headquarters—heroes like ex-Interpol Agent Oleg Saratov, KON Operative Avery "Chevy" Hewitt, and ex-CIA PRS Agent Wes Trimble with his wife, Wynter, Titus' younger sister.

By one-eyed Wes Trimble's counsel, Titus has implemented a small misinformation campaign to throw off the PSDF from fully identifying ELM's leadership and strength. The PSDF wants the superior non-lethal battle rifles that ELM uses, as well as the influence the Casperteins hold to sway public opinion within the city's struggling population. The misinformation spread by Levi and Wes is meant to subtly offer the fictional name Maddix Striber as a benefactor of ELM. If ELM's enemies chase a ghost, Wes has reasoned, then ELM will be safer. The Maddix Striber name has been dropped in the hearing of outsiders who wish them harm, and will hopefully serve as a smoke screen.

During one rescue mission, Levi crosses a man named Dooley, who'd shot and grilled a traveler's horse. One of the women with Dooley is mistakenly tranquilized and Levi shares the horse meat with the starving townspeople. Dooley leaves the area, but not before threatening Levi.

As Jesus Christ tarries His appearing, His people will seek to remain obedient in San Diego—sharing the gospel and standing against violent threats in the region. No one will be ignored. Every soul is important. After all, every life matters to God.

Chapter One

It was evening. Oliver Gleason stood on the street in front of his house and watched the orange glow of flames reflect off low, dark clouds. Either someone's cook fire had gotten away from them or anarchists were starting fires. This wouldn't be the first time. The blaze was creeping closer to where Oliver had barely provided for his girlfriend and son the past six months.

He glanced toward the front door. Milli Lusis, his sweetheart since junior high, had crawled through the hole in the otherwise barricaded door and now stood gazing up at the evening sky as well. The smoke was heavy in the air. There was no hiding this potential danger from her. Her fragile soul needed constant attention and reassurance. Sometimes, he kept the truth from her entirely—when their water was low or when he'd found yet another neighbor had been killed.

Six months had passed since Pan-Day—the collapse of American society, including the electrical grid. The Meridia Virus had sparked quarantines across entire cities. Oliver had fortunately listened to his parents who'd helped him stock up on food and water for his small family in the middle-class suburb of San Diego. But the food had run out. The twenty-five-year-old had plucked a rifle off a dead body and learned to load and shoot it accurately. His family had lasted this long on the meat of stray dogs and bartering for vegetables within a tiny community network. But the approaching flames threatened everything. They had nowhere to go!

"Why would they be burning?" Milli asked as she joined his side. Her unwashed red hair was tucked under a ratty blanket she used as a shawl over her shoulders. "What is it, Oliver?"

Shifting his bolt action rifle to his left hand, he took her hand in his. Smiling, he lied to her as he had a hundred times before.

"I'm sure it's nothing." He cleared his throat against the heavy smoke drifting like swamp fog. "See the breeze? It's blowing toward the desert. Go ahead to bed. I'll keep an eye on it."

She watched the darkening sky another moment.

"If you're sure." She kissed his bearded cheek. "I'll take in your jeans tomorrow, okay?"

"Okay." He grimaced at her reminder that they were still losing weight. It was shameful that he wasn't a better provider. But he'd only been a minimum wage construction laborer straight out of high school with no vision for the future. Like most people his age, he'd been too wrapped up in social media and material possessions to build necessary skills for Pan-Day's aftermath. "I'll come inside in a little while."

Milli left and ducked through the hole in the door. Their son, Rory, was probably still awake in his room. Oliver had taught the six-year-old to be sure to blow out his candle when he was done playing. The youngster had become obsessed with the game of chess since Oliver had taught him a few months earlier how the pieces moved. Keeping the child well-supplied with homemade candles for his mock-chess games where he played both sides was a minor inconvenience for Oliver. The well-mannered boy kept himself entertained, and that allowed Oliver to scavenge for food and supplies, or to comfort Milli through her spells of despair.

Night fell on the neighborhood, but the stars couldn't be seen through the smoke above. Oliver's eyes stung and his lungs burned. He tried to tell himself that the glowing night sky northward was moving east or that it only seemed brighter since the sky was now darker. But, no.

The fire was drawing nearer. And the building noise was unmistakable, like a commercial jet engine upon takeoff.

Oliver turned from the orange sky and faced west. He'd scouted around the area only a few hundred yards, searching abandoned houses for forgotten supplies. It gave him a chill to think of the horrors that lay beyond the areas he'd explored. There had to be more survivors out there, like the couple of families he'd found two blocks south. They'd taught him how to butcher a dog for meat and how to plant sweet potatoes in the spring and to harvest them in the fall. They were probably watching the looming disaster approach them as well.

It was unlikely that Oliver would've met his neighbors or learned from them if he hadn't first been approached by Levi Caspertein, the blond, lone traveler who'd spoken volumes in just a few minutes of interaction three months earlier. Levi had changed his life, given him hope, and equipped him with bits of truth that had given Oliver the ability to endure. And it was Levi who Oliver now considered going to find. If this fire really was approaching as he feared . . .

The Casperteins lived downtown. A couple others in Oliver's small network had heard rumors of the heavily armed and self-sufficient family who kept the peace around Seaport Village and provided safe refuge for the needy who came to them. Oliver hadn't even given his name to Levi that fateful day, but he'd sensed the stranger's genuine offer of hospitality. However, Seaport Village was all the way downtown—several miles of the unknown stretched between downtown and where Oliver now lived. And Oliver had Milli and young Rory to think about.

From his back pocket, Oliver drew out a rolled-up book, its cover wrapped entirely in duct tape. One of the pieces of advice Oliver remembered from Levi was that Oliver should find a Bible. After searching for three nights, he'd found one in a house office one lane to the west. He'd even begun reading it when he knew Milli was sleeping, busy with chores, or playing chess with Rory. The Bible didn't make much sense to Oliver, but he didn't doubt that Levi Caspertein could help him understand its promises and message of compassion. However, Milli had always sworn there was no God. To avoid upsetting her further, he'd kept his Bible reading quiet, and even plastered the cover with duct tape so it looked like a self-help manual or something a plumber might carry in his back pocket.

Flames over the house tops to the north licked at the sky. Oliver flinched at the sound of a gunshot from far away, then another closer. This wasn't an accidental fire. Something terrible was happening! Destruction approached, though it was unthinkable that there could be a more destructive force than the isolation and starvation already plaguing the land.

Far, far up the dark street to the east, a handheld torch seemed to float across an intersection. Oliver crouched low, realizing the torch wasn't floating—someone was carrying it. Then two more torches followed the first. As he watched in disbelief, flames grew in the wake of the torch bearers. He heard shouting, then a gunshot.

They were burning the houses! Oliver didn't know who they were or why they were doing it, but they were coming his way!

He rushed back to the door and leaned his rifle against the outside of the house. After kneeling, he crawled through the door, his mind burdened with thoughts of personal inadequacy to flee with his family. His survival thus far could be traced back to his familiar environment and the kindness of strangers he'd met since Pan-Day. How could he survive with Milli and Rory if he led them into unfamiliar neighborhoods where unkind survivors hoarded and defended what little they had?

"Get up, Milli!" The roar of the approaching flames was loud even inside the house. "Get Rory ready. Hurry! I'll grab our stuff!"

Regardless of her fragile spirit, she leapt from the mattress that lay on the floor and drew on trousers. Months earlier, they'd burned the wood bed frame, and the rest of the room consisted only of piles of clothes and a large cooler they used as a pantry. But the pantry was usually empty.

A candle still burned in the living room where Oliver's eyes darted over the heaps of gear he'd scavenged and collected. What to take now? He tugged an empty backpack from a hook on the wall and began shoving items inside—dome tent, two water bottles, a bag of lighters, water purification tablets, an extra knife. After stuffing in a few more necessities, the backpack was too full to zip closed, but he hung it over one shoulder, anyway. They were leaving so much behind!

"Oliver, what do we do?" Milli held Rory by the shoulders. The boy carried only his travel chess set, hugging the box against his chest like a life preserver. "Is that the fire? I thought it was burning toward the desert!"

"Get your coat!" Oliver snatched up a tarp and an assortment of clothing. "Go outside! We have to get clear of the house. Now!"

Milli found her coat, then she hustled Rory to the hole in the door. She crawled through first, then drew Rory after her. Oliver thrust his armful of gear through the hole, then pushed the backpack into Milli's hands. For a moment, he surveyed the interior of the house. The candle in the living room was still burning. It hurt him deep inside to leave the home in which he'd raised Rory, where they'd found refuge during the long months of danger and hardship. The blankets were still nailed over the windows, and a hose he'd attached to the rain gutter outside was still taped to an empty water jug. All his projects and safekeeping—now abandoned.

In front of the house, Rory was the one weeping instead of Milli for a change. The firelight flickered on her face, revealing sheer terror.

After giving Milli the overflowing backpack, Oliver took up his rifle, tarp, and sleeping bag. The clothes he'd haphazardly gathered were left behind as he led the way to the street.

"Back! Back!" He ordered their retreat back to the house as he noticed the men with torches were only one house away. The street was lit up like apocalyptic daylight. "Over the back fence!"

"Oliver!" Milli cried in panic as she obeyed, dragging Rory with her.

"Shhh!" he hissed, worried they might be heard over the roaring noise. "No talking!"

The chain link fence at the back of the property was only five feet high, but Rory wasn't very coordinated at only six years old. The youngster had spent more time playing on his phone when the power had been on than running around the neighborhood as boys should.

Quickly, Oliver helped Milli over the fence, letting her tumble onto the dead grass. Then, as fast as he could, Oliver tossed their few belongings over the fence, some of it landing on Milli's head and shoulders.

The men with torches were at their house!

He lifted Rory over the fence. As soon as Milli reached for her son, Oliver let him go. Mother and child collapsed together on the dry ground. Galvanized steel gouged and tore at Oliver's forearm as he climbed over and gathered his family.

"Over here, quickly!" He didn't give them time to find their feet or gather their things. He tugged them in the flickering light to the edge of a backyard pool. "Milli, go first!"

The waterless pool was anything but empty. It had become a garbage dump and septic tank for the neighbors before they'd died of the Meridia Virus. Whatever disease might've hidden in the smelly refuse, it was now their only refuge.

Milli dropped into the deep end of the pool and into several inches of muck. Oliver lowered Rory to her uplifted arms, then he dropped into the concrete pit with her. Somewhere above, he'd lost everything he'd brought from the house, even the rifle!

Men whooped and hollered at each other, then they moved on as the flames grew and rose and the heat radiated closer to the family. Oliver held Milli who held Rory against the side of the pool. Embers floated on the night breeze and caught fire briefly on the piles of debris.

The smoke was suffocating. Oliver tore off his t-shirt to cover Rory's face, then he gave his thermal to Milli to breathe through. He buried his own face in Milli's red hair and mentally willed his lungs to function through the ash and black smoke and choking odors of superheated toxins all around them going up in flames.

Minutes passed and their situation worsened as the neighbor's house that bordered the pool was also set afire. But then the night breeze shifted and the smoke lifted to float southward. Rory and Milli coughed aloud, and Oliver let them. The evildoers rampaging through the neighborhood seemed to be gone, but the heat from the structures was still too intense to climb out of the pool.

Thirty minutes passed. Oliver gathered a few pieces of cardboard nearby for his family to kneel on instead of standing as they waited out the fires. A distant scream and gunshot reminded Oliver that even while the fire danger was past, the violent danger was still present.

Finally, Oliver climbed his way to the shallow end of the pool and ascended to level ground. The flames were low. His house had been reduced to rubble no higher than his shoulder. Neighboring houses fared no better. Smoldering or burning structures haunted the landscape in every direction. Everywhere Oliver gazed, the world seemed remarkably flat and empty, unrecognizable.

He lifted Rory out of the pool, then Milli. After they climbed back over the fence, she began gathering items they'd dropped.

"What do we do?" Milli asked him softly, clearly guarding her voice from Rory. "Where will we go now?"

"I don't know yet." He drew on his long sleeved thermal again and unrolled the sleeping bag. Whatever items couldn't fit inside the backpack, he stuffed into the sleeping bag. "Milli, you carry the backpack. Rory, you okay, son?"

"Yeah." The boy examined his bare arm. He'd pulled on jeans after he'd been hauled from his bedroom, and he wore only a thin t-shirt. "I got burned from a spark."

"Can you make do?" Oliver was still choking from the smoke in the air making his voice raspy. "We can put a bandage on it when we get out of this mess."

"I'm okay." Rory held his chess set closer. "But now it's cold."

Oliver fit his own t-shirt over the boy's head for an added layer, then he picked up the sleeping bag of gear. He hefted the items over his shoulder and Milli handed him his rifle for the other shoulder.

"Let's see if Bruce and his family made it." Oliver faced southeast. "Let's go this way. Stay together. And no talking."

Bruce Ramis had taught Oliver how to field dress a dog for meat. Oliver had proven himself as a marksman, so the Ramis family had traded vegetables from their garden with Oliver and he shared his meat with them. Their relationship was strained since they competed for what seemed to be a dwindling food supply, but Oliver didn't know anyone else who might give him advice or help.

The Ramis family lived only two blocks away, but it took Oliver twenty minutes to lead Milli and Rory over and around the blackened and smoldering structures. Oliver had never shot at a man before, and he wasn't sure he could, so he preferred to move cautiously along the way rather than keep his rifle ready to fire.

The swath of fire destruction spanned several blocks wide and continued southwesterly toward the ocean. Bruce's house was one of the buildings that'd been lit on fire along the eastern side of the turmoil. Oddly, the houses farther on remained dark and untouched.

When Oliver walked up, Bruce was stumbling through the ashes of his residence.

"Stay here," Oliver told Milli. He dropped the sleeping bag and proceeded alone. In the last three months, he'd not exposed Milli or Rory to outsiders. No one could be absolutely trusted. "I'll talk to him."

Stepping into the ashes, he reached Bruce, who didn't seem to be his normal alert self. Bruce was a survivalist, the one from whom Oliver had learned how to collect rainwater and plant a garden. Now, the man sobbed openly and carried no rifle.

"Bruce?" Touching the man's arm, Oliver turned him. "Where's—?"

He didn't want to say Bruce's wife's name, or his son's name. The answer seemed obvious.

"Come over here, Bruce." He led the distraught man to sit on a metal water tank that had weathered the flames inside what had been the garage. "Take a swallow."

The man accepted the water bottle from Oliver, took a gulp, then passed it back.

"It's all gone." Bruce's face was blackened except where tears had left streaks. "*They're both gone!*"

Oliver glanced back at Milli where she stood watching from the edge of the charred property. He didn't want to be insensitive toward Bruce, but he needed to get his family out of there.

"Who was it, Bruce?" Oliver coughed up ash from his lungs, then wiped his mouth. "Why'd they do this?"

"They surprised us." Bruce shook his head. "We were all sleeping. Now, look . . ."

Where was the tough survivalist he'd once known? Oliver hadn't come here to comfort Bruce but to be guided by him. Levi Caspertein had encouraged them to work together to endure, but Bruce had always been the one Oliver had relied on—until now.

"Do you have any gear stashed someplace?" Oliver asked. "You can't stay here. They could come back."

"It was that Dooley Gang." Bruce suddenly looked up. "He's insane! He shot my boy right out front there, right on the porch. He asked only one question."

"What question?" Oliver wasn't sure Bruce was thinking straight. The man had never before mentioned anyone named Dooley. "What did he say?"

"He asked for someone named Maddix Striber, then when Bruce Junior didn't answer, Dooley shot him then and there, on the porch. Nothing left. Nothing . . ."

Indeed, Oliver studied the front door area of the ruins, but saw no body—of the son or the wife.

"Who's Maddix Striber?" Oliver leaned forward. "Bruce?"

"How do I know?" Bruce stood and wrung his hands with a fresh bout of sobs. "It makes no sense, burning us all out just because he's looking for someone."

"Bruce, we need to get outta here. What do you think about going to the bay? Maybe find Levi Caspertein. Remember him? There's gotta be something to the rumors about them, right? We'll be safe there."

"Nobody's safe from Dooley. He's insane." Bruce suddenly spun on Oliver and clutched his arm. "Don't go, Oliver. You'll never make it. It's too dangerous. Think of the distance. The cutthroats are everywhere. Better to go back home. Home . . ."

"Hey, Bruce, I have no home left, either. Come on. Why don't you come with us?"

"No home." Bruce wandered away. "No home . . ."

Oliver watched the man fall to his knees in the ashes. He hadn't explained who the Dooley Gang was, but now

Oliver understood they'd caused this carnage in their search for someone. Unfortunately, Oliver couldn't take care of both his family and Bruce at the same time.

Returning to Milli, he rested his hand on Rory's shoulder. The fires dwindled in the distance, but the barren landscape was still visible.

"What'd he say?" Milli asked.

"We're on our own." Oliver knelt and drew his son closer into one arm. "Remember the young man I told you I met a few months ago? Levi Caspertein? His family lives on the bay, down by the shorefront. They're good people."

"How do you know they're still there?" Milli hugged her midsection. "There are no good people left, Oliver."

He felt the bulge of the duct-taped Bible in his back pocket, but he didn't want to tell Milli he'd begun searching for God on Levi Caspertein's advice.

"It's not safe anywhere around here." Oliver sighed. "I'm sure we can find our way to the ocean, and maybe find the Casperteins. We have to try. There's nowhere else. And we have no supplies . . . or food. We'll need to work together. Be strong together. Like we have been."

"Are we gonna die, Dad?" Rory asked.

Though Oliver was inclined to recall something hopeful he'd read in the Bible about God, Milli was watching him and she didn't believe God was real. He didn't want to upset her further.

"We'll be okay," Oliver said instead, "if we can find the Casperteins."

☩

Neil Dooley stumbled out of the bunk house, leaned over the wooden rail, and vomited into San Diego Bay. Remaining there for a few minutes, he drooled and tried to remember what had happened the night before to cause his eyes, lungs, and throat to burn like they were. Had someone sprayed him with mace? As someone with asthma, he fumbled for his last inhaler and sucked a dose into his lungs.

His hangover that morning slowly gave way to the blurry memory of the fire party he and his gang had had the evening before.

"Wow, I shouldn't drink so much."

He wiped his mouth and stood upright, sucking the clean ocean air into his smoke-scorched lungs. Fifty yards away, two of the men in his gang were fishing off the pier over the long, southern branch of the bay. A bucket sat beside the fishermen. Dooley hoped they'd caught something. Anything was better than numbly gnawing on the bland pretzels they'd stashed—millions of them from the local factory.

Footsteps on the boardwalk caused Dooley to feel for his sidearm in the shoulder holster under his left arm. He'd slept with the gun again, and now his ribs hurt along with his pounding headache. Kid Irling, his trusted companion of mischief, walked toward him. Though Kid was ten years older, he'd never questioned Dooley's leadership. Until recently, Dooley had kept his gang fed, drunk, and partying. But he'd heard their complaints. Everything had changed that fateful day when they'd crossed the blond youth over grilled horse meat. Their luck had gone downhill after that confrontation. Even his girlfriend, Fran, hadn't been the same.

"We've got a problem." Kid rested his forearms on the rail. He was a long-haired, scruffy, tattooed ex-con who'd once worked at the nearby trampoline park, servicing rich families who visited Pepper Park. Now, Kid carried an assault rifle with a sliding stock and a flash suppressor painted red. "We lost two guys at the farm. They ran off with our last two pigs."

Dooley cursed. Since he'd spent most of his adult life as a law student, he didn't know much about running a farm or fishery. But he knew they needed animals to make more animals, and that was impossible when his people kept killing and eating their stock.

"Add them to the list. You know their names?"

"Yeah. It's getting to be a long list."

"Everyone who's crossed us, we'll repay one at a time. Who's going to stop us?"

"Nobody around here." Kid spit into the water. "That was a pretty wild night, huh?"

"We left our mark. That was the point." Dooley wouldn't admit, not even to Kid, that he'd lost control the evening before. At least the neighborhood they'd torched was poor and had nothing. It wasn't rational to indiscriminately burn houses down that they hadn't fully searched. But he couldn't confess he was possessed with one goal: finding Maddix Striber—the only name the young blond soldier had boldly left him over a month earlier. "We'll find him. Someone will talk eventually."

"Maybe we could try a different tactic," Kid said as he lit up a cigarette. "I have an idea but I wanted to run it past you without the others around."

"Well, speak up."

"So, we've been raiding pretty much everything in sight for weeks. What do we have to show for it? You don't even have a bunch of inhalers like you wanted to have. You must be running low, right? And there's still no sign of Maddix Striber."

"It's just bad luck." Dooley cursed, took Kid's cigarette from him, and threw it in the water. "Didn't you get enough smoke last night? Yes, I'm on my last inhaler, so don't make it worse."

"Listen." Kid checked the boardwalk for anyone nearby. "We have enough information about a stronghold within a day from here. A few of us could sneak in there, you know, like refugees, instead of raiding them. Maybe we could go there one or two at a time undercover, and figure out how to take whatever they have. You know, take them down from the inside. And we might even come across someone who knows Maddix Striber."

"Hmm, it's an idea." Dooley licked his lips. "From the inside, huh? We could change our names and no one will know it's even us."

"We've hardly left any survivors where we've raided. No one will know what we look like."

"You'll need to get a haircut." Dooley nodded at his man's stringy hair. "Have Fran give you a nice fade."

"Nah, I'm no gentleman." Kid scoffed. "I can't pull off the clean-cut look like you can."

"Not even for a serious score?" Dooley faced Kid. "You've thought about this. What's our target? We've avoided strongholds because they're usually armed better than we are."

"The people we've questioned have talked about downtown. There's supposed to be some refuge that takes walk-ins. Where there's people, there's definitely water."

"And probably inhalers." Dooley stifled a shiver. "I'll shoot myself before I suffocate to death."

"So, downtown?" Kid asked. "Even undercover, we'll need to be really careful. It'll be dangerous."

"That's never stopped us before. We'll know after a day with them what they have to take."

"There won't be much room for error with the Pacific States Defense Forces right across the bay."

"We won't know until we look around down there. It's a good plan, Kid. And Fran will like it. She won't let me rest until I find this Maddix Striber."

"Women, huh?" Kid chuckled. "They take everything so personal."

"I'll be just as happy to see that blond guy put down. That was a week's worth of horse meat he stole from us. And he gave it to all those people! A total waste."

"Hey, we'll show them all. They'll regret they ever crossed us."

Quietly, they spoke of their plans to infiltrate whatever downtown civilization had been rebuilt. Dooley would go in first with Fran. He'd introduce himself by his first name only and seek out whoever was in charge. Kid and the rest of the gang would wander in a day later and blend in with whatever common people were around, prying them gently for information about resources, weaknesses, and local news.

Dooley returned to the bunkhouse and found Fran washing her face in a tub of fresh water. One reason he always returned to Pepper Park was for the desalination tanks they'd taken off the abandoned vessels at the nearby boat launch. Hundreds of them! They had an adequate supply of fresh water, and several of the park's buildings had been converted into living quarters for those eager to partake of the spoils of Dooley's raids. But the spoils had been light lately, which made Kid's change in tactics important to the survival of them all.

"We're leaving on a trip tomorrow morning." Dooley sat on the counter next to the water tub. The counter shelves had been removed where snacks and fishing tackle alike had been sold to tourists and visitors. "Should be exciting."

Fran dried her face on a mildewy towel, but she wasn't too fussy about the accommodations. He'd found her living on the street as a petty thief not long after Pan-Day. She was in her mid-twenties, and her wide, brown eyes gave her the impression of a gentle soul—at least until she spoke. But Dooley loved her for her cold mercilessness. It was hard to imagine her as a pretzel factory worker just a few months earlier—a quality control supervisor. Their current stores of pretzels were attributed to her idea to return to the factory and raid it before hungry civilians found the stash of snacks.

"So now you're deciding all alone where we go?" The bite in her voice made him feel small, but he hoped only she knew that. "We just got back last night."

"It's Kid's idea. We know there's a refuge for people downtown."

"You're forgetting that the same ones who told us about those people also said they're heavily armed. Are you trying to get us all killed?"

She pulled her brown hair back into a ponytail with eyes daring him to contradict her. Somehow, her wildness when drunk or high was worth being with her through her more critical moods.

"That's why we sneak in there. I mean, we go undercover. You and I can show up with some worn-out packs and moldy pretzels. They'll think we came from a long way off."

"I told you already, Dooley!" She stepped close and held up her finger with a dirty fingernail. "Keep our priorities straight. We find that creep who shot me and took our meat. Nothing else matters until we find Maddix Striber."

"Babe, I know, but we have to survive. We can go downtown and talk to people. They might know about Striber."

"Dooley, I want his head!" She fit on her own sidearm, one that she'd used to gun down fleeing civilians the night before. "I thought you cared about me. You don't know what it was like getting shot like that. I didn't know it was just a tranquilizer. I could've died! I thought I was dead. And you want to go socializing downtown? You're such a coward."

"Hey!" He fixed his sternest glare on his face. "Nobody steals from me, and nobody disrespects you, not while I'm alive! I'll kill Maddix Striber and whoever he's with. You'll have his head, babe, I guarantee it. We just have to keep moving to survive."

"That's more like it." She softened her tone and kissed him, touching his cheek like she hadn't belittled him moments earlier. "I'm good for you, Dooley. I keep you thinking about what matters. No one can treat us like

Maddix Striber did. We live in a new world now. We have to be jackals or we'll die with the herd. Do you love me, sweetie? Do you?"

"You know I do. Always and forever."

"What do we think of the weaklings around here?"

"They're only here for us to dominate."

"Dominance or death. Exactly." She smiled. "Is that what we're going downtown to do? To dominate?"

"Absolutely."

"And Maddix Striber?"

"Someone down there has to know his name. I'll find a way to get to him."

"How many are going with us?" she asked.

"You and I will go in alone, then Kid will come in with the rest as strangers to us the next day. But you'll need to call me Neil."

"Why Neil?"

"It's my first name. You can't call me Dooley. People know my last name."

"Neil is your first name?" She scoffed. "No wonder you use Dooley. Neil is a weak name for a weak nobody. Good thing it's temporary. Dooley is the man who takes care of business, isn't he?"

"Yeah, you know I am." He embraced her, but she pushed him back. "What is it?"

"If we leave tomorrow, you have to make sure things keep running around here. We need more eggs. And I'm not eating any more lizards. If we come back from downtown empty-handed, I don't want to starve. Make sure your guys come through for a change."

Dooley walked outside and stalked angrily to the park's entrance. Fran's favorite animal was the jackal, so he wasn't surprised she was such a predator toward him.

At the entrance of the park, he found one of the two sentries asleep. Dooley didn't blame the man for trying to catch up on lost sleep from the night before, but he still had to punch the careless guard in the mouth once he'd woken him. Vigilance was important. Besides, after the way Fran had talked down to him, he needed to do the same to someone else.

"Do your part or you're out of here!" Dooley yelled at the bleeding man. The park was only five acres along the waterfront, so others would've heard his warning as well. "There's always someone out there trying to get in here to take what's ours. Don't let me find you sleeping on shift again!"

He stomped away, knowing he'd let the sentry off easy. If Kid would've found the man sleeping, he would've put his boots to him.

Fran was right. Arrangements needed to be made for their absence. There was no telling how long they'd be gone downtown. Maybe they'd just take over the enterprise on the shoreline and move their operations there. Much depended on the stability of the resources in the city. How did they even get their fresh water? Probably desalination filters, he thought, but their filters were probably running low like his own. Other fresh water sources needed to be found.

But going undercover! It was risky, but not as dangerous as raiding communities across the South Bay and Lemon Grove. If everything went well, he'd find himself an even greater position to dominate the remnant sheep of the city. Dominate or die, as Fran always said.

And hopefully, when he got downtown, there would be something more than pretzels to eat!

Titus Caspertein bowed his head in his radio room. His heart was heavy, but there were no tears flowing. Maybe he was all cried out. The radio contacts he'd spoken to near and far reported very little good news. Ever since the Riverside Guard troops had been defeated in the north, subsequently expanding the PSDF territory, all frequency jammers had been switched off. Now by contacting radio operators across the nation, Titus had received reports that seemed to indicate the worst of humanity was prevailing in the wake of Pan-Day.

Society's condition before Pan-Day seemed to have uniquely prepared hearts to commit the worst crimes on a mass level. And where neighbors weren't attacking neighbors, survivors from Pan-Day were committing suicide at a rate Titus had never seen anywhere during his world travels.

Very few followers of Christ seemed to be effective lights in the midst of the darkness—at least in other locales beyond San Diego. Or maybe the saints in other cities and towns had all perished?

The radio at Titus' elbow crackled, interrupting his burdens of isolation and responsibility.

"Refugees incoming, Titus." It was Oleg Saratov's voice, his Russian-born partner from their COIL years. "I count eight. Over."

"Copy. I'll be down in a few minutes. Over."

He picked up his binoculars and left the radio room. His wife, Annette, wasn't in the kitchen where she was usually preparing meals—most often to feed other refugees who'd come to live in the apartment buildings next door. She was probably either on the roof tending to the chickens in their coops or next door visiting with other families.

The screen door slid aside easily and Titus stepped onto his fortieth-floor apartment balcony. It faced south, but by standing on the left side, he could use his field glasses to gaze east. All day, they'd kept an eye out for expected refugees fleeing the devastating fires that had swept across the neighborhoods to the southeast. But only eight? Surely, there would be more to come.

The distant swath of burned residences was still smoking that afternoon. From Titus' height, he could see the path of burnt structures six or seven miles away. The damage couldn't have been caused naturally overnight.

Fires didn't burn in a straight line like that—across the wind. No, someone had intentionally set the inland neighborhood houses on fire. Maybe as many as one hundred homes had been torched.

He shifted his binoculars downward. The eight refugees approached the perimeter around their six tall apartment buildings. Titus and his men had built the perimeter from abandoned vehicles that had previously choked the streets. Oleg was at one of three perimeter gaps, waiting to meet the refugees. Though Titus couldn't hear what was said, Oleg's hand was raised in greeting and his battle rifle was slung on his back. Weeks earlier, Oleg had been shot in the hip by frightened civilians during a rescue mission, but the forty-seven-year-old veteran was beginning to lumber around like his old self. However, he was a few pounds heavier from lying around, eating Annette's cooking and enduring Carla's affections.

Alongside Oleg below was one-eyed Wes Trimble, Titus' brother-in-law, married to his sister, Wynter. They'd recently announced that Wynter was several weeks pregnant. His little sister was having a baby! It made his heart tremble with apprehension. A baby in this despairing world? It was possible that Titus was more concerned than the expecting parents. Of course, Annette was already doting over Wynter who hadn't even begun showing yet, and Wes was beaming and talking about fatherhood with all the family men next door.

Titus returned to the apartment and exchanged the binoculars for his Bible on the dining table. At the door, he donned his ammo vest and clipped on his battle rifle. He admired the rifle model that had earned the nickname "bullpup" in years past for its snub-nosed and stubby appearance. The action rested behind the trigger guard, but the .308 caliber still sported a mighty eighteen-inch barrel with a maximum range of six hundred yards. Though he had lethal rounds for the assault rifle to hunt deer and other wild animals, he kept it loaded with non-lethal tranquilizer rounds they called gel-tranqs.

Every time he picked up the rifle, he remembered the agreement he had with the others. Everyone on his team had agreed to use the non-lethal rounds to stand against potential aggressors. But not everyone in the ELM building believed as Titus did—that he didn't kill their enemies because Jesus Christ wouldn't want them to. Those who lived in the ELM building at least agreed that every life mattered, the motto Titus had implemented three months earlier to facilitate the gospel message that God offered through the Holy Scriptures. Since every soul matters to God, Titus couldn't with a free conscience commit to killing others made in God's image. No, his killing years as an international arms smuggler were long past.

In the hallway, Titus tugged on leather gloves to pull on a cable hand-over-hand to lower the dolly platform to the floors below.

"Going down?" Carla Criswell emerged from her apartment, plastic food containers in her arms. She rarely carried her rifle inside the ELM perimeter anymore, but she always carried the handheld radio to stay in contact with the team about their activities. "Perfect timing. Eight refugees, huh?"

"Yep." Titus stepped onto the platform, then waited until Carla braced herself. "Is that Oleg's dinner? I should probably taste-test that before he wolfs it down."

Turning slightly away, Carla acted as if she were protecting the containers from his very gaze.

"I've seen you Casperteins eat. Once you start, you don't stop."

"It ain't easy having an endless appetite!"

He laughed as he lowered the platform to the bottom of the first stage. As they descended the stairs two floors for the next stage, Titus reflected on how far the woman next to him had come.

Carla had recently shed her arm brace from a broken collarbone. Her injury had occurred not long after she'd been burned and horribly scarred from jet fuel. The right side of her head and face had been burned so badly that her frizzy platinum hair no longer grew on that side of her head. But she'd found a companion in Oleg, who was only a few years older than her forty-two years. The two were very opposite in personality, but Titus had witnessed Carla's attachment to the oftentimes ungroomed Russian. There was safety in the ex-Interpol agent's presence, and though Carla hadn't yet received Jesus' gift of salvation from sin's penalty, Oleg wasn't one to push anyone away.

Titus alone knew Carla's secret, and he had assured her that it was hers to reveal when or if she wanted—that her last name was Criswell. Her father was President Arthur Criswell of the Pacific States, residing in the government capital across San Diego Bay on Coronado Island. Since Carla had arrived at the ELM building, she'd apparently preferred the company of Christians over the might of the Pacific States Defense Forces with her father. The PSDF was a force led by General Brogdon, who was sometimes at odds with ELM's passive stance in government affairs, but for a few weeks, there'd been peace between the two parties.

"Shouldn't there be more than eight refugees?" Carla asked as they rode down the second dolly stage. "After so many houses were burned?"

Becoming used to Carla's inquisitive nature, Titus expected such questions from her. She'd once been a journalist who'd flown on Air Force One, advocating for many of the administration's progressive ideals. She seemed to have recently realized her old beliefs put her at odds with her own survival, like her old push for gun control, but her journalistic tendencies had persisted.

"Eight isn't many." Titus frowned. "Let's pray that's all who were living over there, or other refugees fled elsewhere."

"Where else is there for people to run? I mean, where else is safe?"

"I don't know," he said somberly. "Things are still shifting a lot east of Interstate 5. We don't know what infrastructure exists out there, but there probably isn't much."

He made a conscious decision right then that sharing bad reports from his radio conversations would be unnecessary for his family and friends, unless they needed to know for tactical reasons. There was just too much discouraging news out there.

When they reached the first floor, Titus looked in on Gabby Hillerman, his and Annette's adopted daughter with Down syndrome. As usual, she was among the Toggenburg goats that Titus had welcomed into the building with their shepherd, Gustavo Hernandez. The tall, elderly Hispanic man sat at a desk where he often made his milk distribution calculations on behalf of ELM. Three milking stations had been set up, but at that afternoon hour, only bearded Conrad Prosky sat milking one doe.

The fifty-year-old jowly man still bore the scar above one ear where a bullet had grazed and left him with debilitating brain damage. He'd once been a rancher who'd commanded a violent private army, but now he followed the orders of Gabby. It made Titus smile. She couldn't speak herself, but her unintelligible sounds accompanied by her commanding gestures kept the ex-rancher in line like he was her little brother. Conrad was quickly becoming known as the Goat Man, since he could often be found in the goat pen with Gabby, caring for the small herd.

Titus passed through the steel door on the north side of the building and turned east with Carla fast-pacing to keep up with his lengthy stride. Oleg was leading the eight refugees through the vehicle perimeter as Titus approached. He used his left hand to comb his blond hair aside, hoping he was presentable, but then noticed the refugees' appearance. Their faces were blackened by ash and smoke, and their possessions were few.

"Oh, perfect timing, Carla!" Oleg welcomed her by accepting the containers of food and passed one to Wes. Together, he and Wes opened the containers of bread, beans, fish, and vegetables to offer to the new arrivals. "Here, there's plenty for everyone."

With amusement for Titus, it didn't seem to dawn on Oleg that he was giving away his own dinner, which Carla had fixed especially for his robust appetite. She opened her mouth to object, but Titus touched her shoulder and nodded at the refugees—four adults and four children, two families. They gobbled the food with their fingers like they hadn't eaten in days. And perhaps they hadn't since their clothing hung off their slender frames like victims of starvation.

Carla lowered her eyes to the last bowl still in her hands, then popped off the lid to offer fresh nut bread to all.

Annette arrived at a jog from one of the other apartment buildings ELM had placed under its protection. Avery "Chevy" Hewitt followed, his Bible in hand and a smile on his face to welcome the new people. The engineer and mechanic had received a giant Chevrolet tattoo on his chest during his many years in a state prison, but now he eagerly welcomed new arrivals who would undoubtedly make demands on his own time and expertise. After all, he was the one who would make more apartments hospitable with electricity and plumbing.

In seconds, the eight had been whisked away by the ELM greeters, and Titus was left standing on the swept pavement between the high-rise apartment buildings. The courtyard area was kept clean of wind-blown garbage only because they'd employed two whole families to be responsible for cleanliness inside the ELM perimeter. Payment came by way of food and supplies gathered or grown. There was no shortage of people now that Levi, Titus' son, had brought the Hillcrest Hopefuls downtown. Fifty men, women, and children now occupied one building. And a third building had been opened and prepared for additional residents, to which the eight were escorted.

The odor of fish reached Titus' nose. He turned to find Levi leading the daily fishing crew back from the bay. Looking at Levi was like looking at his younger self in a mirror, but Levi might've been even taller at twenty than Titus had been at that age. His narrow shoulders were slowly broadening from hard work, and he'd already received a few scars from conflicts in the past six months.

Though the fishermen and women appeared weary from a day of catching, cleaning, and filleting fish, Levi's gait was bouncy, even as he strolled beside one of two carts laden with fish. Titus guessed they had more halibut, unless they'd gone for yellowfin offshore. They'd been averaging about fifty fish a day over the last month, aided by a professional named Raymond Weaver who lived on the shore in a sailboat. Thanks to Ray joining ELM's network through Levi, the ELM residents had plenty of fish to distribute and often enough to barter with PSDF soldiers who patrolled inland from Coronado. Such commerce gave ELM unofficial safe access to the waters around the island and all the way out to sea.

"It ain't easy making a living with fish hooks stuck in your thumb!" Titus laughed as Levi walked up. The two shook hands like old friends. Levi had matured in Christian character and had learned to carry himself as a man who respected his elders. "I think that's a fresh piece of tape on your thumb."

"Yeah." The young man scowled at his taped left thumb—one of four digits taped if not stitched. "I think I should be given blunt-ended hooks and child-proofed fillet knives when I go fishing."

"Hey, at least you still have all your fingers!" Titus said. "I'd probably be missing an eye or two by now if I were doing your job every day."

Levi gestured at one of the buildings as his fishing crew took the fish into the Hopefuls' building from where they'd be distributed.

"New arrivals?" he asked as he stood next to his father. "From the fire?"

"Yeah." Titus frowned and rested his hands on his hips. "But only eight."

"Any word about what happened out there?"

"Wes is in there with your mother getting them settled. If they know anything, he'll find out."

Dustin "Dusty" Howard emerged from the Hopefuls' building, his arms burdened with wrapped fish fillets, enough for the twelve residents in the ELM building. Titus watched the reformed street bandit who Levi had taken in and led to faith in the Lord over a month earlier. In his mid-thirties, Dusty was skinny and much lighter than Levi, but he'd attached himself to the younger Caspertein like a brother. Together, they'd finished burying the deceased from the streets of the city and renewed the fishing industry on the shore—all in the last two months.

"I think I've earned a hot shower today." Dusty's exhaustion was obvious. "I'll drop the fish off with Wynter."

He didn't stop as he headed back to the ELM building where he lived as a roommate with Conrad and Levi.

"I'll be up in a little while," Levi called after him, then to his father, "I want to hear what happened from Wes before I wash these fish guts off me. But it probably ain't easy standing downwind of me right now."

Across the courtyard, a family of gatherers who lived in the Hopefuls' building were pushing a grocery cart up to the ELM building. The cart was filled with bark, twigs, and bushes—the preferred diet for the goats. The family would be paid in milk, fish, or vegetables from the gardens that grew safely on each balcony space above.

"Uh-oh." Titus took a deep breath. "Look at Wes's face. We've had two months of calm. I guess we're due for some more testing, huh?"

Levi nodded, then shook Wes's hand as the one-eyed man joined them. Wes glanced over each of his shoulders, then shifted even closer so only father and son could hear him.

"We were right. The fires were intentionally set. About ten guys with torches last night, shouting threats and shooting anyone they saw. One guy in there said he recognized them as people from who they call the Dooley Gang."

"The Dooley Gang?" Titus shook his head. "Never heard of them."

"I have." Levi lowered his head. "I crossed a Dooley a couple days east when I was coming back with Sergeant Lesage. Dooley and his people are the ones who shot Conrad. That's their handiwork."

"Well, apparently Dooley's operating a little closer to us now." Wes sucked air through his teeth like he didn't want to share the rest of his news. "While they were burning houses and shooting anything that moved last night, one of our recent arrivals said Dooley's people were shouting for someone named Maddix. If anyone didn't know the name, they were shot. I guess they were burning houses to get people out to question them."

"Levi? Fill in some more blanks for us."

"After Dooley shot Conrad, he took his horse. His gang was grilling up horse meat when Lesage and I showed up and made them share the stolen meat with the starving townspeople. I ran off Dooley after I planted the name Maddix Striber as a bogus calling card, as we'd agreed."

"Unintended consequences now." Titus winced. "Maddix Striber was meant to be a ghost for an enemy to chase down instead of chasing after us. It seems we've created a monster."

"The monster was already there," Wes said. "Levi just gave him a name belonging to nobody to go after."

"That's not all." Levi eyed both men like he hated to admit something. "Lesage accidentally tranquilized a woman who was with Dooley. Maybe he's looking for revenge."

"Regardless of his reasons, he's looking for Maddix Striber," Titus concluded, "and he knows your face, Levi."

"The question might be," Wes said, "what else will he do to find the one who took his meat and shot the woman?"

"He's overreacting." Levi shrugged. "We took only a portion of the horse meat, and the woman was only tranquilized, not harmed."

"It's like before Pan-Day," Titus said. "People build up offenses in their minds and they fixate on perceived wrongs done to them. Levi, you couldn't have known this Dooley guy would lose his mind looking for vengeance, but now we need to sort this out. Maddix Striber was our invention. So, this is our job."

"The ruse is still a sound plan, long-term," Wes said. "If ELM has a benefactor, a false one in this case, an enemy like the PSDF chases that ghost instead of chasing ELM. Except Dooley's not chasing Maddix Striber. He's killing people until he finds out who knows him."

"I have to find him and stop this," Levi said.

"No, you have the fishing industry you're building up," Titus said. "That's a commitment you need to see through, Levi. Dusty's not the leader you are, even if he's a good hand."

"Well, I should probably stay near Wynter for now," Wes said. "Even if I volunteered to go search for Dooley, which I wouldn't mind, she'd blame you."

"Yeah, and I'm content to steer clear of that pregnant whirlwind," Titus said, "even if she is my sister. Oleg's not yet up to full strength. Chevy is needed here to keep the buildings running. But I shouldn't go alone. Levi, can you spare Dusty?"

"Sure, I think he'd want the break from fish guts, anyway." Levi nodded, but Titus recognized the disappointment that Levi hadn't been chosen himself. "He knows those neighborhoods to the east, too."

"So, you and Dusty," Wes said to Titus. "What'll you do with Dooley?"

"That's something to pray about." Titus sighed. "I don't know just yet, but he might need more than a public paddling like we did with those lost boys by the railroad."

Levi chuckled recalling his father laying down a type of civil punishment for rule-breakers. The wooden paddle had been used on four criminals two months earlier. The story had spread, and the paddle hadn't been needed since, but it was leaning against the wall behind the door in Titus' apartment just in case.

"Dooley feels wronged," Titus said. "I'll trust God to find a way to reconcile with him that keeps our Maddix Striber counterintelligence intact."

"Well, this is something to take to the Lord," Wes said. "You'll need to leave before the Dooley Gang burns down anything else or shoots someone else."

"I'll leave in the morning," Titus raised his head, "but only because I know I'm leaving things here in capable hands."

✝

Sergeant Dom Lesage walked alone down Silver Strand Boulevard under a starry sky. He resisted the urge to turn and look back at everything that had given him hope and purpose the last few months. The Pacific States Defense Forces had been his home since Pan-Day, but duty now called him to a short recon mission inland. The lights and noise on Coronado Island were gradually left behind for the dark unknown of a city in despair.

For two months, the PSDF had experienced peace with its neighbors, particularly because the Riverside Guard to the north had been defeated, and their resources absorbed. With new territory claimed for President Criswell came opportunities for diplomacy. But Dom was a soldier. He had no use for peacetime. Even recent patrols off the island had offered little action. The world seemed to be settling into its new reality after Pan-Day. Survivors were learning how to avoid PSDF patrols or submitting without resistance to confiscation requirements.

Instead of his crimson-colored jacket that identified him as a PSDF soldier, bald-headed Dom wore a dark blue windbreaker and jeans. He'd even abandoned his black armband that boasted his status as the leader of the military's elite Flash Troops. Also absent was his rifle, but he'd kept his sawed-off shotgun in a scabbard on his back and his Bowie knife under his windbreaker across his chest. As much as he dared, he'd temporarily given up his mighty military position for one week to explore the mainland, searching out its potential threats and hidden resources.

The great fire inland the night before had been witnessed by everyone on Coronado Island. It had offered Dom the perfect excuse to convince General Brogdon to let him leave the island to recon the area. Brogdon's face had shown concern over Dom's leaving, even temporarily, but Dom was his most trusted officer, and refusing his request could have hurt their relationship. Besides, the general needed fresh intel on the latest happenings in the South Bay area.

Now alone in the darkness, the highway before him and the sea beside him, Dom felt free from the pressures of military life. He enjoyed the violence and superiority of his position, yet he'd been finding himself gazing toward the tall, downtown buildings more often lately. That was where the Casperteins lived—particularly, where Levi lived. Dom still bore the scar on his ankle where he'd been shackled and tortured as a prisoner up in the hills, but the young Caspertein Christian had risked his own life to rescue him.

Levi Caspertein was his friend. And Dom had never had a friend before.

Together, the two had spent almost a week out there, braving the elements, facing dangers, rationing food, and slowly working their way back to the bay. It was impossible for Dom to think lightly of Levi's role in his life two months earlier, even if General Brogdon had expressed his distaste about the Caspertein influence within San Diego. Of course, Brogdon was still sore about losing two small gun battles with the Casperteins as well.

Dom reached the end of the bay and turned east around the salt evaporators. The cross streets were quiet and barely littered with bags of trash, almost as if the locals had escaped the area months earlier rather than try to hold onto their property. During PSDF patrols, Dom had noticed many civilians residing along Highway 75, so he guessed there were resources still to be discovered. And stolen.

Though he wasn't originally from San Diego, Dom had learned to call Coronado his home. He'd probably never get back to Canada, and he saw no point in trying if Brogdon kept him on as an officer.

After midnight, Dom was approaching Interstate 5 when he observed a light flicker a block to the south. It was such a brief flash of illumination that Dom wondered if he'd seen only a reflection of starlight off a shard of glass or windshield. However, he was out there to investigate the area, and any local he met could offer him intel he could take back to the general.

Skirting two cars parked on the shoulder of an avenue, he came upon a metal storage container that seemed very much out of place, as if it had been dumped off a truck or fallen haphazardly off a train. The container all but blocked the entrance to a factory of some sort. Only a narrow gap remained open behind the container to walk through a chain link gate.

He sniffed the air. Normally, while on patrol, he had a dozen men with him, scouting and polluting the scene. But tonight, he was free to investigate the scene alone—though ever wary of danger.

There was an aroma of sweetness in the breeze. A cook fire was difficult to hide, but survivors had been learning to cook by meager forms of electricity to hide more traces of their existence. Rather than a scent of fire, he smelled the scent of cooked food, even spices.

However, approaching anyone in the dark of night was a sure recipe for disaster. Dom surveyed what he could see of the factory, then he retreated to the far side of the container. He'd found sign of the locals. Hopefully, they would be friendly and willing to share a little intel with him—a harmless and lonely traveler searching for his family. During his long march from Coronado Island, he'd devised the perfect cover story. After all, he couldn't possibly tell people he belonged to the PSDF; he'd stolen and killed without restraint during patrols all over the area.

There was no media in those days, but Dom guessed where people still survived, there would be a network of communication. Neighbors would talk. The PSDF was probably feared, but as long as his cover story held, he hoped to draw information from the local grapevine.

With his back to the container, he took off a light pack and sat down on the dusty asphalt. To offer the illusion of a hard-up traveler, he'd packed meagerly. During his military training in the Canadian Special Forces, he'd often undergone starvation under heavy exercise routines, so he'd learned his limitations. Those limitations had been tested two months earlier while trekking with Levi, but now Dom wasn't wounded or limping along on a makeshift crutch. If necessary, he could make his food and water last the whole week abroad.

His hand rested on his shotgun in his lap, and he allowed his head to bow for a little sleep. Though he was vulnerable and exposed to threats on the street, he was a light sleeper—and he welcomed anyone who thought he might be prey. His reputation among his men and on patrols was one of cruelty. Anyone who intended to harm him now would find that he'd respond with brutal swiftness.

"Bad place to catch a wink of sleep," a calm man's voice said.

Dom slowly lifted his head. He hadn't even drifted to sleep yet! Whoever the speaker was must've been there the whole time, shrouded by darker shadows nearby, remaining perfectly silent as he'd scouted the entrance of the factory.

The stranger wasn't yet visible, but he was probably around the corner of the metal container. Under the starry sky, Dom guessed his shotgun on his lap could be seen easily, but he didn't dare raise it. Chances were, the speaker wasn't alone.

"I'm just passing through," Dom stated softly, aware that some people could pick out his foreign accent since he'd spoken French since childhood. "I'm a stranger in America, searching for my relatives."

There was a long, silent pause.

"That doesn't explain why you stopped on my doorstep."

Dom's eyes shifted. Yes, the stranger was definitely remaining behind the container corner. Smart. And so calm!

"I meant no disrespect. I can move on. But I was hoping there'd be someone friendly around here to give me some directions."

"No one in the world is friendly any longer," the local said. "What directions do you need?"

"My name is Dom Caspertein, and I'm looking for my relatives." He paused. "They're supposed to be around here somewhere—the Casperteins."

Dom had imagined the Caspertein name had reached this far south. It was the perfect cover—and one that he thought Levi would find amusing if he learned that he'd used it to fit in peaceably with the locals.

"You're a Caspertein?" The man sounded skeptical. "I met some Casperteins last month. We searched them out when I heard they were helping people in special ways."

"What'd you find?" Dom smiled knowingly. "My extended family is a little bit . . . different, wouldn't you say?"

"They shared a cup of goat's milk with me, then I moved on. I'm searching for someone myself." Another pause. The street remained quiet. "I was there only an hour, but Dizzy and I learned to take the Casperteins seriously."

Dom wondered what kind of a name Dizzy was, but regardless, this local wasn't alone.

"Then you also know I'm no threat to you," Dom said.

"Maybe." The shape of a man moved into view from around the container corner. "If you're a Caspertein, where's your tranquilizer rifle? I heard you people don't use lethal force, but I see you're carrying a sawed-off shotgun."

"It's just for show—and stray dogs. May I stand?"

"Slowly. Leave that blaster on the ground."

Setting the shotgun aside, Dom climbed to his feet. He held his hands wide, his palms open.

"If you know the Casperteins, then you know we look after our own." Dom felt panic without his weapon. What if this stranger took advantage of him? All he had was the Bowie. "If anything happens to me—"

"Quiet. Dizzy, search him."

Dom flinched as a shadowy form darted towards him. The muzzle of a dog sniffed briefly against his jeans, his boots, and his small pack on the ground. The canine backed off seconds later, but only a few feet. She held her head low, her ears flat, ready to attack.

"Your dog can tell if I'm dangerous or not just by sniffing me?"

"No, my dog can tell you that we're dangerous if you try anything. Watch him, Dizzy." The man stepped forward, picked up the shotgun, then backed away. "If you're really a Caspertein, then you'll want to hear what I have to say."

"Sure." Dom tried to imagine what Levi would say. "It ain't easy trusting a stranger, but I'm sure we'll be like neighbors in no time."

"I'm not looking for a neighbor, and I'm definitely not interested in trusting anyone. But you might be able to help some people I know. Let's go. Dizzy, let him come."

The dog spun around twice on her hind legs, then heeled next to her master. The man paused another second, then walked away and around the corner of the container.

Following the man, Dom knew he'd been welcomed, but he was still unsettled about being unarmed. However, he scolded himself to show confidence. A Caspertein wouldn't care if he had a weapon or not, because he would trust in his God.

On the back side of the container, the man reached above to the edge of the metal frame. In the moonlight, Dom saw the stranger pull down a narrow stepladder. He ascended to the top of the container, then stood and looked down. Though Dom was about to climb up to join him, Dizzy instead dashed past him and climbed the ladder twice as fast as a man could.

"That's some trick." Dom grunted his approval.

"It's no trick. She's trained. Dizzy's a search and rescue dog." Both master and canine watched him. "Well, you coming?"

Dom climbed the narrow steps. As soon as he reached the top, the stranger knelt and pulled up the ladder. On the other end of the container, he opened a hatch and Dizzy descended into darkness. The factory wasn't his home—the container was!

"Go," the stranger ordered Dom.

He obeyed, feeling his way into the box, pitch black with an odor of . . . mint? And other spices. So, this is what he'd smelled earlier.

A moment later, the hatch above was closed and Dom moved aside so the man could turn on a bright LED lamp.

Dizzy lay in a wicker bed next to a locker. At the opposite end of the long container, a bunk bed sat with an army blanket tucked tightly at the corners and sides. A cooking counter, work bench, and three shelves of canned food completed the habitat.

"The name's Brand," said the man as he set down Dom's shotgun on the work bench. "Sit. I'll fix some tea, then we can get some sleep."

Sitting on a stool, Dom eyed the canned food. He'd laid siege against civilians for less.

"I picked the leaves myself yesterday," Brand said. Now seeing the stranger in the light, Dom guessed he was about fifty with a gray crewcut. His shoulders were broad and muscled, and his hands appeared to be calloused. "You can stay the night. I'll take you to the O'Shea family in the morning."

A kettle over a propane burner whistled, then Brand poured water into two tin cups. He stirred mint leaves into the water, then handed a cup to Dom.

"O'Shea family?" Dom blew on the hot liquid and took a sip. It was refreshing. On Coronado Island, sugar was in short supply, so he wasn't surprised the tea outside the city center was unsweetened and bitter. "They live nearby? They know my family?"

"No, I doubt the O'Sheas have met your people, but I've told them about the Casperteins. The O'Sheas need you. The Casperteins help anyone, right?"

Dom felt trapped. He'd used the Caspertein name to gain favor, not to be given a task. But maybe it would all add to his intel gathering mission.

"We don't deny anyone a helping hand. It's our Lord's way."

"Well, they need it." Brand exhaled loudly. "They lost two teenage kids, a boy and a girl, to some bandits last week. No one around here knows what to do. The kids are probably still alive. You Casperteins do this sort of thing, I've heard."

Dom glanced at Dizzy and back again at Brand.

"What sort of thing, exactly?"

"Rescues. They were kidnapped. The O'Sheas need your help."

"You're armed." Dom gestured to a semi-automatic in a holster on Brand's hip. "Why didn't you help them? A kidnapped boy and girl . . . after a week with bandits? They can't be in good health."

"What? I didn't think you Casperteins were hesitant about tough cases. The word is around here, you guys don't care about the odds against you. You even have the PSDF on the run."

"Not on the run," Dom corrected carefully, only mildly offended. "We try to reach an understanding with people to keep the peace."

"Then now you can do that with these bandits." Brand was watching him closely, as if he were still suspicious that he wasn't who he claimed to be. "You Casperteins are Christians, right? Those kids might be in bad shape, but you folks help people get their lives back on track. Come morning, the O'Sheas will be counting on you."

Dom was shown to a floor space near Dizzy where he could sleep on a thin throw rug. The lamp was extinguished and Brand went to his bunk, but Dom didn't fall asleep right away. In the pitch blackness, he could feel Dizzy's eyes on him, as if she could detect his lies.

And he had no idea how he was supposed to help anyone like the Casperteins did.

Twenty-eight-year-old Emily Pickford huddled against the ground. She barely breathed among the flowers, leaves, and trimmed bushes. Sazon was searching for her. Her eyes were fixed on the stone path that led from the chapel to the private villas. If she were found, Sazon would be the one to kill her, but anyone in the community would turn her in. It was the CARE Protocol—their law.

For the last six months, Emily had found shelter in the small community that straddled the Stillwater River, fed by the Stillwater Reservoir. As a paraplegic, she'd been thankful to find refuge among friendly people who were willing to moderate and regulate their resources. Since the community was already gated, it made for a natural stronghold against the terrors that were happening *out there.*

The residents called it the Garden.

But things had changed in the Garden since Emily had first pushed her wheelchair down its swept path and garden walkways. The changes had happened so slowly that Emily never dreamed they would one day target her for a "sympathy" death! No matter what euphemism they used, it was still murder.

It had begun when the Garden's mayor, Ridley Malden, had proposed they regulate and disperse their few resources to those residents most able to contribute to their community. The initial response from the eighty residents had been to throw themselves into meaningful tasks that proved their worth.

Since Emily was wheelchair-bound, her contributions weren't based on physical labor. Prior to Pan-Day, she'd been a property manager's executive assistant, so she took charge of the Garden's housing assignments and gardening responsibilities. The mayor approved of her proposals, and everyone who lived in the Garden became dependent on Emily's management. She'd created her own valued position and gloried in the fact that she was a valued member of the Garden. Even as a paraplegic, she showed herself as someone able to contribute to the quality of life of everyone. Because of her ideas, people within the Garden's exclusive property would survive even while the rest of the world suffered and died from crime and the Meridia Virus.

The implementation of the CARE Protocol had been proposed by Mayor Ridley Malden's girlfriend, Doctor Jaimie Ferguson. She specialized in neurology with a Master's in psychology, so no one argued with her scientific approach for the good of the community. The CARE Protocol was based on the three *Rs: Recover Humanity from Disaster, Restore Health from Disease, and Return Honor from Disgrace*. All eighty residents had unanimously agreed to the CARE Protocol. CARE stood for: *Cleansing All, Restoring Everything*.

It had been so exciting to be a part of a new movement!

But then death arrived in the name of quality of life—"sympathy" killings. The CARE Protocol was revealed to be the subtle vehicle to convince the residents that those in their midst who had diminished abilities or drew too much on their resources or attention—needed to be compassionately "put down."

Emily was only too relieved that the Garden meetings held in the chapel didn't propose the doing-away of disabled people like herself, but only the mentally ill in the Garden. Dr. Jaimie Ferguson was uniquely qualified to determine who was mentally ill and who was not.

Five residents were nominated as being too mentally diminished to contribute meaningfully to the community's well-being. Their quality of life was so low that, according to the doctor, a sympathetic "passing" needed to be orchestrated—for the good of everyone in the Garden.

The population of the Garden dropped from eighty to seventy-five in one night, but only after a muscle-bound yet soft-spoken man was chosen to be the Garden's chief "Sympathy Agent." Ferguson armed him with a syringe and a fatal toxin she'd designed for this purpose, and the five undesirables were "released" from their diminished quality of life.

The cemetery plots among the Garden's orchard trees for the five were in Emily's charge. They were summarily buried the next day after a beautiful ceremony. The whole community had come out for the celebration of life. Someone had written a song and it was sung as a blessing of life unto death.

At a Garden meeting in the chapel two weeks later, the doctor proposed that the CARE Protocol needed to extend to the elderly. There were nine over the age of sixty-five she'd listed by name who needed to be examined for quality-of-life approvals. Emily still remembered the chill she'd felt at that meeting. The nine had been seated amongst them—and they had no choice but to submit to the science. Indeed, their quality of life had been determined to be diminished, according to the doctor's standards of youth and mobility.

The nine had been quietly disposed of that night. Sazon was again their sympathetic executioner. Their compassionate passing was celebrated during the funerals the next morning. Emily had arranged everything. The blessing was sung. The community grieved. But the deaths were necessary, it was agreed, for the good of the community—and for the people who'd suffered so terribly from old age.

The population of the Garden fell to sixty-six, and Emily knew she was next.

Sure enough, following Dr. Ferguson's flawless science, Emily and four others with physical disabilities were quietly nominated as having diminished quality of life. No meeting was called this time. Sazon acted on Mayor Malden's word with Dr. Ferguson.

A man with a prosthetic leg was sympathetically killed. His widow was threatened with exile if she raised a protest, and no one wanted to leave the Garden for the chaos outside the gated community.

Then a man who had nerve damage in one hand was selected. After all, a man with only one working hand couldn't contribute wholly or appreciate life in comparison to a man with two functioning hands. His sympathetic killing had been welcomed by everyone since he'd had an obtuse attitude anyway, often complaining about the food and the taste of the water filtered from the reservoir.

Emily had known Sazon would come for her next. There would be no hearing. No appeals were allowed to scientific logic. And how could she argue against the science? After all, she really was disabled, unable to feel her legs or body from the waist down. The car accident ten years earlier had left her as an eighteen-year-old paraplegic. But she'd learned to care for herself and pull her own weight. Yet now, the CARE Protocol didn't care that she'd earned her real estate license and didn't rely on any aid in the villa apartment she'd been given.

Though she loved her life and enjoyed her job, the science said otherwise. Her diminished quality of life, in comparison with an able-bodied person, made her a candidate for Ferguson's toxin and Sazon's syringe. The science was flawless. The CARE Protocol knew best, and everyone had agreed to the three *Rs*.

Sazon had come for her during the day. She'd chanced a look out an open door into the villa courtyard and had seen his muscled frame weaving through the manicured lawn and fountains. Trapped, Emily had opened the shutters of her bedside window and boosted herself onto the windowsill. Her wheelchair, clothes, even water and other possessions had to be abandoned, but for what? For a few more minutes to continue breathing?

Now, from where she lay among the flowers behind her villa wall, she heard voices over by the gate. It was a miracle she'd dragged herself this far from the window after tumbling out of it. And another miracle—that Sazon hadn't tracked her handprints and drag marks from the window to here, only fifty yards from the villa!

There was only one place to go now: outside the Garden. She'd agreed to the CARE Protocol when it hadn't targeted her. The others who'd been killed had been necessary for the good of the community, but she wouldn't be so willing to die for the community! Who were they to decide if she enjoyed her life or not? That personalization forced her to realize the others who'd been sympathetically killed had been murdered. How gradually and cruelly everything had become so inhumane!

The way seemed clear. Emily sat up and scooted herself through a flower bed and onto an adjacent lawn. Thankfully, the heat of the day had forced most of the remaining sixty residents indoors. But she imagined they'd all be up in arms and searching for her by evening. If she were allowed to escape the Protocol, then others might try to do the same. Anarchy would ensue in the Garden. No, they'd have to kill her now, or the Garden's entire quality of life system would be undermined.

Emily reached the edge of the lawn where the grass ended and woodchips had been scattered on the bank of the river to ward off erosion. The river had been diminished to a shallow creek since Mayor Malden controlled the reservoir's floodgates upriver. Though Emily didn't know where the river ran, she could think of no other way to escape the gated community. Dragging herself back through the villa acreage to reach the front gate—that wasn't an option. Besides, the gate would be closed and locked and probably guarded by at least one sentry with a firearm.

She wore tennis shoes on her limp feet, which now left scuff marks through the woodchips as she dragged her legs to the water's edge. After one look back at her villa, she slid belly-first into the slow-moving water. Using just her arms to tread water, she allowed the current to draw her westward. The water tugged at her slacks, but she wasn't about to lose her clothes to swim easier. She'd already abandoned her wheelchair! Besides, after ten years of pushing herself around in her chair, she'd developed good arm strength that could overcome the current's tug against her clothes or shoes.

A couple of minutes of floating downstream brought her to a widening of the river. The culvert under the wall was clogged with debris and garbage, causing a natural dam. Emily gasped as she swam backwards, buying herself a few more seconds to determine a way over or through the wall since the culvert was certainly impassable. But there was no other way.

Allowing herself to drift up to the trash, the current was strong enough to hold her in place against the garbage as she took a tree branch from the blockage and threw it toward the north shore. For several minutes, she worked through plastic bags, discarded clothing, and soggy cardboard before she realized she was sobbing. Stopping her work, she let herself wail against her arm to muffle the noise. What was happening to the world that she was running for her life? And what anguish awaited her now that she was about to enter a society she imagined was unhinged? A normal, able-bodied woman would've been hard-pressed to survive where no law existed. How was she supposed to live as a paraplegic in civilization with no wheelchair?

The culvert mouth gaped wider the more she worked. Some debris was too large and heavy to remove, like part of a bed frame and a car door. Over these she climbed to move or toss aside anything else that barred her escape from those who hunted her.

Finally, she peered into the mouth of the culvert at the daylight on the other side. With a shudder, she braced herself before entering the metal tube. The optical illusion confused her eyes from determining the length of the culvert. All she knew for sure was that the water was moving more swiftly here, and the length of the culvert was still littered with some boards and bushes—and there was no telling what spiders or snakes she might encounter in the darkness.

Emily let go of the edge of the culvert and guided her way over more garbage and broken containers with sharp edges. Since she couldn't feel her legs, she could only imagine the scrapes she was receiving on her knees, thighs, and shins. Wearing a short-sleeved t-shirt, her exposed arms were scraped and bleeding in more than one place. However, it helped to tell herself that she'd been through worse. Recovering after her car wreck that had severed her spine had been more traumatic, painful, and life-changing. If she could rise above her paralysis, she could rise above a few superficial gashes from a smelly trash heap.

Suddenly, she found herself snagged midway through the culvert. Water rushed up her neck and threatened her head. She felt down each leg and found barbed wire had caught her slacks. With desperate strength, she ripped herself clear and clawed her way through the rest of the culvert length.

The mouth at the other end of the culvert emptied into a wide pool of swampy water, by way of an eight-foot drop. After the drop, Emily surfaced, sputtering and wiping her face free of slime and gunk. With the current, she breast-stroked to the south bank that consisted of clay. An inch at a time, she clawed her way up the embankment and didn't stop until she reached level ground.

A city street littered with paper trash was her first impression of the world outside. Her second impression was that she wasn't alone. A man, woman, and child each carried full water containers as they hustled past her and away from the water's edge. From the street, the man looked back at her. Emily wondered if she would see any pity on his face. But in the setting sun, she saw only blank eyes. Like the world before Pan-Day, apathy ruled a people who cared only for themselves. How remarkable, Emily thought, that her own near-demise had opened her eyes to such gross attitudes. For a time, she'd even gone along with the removal of innocents, as long as it was for the good of the masses.

The family moved on with their water containers. Emily couldn't imagine drinking that water—polluted from the waste that ran from the Garden. But truly, she wondered what she might have to eat or drink herself just to stay alive now.

Buildings, houses, and shops lined the street not far away. Emily checked her legs and found that her trousers were torn in several places, but she didn't seem to be bleeding too badly.

Stifling her whimpers and fear, she began to drag herself toward the nearest building. She'd escaped the Garden walls, but she wondered if Sazon would come after her. He'd been rumored to have left the Garden a time or two, but Emily didn't know what for. Could Mayor Malden allow his authority to be undermined by dismissing her escape? Could Dr. Ferguson allow her precious CARE Protocols to be ignored?

Emily already knew the answer. But she saw no way to avoid death, whether from the residents of the Garden or from the civilians outside. She was on her own now, and without a wheelchair, she would be an easy target.

Chapter Two

Oliver Gleason lay motionless on his belly, barely breathing. His right hand gently held a length of red yarn that traced halfway across a dusty parking lot to a pine tree. In the shade of the tree were a few pine cones where small birds were pecking and fighting one another for seeds or insects.

The red yarn, acquired from a derelict hobby craft store that morning, was attached to a crooked stick. The stick supported one end of a cardboard box. As the tiny birds fluttered about, they intermittently landed on the ground under the box.

Twenty yards away, six-year-old Rory yawned and stretched in the shade of a bowling alley where he was resting with his mother, Milli. They'd both marched stoically through the night. Oliver had led them southward and out of the burn zone, though he'd done so only to avoid those who'd set the fires, who he believed were to the west of them. Somehow, he needed to find a way around them to reach downtown where he knew Levi Caspertein lived.

The birds ignored Rory's yawn and fussed over potential food under the box. Oliver tensed. One bird was just a mouthful for Rory. Two birds might become a meal for both Milli and Rory in a light broth. But three birds? Three were unlikely, but it might mean Oliver could tease his stomach with something edible as well.

Two birds tackled another—directly under the box! A fourth came to the aid of the first. Oliver jerked on the yarn. The stick flipped into the parking lot and the box settled on the ground. The remainder of the birds under the tree flew away, abandoning their four companions trapped in the box.

Oliver could barely believe his luck. *Four birds!* Sure, they were small, but fixed properly, he could offer his family a broth with a little meat. He'd already collected edible leaves after the sun had risen that morning, and a tin can he'd cleaned out would make a nice cooking pot.

He spooled his thread onto a popsicle stick as he approached the box. Trapping four birds was one thing. Fetching them from the trap was another feat altogether! But he'd thought ahead and had already cut a hole in one side, currently plugged by a washcloth he'd found in a sidewalk gutter.

On his knees next to the box, he licked his lips, imagining just a nibble of bird meat. They hadn't eaten since supper the afternoon before, and the night had been exhausting.

His hand hesitated over the wadded-up washcloth. Finally, he plucked it out and covered the hole with one hand. With the other hand, he shook out the cloth and spread it to serve as a net. When he removed his hand, one bird squeezed out of the hole. Oliver grabbed it with the cloth, then covered the hole with his hand again. With a pinch of his thumb, the little creature expired, and he repeated the same tactic three more times.

After plucking the feathers, he caught his breath with concern as he studied the little creatures. He glanced toward Milli and Rory, restlessly sleeping against the building. They would never know if he'd gulped down one or two birds. It would barely dent his craving for food, but it would be enough to keep his energy fueled for a few more hours. How was he supposed to hunt on an empty stomach day after day?

But self-sacrifice had been on Oliver's mind a lot lately. For months off and on, he'd denied his own appetites for the sake of his family. And from reading the Bible, he realized that true sacrifice was about more than merely preserving others. It was also about more than loving others. It was about behaving like Jesus who had sacrificed Himself on a cross. The more he read from the Bible, the more he realized this sacrifice of Jesus was the single thing that was meant to inspire His followers. It seemed to Oliver like there was more to being a Christian than behaving like Jesus, but he hadn't put it all together yet. Hopefully, Levi Caspertein would clear up those questions for him.

He cleaned the four birds and carried them back to the shade of the bowling alley to build a small fire. There were houses and shops they could use for cover, but Oliver never knew who else might be hiding inside. Until he found a safe place for them to sleep that night, he preferred to remain outside where he could see people coming. At least the weather was comfortable.

Using his pocketknife, he sliced the tiny breasts of meat and plopped them into the boiling water over the crackling flames. He dropped in green leaves and slowly stirred the soup. The meat wasn't much, but it was strong and oily. In time, Oliver knew he could find some spices in nearby houses, but scavenging was dangerous work. Since he'd seen fresh shoe prints in the dust that morning, he knew there were other people around.

"Ugh, that stinks, Oliver." Milli sat up beside Rory, the sleeping bag unrolled under them. "What'd you put in there?"

"Bird meat." He sniffed the smokey flavor. It was a little gamey. "We need to eat something. It's good food, even if it tastes a little—"

"Nasty?" Milli sighed and tugged on her shoes. "Sorry, Oliver. I know you're trying."

Oliver stared at the cooking tin and felt like crying. He'd spent nearly three hours trying to catch the birds, and she was right. They smelled terrible, but what else was there to eat? Bruce Ramis had still been giving him survival tips when their lives had changed by the fires.

Levi Caspertein was young, he remembered, but Oliver guessed he'd know how to care for others much better. Now *there* was a man no one probably ever messed with!

Milli suddenly grasped Oliver's arm. He lifted his eyes to the street, knowing it could only be danger. Sure enough, a sizeable man in a sleeveless, plaid shirt and long, brown hair walked up the middle of the street. His exposed arms showed thick muscles, twice the size of Oliver's.

Moving his rifle into his lap, Oliver roughly pointed it toward the stranger. Though the man had no rifle or pack, he carried a holstered sidearm on his left hip.

"The fire!" Milli whispered.

But the stranger had already noticed them. Oliver had met only a few people since Pan-Day. Milli had seen no one else for months, so her usual dread was certainly heightened.

Though he felt no courage, Oliver stood tall like he was an experienced survivor.

"Hi there!" The stranger waved and smiled. His face was tanned and his eyes were bright and seemed friendly. "I smelled your fire."

"We're cooking up a few small birds." Oliver cleared his throat. "Do you live around here?"

"About a mile south on the Stillwater River." The man's eyes took in Oliver's meager possessions, then he noticed Rory and his gaze lingered on him. "You three have been through some real challenges, huh?"

"Yeah." Oliver didn't like the way he was looking at them. "The fires last night chased us from our home."

"I saw them from the Garden." The man crouched low in front of the small fire. "That's where I'm from, the Garden. It's a Garden of Eden compared to all this wasteland out here. Are you three healthy? No diseases?"

"We know the rules." Oliver swung his rifle onto his back. "But we haven't been around people enough to catch anything."

"How about disabilities?" The stranger looked from Milli to Oliver. "Blindness? All your arms and legs work well? You've taken care of your teeth?"

"Yes." Oliver frowned. "Why?"

"The Garden would welcome you three if you're in good health and willing to work with the rest of us. We have food and water, plenty of nice homes to live in. You'll be safe there."

"Stillwater River is south." Oliver felt Milli's pleading eyes, but he'd already made up his mind. "And we're going northwest, toward downtown."

"There's nothing good downtown," the stranger said. "You'd just be closer to the military. You don't want to be anywhere near Coronado Island. They steal food and fuel from anyone who has it."

"Well, there's a family who lives downtown," Oliver said. "They're good people—the Casperteins. They invited us."

"The Garden would love to have you. We have whole gardens full of flowers and vegetables and fruit trees. Whole orchards surround the villas! It's a paradise, I'm telling you. Mayor Ridley Malden will welcome you himself. There's plenty of water to wash in and fresh clothes to wear. We even have some electricity flowing in the evenings to play a little music.

"Oh, Oliver," Milli pled, "let's go there."

"I'm Sazon." The large man offered his hand and a smile to Oliver. "I work for the mayor."

"Oliver." Milli moved up beside him. "How could things downtown be better than what's at the Garden?"

"There are more important things than food and water," Oliver said, frowning as Sazon continued to watch Rory in his sleep. "Life isn't always about what we have, Milli. We've been invited downtown. Levi Caspertein is waiting for us."

"But, sweetie, now we're being invited to the Garden. We want to raise Rory someplace nice, right? They even have a mayor."

Though Oliver wanted to ask Sazon if anyone in the Garden could explain the Bible to him, he dared not ask in front of Milli.

"Maybe we'll check it out." Oliver forced a smile to Milli and put his arm around her. "Any place called the Garden can't be that bad, right? At least we'll all be together."

"Come on." Sazon waved a friendly gesture. "I'll help you carry your things. Did you guys want to eat first?"

"Oh, no!" Milli giggled. Oliver hadn't heard her laugh in months. "I don't think I could get whatever that is past my lips!"

Oliver doused the fire under his boot, but set the cooking tin aside to cool off as he packed up their few things. Nothing they owned was new. Nor did anything they had smell good—after living so long without much water to wash regularly. Sazon's plaid shirt and jeans appeared new and his long hair was shining from a recent shampooing.

"Hi there, young man!" Sazon shook Rory's little hand as the boy blinked sleep from his eyes. "Are you hungry? Can you growl? Let me see your teeth like you're a hungry bear."

Rory barred his teeth and gave his best effort to growl like a wild animal. Sazon laughed, tossed his hair back, and offered his hand for Rory to walk beside him.

"Come on, Rory. You'll love the Garden. Everything there is beautiful! Milli, the flowers in the Garden are almost as pretty as you are!"

Milli laughed carefree beside the stranger as they walked away. Oliver bound the sleeping bag to his backpack, collected his coat, then swigged down the bird soup. The taste made him gag, so he knew not to bother chewing lest he vomit, but at least his stomach had something in it.

A moment later, he caught up to his family and walked behind Sazon, listening to the man explain the Garden's only three rules, which he said every resident needed to live by: Recover humanity, Restore health, and Return honor.

"It sounds amazing!" Milli sighed as if speaking of heaven itself.

The iron gate to the Garden stood tall in the brick-and-mortar wall that surrounded the community inside. After smelling his own dirty laundry and the charred buildings recently, Oliver was startled by the sweet aromas that wafted from the greenery of the Garden. The gate was opened by two sentries who carried only sidearms. Sazon led them up a swept driveway, over an arching bridge, and stopped at a chapel surrounded by flower beds. Small villas with individual apartments lined the path behind and beside them.

"Where is everyone?" Milli asked. "There must be an army of people who take care of all these plants!"

"They're inside." Sazon held his finger to his lips. "It's a funeral ceremony. Come on. We'll sit in the back until they're finished."

Oliver was in awe of the colors and smells as he followed Sazon and his family up to the chapel's double doors. There, Oliver leaned his rifle and dumped their belongings against the outside of the chapel below a stained-glass window. Sazon opened one door and the family entered.

". . . We don't grieve now as we grieved when she was alive." A man with thinning blond hair spoke softly from the front podium. "She suffered and now she is suffering no longer. With our sister's passing, the Garden recovers a little more. We are restored a little better. And we all return to our former glory. Let us sing."

Sitting in a pew, Oliver listened to the congregation of fifty or so parishioners dressed in their finest suits and summer dresses. Inside the chapel, it seemed as if Pan-Day had never happened.

The people sang in a slow, melodious tone:
"A life returned, no more to burden;
No more to anguish, no more to lend;
A life let go, yet remembered still;
Strength remains as our hearts are filled . . ."
The words were very odd, Oliver thought, since they seemed to honor the deceased in death, but still called her a burden when she'd been alive?

"It's the hymn we always sing," Sazon whispered to him as several more verses were sung. "It's called, '*Where Memory Lives in Beauty.*'"

Oliver nodded and noticed Milli softly weeping. This wasn't one of her sobbing fits, but tears of joy. He'd not seen her so happy since before Pan-Day. The trials of living from meal to meal seemed to be in the past for them.

When they'd finished singing, four men solemnly picked up a sheet-covered pallet near the podium and exited the chapel sanctuary by a back door. Oliver glimpsed green trees and garden flowers through the open door. He couldn't remember ever seeing such beauty.

Sazon rose to his feet, his height towering over everyone else, and signaled with one hand to the blond man who'd presided over the ceremony. Oliver stood and shook the man's hand.

"Mayor Malden, this is Oliver and his family, Milli and Rory." Sazon moved aside. "This is the mayor of the Garden."

"Look at you all! It's wonderful to meet new friends!" The mayor had freckles and green eyes. Oliver guessed he was in his mid-forties. Though he smiled, his eyes seemed somehow expressionless. "You're the first outsiders we've welcomed to the Garden in months. We expect much from our residents, you understand."

"We're just checking things out first." Oliver nodded in greeting to others in the chapel as they filed past. Their faces didn't show the same welcome, but perhaps suspicion. "We were actually invited to go downtown to the Casperteins. Have you heard of them?"

"There are many rumors these days." Mayor Malden squeezed Oliver's upper arm, touched Milli's unwashed cheek, and brushed a finger under Rory's chin. "Such youthfulness. Sazon will help you get settled. I can't imagine a more wonderful place to raise a family than what we've built here. Sazon?"

"I'll get them settled, sir, then come find you."

Sazon led them outside and down a path west of the chapel to a pair of villas. Residents avoided them by closing their apartment doors and watching from curtained windows. Each horseshoe-shaped villa, Sazon explained, contained four apartments. The Garden had eight villas, and each villa had its own courtyard, garden, and fountain.

When Oliver was shown to an apartment for his family, he noted that they were being housed in the villa farthest from the front gate, and there was no obvious path to a rear gate on the immense property. As Milli lingered outside with Sazon, who was pointing out edible vegetables planted in that very courtyard, Oliver carried their belongings into the apartment and dropped everything on the floor. Rory carried only his chess case as he explored two sterile bedrooms. Then at a glass coffee table on a carpeted bedroom floor, the boy began to set up his chess pieces.

Oliver walked to a bay window that faced south and drew aside the lace curtain to see the leafy forest and garden behind the villa. How could everything seem so wonderful, yet scream at him simultaneously to escape with Milli and Rory that very minute? Maybe it had been the way that Sazon, first, and then the mayor, had looked at Rory. Or maybe it was the friendliness by which they'd been welcomed. But the residents themselves hadn't shown such hospitality. Something was amiss here.

Milli laughed at the front door. *She was actually laughing!* And Sazon mumbled something else Oliver couldn't quite hear, but Milli giggled more, then entered the apartment and wrapped her arms around Oliver and kissed him.

"Isn't this amazing, Oliver?" She stepped back and twirled like a child with her arms out. "It's like we've entered another reality. We're saved, Oliver. We're really saved!"

Swallowing nervously, Oliver knew he needed to tell her about his Bible reading. It was time she knew about what he was trying to figure out—true salvation. There were things about God they needed to teach Rory as soon as possible, while he was still young.

"I'm gonna take a bath!" She squealed with delight and ran into the master bedroom where she slammed the door. A few seconds later, Oliver heard water cascading into the tub.

"Mom doesn't get it," Rory said without looking up from his chess set where he moved a pawn to threaten a knight.

"Doesn't get what?" Oliver sat cross-legged across from Rory and assumed the black pieces.

"This place is weird." Rory tapped his forefinger on his chin in thought, then moved a white bishop. "Really, really weird."

Oliver didn't say anything, but he agreed with his son. Lots of things were *off* about the Garden, but they were things he couldn't fully identify. Or separately, they were things that might not be that strange. Maybe they just needed to get used to being around people again.

"Hey, how about that stream we crossed when we went over that bridge, huh?" Oliver said. "There might be fish in it. We could go fishing."

"I don't think so, Dad." Rory moved a piece.

"I've never been fishing, either, but it'd be good for us to learn new things."

"Yeah, I want to learn to fish, but I don't think they want us doing those kinds of things here."

"How can you tell?" Oliver frowned. "We just have to ask for a fishing pole."

"Okay, but I'm not sure they'll give us one. They already took your rifle."

Leaping to his feet, Oliver stared at the heap of belongings he'd set inside the front door—which was still open. *Rory was right!* Before entering the chapel, he'd leaned the rifle against the wall. Upon exiting, he'd picked up their gear but his rifle hadn't been there!

"You don't miss much, do you, Rory?" Oliver said as the boy continued to study the chess board. "We need to get out of here, son, if we can. Whether they let us or not, we need to leave."

✝

After a few hours of restless sleep in the storage container, Dom Lesage was relieved that survivalist Brand Windfield had returned his shotgun to him. Somewhere southeast of the bay, Dom followed Brand who was following his Labrador retriever, Dizzy, through the destroyed neighborhood. Since they'd set off before dawn, Dom wasn't sure if they were east or west of the interstate.

Twice that morning, they'd seen a PSDF patrol in the distance. No one but the general knew where Dom had gone, so he hoped he didn't cross a patrol that might blow his cover.

Dom had considered himself to be an elite soldier for nearly half his life. Now at thirty-five, no one on Coronado Island was a match for him when it came to hand-to-hand fighting, stamina on the obstacle courses, or marksmanship. But that early morning, he struggled to keep up with Brand and Dizzy.

Brand was at least fifty years old, but he reminded Dom of the way Levi had stalked the streets when escorting him home. Dizzy had taken point as if the canine knew exactly where Brand wanted to go. Dog and master were a single unit, pausing at cross streets, darting ahead, studying everything. Dom noticed that Brand even sniffed the air when his black Lab did.

Winded, Dom hustled to catch up to Brand where the local crouched next to a trailer with a twenty-foot motorboat on its bed. The trailer and sports craft sat on a residential street, presumably abandoned in the rush of Pan-Day.

"That's the house." Brand pointed to a three-story structure with boarded up windows. "There are others a few houses away. We don't want to expose them to threats any more than we have to."

Sniffing the air, Dom could usually smell pockets of survivors from their cook fires or sewage.

"I taught them how to dispose of their waste," Brand said, reading him accurately. "You would never know they were here. Dizzy, scout around."

With a finger and a circular motion, Brand signaled to his dog. The Lab darted away from the cover of the boat and ran down a side street. She wore a camouflage doggie vest with pockets and pouches, but the gear didn't seem to slow her down. Dom guessed the vest was bulletproof since Brand would know anyone with a rifle would be interested in eating his search and rescue companion.

"Looks clear," Dom whispered. "Am I missing something?"

"It's not clear until Dizzy says it's clear." Brand took off his pack, which was twice the size of Dom's. He drew out a knapsack and handed it to Dom. "Take this. Give it to them when we get inside. I bring them something every time I visit. They need it."

Without opening it, Dom felt the sack's contents—cans and pouches. Food. He desperately wanted to know where Brand had stored so much food to stock his home and to give so much away, but he had to maintain his façade as a Caspertein. Levi and Titus would never bother others for what they had. They'd rather go without than allow someone to sacrifice for them. Even when Levi had walked him home, the young Caspertein had always offered Dom the choicest bits of food and the greatest amount of water when they came upon it.

"How will you know if it's not safe?" Dom asked.

"Dizzy will bark." He pointed at the street to his left. "Or she'll come around that corner in about thirty seconds. She knows her job. You worry about doing yours."

Mine?—Dom wanted to ask, but held his tongue, still concerned about what was being asked of him.

Sure enough, Dizzy trotted around the nearby intersection corner. Her tongue flapped as she panted and her tail wagged as she returned from the scouting mission. She was welcomed by Dom's embrace, like they'd been apart for days instead of minutes.

"Let's go!" Brand rose and ran from the trailer.

Dom clutched the sack and jogged after dog and master into the yard of the three-story residence. They skirted the front porch by way of a paved path on the east side of the house against a chain link fence. At the back door, Brand knocked loudly three times, then waited for a full minute.

"No one seems to be home." Dom eyed the houses next door, the cluttered yards and shuttered windows. "Maybe they relocated since you were here last."

"They're home." Brand petted Dizzy's head. "It just takes them a couple minutes to disarm the countermeasures and reach the door."

"Countermeasures?" Dom gulped and stepped back. "Traps? Inside?"

"I installed them myself. Unfortunately, O'Shea's kids were taken when they were out there." Brand gestured at the neighborhood in general. "He regrets not keeping them inside, but that would've made them prisoners. You can't stay inside forever."

"Right." Dom tried to act like what Brand shared was common knowledge to him, but he actually had no idea how common civilians survived on the mainland. He'd thought they'd all lived like filthy animals in hiding for months, but Brand was revealing a network Dom could only imagine.

Finally, there were footsteps from within the house. Dom watched Brand for cues, but not even Dizzy reacted adversely.

The door opened a couple of inches. A red-bearded man about forty examined the visitors, then visually checked the yard behind them.

"Quick!" The resident opened the door wider and stood aside.

Brand and Dizzy entered first, then Dom with his sack. The door closed and Dom's eyes adjusted slowly to the dimness. Light pierced the otherwise dark room by way of peep holes probably drilled intentionally in the plywood window covers.

"Follow me exactly," Brand told Dom. "Touch nothing."

No one gave him orders on Coronado Island, not even General Brogdon. He'd put men in the stocks or suspended their food rations for insubordination. Perfect order needed to be strictly maintained within the military. But here, Dom didn't object or question Brand. A Caspertein led by serving and helped others by submitting.

On the way to a flight of stairs, Dom noticed a counterweight fashioned from an old refrigerator. A thin cable was attached to the fridge, then looped over a pulley on the ceiling. He imagined some horrible spear or set of knives ready to be triggered in the shadows somewhere.

It was suddenly daunting for Dom to think that he'd joined his PSDF scavenger teams to explore houses all over the city just like this one. If civilians were setting up defenses in one place, it was likely they would set them up elsewhere. After all, Brand seemed to be a man who shared his tricks and resources with others. So why hadn't he rescued the missing teens?

On the second floor, they walked down a hallway and past other disarmed countermeasures: a compound bow locked with three arrows, a hatchet on a horizontal staff held by a rubber strap, and a propane tank with a nozzle aimed down the corridor.

They followed the bearded man into a back bedroom, then he closed and locked the door. He reached overhead to a ring on the ceiling and drew down an attic ladder.

With a hand gesture, Brand ordered Dizzy up. She vaulted up without questioning her master and disappeared into the attic that had a wood and cinnamon smell. Brand was next, then it was Dom's turn.

His head emerged from the hole and he quickly took in the attic space—much larger than expected with more people than he'd anticipated.

Two young children rolled on the attic floor as Dizzy spun in a circle and tackled them. They laughed breathlessly at the play wrestling. A half-dozen adults watched wide-eyed from where they sat on cushions under the sloping eaves of the roof. A curtained area probably contained a bathroom, and farther back maybe more people and living quarters.

Dom walked hunched under the low roof and offered his sack of goods to a woman who had the look of a matriarch. She sat on a short chair at a makeshift counter where she was dicing fresh vegetables. A cooking pot boiled on a propane stove beside the counter. Crafty—no wood-burning. People were getting smarter, learning to hide all traces of themselves to outsiders.

He sat on another wood chair, its matting well-worn, and set his shotgun and pack aside. Brand sat on a piano bench, its legs sawed off half-length and unevenly, and the bearded man knelt next to him. Though Dom wanted to appreciate the rare laughter of the children playing with Dizzy, he did his best to give his attention to Brand and the bearded man.

"Noah O'Shea, this is Dom Caspertein. I thought you two should meet."

"Caspertein!" The bearded man stared at Dom. "We've heard of you."

Shifting uncomfortably on the short chair, Dom's knees were bent awkwardly. He didn't feel like he could rise or fight effectively while cramped in the attic.

"You've probably not heard of me but of my heroic cousins, Titus and Levi Caspertein," Dom offered apologetically. But when he saw the disappointment on Noah's face, he couldn't resist adding more. "But I am a Caspertein. You know, we have our . . . ways."

"Your whole family are Christians, right?" Noah touched his chest and his face softened, as he seemed perhaps close to tears. "We are as well. My daughter Mae and my son Isaac were on a supply run with another man who used to live here. They killed him and took my children."

"Tell him who the kidnappers were," Brand urged. "Go on. He might be able to help if he has all the facts."

"I met some of them about a month ago," Noah said. "They were just kids, really. Mostly teens and maybe some in their early twenties. I had my rifle with me, even though I have no bullets left, but they didn't know that. Mae and Isaac were with me. I think that's when those hooligans got the idea to take Mae and Isaac. I told them to stay clear of this street and we'd have no problems."

"Dizzy and I caught one of them about two weeks ago," Brand said, his eyes full of mischief. "Just to question him, see who they were. The kid said he and his pals left downtown because the Casperteins had run them out—after *spanking* them!"

Dom blinked in surprise. He'd actually watched Titus Caspertein use a wooden paddle on several youths who'd preyed upon two ELM women. Though Dom had been too injured at the time to assist, he'd witnessed the fear that the gang of youths had learned to have of Titus.

"Cousin Titus has a unique way of handling criminals." Dom nodded. "At least you know who took your kids, Mr. O'Shea. Are the bandits around here now? Do they have a new hangout since leaving downtown?"

"It's a little farther down the interstate," Brand said. "Dizzy knows the way. Then you can confront them the Caspertein way."

"Yes!" Noah licked his lips. "Praise God, He's brought us a Caspertein! I'll go with you. If anyone can get Mae and Isaac back, it's you, Dom. Thank you so much for coming!"

Feeling both empowered and terrified, all kinds of concerns flooded into Dom's mind. If he'd had a convoy of Flash Troops from the island, he'd obliterate the kidnappers once and for all—not give them a spanking! But he was a Caspertein as far as these people were concerned. He needed to earn their trust if they were to share the secrets of their provisions. The PSDF couldn't control the population of survivors until they discovered how they were surviving.

"We'll need to watch out for the PSDF," Brand warned. "Their patrols are all over this area. Dom, you're new here, so I'll tell you—they're our greatest fear. They've pillaged this whole area of all obvious resources. We've had to move everything underground just to survive."

"That's good you have stores hidden away." Dom's eyes drifted to the shelves of the attic. They were bare. Wherever Brand's stores were kept, it wasn't here. "These bandits—do they want you to pay ransom with food or what?"

"No demands have reached us," Noah said, "and they know where we live, so there's got to be another motive."

"Dizzy and I think they're just recruiting," Brand said. "They want other youngsters like themselves to run around with. And Mae, she's a pretty girl for somebody. Sorry, Noah."

Watching Noah shudder, Dom reached out and touched the father's shoulder—like he'd seen Levi comfort others before.

"Don't think about that," Dom said. "Mae's your daughter. We'll get her back. Somehow, I'll . . . deal with these fools and this won't happen ever again."

Dom settled his own heart, vengeance and wrath rising up inside his chest. He'd lead the PSDF down there and scour the streets for these rapists and murderers— and execute them himself! But then he remembered his men had been just as abusive against the citizenry in the area. They'd indeed pillaged and murdered for provisions, and in some less restrained situations, some of the men had taken women. However, this personal look at the effect of such behavior angered Dom like he hadn't thought possible.

"It's still early," Brand said. "Dizzy will get us to the school before noon if we have no problems. That's where they hang out now, at a school. Then you can do your stuff, whatever it is that you Casperteins do."

"Right." Dom's breath seemed to catch. His stomach trembled. "I'll do what we Casperteins do."

"God's still working on ol' Brand's soul here, Dom, but you and I are believers," Noah said. "Don't you think we should pray about all this? Brand has brought you to get my children back, but God's the One who moves hearts, after all. Go ahead and pray."

"Of course." Dom looked from man to man, then at the elderly woman who was stirring the contents of the pot. He wasn't sure if he'd ever prayed to God before, but he'd spent days with Levi, and that young man was a praying maniac! Morning and night, before meals, and before and after hardship—Levi was always calling on his God. How hard could it be? "Let's pray."

"Count me out." Brand started to rise.

"No, stay," Noah said. "This is important. Speak to our Lord for us, Dom."

"Right." Dom bowed his head and everything inside him seemed to freeze in panic, uncertainty, guilt, and fear. How was he truly to face these bandits unless he had the supernatural protection the Casperteins had often wielded? "Uh, God, we're nothing without You. We don't know much about what's happening in this world and we sure need Your help today. Please help me, I mean us, get Mae and, uh— What's the boy's name again?"

"Isaac," Noah reminded.

"Isaac. We need them back, God. Uh, You've been good to us Casperteins for a long time. I beg You for, well, that maybe You'll extend something special to all of us. Um . . . amen."

"Amen!" Noah took a deep breath and wiped his eyes. "This is what we needed, huh, Brand? A praying Caspertein on our side!"

"Hey, I've got my own troubles." Brand scoffed at them both and rose from the piano bench. "I'll see if Dizzy's ready to get back to work."

Alone with Noah, Dom felt uncertain of what to say to the grieving father. He'd never consoled anyone in his life.

"Uh, their mother?" he asked. "Your wife? Is she still with us?"

"Melody," Noah said softly. "Her suffering's over now. She was a solid Christian woman. She raised the kids in the Scriptures, too—more than I did. But now my faith is stronger. I want what He wants for my kids."

"That's good." Dom noticed across the attic floor that Dizzy was spinning in circles on her hind legs at words from Brand about leaving. "I've heard that God uses tragedy to get our attention. I mean, that's what I've heard, anyway."

"Of course, you've heard that!" Noah chuckled and slapped his thigh. "Isn't that one of the major themes in the Bible?"

"Right." Dom smiled nervously. As a child in Canada, he'd learned some of the Bible stories from his grandmother, but he'd always thought such fantasies were for the gullible masses who needed such dreams. He was just a military man, after all.

However, as the three men left the attic, Dom hoped there was some truth to the God of those Bible stories, because he had no idea how to get those kids back from a gang of wild youths!

✝

Neil Dooley trudged slowly up the dusty street next to Fran Garrick. She was still complaining, but his mind was on the buildings and barricade ahead. Something indeed was here in downtown San Diego. On the balcony of a high-rise apartment, a woman shouted and laughed to a neighbor as she hung laundry on a clothesline that spanned the distance to another building. And a man, woman, and child who carried bundles of twigs and bushes merged with the street Dooley was on.

"You're not listening to me!" Fran slapped him on the side of the head. "I said, I can feel fleas in these filthy clothes you picked for us!"

Rubbing his burning ear from her slap, Dooley distanced himself from his girlfriend by an arm's length. He thought about hitting her back. It'd been a few weeks since he'd struck her, and it had only infuriated her further rather than bring her into compliance. Their relationship was mostly physical—except when they were pillaging and killing. In those moments, her ruthlessness was unequaled, and she'd saved his life several times by shooting civilians who would've otherwise shot him in the fray of a gunbattle.

But in these lulls of inactivity, she was nearly intolerable.

"You're supposed to be a man." Fran scoffed. "What man gives up his gun to infiltrate a stronghold?"

"I told you—my pistol is in the bottom of my pack." He unzipped his tattered coat under the mid-morning sun. "We won't be welcomed as harmless travelers if we're armed as we usually are. Let's find out what we can. Play your part and we'll walk away from this place with more than we've ever gotten anywhere else. Look, there's plants up on all those balconies. See through the railing? This place is thriving!"

"Maddix Striber is the only one I want to find out about." She lowered her voice as they approached a barricade of vehicles, three or four rows deep, with space to walk through in only one place. "I'm seeing signs of a lot of people here. I bet if we do this right, if you don't mess this up for us, we'll never have to eat another pretzel again."

Dooley led the way through the vehicle perimeter behind the family who was carrying firewood, then emerged into an open courtyard of swept concrete between several tall buildings.

"Welcome to ELM," said a young man seated on an elevated stool under a covered booth. Dooley had nearly missed the gatekeeper or doorman directly inside the perimeter. A large bell hung from a wooden frame at his shoulder. He thought it odd the young man didn't rise from his stool to stand until he noticed his left leg in a brace over his jeans. The leg itself seemed to be smaller, possibly withered. "Are you new to ELM?"

Swallowing, Dooley chose his words carefully. He was used to ambushing travelers or burning families out of their homes to take the valuables they fled with. This undercover acting was already trying his nerves.

Obviously, the young gatekeeper would ring the bell if he sensed someone contrary had passed through the perimeter.

"We heard we might find a safe place to sleep around here." Dooley gazed across the courtyard. Civilians came and went from open doors to at least two different buildings, and two little girls were twirling a jump rope on the concrete as a third sang a ditty and hopped in rhythm. "We were run out of our home in the Lemon Grove fires."

"A lot of that happening lately." The young man still didn't descend from his perch, but he pointed toward the northern-most apartment building. "That's ELM headquarters. You'll see an elm tree painted on the front. See the one-eyed guy on the balcony? That's Wes Trimble. Go see him for a housing assignment. Whatever you need, he'll take care of you."

"Wow, thanks!" Dooley smiled and studied the gatekeeper closer. No visible weapons. Just the bell. Easy pickings so far. He hadn't even checked their backpack for a sidearm—which he'd explain away as a precaution if necessary. "What is all this? ELM, you say?"

"Every life matters." The gatekeeper nodded. "It's the motto of this whole place. The founders set everything up for us to start new lives here."

"The founders?" Dooley's eyes narrowed. "Who are they?"

"The Casperteins mostly. They're good people. Go ahead. Go talk to Wes Trimble. He'll tell you more."

"Is Maddix Striber here?" Fran asked sharply. "Do you know who Maddix Striber is?"

"No, but you could ask Chevy." The young man scratched his head. "People come here looking for family all the time. If you're looking for someone, Chevy's the one to talk to."

Dooley took Fran's hand and led her away—though he knew she didn't like her hand held. She said his hands were too clammy. But for appearance's sake, she didn't shake him off as they left the gatekeeper and advanced on the ELM building. A boy of about twelve approached from the west carrying a small cooler in one hand with a cocker spaniel on a leash in the other.

"What do you have in the cooler there, boy?" Dooley asked.

As the boy's small hands fumbled with the cooler lid, he slowed and his dog sniffed at the newcomers.

"Just eggs I couldn't sell." The boy presented the cooler with several chicken eggs on a bed of shredded newspaper. "You want one? One for each of you?"

"How much?" Dooley's mouth watered. *Fresh eggs!* "We don't have much left."

"You can just have them. I already made a good profit."

"Who do you sell to?" Dooley selected what seemed like the two largest eggs. "And for what?"

"To the soldiers. Look." The boy told his dog to heel, then dug into his pocket to produce a handful of lighters. "I can sell these for more eggs from Mrs. Caspertein, or get fish from Levi. I'm the best barterer around."

"Not if you keep giving your eggs away." Fran scoffed and took the two eggs from Dooley. "I'll keep these so you don't smash them."

The boy scowled at her ingratitude, then pocketed his profits as he continued to a nearby building.

Below the balcony where the one-eyed man stood, Dooley smiled and waved.

"You Wes Trimble? The guy at the little booth back there said to come talk to you about somewhere to stay for the night."

The man above adjusted his eye patch and angled his head as he leaned over the balcony. Dooley was distinctly aware of the rifle sling over the man's shoulder.

"Did you come far?" Wes asked.

"East side of Lemon Grove." Dooley wrung his hands, acting exasperated. "Some people ran us out with those fires. We were short on water as it was."

Wes said nothing for a moment as his one eye stared down. Dooley couldn't remember being scrutinized so carefully by a man with two eyes. They'd traded their clothes for rags and their packs for sacks with straps. But a careful eye might pick out some inconsistent detail that Dooley hadn't thought of.

"Been traveling awhile, huh?" Wes asked.

Dooley gulped. This man knew. Why else would he ask the same question in a different way? What would they do to liars? No, they couldn't prove anything. No one knew who he was. Almost everyone he'd ever hijacked for food or gear, he or Kid had killed without mercy.

"A couple days." Dooley gestured to the nearest apartment buildings where people were frequenting. "Quite a community you have here. Someone out on the interstate said we'd find a friendly face downtown. Haven't seen much friendliness lately, Mr. Trimble. My wife here lost her sister to Meridia, then we lost our daughter two months ago to malnutrition or something in our water. We had to bury her without knowing what it was exactly. I know it's been tough for everyone, but we're ready to settle in somewhere if we can start fresh. Maybe here?"

Turning, Wes looked west at something perhaps out on the bay. Dooley knew they were just a couple blocks away from the shore. He could smell the sea. But what was Wes's hesitation? Or maybe they were this cautious with every new arrival. Finally, Wes turned his attention back to them.

"The building there—we call it Overcomers' Refuge." Wes pointed past the nearest adjacent building. "You'll find a man named Chevy inside. He'll tell you which apartments have running water and electricity."

"Running water and electricity?" Dooley glanced at Fran. "Did I hear you right?"

"Hey, Chevy's the engineer." Wes shrugged with a smile. "You can ask him how he's doing it all."

"Thanks, Mr. Trimble!"

"Call me Wes," the man said.

"All of this—it's amazing!" Dooley flapped his arm at a couple of women walking inside the perimeter barrier as if they had no care in the world that the country had fallen apart and bandits were still preying on the innocent. What a thrill to be moving amongst them, so unsuspecting! "It's an oasis, Wes."

"We're just sharing what the Good Lord has given us," Wes said. "Glad to have you. And sorry for your troubles. Hopefully we can help you move beyond those challenges. Until the Lord comes to take us home, we're just growing together here on earth."

"Praise the Lord for that," Dooley agreed. He'd never said such words except in mockery, but he hoped they sounded sincere this time.

"Ask him!" Fran jabbed him in the side.

"Hey, uh, Wes?" Dooley cleared his throat. Fran didn't seem to have any sense of timing when it came to undercover work. "We were hoping to catch up with an old acquaintance named Maddix Striber. Has he been through here? I mean lately?"

"Oh, you two know Maddix?" Wes chuckled. "Him on that bicycle of his, huh?"

"Yeah." Dooley chuckled nervously. "Is he around? We'd sort of like to surprise him."

"Well, he's a hard guy to pin down," Wes said, then wagged his finger. "If you see him before I do, tell him I'll trade my best eye patch for his saltwater taffy recipe."

Dooley laughed and waved, then pulled Fran with him as he started toward the Overcomers' apartment building. The rope-jumping girls kept singing their song as they walked past, and a man with a push broom nodded his greeting to them as he moved toward the ELM building.

"Maddix Striber is here!" Fran hissed in Dooley's ear. "I knew these people were responsible for shooting me—and embarrassing you. Losing all that horse meat made you look like such a fool!"

"How about those free eggs, though, huh?" He tried to temper her sharpness. "I'm scrambling mine as soon as we get—"

"They're all idiots!" Fran cursed. "Giving eggs away, and putting an unarmed cripple at the gate, and giving that overseer position to a one-eyed man? We could so easily move in here and take over. Just wait until Kid and the others get here tomorrow. Usually, you have dumb ideas, but this is something we could do. They're just a bunch of unarmed nobodies—with so much to take away!"

"Don't forget that blond guy shot you. They're not totally unarmed. Wes's rifle sort of looked like that gun that left you unconscious. If Maddix Striber is here, I don't think he'll be so easy."

"You're such a coward! Look, these people have opened their arms to us after you told your lame story about a dead daughter. They'll never see us coming. All we have to do is get the others in here tomorrow."

"Kid will be here in the morning."

At the Overcomers' building, they entered the open door that bore a sign that read, "This door will be closed and locked at sundown."

In the lobby, Dooley stood with Fran and watched a crew of three men disassembling the old elevators from the four elevator shafts in the middle of the lobby. Dooley identified the stairs when a door crashed open and two young boys ran out, giggling and chasing one another. They tore across the lobby and leaped across a marble containment wall that had probably held a fish pond prior to Pan-Day.

"Excuse me," Dooley said to the work crew. "I'm looking for a man named Chevy."

"Oh, that's me." A wiry man of about forty-five offered a smile then his hand. His gray eyes had a subtle fierceness to them. His shirt was half unbuttoned to reveal a broad Chevrolet tattoo across his chest. "You two must be new arrivals?"

Dooley matched the man's smile and shook the hand. Everyone seemed so gullible and accepting. They were perfect targets.

"Wes Trimble said you'd point us to an apartment." Dooley put his arm around Fran. "My wife and I are ready to settle down after a few hard months."

"Sure, sure." Chevy wiped his brow with his forearm and buttoned his shirt. They followed him across the lobby to a pile of gear: ammo vest, rifle, and a black book. "The next apartment available on the lowest floor is on ten—unless you want something higher."

"How high do they go?" Fran asked.

"Forty stories. We're installing a dolly system once we remove those old elevators." The crew of two dropped a wrench, then kept working without Chevy. "I've got water tanks set up, and electricity is trickling in from solar panels on the roof. It's not much, but it's something."

"Water tanks?" Dooley frowned. "But where do you get the water? How many people live around here?"

"Well, there's fifty in the Hopefuls' building. Here in the Overcomers' building, we have only twenty-two so far. Solar panels aren't much of a mystery, of course, but the water is a trade secret. I'm teaching some of the other engineers we have here to help me maintain them."

"Oh, it's a secret?" Dooley nodded. "I get it. You have to protect—"

"No, not like that. We tell everyone we can what works. All we do is use a little electricity to cool copper pipes on the roof, which collects condensation from the air day and night. The air here is humid, so we're pulling in gallons every day. With more piping, we can fill the demand of more residents."

"Water out of the air?" Dooley blinked. "That works? For real?"

"Reverse humidification, I call it. No one goes thirsty once they understand the science behind it. Of course, we all need to work together to conserve what water we can, but it's enough to shower every other day and drink whatever you want."

Dooley glanced at Fran, who seemed equally shocked. Their short supply of desalination filters would no longer be a worry.

"What about food?" Dooley asked.

"We'll get you set up," Chevy said, "then it's up to you to make a living. We have lots of little tasks—gathering brush for the goats, milking the goats, fishing at the bay, or cleaning the fish. Other stuff, too."

"What do you mean you'll get us set up? Who's doing this?"

"*ELM*. Every Life Matters." Chevy held up his black book. "I'm a follower of Jesus Christ. Since every life around us matters to Him, every life matters to us, His people. The elm tree is our symbol since every type of elm tree has a different usefulness, but each type is important. There's a forestry guy in the Hopefuls' apartments who's actually pretty knowledgeable about the different uses and types of elm wood."

"What do the trees have to do with anything?" Fran scowled. "That makes no sense. I see no trees around here."

"He's saying *they* are the trees," Dooley said to Fran. "It's just a symbol, Fran. Look, Chevy, we're not religious or anything, but could we still get an apartment upstairs? Whatever's on the tenth floor is fine with us."

"That's a lot of stairs to climb!" Fran crossed her arms. "Who wants to do that ten times a day?"

"I live on the twenty-seventh floor in the ELM building." Chevy chuckled as he picked up his gear. "You'll learn to make every trip count. Once we have the dolly working, it won't be that bad. Come on. I'll walk you up there."

Chevy told his two workers he'd return to them soon, then he led the way up the stairs.

"Hey, that's some rifle you have there," Dooley admired. "You're carrying it all the way to the tenth floor? It looks heavy."

"Gotta stay ready for battle." Chevy climbed the first flight. "The world is an evil place and it's important we take a stand where we're needed."

It took all of Dooley's discipline to resist asking if the rifle was loaded with some sort of tranquilizer, like the one Fran had been shot with. He couldn't reveal his intentions quite yet, and for once, Fran had the sense to keep her mouth shut about it.

Dooley was used to walking a few miles each day, but straining himself was against his code. He'd ambushed people for what they'd gathered so he didn't have to work hard for it. Chevy was clearly more fit since he was still going strong by the fifth story landing. Fortunate for Dooley, Fran asked for a rest before he did—so he could save face. Turning his back to Chevy, Dooley sucked twice on his inhaler.

Fran collapsed on the nearest stairs and panted for breath. After the dose from his inhaler, Dooley was more easily able to hide his exhaustion by leaning against the wall opposite Chevy. Obviously, the ELM people weren't the all-night partiers like Dooley and his gang were.

"What kind of deal do you guys have with the PSDF?" Dooley asked. "I thought the Pacific States went after anyone who had anything."

"We've started up a few industries that help the families on Coronado Island," Chevy said. "But more than selling them eggs, milk, and fish, the Casperteins have a way of leaving an impact. Levi saved the life of Sergeant Lesage, General Brogdon's top officer, so there's peace between us. That's the way God starts working in lives. He opens doors for reconciliation, but we have to be willing to step through the door."

"I'm more familiar with looking out for number one," Dooley said, then remembered Fran. "And taking care of my wife."

"Don't be fooled," Fran said with more bite than Dooley thought necessary. "He doesn't think of me that often."

An uncomfortable silence passed before Chevy encouraged them to continue.

Finally, they reached the tenth floor and Chevy showed them apartment one, which faced south.

"You'll have sun here all day." He led them to the suite of two bedrooms and a large kitchen and living room. "It's the best apartment on the floor for growing vegetables on the balcony. And look here. This'll save you trips up and down for little things."

He showed them a spool and fishing reel of heavy gauge line attached to a bucket that could be lowered outside to the ground floor. Next, he pointed out the switches for the kitchen electricity and the hot water tank heater—meant only to be switched on prior to use, then switched off. Lighting in the buildings was to remain dependent on candles or lanterns so electricity could be saved for hot water and cooking.

After Chevy left, Dooley wandered around the suite with Fran as they took in the furnished apartment—even folded sheets, blankets, and towels in the closet.

"This is pretty nice." Dooley admired a cupboard of pots and pans. "I could get used to this."

"You better not be having second thoughts!" Fran punched his shoulder, knocking him sideways. "I know you saw his rifle. It's the same kind that I was shot with."

"Hey, easy!" Dooley rubbed his arm. "I'm not having second thoughts. I'm just enjoying the vacation. Don't worry, babe. I'm seeing everything. With Kid and the rest of the boys, we could take over this whole operation. Living like this could be permanent for all of us."

"I'm not going to climb those stairs every day." Fran picked up a throw pillow and sniffed it before tossing it back to the sofa. "You need to find out who these Caspertein people are. I bet they have some sort of penthouse somewhere and never climb any stairs."

"But this isn't that bad, right? I mean, compared to what we've been living in? We could do this temporarily."

"Well, I'm not growing vegetables!" Fran swore. "I'm not with you to become some farmer. Get rid of whoever is in charge here and we can live like royalty. If it's Maddix Striber, then I want him thrown off the balcony. If it's these Casperteins, then we'll get rid of them, too. We can make everyone else here work for us. And no one is telling me I can't use all the electricity I want. No one, Dooley!"

"We just need to play along for a few days, Fran." Dooley unpacked his bag on the dining table. "Let's go next door and visit with some neighbors. We might find out more about who needs to be removed."

"No, I'm not going down there again." Fran laid back on the couch. "These people disgust me. They're weak. Just go and do whatever you need to, but leave the gun."

"Fran—"

"Leave the gun!" She sat up and glared at him. "I'm not going to be left defenseless. Go scout around. No one'll suspect you."

"That's not what I'm worried about." Dooley set the handgun on the table. "Just . . . don't shoot anyone. We've only glimpsed what they're doing here. This place isn't like the suburbs. They're organized here. Let's wait for Kid and the others before we decide anything."

"Just go." She rolled over on the sofa. "Your voice is giving me a headache."

Dooley made a face, but said nothing more. It'd been several days since she'd said anything pleasant—since before they lit all the house fires. When she was in the mood, he enjoyed himself with no one more, but lately, her mouth stung him like acid.

Making his way down the stairwell, he heard people far below come and go from their apartments, and clanging metal told him that Chevy and his men were hard at work, getting the dolly system working. It all seemed so futile and fragile—trying to rebuild what once was. In a single night, Dooley guessed he and his gang could storm the buildings and loot whatever stores they had. They had become experts at destruction. Then they could replace the ELM leadership and force everyone to work for them. Dooley liked the idea of living like a king. Having electricity again suited him just fine, too! ELM could be his retirement plan.

In the courtyard outside, Dooley stood against the Hopefuls' building as two men with sledge hammers broke through several concrete squares. Young children hopped excitedly and clung to their mothers who encouraged their kids to be patient. Dooley thrust his hands in his pockets and wondered what they were building.

Suddenly, a woman with horrible facial scars wandered across the courtyard and stood nearby to watch as well. Dooley was so captured by her ugliness that he didn't look away when he realized she was staring back at him. She had no shame—bearing such scars where no hair grew on one side of her head. It was in plain sight of everyone! Most people who'd been injured so severely during or after Pan-Day hadn't survived since no hospitals existed any longer. Such chaos had enabled him to range where he'd wanted and victimize whomever he'd desired.

Scoffing, Dooley recalled the damage he'd done across the city to shut down such facilities like hospitals. This woman's scars appeared to be from a fire, but Dooley doubted they were from a recent fire he'd started since she seemed to have recuperated.

He straightened up to stand taller next to the building as she walked directly toward him. Though he wasn't a tall man, he'd relied on his gang and their weapons to intimidate the populace. Here, he had neither.

"You're new here." She offered her slender hand. "I'm Carla. I live in the ELM building."

Dooley tried not to stare at her scars—where her platinum hair ended high on the right side of her skull. Her ear even appeared to have melted against her head!

"Neil." He shook her hand. "I was just watching, wondering what they're working on. They're digging something up?"

Carla turned to stand beside him. She smelled like soap and other sweet smells he'd forgotten existed. Maybe Fran would smell like that after she cleaned up. The women who'd joined the gang had smelled no better than the men—forced to endure body odor and filth since water was so cherished and scarce. Most didn't like bathing in the salt water in the bay since the salt caused sores on some who couldn't rinse off adequately in fresh water.

"They're building a sandbox for the kids to play in," she said. "They need to get outside more. Titus said this would be a good spot because the buildings will shelter the kids if there's any gunfire."

"Gunfire?" Dooley stiffened. "Who would attack a place like this? You guys actually worry about that sort of thing?"

"Oh, the Casperteins don't worry about anything." She chuckled. "You apparently haven't met them. They say they trust God for everything and remain prepared for anything."

"So, this Titus—he's a Caspertein?"

"Yeah, he pretty much runs all this." She nodded with a far-off look. "He's amazing. I've known a lot of powerful men in my previous line of work—men who were influential and proud. But no one's like Titus. And don't get me started on Levi, his son."

"Levi?" Dooley thought she blushed a little. "What's his son like?"

"He's only twenty, but he's already like a mini version of his dad. They're pretty special guys. Confident. A little delusional about their God, but I've learned they're pretty harmless since all they do is care for people."

"There is no God." Dooley grunted. "I share your point of view. I'm glad there's someone here who thinks like me and my wife."

Carla smiled, maybe just to be polite. Dooley wondered if he'd said too much. Once he took over the ELM complex, it would be helpful to have like-minded people from the old regime to carry on—if anyone was still alive.

"I'll have to meet this Titus character pretty soon." Dooley leaned back to scan the upper floors of the ELM building. "My wife and I are probably going to be sticking around."

Men with wheelbarrows arrived with loads of sand and dumped them next to the squared-off section.

"Titus left this morning with a guy named Dusty to go investigate the fire from a couple nights ago. That's why you and your wife are here, right? The fire?"

"Yeah." Dooley nodded. "The fire. But we're realizing this is where we need to be, anyway, so it's all working out."

"The Casperteins would say that their God purposed all that for you."

"Oh, yeah, right." Dooley rolled his eyes. "I see what you mean by delusion. How about Maddix Striber? I heard he might be around here somewhere, too."

"I think I've heard that name once." Carla frowned. "You could ask Levi when he gets back from fishing this afternoon. He's met more people than anyone in the city—even outside the downtown area. He'd be the one to talk to if you're looking for someone. I mean, besides Chevy, who knows everyone here."

Dooley had so many questions for this woman, but he didn't want to seem suspicious. He wanted to know how strong Titus' fighting force might be. How many guns could be put on the above balconies? How vulnerable would they be if Dooley or a couple of his men got inside the ELM building, say, at night?

"So, what's it like living in the ELM building?"

"About the same as the other two buildings." Carla shrugged, then winced and held her shoulder like she'd injured it recently. "Chevy installs all the same utilities inside each building and on top of each roof—electricity, water, gardens, and so on. No one was more prepared for Pan-Day than the Casperteins, but they're not hoarders like you'd think most preppers would be. I think their beliefs push them to share everything they have, even if it'll cost them down the road."

"But they must have some serious stores in that building if they can accept travelers like me right off the streets."

"They try to get everyone to become self-sufficient as soon as possible," Carla said, noticeably dodging his question. "You'll find something to do to make a living. Your wife, too. I can tell Levi to find you when he gets back from the bay—if you want to join the fishing crew. I hear it's hard work, but you'll own what you catch. Everyone needs something to barter with."

"What do you do?"

"Gardening and laundry. Annette Caspertein, Titus' wife, got me started. I have a pretty good system in my building. At least I have everything I need."

"I'd sure like to see something like that. I mean, your laundry system. Maybe we could set up something like it in our building."

"Oh, no one's allowed inside the ELM building except us twelve residents."

"Twelve?" Dooley's heart skipped a beat. *Only twelve!* "So, you guys have all kinds of space over there, huh? Lots of empty apartments and floors?"

"Titus calls it our last line of defense. That's why no one's allowed inside to see what's in there."

"Sounds like a little paranoia. From what I hear, not even the military will bother you guys."

"There are other enemies, Titus says, who may be lurking. They're prepared here for everything as far as I can tell. That's one reason why I stay here. They're good people."

"Even with their religion?"

"It's not that bad, really."

"What about Titus? When do you think he'll be back so I can meet him?"

"I don't know. Maybe a day or two if he doesn't get sidetracked. Of course, if he's anything like Levi, Titus and Dusty will find someone to help or escort. They could be gone for a week, or they could be back tomorrow."

Dooley watched the filling of the sandbox, then the men carted away the fragments of removed concrete. For once, he didn't want to destroy a place, only assume command. Force would be necessary. Blood would be spilled, but that didn't bother him. ELM would be his, but he'd have to make his move soon.

He excused himself from Carla and climbed the ten stories to find Fran still in the tub. She seemed to be in a better mood, so he sat on the toilet seat and quietly shared his latest idea. Though he believed they were the only ones living on the tenth floor, he took no chances and spoke in hushed tones.

"So, we need to attack them tomorrow," Fran said, "before this Titus person returns from the burned-out area."

"Exactly. Titus and his friend Dusty are gone. That leaves ten in the ELM building. They can't all be armed. Carla wasn't. Once Kid and a couple others arrive tomorrow morning, we can surprise whoever might resist. We'll kill them all. Whenever Titus and Dusty return, we can ambush them easily. Everyone else, all the civilians, will fall in line. You'll see."

"This is better than your usual stupid plans," Fran said. "I could get used to bubble baths and eggs, Dooley. Don't mess this up."

"I won't. We won't. It'll be easy. They let us in the front door. It's almost like they want to give us the throne here. There's just one thing."

"What?"

"Titus' son, Levi. Carla says he's only twenty, but he's some sort of leader who's gone out fishing most days. He's probably the only one who'll be any trouble for us. She didn't mention anyone else. Chevy looks like we can take him by surprise since he's always busy working. He sets down his rifle to work with his hands."

"And Wes has only one eye." Fran shook a bubble-coated hand at him. "And don't forget about Maddix Striber. He's around here somewhere."

"Maybe." Dooley scratched his chin. "He can't be in the ELM building. Carla didn't even know who he was. I don't like not knowing where he is."

"We'll find him eventually. But first, we'll need to kill the ELM people," Fran said. "It will keep the others in line. Make it public. Throw them off one of the balconies so everyone will see we mean business. Then we'll move into the ELM apartments and control everything from there like they do."

"This is why I love you." Dooley kissed her hand. "We have the same heart."

"Before Kid arrives tomorrow, find out for us exactly how many guns we'll face. You have to know, Dooley. And Kid will want you to tell him everything we find out."

Dooley returned downstairs to the courtyard, then walked alone inside the perimeter of vehicles which had been lined up at every intersection to keep out vehicle traffic. It took him an hour to walk the whole perimeter, stopping at all three gaps of the arranged vehicles to study what lay beyond the barrier. The ELM people had indeed cut off for themselves several blocks of the city to continue to thrive, and the rest of the city seemed abandoned to dust and rust, wind and garbage.

Though Dooley was rarely this cautious while attacking other targets, taking over ELM was an entirely different kind of venture. He would need to remain sober and disciplined, even if the rest of his gang indulged themselves with the civilian women and resources when they arrived. This was an investment, a plan for the future that could secure him for years to come. All of ELM could become both his empire and his playground!

As he returned to the central courtyard where the three occupied buildings stood—among the six within the perimeter—he noticed a procession of a dozen people approaching ELM from the bay. Right away, he knew this was the fishing crew. Sure enough, they pushed or pulled two carts with heaps of what was probably their catch for the day—and it smelled like it. Dooley anticipated spying on their whole fishing process eventually, but for now he stood against the ELM building to wait for them to pass by. Most of all, he wanted to meet the son of Titus Caspertein, since he'd learned it was this formidable family he would need to replace unconditionally.

Identifying Levi Caspertein was effortless for two reasons. First, the twenty-year-old stood a head taller than his fellow fishermen, and second, Dooley recognized him! He was the blond, young man he and Fran had crossed two months earlier during a dispute over horse meat.

Rather than stand there and wait to be recognized himself, Dooley dropped to his knee to retie one of his shoes. Hiding his face seemed perfectly timed as people from the Hopefuls' building emerged to welcome the fishermen and receive their catch for distribution.

Dooley looked up only after he was sure the parade had moved beyond him. So, Levi was responsible for tranquilizing Fran. Though she would be spitting mad at the young man for his role a couple months earlier, Dooley knew they couldn't act with vengeance too rashly. They needed to stick to a plan. After all, Levi could still recognize him or Fran before the following day when they hoped to implement the takeover with Kid and the others.

Wandering widely across the courtyard, Dooley was thankful to blend in with more residents who spilled out to admire the catch or barter for their share. Carla was there, as well as a tall brunette whose beauty and poise seemed out of place in the drab, broken-down world. By the way she stood and laughed close to Levi, he figured they might be family, maybe an older sister. And Carla took two wrapped meat packages and handed them to a stout-looking man who carried one of the stubby rifles of the ELM defenders. The way he moved, he would need to be dealt with carefully the following day. Hopefully, there were no other soldier-types inside the ELM building that Dooley hadn't met yet.

So far, Dooley saw no real concern that would make him hesitate to proceed. Though he and Fran had only one handgun at the moment, it wouldn't be difficult for him to get his hands on one of those assault rifles a few of them carried.

Across from the ELM building, Dooley stopped where he could see directly into the headquarters' open door. The large elm tree painted above the door would need to be painted over once Dooley took charge; no symbols of the past leadership should remain. He'd destroyed enough property in the last few months to learn also how to destroy people's loyalties or convictions. There were ways to ruin lives in such a way that they became passive, inconsequential, and nonthreatening.

Once he had control of the fishing, gardening, power, and water systems in each building, any dissidents would fall into line and follow him. A little discomfort was all that was necessary to force people to sell their souls—for a cup of water or a bite of food. Yes, he'd control all of this by sundown tomorrow!

From that angle, Dooley could see through the ELM door and make out the goat pens. He couldn't wait to get his hands on the milk production. Fran would probably want to take a milk bath—just because she could!

He merely needed to avoid being recognized until the following morning when Kid arrived. ELM would soon fall!

Chapter Three

Titus walked cautiously up a street surrounded by blackened properties. Entire homes had been reduced to heaps of ash. Only a few refrigerators, fireplaces, and vehicles remained. Even the trees that hadn't been chopped down for firewood had been reduced to solitary skeletons, black posts standing between house lots.

Dusty stood near a mailbox twenty yards ahead, waiting for Titus to catch up, but Titus took his time reaching him as he read sign on the dusty street and studied the burn pattern of the fires. Using a piece of white chalk, Titus drew an elm tree on another mailbox. In time, he hoped people would learn about Jesus Christ, who'd inspired their motto, but for now, he could only leave it on broken remnants where people might pass by.

"What do you think?" Dusty asked softly. The air was still and uncomfortably quiet. Not even the birds had returned to the neighborhood. There was nothing for them to return to. "Why would they burn all these houses through here, but not those up the street?"

"I'm not sure yet." Titus slid the chalk into a breast pocket, then held his battle rifle ready to fire. Though he'd been on one excursion with Levi away from ELM, this was his first time abroad in the heart of San Diego's suburbs since before Pan-Day. "Their tracks indicate about a dozen men. A couple women. They worked in pairs, lighting each house as they came through here from the northeast and moved southwest."

"Why pairs?"

"Probably one to pour lighter fluid or gasoline on the houses, and the other to ignite the accelerant."

"Stinks pretty bad." Dusty wrinkled his nose. "So, you think we should follow them south?"

"Yeah, they're probably holed up somewhere, maybe near the shore."

Titus had already begun to think of Dusty as his adopted son, even though the thirty-four-year-old had been living with them for only two and a half months. As a roommate and companion of Levi's, the ex-con had been impacted by the bondage breaking grace that Levi and the others at ELM lived out daily. Dusty had become a new man.

Only because Titus believed Dusty's conversion a few weeks earlier had been genuine was he allowed to come on this type of mission. Any mission outside ELM's perimeter was inviting potential death. As a believer in an everlasting reality and eternal judgment, Titus wouldn't have risked the soul of an unbeliever accompanying him. But Dusty needed to exercise his faith outside of Levi's shadow and the fishing enterprise down on the bay. Besides, Dusty had a pleasant disposition, thanks to the humbling power of grace and his born-again curiosity to experience the world as a sober and moral man.

They walked south until they emerged from the burn zone, then followed the edge of the trail of destruction southwesterly. Dusty had been instructed by Levi how to take point and move as a unit in cover formation, so Titus didn't need to correct the younger man along the way. He walked a little ahead and to the left of Titus, glancing over his right shoulder occasionally to check on Titus' heading. Though Dusty had been target practicing only a couple of times with Levi down by the docks, Titus was confident he'd become more proficient with the battle rifle while in the field.

Suddenly, Titus crouched and examined drag marks across the littered street. He whistled a black-capped chickadee call to Dusty, like he'd used since a youth in

Arkansas, and motioned for Dusty to study the tracks with him.

"Which direction are they going?" Dusty asked after a few seconds. "Somebody's dragging some loot maybe?"

"That's the curious thing." Titus pointed to the marks beside the drag marks. "Look at these. Hand prints here, here, here, and they keep going. Small hands. Maybe a woman. She's alone. Looks like she's scooting along on her backside. See?"

"I don't get it. Why?"

"Maybe she's wounded." Titus gazed south. "She came from back there. See those green trees and the dip in the terrain? That's got to be the Stillwater River. And this lady is shuffling herself away, heading north."

"She won't find anything in the burned-out area."

Titus stood tall and used his rifle scope to scan south, then north.

"We need to have a chat with Dooley and his boys," Titus said, "but sometimes the Lord puts someone in our path who interrupts our day. The needs of one person comes before our own plans today."

"This woman?"

"Yep. These tracks are fresh, maybe even from this morning. See the rigid clarity of her handprint? The wind hasn't even had time to blow sand into the prints yet."

"Moving on her hands like that, she can't get too far. Forget Dooley. Let's help her."

"I'm with you." Titus started to follow the tracks north. "When you're tracking something, you always preserve the sign. Be careful where you step so if you need to come back and study the sign again, it'll still be there. And don't forget to watch your surroundings at the same time. We'd feel pretty foolish if our eyes were on the ground and we walked right into an ambush."

"Ambush?" Dusty licked his lips. "You think she's dangerous?"

"It ain't easy preparing for every eventuality, but that's what we're here for."

"How can we be prepared for everything?" Dusty asked as he walked along the trail opposite Titus. "Is that even possible?"

"No, I suppose not, but we can trust God in these moments to prepare us for whatever we find."

"You really know how to make a guy nervous."

"So, it's a little more exciting out here than burying the dead or fishing with Levi, huh?"

"Hmm, I'm not sure exciting is the right word."

The trail of drag marks led to the left and tracked in front of a music store. The glass windows were gone, the store looted and emptied from Titus' viewpoint. Next to the music store there was an alley that led directly north.

"She's going right into the burned-out zone," Dusty said. "You think she's armed? Or it's an ambush?"

Titus checked their back trail.

"I'm not sensing a trap, but just the same, let me go in. You stay out here and cover the street. And watch the rooftops. Levi said Dooley used roofs to shoot down at travelers. Stand with your back against that corner. If it looks safe to follow me up the alley, I'll radio you."

Dusty nodded and pressed his back against the building. As Titus started away, he noticed his partner's lips moving, like he was praying for courage and fidelity.

The alley was like a dim tunnel between two buildings over three stories tall. Trash bags—many ripped open— would block vehicle traffic, but a walking path had been preserved. The trail continued halfway up the alley where the woman's handprints swerved to the left and into a dark doorway. The metal door hung off its hinges from looters, but judging by the tracks on the ground, the woman was the only one who'd passed this way recently.

Leaning into the doorway, Titus waited for his eyes to adjust to the dim lighting.

"Hello in there," he said without yelling. The woman had to be nearby. The rails and shelving of a dry cleaning and laundry service spanned that section of the first floor, but the clothes were gone. "My name is Titus Caspertein. I saw your drag marks and handprints leading in here. My wife would never smile at me again if she knew I'd overlooked someone in need out here. Let me know that you're okay. Just call out."

He waited at the door, but heard no response.

"I have food and water. And I'm a follower of Jesus Christ, so it's not in my nature to move on until I know you're safe and in good health." He sighed, then chuckled. "Come on, now. You're not making this easy on me. Just call out and I'll come to you. Meeting people out here is pretty dangerous, but I'm only here to care for people because God cares for people, all people. Whatever your situation, well, I love a good challenge."

Still no response.

Titus swung his rifle onto his back, then drew his flashlight. Her trail continued into the store to the right. He walked softly into the dim room and left the bright doorway behind. A row of washers and dryers stood against a dividing wall. Cautiously, he peered around the corner and shined his beam on a woman who was sitting on the floor with a metal pipe in her hand, raised and ready to strike.

Instantly, Titus lowered his light from her eyes. Her thin legs were bundled and rags were tied onto her backside to protect her skin from dragging as she'd shuffled along. Since she seemed to have no pack or supplies, Titus guessed she'd entered the laundry in search of drinkable water or safe shelter. A deep sink indeed hung on the wall nearby, but Titus doubted any water would flow from its faucet any longer.

"Don't worry," he said. "I'm not coming any closer unless you say so. Besides, it ain't easy getting clocked with a metal pipe like that one."

Her eyes were wide and wild, and her dark hair was tangled, half-obscuring a pretty but dirt-smudged face. She appeared to be in her late twenties, perhaps tall and slender if she were standing upright.

"When was the last time you ate?" Titus drew wrapped food from his ammo vest pocket. "This is my wife's recipe—her first yogurt energy bar. It's homemade from goat's milk. It's pretty terrible, but I'm confident they'll improve. At least it's edible, right?"

He tossed the bar underhandedly onto her lap. She lowered the pipe in her raised hand, yet didn't let it go. With her other hand, she picked up the health bar and sniffed it.

"It doesn't smell too bad." She spoke weakly. "I . . . could use some water more than anything."

Titus tugged off his water bottle.

"Here. It's heavy. Here it comes."

She let go of the pipe and caught the water bottle with one hand. There was strength in her arms regardless of her condition. After unscrewing the cap, she sniffed the contents.

"Fresh water? It's clean?"

"Straight from our reverse humidifier and filtered through some sort of contraption my buddy Chevy rigged up."

"Chevy?" She guzzled a few swallows and took a bite of the yogurt bar. "Who's that?"

"He's an engineer who keeps a few buildings downtown running with water and electricity."

"Electricity? Downtown?"

"Yep. I don't think my wife would tolerate me if I didn't shower a couple times a week at least. And if I have to shower, I'm too old to use cold water. We have hot water tanks and everything."

"You don't look too old. What's your wife's name?"

"Annette. If you're old enough to remember the supermodel named Annette Sheffield, well, she's Annette

Caspertein now. She'd never admit it, but I know she married down, maybe out of pity."

"Funny." She slurped from the bottle, then wiped her mouth on her sleeve. "People don't joke much where I'm from."

"If we weren't supposed to use our sense of humor, God wouldn't have made so many of us so funny-looking." Titus chuckled. He kept the flashlight beam on the floor while she finished the bar and half the water. "Keep the bottle. It's yours. It looks like you need it. I have a couple more in my pack."

"Thanks. I . . . do need some help." She was very still while he waited for her to explain. He knew it was difficult for anyone to trust a stranger, so he didn't push her. "I'm a paraplegic."

She watched his face, maybe for confusion or disgust or surprise. But he only grunted.

"Seems like there might be other ways for someone like yourself to move around out here."

"No kidding." She scoffed. "I had to climb out a window and leave my wheelchair behind. I barely survived. They were coming to kill me for being disabled. The Garden doesn't allow anyone to live who's unhealthy or old or mentally ill."

"The Garden?"

"It was a rich people's retirement center not far away. Now, it doubles as a cemetery. I lived there for a while. Everything was cool until they started killing off undesirables. And I didn't even use more resources than anyone else. But that didn't matter to them."

"How long have you been out here alone?"

"Like a day and a half maybe. I really need to find a wheelchair so I can move around easier. Besides that, I have nothing because I had to leave everything behind when I escaped the Garden. I had to crawl through this nasty culvert where the Stillwater River runs through."

"So, your wheelchair is still there, right?" Titus took off his pack and rifle and sat cross-legged on the floor. "Seems like if you have a wheelchair that works for you, you should keep it. I'm guessing it's measured to fit your body, right?"

"Custom? Yeah, but anyone would be stupid to go into the Garden after leaving. They murder people while patting themselves on the back for doing it. I saw it for weeks and didn't do anything until they came for me. My chair is gone."

"Hmm. You don't know me, my new friend, but fetching back your wheelchair is just the excuse I need to get into a place like the Garden."

"What? Are you dense? I just told you they'll kill you!"

"Are they heavily armed? Have lots of guns or something?"

"Well, no. Mayor Malden allows some of his men to carry handguns, but this guy, Sazon, he's called a Sympathy Agent. Sazon does the executions and carries a little syringe of this deadly stuff on his belt. He's this big muscled guy who nobody messes with."

"Sounds like someone I need to meet. But we need to get your wheelchair back first. I'm guessing they kept it. You've only been gone a couple days."

"The Garden has rules. Laws."

"If they're that dangerous," Titus said, "then I need to meet them for myself and assess the threat."

"You can't just walk in and out of there. If you live downtown, then you must know where a medical supply dealership is, or a hospital. I don't even need a nice wheelchair. Anything that rolls will beat dragging myself around."

"Sure, but what would happen if no one stands up to this Mayor Malden?"

"I'm not standing up to him."

"Sure, you will. Who do you think is going to give me an introduction?"

"I— You're—" She swore. "I'm not going back into the Garden!"

"Well, at least not until you tell me your name, right? Then I'm going to walk you right into the Garden and set you in your own wheelchair."

"Set me in my wheelchair?" She guffawed. "What, you're going to carry me right in there?"

"How else? You're not dragging yourself anywhere else, not when the Good Lord gave me a strong back for moments like this. I'm getting older, but I'm not too geriatric yet."

"If you were, Sazon would kill you." She sighed. "My name is Emily. Emily Pickford."

"It's a pleasure. Call me Titus."

"You're serious about this? It's pretty dumb, but they probably won't kill a stranger outright. They probably won't even let you in the front gate."

"Maybe we'll avoid the front gate altogether." Titus smiled. "You know, find another way in there. But not through that culvert. I can imagine that was disgusting."

"It was. But I should probably wait for you outside the Garden when you go in. I can tell you where I left my wheelchair. And if you go in at night, you could probably get in and out without anyone noticing—if you're lucky."

"How will I get a sense of who this Malden guy is if I go in at night and in secret? No, we should go in while it's daylight. We should go in right now."

She shook her head, then gestured at him.

"That's a gun, right? You better know how to use it."

"Well, I don't keep it as an ornament."

Titus notified Dusty on the radio that he'd found the woman and they'd be out in a few minutes. But it took more than a few minutes for him to fashion a harness while Emily held the flashlight. He used a wool blanket from his pack as the basis for the harness, then cut leg holes for Emily to sit in it like a baby carrier. However, attaching shoulder straps to support her weight on his back seemed untenable. Finally, he emptied his pack, then cut holes for her legs.

"You're sure doing a lot for someone you don't even know," Emily said. "And I'd say you're more than a little stubborn about being gallant."

"This isn't gallantry." He gathered his pack's contents in his nylon rain poncho and tied it in a bundle to carry in front of him. "Us Casperteins—you'll learn we don't mind doing things the hard way if we know God is showing us His will."

"I don't know anything about God's will," she said as he knelt in front of her, "but I think I'm about to learn something about discomfort."

"Help me with your arms." He fit one shoulder strap up his arm. "Hopefully, we don't have to do this but once—and the Stillwater River isn't too far away! Wait just a minute . . ."

Titus touched his ear as his radio receiver crackled. It wasn't Dusty outside, but someone was definitely on their frequency.

"ELM333, this is ELMHQ." It was Levi's voice. "Pops, we have news on Dooley. He's here at ELM scouting around. I repeat, Dooley is at ELM, but we are being hospitable. You're out of range to respond probably, but I figured you'd want to know that you can come home now. Out."

Emily watched his face, certainly curious as Titus considered his son's news. If Dooley was truly at ELM, and Levi was dealing with him, then there was no need to hurry back. He could focus entirely on this new adversary—the Garden.

"Sorry, Em. That was the home office giving me an update. Okay, let's do this!"

Piggyback style, Emily clung to his shoulders as he fit the pack on and tightened the shoulder and chest straps. Next, he collected her legs and used a shirt from his pack to tie her ankles in front of his waist. Finally, he bent over and picked up his rifle and the bundle of gear. Her arms circled his neck under his chin, leaving his arms free to carry his belongings and rifle.

"Can you tolerate this for a little while?" He headed for the alley entrance.

"If you can tolerate me breathing in your ear for a little while." She scoffed. "An hour ago, I was alone. Now I'm draped over you like a pet monkey."

"It ain't easy getting familiar so quickly, but sometimes our needs have to come before our bashfulness."

"I can't imagine you being bashful about anything."

"Well, I used to be a little self-conscious about my ear hair, but my partner Oleg teased me so much about it that I've just owned the fuzz entirely."

"You have a weird way of looking at things."

"The last few years, I've learned life is easier when I just admit my weaknesses and foolishness instead of posturing or bluffing. Besides, the Bible says our humility makes way for God to show us favor. If Oleg were here, he'd agree and say guys with as much ear hair as I have need lots of favor."

They reached the alley and Titus marched toward Dusty.

"All's quiet?" Titus asked as they reached the cross street.

"Nothing's moved. You heard Levi's message?"

"Yep. It sounds like we can take our time returning since they've got things under control back home."

"If you say so." Dusty nodded at Emily. "Hey. I'm Dusty."

"Emily." She lifted her hand in greeting over Titus' shoulder. "Your pal here wants to go get himself killed. Maybe you can talk him out of it."

"What's the plan?" Dusty asked Titus. "Something new?"

"Something worthy." Titus indicated their way southward as he explained their need to recon a threat in some place called the Garden. "I don't mind carrying you around, Em, but having your wheelchair will be more comfortable for you."

"And I'd have less ear hair in my face."

Dusty choked with laughter and Titus nearly stumbled, appreciating her quick humor. Emily was no more than one hundred and twenty pounds since her paralyzed legs had atrophied, even though her upper body was muscled from pushing herself around for years.

As they walked, Titus asked her questions about the layout of the Garden's buildings and driveway inside the front gate. Once he knew what to expect, he explained what Dusty could do to cover Titus while staying hidden—yet enter the Garden covertly from another direction.

"We'll stay in radio contact," Titus said, "so you'll know when or if I need you for cover fire. We need to get Emily's chair first, then I'll be getting an introduction one way or another to this Mayor Malden character."

"And Sazon," Emily added. "He's the real killer. But there are others, too. You'll be very outnumbered."

"That's why I brought lots of ammunition. But if all else fails, I throw the monkey on my back at them."

Titus's jokes came to an end when the gate of the Garden came into sight. It was tall iron, reinforced at the hinges with extra welds to withstand anything less than a tank. Dusty jogged past the gate and plunged into the bushes alongside the wall where he disappeared into the thick foliage and beyond.

Turning right, Titus followed the wall in the other direction and along the street.

"I'm tempted to demand that you leave me out here," Emily said with a sigh, "but I resigned myself to dying two days ago, and I sort of want to see their faces when I show up like this. They'll be totally surprised."

"And exposed. They'll know you told me all about their evil deeds, but the way I'll treat them will throw them off balance."

"What do you mean? You're just going to shoot them, right? I'll tell you who to kill and you kill them. The others can figure out their own lives. Like I told you, they only have handguns. I've never seen any rifles."

"Oh, I'll definitely be shooting if there's a need for it, but I won't be doing any killing."

"Wounding?" Emily asked with hope.

"Not even that."

He shared with her the ELM motto and the reason for Christ's sake that he no longer killed his enemies—even at the risk of his own life.

"Tranquilizers!" Emily stuttered through several words, then finally said, "That's ridiculous!"

"I know that." Titus smiled. "But it's often the ridiculous measures of grace that touches hearts. I'd rather win over Sazon than send him to hell."

"Well, I don't have the same sentiments."

"That's okay. That's why I'm the one with the guns and you're along for the ride." He stopped in front of the wall. "How's this spot?"

She described the orchard on the other side of the wall in that area of the property.

"But you'll need a ladder to get over it. It's got to be fifteen feet high. Maybe use that tree—"

"We've got this." Titus backed up and stood idly eyeing the wall a moment. He set down his bundle of belongings behind thick bushes, then handed his rifle to Emily. "Hang onto this until we get onto the wall."

"I'm very skeptical about this plan," she said.

"You'll learn that I ad-lib more than I actually plan."

Emily started to respond, but he charged the wall at that moment. She shrieked the instant he planted his foot on the wall and surged upward. Their combined momentum carried him high enough to slap one palm over the top of the wall. Once his second hand grasped the top, he swung his body left and right, then pulled up until he could hook a foot over the top. Emily reached past his head and set the rifle on the wall, then she used her arms to pull her weight up with him.

Panting, Titus reached the top and sat down. With Emily on his back, his balance was off, and he felt as if they'd fall over any second. Since they were as exposed as a bird on a branch, he grabbed his rifle and dropped off the wall straight down, landing with a thud and rolling to the side. Fruit trees grew thick a few yards away where he crouched and refastened his rifle to his vest.

"Which way to the path?" he asked.

"The path and bridge are that way." She pointed over his shoulder. "It's the best way to cross the river. The villas and chapel are on the other side."

Titus stalked through the trees, his heart beating wildly with excitement. Emily was a burden, but he'd carried heavier packs during various operations for COIL in Africa and Asia.

"I'm over the wall," Dusty reported in his ear. "Now I'm moving west. I can see some sort of building ahead. I think it's one of those villas she talked about. Over."

"Okay, Dusty." Titus paused at the path that dissected the Garden. The swept walkway stretched left and right before him. "Get closer and stay hidden until you're needed. Over."

Leaning out of the foliage, Titus looked to the left. Only one sentry stood at the closed gate. He seemed focused on nibbling something. While the man was distracted, Titus walked onto the path and climbed the gently arching bridge over the quiet river. Twenty seconds later, he was over the arch and darting through the vegetables growing behind the first villa.

Though his eyes were mainly searching for adversaries, Titus let his gaze drop to see what they grew in the Garden. He recognized carrot leaves, cucumbers, and summer squash. Heads of lettuce were ready to harvest, and blueberry bushes hung heavy with grape-sized fruit against the villa wall.

Around the back side of the first villa, Titus startled Dusty who'd crawled up to the window of the third unit. They didn't communicate, but instead Dusty recovered from his surprise and snuck through the plants between the villas. For an instant, Titus praised God that the man who'd once been a thief and bandit was now using his covert skills for righteous purposes.

"This one!" Emily whispered harshly and patted Titus' shoulder to direct him to the second apartment in the next villa.

He stepped over ground produce, squashed a small melon, then reached the window. Having arrived, he studied their surroundings for a few seconds, securing potential exit routes. Running straight east and exiting where Dusty had entered seemed the most viable.

"Use your knife," Emily coached. "This is the window I climbed out of. Pry open the lock. It's small."

Titus drew his blade and fit it between the panes. With a jerk, paint flaked off and the lock jiggled loose on a single screw. Emily opened one side of the glass and Titus stuck his head into the dim interior. He could see an unmade bed, a cluttered desk, a custom wheelchair, and a wooden dresser. On the left, the bathroom door stood ajar. Curtains blew gently over kitchen counters where another window had been left open.

Easing through the frame, Titus found no step into the room. He fell forward and landed on his hands. His rifle clunked loudly to the floor, then he rolled to a seated position, with Emily still firmly on his back.

"Not my most graceful moment," he admitted softly, checking his bruised palms. "Maybe you should be the one carrying me, huh?"

"Unbuckle me," she urged. "We have to hurry. Someone might've heard us!"

After finding his feet, Titus moved to the bed where he sat down and unfastened the pack straps. Emily frantically arranged her paralyzed legs as Titus moved her chair closer to the bed. Once she'd transferred, she gestured to the bathroom door.

"If we had time," she said, "I'd wash up a bit."

"We have all the time you need." He readied his rifle. "Go. I'll keep watch."

"But Sazon—"

"He's not doing syringe injections with me here." Titus slapped his rifle stock once. "Go on. I'll watch the door and tell Dusty to sit tight. We can even pack up some of your belongings here and make our exit as I intended."

"This is crazy!" Emily blinked through eyes of frustration, but finally relaxed and eyed the bathroom. "Okay, give me ten minutes."

Titus shut the window they'd entered, then spied through the front, curtained windows at the courtyard and path beyond. Several residents wore straw hats as they bowed to harvest or weed between rows of vegetables. If he hadn't already met Emily, he wouldn't have suspected this fruitful oasis held secrets of murder and euthanasia. The only odd thing he noticed was that everyone in sight wore new clothes, even business suits, while they gardened.

He communicated with Dusty, who'd found a hiding spot in the shade on the north corner of the second villa.

"You cover my exit with Emily when it's time," Titus told him. "I want to leave straight out the front gate since she's in her wheelchair now. But we need to meet the mayor first. I want to look into the eyes of that man and let him know that his activities here are in the light."

"Now I know where Levi gets it," Dusty said. "He can never leave well enough alone, either. Over."

After a few minutes, the gardeners looked up as if they'd been summoned. Together, they set aside tools, removed gloves, and walked southward toward the chapel. Titus wondered if the well-dressed residents had been recalled somewhere because he and Dusty had been detected, but he saw no one approaching the apartment or acting frantic.

Emily emerged from the bathroom in clean clothes and her hair washed.

"Normally, a person wouldn't want a wheelchair-bound person in this type of situation." She stuffed clothes into a backpack. "I try not to be a burden on anyone, but it's just a fact that I am. Mayor Malden is right about that much. I have more needs than your average civilian."

"Some need less and some need more." Titus shrugged and didn't take his eyes from the front landscape. "We don't measure a person by the resources they consume, but by the quality of their character. What God values should be what I value."

"Oh, yeah, you're definitely going to clash with the mayor." Emily sniggered as she hung the backpack on her wheelchair seat back. "And Sazon will probably draw his syringe the minute you are seen with me."

"You don't say?" Titus glanced toward her. "Where's he keep his syringe exactly?"

"Um, his right side, like on his hip." She wheeled up to the front door to look at him. "Why? Does that help you?"

"Everything you've told me helps me."

"Well, you said you'd get my wheelchair and you did. We could leave now and never even get into it with the mayor or Sazon."

"Yeah, we could leave." He gripped the door knob of the front door. "Or we could make a point that might change some hearts and clarify the danger that we face."

"Okay, you promise you won't get me killed?"

"I can't promise that. No one can. But I can promise what's about to happen won't be boring." He grinned. "Ready?"

"You're not very good at comforting a person's nerves. There are a lot of people here who don't want me to live. We are very outnumbered."

"It ain't easy trusting God in impossible moments."

"I'm not trusting God." Emily frowned. "I'm trusting you."

"You and I will need to get on the same page eventually." Titus opened the door a few inches and touched his transmitter. "Dusty, Emily and I are coming out. I think everyone's down at the chapel. Hold your position. Over."

"Copy that. Over."

"Stay behind me," Titus said to Emily as he stepped over a wicker doormat. "But move with me."

"Oh, you'll get no argument from me. There's no way I'm taking the lead. I'd go back alone to the front gate if it weren't guarded."

"Soon enough, Wheels." He winked at her, and held the rifle tighter. "Let's go meet the mayor."

Oliver knew he was a prisoner of the Garden, even if he wasn't held in a cell or wearing shackles. He'd glimpsed the high wall through the distant fruit trees around the property, and he'd seen the sidearm Sazon carried. The muscled brute seemed to be Mayor Malden's courteous but imposing enforcer.

And there was still no word on who or why someone had taken his hunting rifle outside the chapel. He didn't dare ask about it. If something happened to him, Rory and Milli would be alone.

"You're Oliver, right?" asked a man in a dress shirt and slacks. Everyone in the Garden wore new clothes, even when gardening and doing other chores. The men were always shaved and the women were always clean with their hair washed. "The major wants everyone in the chapel. It's a funeral celebration."

"A funeral . . . celebration?" Oliver pushed the straw hat back on his head. The summer sun was tempered by the little breeze coming from the northwest. He could smell the sea, so he couldn't be far from the coast. Setting aside his gardening spade, he stood and brushed off his knees. "Another funeral so soon? Is that normal around here?"

"Just come to the chapel. Malden's orders."

The man turned and walked toward the chapel. Oliver could see others streaming toward the building. It all appeared so innocent in the midst of fruitful acres of trees and vegetable plants. He'd never seen so many roses and other flowers! But there was something creepy about the way he and his family had been welcomed. If only he'd continued on his way to find Levi Caspertein downtown!

He dropped his gloves on the tilled ground to mark the spot where he'd continue to weed later. The fresh fruit and vegetables were amazing, but he couldn't look past the odd, cultish behavior of everyone. And now another funeral? Had someone tried to run from the Garden and suffered the consequences?

On his way up the path to the chapel, he touched his clean-shaven jaw. Less than a day in the Garden and his entire appearance had changed. They'd insisted he shave off his beard—citing health concerns. They'd given him a new wardrobe, and again, encouraged high personal hygiene standards. His girlfriend, Milli, had been thrilled to receive new summer dresses, but Oliver would've preferred his old thermal top after a good washing.

Inside the chapel, Oliver searched first for his son, Rory. The six-year-old had been corralled with a few other youngsters and seated on a single, front pew together. A stern woman ordered Rory to put away his chess set and fix his recently washed and cut hair. The boy tucked his travel board behind him, then used his fingers to pat down his hair, now parted on the side, exactly like the other children.

A woman's laughter sounded over the quiet hum of voices as people settled into their seats. Oliver barely recognized Milli—her appearance or her laughter. Mayor Malden leaned close to her and whispered something into her ear that made her laugh even more. His fingers touched her upper arm where the sleeve of her dress ended. Her red hair shone in the sunlight that pierced the stained-glass windows high on each wall above the pews. But she didn't look in his direction. Mayor Malden seated her next to a tall, blond official-looking woman in the front row.

Rory turned in his seat and scanned the sanctuary. Oliver rose halfway from the pew to wave at his son, thrilled that Rory had remembered him even if Milli hadn't. The boy spotted him, grinned, and waved. An instant before Oliver waved back, the stern woman in charge of the children snapped at Rory to face forward with his hands folded in his lap.

Helplessness grappled with Oliver's heart. How could he stand up to men like Mayor Malden or mighty Sazon? He certainly couldn't argue against the health and cleanliness of the Garden environment, even if they seemed to be applying extreme measures in the wake of the Meridia Virus.

Someone suddenly stood over him. It was Mayor Malden. His eyes were green, his face lightly freckled.

"Can I sit with you a moment, Oliver?" The mayor didn't wait for his response, and moved past Oliver's knees to sit on the pew beside him. "We have a few minutes before everyone arrives. I saw you working on that row of squash earlier. And I heard you're on the composting crew as well. You're a valued new addition to this community, Oliver."

"I'm glad to be here," Oliver lied, flinching at the deceit. The Bible back in his villa room made it clear that lying was wrong. "Everything's so perfect and orderly."

"That's what our CARE Protocol is all about: Cleansing All, Restoring Everything." Malden put his arm over Oliver's shoulders, pulling him closer. His cologne was pungent. "Listen, Oliver, Milli said you two aren't actually married. Now, I'm not trying to come between you two, but when I look at your little boy, Rory, it makes me wonder if Milli could have healthier, more masculine offspring if someone else sired a child through her."

"Excuse me?" Oliver felt his cheeks redden as he searched Malden's face. "There's nothing wrong with Rory. What are you—?"

"Now, don't get excited, Oliver, but look at him. He's six years old, and he's hardly as tall as anyone younger than him. He's a runt. And obviously he's not been taught very well or his genes are lacking—because he seems to have trouble learning. Look at him, still playing with that board game after he was told not to."

"It's just chess. He's just six years old!" Oliver gulped. What was happening? "I'm proud of him. Any parent would be."

"Well, Milli thinks she wants another child. Imagine what kind of stout boy she could have if I were the father? We need to think of recovery, Oliver. Restoration for humanity doesn't come by weakness. We all need to make sacrifices. Milli wants this."

"She does?" Oliver stared at the back of her head. "It's only been about a day since we got here."

"Let her do her own thing for now, Oliver. She doesn't want to create problems. I think she'll find her way back to you naturally. Or not. But tonight, she won't be going back to your apartment. Yes, she seems to understand the important role she could play here in the Garden."

"Where will she stay?" Oliver fought tears. Was he just a bug for this man to swat aside? "She'll stay with you? I have all her clothes at our apartment. What about Rory?"

"Rory is a son of the community now, Oliver, even if he is small and ill-tempered. But he's healthy, so he'll serve his purpose as he grows up, somehow. He'll live with you and you'll be his father, raising him in the ways of the Garden."

"I'm not—"

"Thanks for understanding." Malden squeezed the back of Oliver's neck. Such power in this man! "I'll let Milli know that you're on board for what makes her happy. Keep doing a great job at your assignment. A family has to work together like this. Let's get this service started."

Before Oliver could object, argue, or even speak, the mayor stood and walked up the aisle. The tall, blond woman next to Milli rose to her feet and stood behind a litter with a body covered by a single, white sheet. Malden sat in the front row—next to Milli.

Oliver felt the heat on his neck. None of this was real. No, it was a nightmare!

The blond woman spread her arms wide, welcoming the attendees but gazing up at the ceiling. Oliver remembered her name was Dr. Jaimie Ferguson. She'd examined Rory for any ailments the night before. He'd seen her kiss Malden that morning, so he'd guessed the two were an item. But now they both seemed accepting of Milli. What kind of doctor was this woman?

"We're here again to remember a life given and a life returned." Ferguson was taller than many men in the room who were now seated and listening intently. Only Sazon may have been taller than she. "Our brother was plagued by depression, a disease with crippling effects on a community like ours. Let us take a moment of silence to welcome the wonder of life's cycle and the clarity with which we must recover, restore, and eventually return ourselves in this beautiful circle."

All in the room bowed their heads, but Oliver was seated in the back, so he felt no obligation. Even young Rory followed the instructive posture of prayer, which enraged Oliver even more. He'd been on the verge of explaining to the brilliant, little boy how the Bible recorded so much interesting history—and promised a remarkable life in heaven beyond this broken world. And now the boy was being indoctrinated by . . . all this?

The double doors at the back of the sanctuary suddenly burst open. Oliver had thought everyone—man, woman, and child—had been required to attend the service. He turned to see who the latecomer was, but it was obviously no one who belonged to the Garden. In fact, it was two people: a tall, blond man in his mid-to-late forties and a brunette woman in a sporty wheelchair.

Oliver rose to his feet as he recognized the blond man's face—and identified the rifle as a model he'd seen before. But instantly, Oliver knew he'd never met this man, exactly, but his younger self, perhaps, in the face of his son. This man could be none other than Levi Caspertein's father!

A murmur swept through the sanctuary of nearly sixty people. The newcomer and his companion in the wheelchair stopped in the aisle next to Oliver's pew. Oliver wanted to reach out and touch the broad-shouldered gunman to ensure he was real. Recalling Levi's brief presence in Oliver's former neighborhood—perhaps his father could have just a fraction of that kind of impact here! The man's blue eyes surveyed the room critically, as if he already suspected the troubles Oliver was having with the Garden's leadership.

"Welcome, friend!" Malden was on his feet, smiling and moving down the aisle. "We weren't expecting—"

The gunman shifted his rifle muzzle to cover the mayor, stopping Malden in his tracks, but not discouraging his sunny disposition, which Oliver had learned to distrust.

"It looks like I'm interrupting," the man said. "Are you Mayor Malden?"

"Why, yes!" Malden gestured to his flock. "There's no need for the weapon, my friend. We were just wishing farewell to a departed soul from among us."

"Ask him how he died," whispered the disabled woman to the stranger. Oliver guessed only he had heard her urging, but he instantly liked her—a pretty and determined face, unwilling to give Malden an inch. "Ask him!"

"How did he die?" Caspertein had a low, loud voice, one that rang with authority. Yes, just like his son! "I asked, how did he die?"

All eyes looked to Malden for an answer. So, it was true, Oliver thought. He wasn't the only one who'd thought yet another funeral seemed a little odd in such a small community that prided itself on healthy living.

"He was sick." Malden's voice didn't quite express the sadness he may have intended. "He was afflicted for years. Now his suffering is over. We're remembering his life. We were just about to sing of his—"

The stranger raised his left hand so swiftly that Malden's words trailed off and he shut his mouth.

"My name is Titus Caspertein," he said for the room. "All of you here appear healthy, so I expect to hear of no more deaths coming from this place. No more funerals. No more accidents. No suicides or mysterious diseases that lead to sudden fatalities in the night."

"Mr. Caspertein," Malden said, "I assure you that we are a—"

"Your assurances mean nothing to me, Mayor." Titus glanced down at his companion. "You all know Emily here. It's the strangest thing—she left in such a hurry a couple days ago that she forgot her wheelchair. By God's good providence, I came across her and heard her story. You can imagine how eager I was to meet you, Mayor, to see for myself if the rumors were true. And what do I find? Another funeral. And which of you is Sazon?"

The long-haired, muscled man stood from the second pew and stepped into the aisle. He moved past Malden and slowly approached the stranger. Sazon's eyes narrowed and seemed full of disdain.

"I'm Sazon." The enforcer offered his giant hand. "It's a pleasure, I assure you."

Oliver hoped Titus wouldn't shake his hand. The two men were about the same height, though Sazon was heavier. These people didn't deserve any kind of civilized greeting! Sazon's sidearm was in its holster, obvious for all to see. If they were really peaceful in the Garden, why would he need a pistol?

Instead, Titus let go of his rifle and clasped the mitt of the larger man. Their palms slapped with such force that half of the observers jumped with surprise. The battle between the two bulls stretched for several seconds while neither man withdrew his muscled hand or waivered his gaze.

Oliver was closest. He saw Sazon's forearm quiver under the strain. His jaw was clenched, but Titus was smiling slyly, as if he actually enjoyed such contests of strength.

Suddenly, Titus' left hand shot out to Sazon's left hip and closed his grip around a small nylon pouch Oliver hadn't noticed on the big man's belt. A crunch of glass came from inside the pouch.

Sazon yanked his hand from Titus and took a step back to inspect his black pouch, now dripping liquid. Oliver wondered what all this meant, for crushing the glass had clearly been intentional.

"Oh, I hope that wasn't too valuable." Titus' voice was light as he returned his right hand to his rifle. "Tell me what it was if you want me to replace it."

Flexing his right hand, Sazon subtly wrung it at his side. His left hand wiped at the moisture dripping from the pouch.

"It was nothing." Sazon glared at Titus. "I have more in my villa."

Titus looked past Sazon at those in the pews. There was no question that he had everyone's attention. Oliver wanted to run up to the children's pew and bring Rory back to introduce him to this Caspertein—the father of the young man who'd saved their lives a few months earlier.

"I live downtown," Titus stated for everyone. "We have space and food, water and jobs for anyone who wants to join us. You don't have to stay here and tolerate whatever death cult this is."

"We're not a death cult," Malden said from behind Sazon. "This is a caring and compassionate community that values health and liberty from disease."

"Yeah, at the expense of anyone who you say isn't healthy!" Emily shouted.

"When a person's quality of life is diminished," Malden said, "of course everyone around him or her suffers. We respect life enough to honor those who shouldn't have to burden themselves any longer, or burden others with their infirmities."

"The Bible says that God never gives us more than we can handle," Titus said, "all so we learn to value spiritual things and to learn to trust in God's faithfulness and deliverance from spiritual darkness. That's right. I'm a follower of Jesus Christ. There's salvation and fulfillment from sin and death found in no one else. You might have a lot of vegetables and fruit around this place, but I'd rather be sick and diseased under God's loving hand than healthy in the hands of wicked people."

Oliver wanted to raise his hand and call attention to himself—so Titus knew he didn't belong with these people in the Garden. He wanted to applaud Titus' words and leave with him, but what about Rory? And Milli?

"Actually," Malden said, now stepping up to stand beside Sazon, "we've been talking about expanding. More than just our community of compassion needs our CARE Protocol. Emily here may have convinced you that she's happy, but her life as a disabled person is both depressing as well as debilitating to our recovering society. She'll drag us all down. Stay here, Emily. We'll help you . . . the compassionate way."

"You're right," Titus said to Emily, "this place has lost its mind. Cruelty is called compassion and God's care for every human life is ignored."

"This is what you all want?" Emily called to the sanctuary. Many lowered their eyes. "Come with us!"

"No one move!" Malden ordered, his hand raised. "We're the beginning of this restored world. We are! Look at our Garden. You've tasted its fruit, its produce. You can't argue with our results. Imagine all of San Diego thriving like we are—even all of California!"

"Oh, yeah, you're thriving all right." Titus scoffed. "It ain't easy turning from selfishness to your Savior, people, but you all desperately need Jesus Christ. Don't wait too long. Come find me downtown and you'll see that the true God of the Bible accepts the weak and the sick, the lost and the blind. The Garden is not the answer!"

Titus backed toward the door, Emily with him. Oliver measured the distance between him and his son. But Sazon wouldn't let them leave. This was the moment to act, but Oliver hesitated. He couldn't risk his son's safety. Torn and conflicted and intimidated, he watched Titus Caspertein leave through the double doors. His heart sank. The man had left—the very family he'd hoped to find had now come and gone.

The sanctuary erupted in cries of alarm and anger. Oliver slowly sat in his pew as the mayor returned to the front and raised his arms to settle the crowd. Sazon marched swiftly out the doors.

"He can't come in here and talk like that about us!" said one man.

"Sazon should've done something!" a woman yelled. "The man had that Emily with him!"

"People don't understand what we've built here!" fumed another man.

"Quiet, now. Quiet." Malden folded his hands. "Sazon is responding, and our thoughts are with him while he's out there. That Titus Caspertein man spoke unfair words to us, but his mind is shrouded in the past. He's afraid. You heard the way he spoke about his God and his Bible. His delusion is a disease this society should be freed from entirely. Let his visit be an inspiration for all of us to enact the CARE Protocol on the greater San Diego area as soon as possible. We may clash with some like him, but for the greater good, we must restore humanity's standing from disaster, disease, and disgrace."

The people cried out and crouched in their pews as gunshots blasted from somewhere up the path. Oliver hadn't had much experience with firearms, but he'd learned the sound of his own rifle well enough to know the difference between a pistol and a rifle shot. Three pistol bangs were followed by four rifle booms. No one in the chapel moved or spoke for several seconds.

"Are we being invaded?" asked a woman.

Mayor Malden shushed their concerns, then approached the double doors. Oliver noted that Rory was safe in the stern woman's care, so he joined Malden at the door. Down the path, Sazon's sizeable bulk lay near a bed of roses. Farther up, closer to the bridge, the one sentry who had been left to guard the Garden entrance lay dead.

Slowly, Malden turned from the door to face his followers, but Oliver stared at the dead. *Titus Caspertein was a killer as well?* It didn't seem to fit the image he'd built in his head—that Levi and his family were Bible readers—yet they now seemed to somehow justified their own violence and cruelty.

"Sazon is dead," Malden stated softly to the room. "This just confirms what we've believed. Sazon was the picture of health and strength among us. He never hurt anyone. His goals for this paradise matched my own. We must respond to this sacrilegious assault or it'll happen again. We must carry our message to others beyond the Garden."

Still in disbelief that Titus had killed the mighty Sazon, Oliver eased out of the chapel and walked carefully up to Sazon's body. His handgun had been taken. After all, Oliver recalled hearing that Sazon had fired first. But still, Titus and the woman in the wheelchair hadn't even belonged there. What gave them the right to kill?

Oliver felt tears of frustration on his cheeks as he walked to the bridge and knelt over the still sentry. He hadn't known this man who'd been stationed by the gate—perhaps to keep him inside as much as to keep others out. But his life was no more, and now Oliver saw no point in leaving the Garden if those outside were just as dangerous as those inside.

Was it possible that he had to learn to enjoy his new life in the Garden? Malden had taken Milli as his own—and Milli seemed complicit. Rory had been claimed by the Garden's schoolteacher, which left Oliver questioning his life as a father and as a man worthy of a woman at all. Had his life indeed been reduced to composting and weeding? It seemed so—since his family had been stolen from him.

Feeling worthless and hopeless, Oliver left the path and wandered almost sightlessly into the fruit trees beside the river. Just days earlier, he'd been a provider and protector of his family. The Dooley Gang's fires had disrupted all that. Oh, if only he'd never come to the Garden, this deceitful paradise!

For a long time, he stood staring at the slow-flowing water. His eyes dried and he contemplated leaving the Garden alone. Without Milli or Rory, he could forge a new life out there, beyond the walls of this wicked Eden that had taken everything from him, even his hope. Maybe the way the world was now, Rory would be better off under Malden's fathership. Milli was clearly swayed by the man's affections, even if he were already with Dr. Ferguson.

Cries of laughter and peels of astonishment from the bridge reached his ears. Rejoicing wasn't characteristic of the Garden—which he'd discovered in his short time among the residents. So, what was this new excitement in the wake of such bloodshed?

Oliver returned to the path to find both the sentry and Sazon alive and standing in the middle of a crowd of residents! Others ran to see the miracle as well.

"It's a sign!" Malden shouted above the laughter and rejoicing. "We are meant to spread our message abroad—beyond the Garden! Their violence against us will not silence us. Beyond the Garden!"

"Beyond the Garden!" shouted others.

"Beyond the Garden!" Dr. Ferguson repeated. "Beyond the Garden!"

The chant caught on. Oliver watched as they danced and strained to touch Sazon and the sentry, like they'd been raised from the dead. Shocked at their gullibility, Oliver wondered how he could be the only one who'd realized the obvious: Titus Caspertein hadn't fired lethal rounds at the two men. They'd been alive all along!

Oliver found Rory jumping up and down with other children who were repeating the chant. He picked up his son and embraced him. In that instant, Oliver's self-pity vanished and he saw very clearly what he needed to do. He'd condemned the Casperteins for being murderers, but he'd been wrong. Levi Caspertein's invitation had drawn him, and his father's mercy toward Sazon now convinced him. It was time to leave the Garden.

"Where's your chess set?" he asked Rory.

"The mean lady made me leave it under the seat."

"In the chapel?" Oliver set Rory down to walk on his own, but he took the boy's hand. "Come on. We need to go."

Rory didn't argue. Oliver glanced back only once to ensure that no one was coming after them. Quickly, he inventoried what he had on his person. They'd taken his rifle, but he still had a pocketknife. Sadly, he was leaving behind his duct-taped Bible, but he'd find another. There was no time to return for his Bible if they took time to fetch Rory's game board. They were only ten miles from downtown, which they could walk that very evening if they had no interference.

They reached the chapel. As Rory retrieved his chess game, Oliver approached the body under the sheet at the front. He drew back the sheet to look upon a man he'd seen a couple times around the Garden—that very morning! And now he was dead?

"Why aren't you with the others?"

Covering the dead man, Oliver spun around to find Dr. Ferguson standing in the open double doors. She was alone, but Oliver knew she could summon others within seconds. As a sizeable woman, she could overpower him at least long enough for others to arrive.

"Come on, Rory." Oliver backed toward the rear of the chapel. He'd circled the building outside the night before, so he knew where it led. "We're leaving. Don't follow us!"

"No one leaves." Dr. Ferguson lifted the hem of her shirt to reveal a black pouch on her belt, the same as Sazon had. "The Garden is your home. You either participate in the restoration or you're part of the destruction."

From the pouch, she drew a syringe, removed the cap and a plunger lock, then walked slowly toward him. She remained so calm that her intentions hardly seemed harmful.

Rory clutched his chess board and reached his father's side. Oliver picked up a vase of flowers and threw it in Ferguson's direction, though it landed far short.

"Stay back!" he shouted. "You don't control us!"

"Ungrateful people just don't know what's best for them." Then she charged.

Oliver nearly tripped in his retreat. He swiped at potted plants to reach the rear exit. But it was padlocked!

"Dad!" Rory warned.

Without looking back, Oliver heel-kicked the door where the padlock brace had been bolted. The door material cracked then gave way. Father and son burst into a flower bed. Oliver ran with Rory in his arms—beyond the southernmost villa and into the orchard trees. The wall wasn't far away now. He risked a look over his shoulder. Others had joined the pursuit.

Reaching the wall, Oliver shoved Rory up the side. The boy dropped his chess set.

"I'll get it," Oliver assured him. "Just get up there."

He picked up the chess set and stuck it down the back of his waistband.

From several months of scavenging, Oliver had developed a variety of scaling skills. He backed up a few feet and dashed forward, planted his foot, and reached the top of the wall. Rory, who was far from coordinated, still hadn't drawn himself onto the top, so Oliver did so with one arm.

Their pursuers were thirty yards away.

Oliver slid down the far side of the wall, then turned to receive Rory, who needed no coaxing. Rory may have been physically small or weak for his age, but Oliver was thankful he was a child who understood that his father's arms were trustworthy. The boy sprang into Oliver's arms, colliding heavily, then they turned from the wall.

Again, he ran with Rory in his arms. Leafy trees were sparse and bushes were thick amongst tall weeds. The untrimmed grass reached his waist, hiding the uneven ground. Something whistled past his head, then the report of a handgun echoed around them.

"They're shooting at us!" Rory yelled.

"We'll be okay," Oliver managed to promise, but he knew not why.

Two hundred yards later, Oliver tripped and fell. The two tumbled together in the dust and vegetation until Oliver gathered Rory in his embrace and held him against the ground.

"Shhh," Oliver urged in a whisper, his eyes wide to match his son's. "Listen."

For several seconds, there was no sound. Oliver eased his head above the grass. Three men, one of them Sazon, stood on top of the Garden wall and peered in their direction. Slowly, Oliver eased his head back down.

"They're still there," he whispered. "Stay low. Let's crawl. Follow me."

Oliver slithered rather than crawled through the grass, trying not to disturb too much vegetation that might identify their whereabouts. Since he'd met Sazon outside the Garden, he knew the man ranged beyond the walls occasionally, but he hoped that he thought Oliver wasn't worth the trouble. Indeed, Oliver planned on being very troublesome if he were forced to return! But then he realized he wouldn't be allowed to return. The mayor wanted Rory. He was young and pure, even if the boy wasn't seen as physically superior by their standards.

After climbing over a low fence, they crawled through a ditch and reached a paved street. Oliver drew Rory to his feet beside him as they checked the way north and east. The landscape seemed absent of pursuers, but Sazon might anticipate their way and head them off from another direction.

"We need to keep moving." Oliver tugged the chess set from his pants. One side of the board was cracked. "Sorry. We can tape it up or—"

"It's okay, Dad." Rory traced the crack with his fingers. "What about Mom?"

"Well, it seemed like she wanted to stay behind for now." Oliver knelt and brushed his son's collared shirt free of grass and leaves. "These fancy clothes they gave us—now look at them."

"I miss my old clothes."

"Me, too." Oliver smiled sadly but also proudly at his son. "You've been real brave, Rory. We have to get downtown as fast as we can. If anything happens to me, that's where you go. See the buildings way over there? By the ocean?"

"Yeah. I remember the boat ride."

"That's right. We took you for a ride on the tour boat around Coronado Island."

"But it's not really an island," Rory said.

"Good memory. But that's where we're going. If we get split up, that's where you go. You ask for Levi Caspertein. Can you remember that name?"

"Levi Caspertein?"

"Yep. I think everyone downtown will know him, if we can just get there. You saw how his dad handled the mayor and Sazon."

"He shot them by the bridge."

"But he didn't kill them. The Casperteins obey Jesus. They're Christians. Do you know what that means? Have you heard of Jesus before?"

Rory shook his head.

Oliver reached for his Bible, but his back pocket was empty. Of course, he'd left it in his apartment that morning.

"I've been reading a book called the Bible. It's a book about God and Jesus and a bunch of His people. I have a lot of questions myself, but it's a holy book. God is important. He created us and loves us. And He wants us to live right. I'm not sure what else to tell you, but I know it's important. I've read most of it, but I have to find out from the Casperteins what it all means."

"Some nights I've seen you reading it."

"Yeah, I guess you have." Oliver smiled. "You're smart. Come on. Let's get moving."

"Dad, I'm a little thirsty."

"Before we go too far, we'll have to hunt down some water."

"We don't have any of our stuff."

"Oh, we'll get new stuff."

"From Levi Caspertein?"

"I don't see why not. He's a friend of ours."

"But I've never met him."

"Well, you've met his dad there in the chapel. He was with the lady in the wheelchair. Levi is just a younger version of his dad."

"Am I a younger version of you?"

"Younger but smarter." Oliver eyed the buildings ahead as they approached a Chula Vista neighborhood, angling toward the bay. "Now keep your eyes open for signs of water. And a container that can hold some. We can do without food for a day or two, but we need water."

"The Garden had a lot of water, but we won't go back there for anything, right?"

"You've got that right!" He took Rory's hand. "We'll be better off with the Casperteins."

Chapter Four

Levi Caspertein held his breath as an infant cried in the night. The noise seemed so loud from where he listened on ELM's second floor balcony.

"That's everyone," one-eyed Wes Trimble notified on the radio. He stood below in the courtyard outside the Hopefuls' building. "Be safe, young Caspertein. Over."

"Don't get yourself killed over our belongings, Levi!" Annette warned on her own headset. She was somewhere in the front of the procession of escaping ELM-dependent residents, but Levi knew his mother couldn't leave him behind without also leaving her two cents. "Just stay in hiding until we leave. Over."

"Just pray for me," Levi stated softly. The last of the people below disappeared in moon shadows, heading northeast toward the zoo. "I won't be reckless, I promise. Out."

Alone now, he checked his watch. It was nearly three in the morning. The evacuation of everyone in the Hopefuls' and ELM buildings had taken hours. The Overcomers' building evacuation had occurred suddenly so as not to alert Dooley or his lady friend, Fran.

It had been Wes's idea to evacuate everyone as soon as he had confirmed with Levi that Dooley was indeed the murderer Levi had crossed a couple months earlier east of the city center. Dooley's inquiries for Maddix Striber had been too much for Wes to ignore, and Levi knew the killer by sight, so they had to respond.

Dooley's deceitful presence at ELM, impersonating a distant traveler, could mean only one thing—the Dooley Gang was making a move against ELM. No one knew when Dooley would act upon his plan, or when the rest of his gang would arrive, but with all of ELM evacuated, Levi could address the threat alone and from the inside. The perimeter was now free of innocent civilians. Even the three perimeter booths had been vacated.

Only Oleg had remained onsite and hidden in a vacant apartment inside a fourth high-rise beyond the Overcomers' building.

Levi descended the stairs to the lobby of the ELM building. The floor no longer housed the popular Toggenburg milk goats. He could only imagine how Wes, Chevy, and Wynter were coming with the goats on leashes as they trekked north to stay for a couple of days. Of course, the goats were too valuable to be abandoned and left behind for someone like Dooley. The ambusher had a history of killing useful animals and grilling their meat.

Descending lower, Levi reached the parking garage under the building where several vehicles had been cannibalized for parts over the last few months. Garbage and other litter had been intentionally left scattered between huge, round, support columns. The space was otherwise empty and unvisited—or so it appeared.

Near the far wall of the garage, Levi carefully stepped on newspaper trash and flattened cardboard boxes so he didn't leave any footprints in the dust. He reached the wall and touched the concrete between cinder blocks. It was almost dry. Except for the smell, the new cinder blocks appeared to fit with the other blocks set in the rest of the garage walls. But actually, the ramp behind the new wall led to an entire second subterranean level where pallets, containers, and barrels remained stacked to the ceiling. These were Titus' provisions set aside before Pan-Day had struck.

ELM provisions couldn't fall into the hands of infiltrators. By dawn, the cement would be completely dry and nothing short of a sledge hammer at just the right section could break through the cinder blocks.

Returning upstairs, Levi used the dolly to arrive at his own apartment on the fortieth floor. The water tanks had been almost drained to fill containers for the evacuees, so Levi didn't bother showering. He leaned his rifle against the wall and stripped off his ammo vest. On the night stand next to him, he propped up his radio transmitter.

"Oleg, you there? I'm gonna catch a few *Zs*. Over."

"I copy," said the Russian. "Don't sleep too long. You want a wake-up call? Over."

"Around dawn, unless you see movement before that. Over."

Levi lay on his bed, still fully clothed and battle ready. It had been Wes's idea to secretly evacuate ELM, but Levi was still reeling that his father's companions had agreed that *he* be the one to remain inside! He was only twenty, but Wes, Oleg, and Chevy had agreed that no one was more familiar with the buildings, and no one was stronger than he to climb the stairs as needed—or to use the ziplines outside if need be. Besides, Carla had reasoned, Levi had experience with all kinds of aggressors as well as Dooley himself.

Only Aunt Wynter had objected to him being the one to remain behind with Oleg. She'd recommended Chevy, but Chevy had spoken up, suggesting his engineering skills might be better used at the zoo where the evacuees would shelter for a couple days. After forty-eight hours, their food and water would run out, and they'd need to return to ELM—to take it back by force if Levi hadn't already resolved or interrupted the Dooley threat.

Oleg had been the final voice of reason in Levi's favor.

"One or two men in hiding can be more effective in this urban setting," he'd said. "Levi is agile. I'm not—since my hip is still healing. But I can stay back and cover him from another building. He won't be alone."

"And if I get into trouble or get cornered," Levi had added for Annette's benefit, "I can just ride a zipline down to the train depot and abandon ELM. When Dad and Dusty get back, we can retake the whole place."

But Levi had no intention of abandoning ELM or any of the buildings. This was his home now. And it was the home of nearly a hundred others who relied on the Casperteins to keep them healthy, safe, and neighborly. Chevy, Wes, and Wynter had been holding various discipleship classes with new believers throughout the week, so if ELM fell, God's work would be hindered as well.

Remaining back with Oleg caused Levi to view it as making a spiritual stand for Jesus Himself.

"Time to get to work." Oleg's voice shook Levi from his slumber. "You there, Levi? I see no movement yet, but the sun is coming up. Over."

Sitting up, Levi blinked his eyes, cleared his throat, and picked up his radio.

"I'm up, but I may be sleepwalking most of the day. Over."

"Throw out the welcome mat," Oleg said. "Let's see what these people have in mind. Over."

As he ate an egg and goat cheese sandwich in the kitchen, Levi's stomach flip-flopped with excitement. Before he left the apartment, he checked from his balcony the Pacific States Defense Forces out on Coronado Island. All seemed calm over there, just as it had been for the last couple of months. General Brogdon seemed to tolerate the Caspertein presence downtown only because Titus had brought stability and commerce to the city. But their relationship with the new local government was fragile, Levi knew, and most definitely conditional. Dooley threatened all that the Casperteins had prepared and built.

His eyes narrowed at the small ferry landing across the bay. Sometimes, he thought he saw Sergeant Dom Lesage alone there among the palm trees. They had become friends during a tumultuous time weeks earlier, but Levi guessed the soldier had moved on, thinking little of him or their time together.

When Levi exited his apartment, he left the door wide open for guests—if Dooley or his men bothered to reach the fortieth floor. All of their apartment doors had been left unlocked if not open per Wes's advice: why invite Dooley to cause damage when they could just welcome him in?

It bothered Levi that a stranger who intended them harm would be walking through their buildings, taking what he wanted, though most valuables had been carted away in the night with the evacuees. Some items, like Titus' radio equipment, couldn't be packed up on such short notice. And the garage storage space contained many necessities if ELM needed to be completely restocked after the Dooley Gang's looting.

Instead of taking the dolly down, Levi locked the dolly upstairs by disabling its track. He took the stairs down to the next two dolly stages and similarly disabled them. Again, taking Wes's advice. They were turning over the buildings temporarily to avoid bloodshed, not trying to make it easy on the invaders to access the upper floors where most of the living quarters were in the ELM building. Dooley and his people would need to use the stairs if they wanted to get up there.

On the ground floor, Levi opened the front, metal door halfway and stepped outside. *What silence!* By now, the people would've reached the zoo and found shelter. Wes, Wynter, Annette, Carla, and Chevy were heavily armed, but they were only five rifles to protect so many.

Visually checking the Hopefuls' building, Levi noticed the front door was open. The whole compound was like a ghost town.

"Okay, Levi, I have movement in front of the Overcomers' building," Oleg warned. "It's Dooley. No sign of Fran. Over."

"Copy."

Withdrawing to the inside of the ELM building, Levi ran across the lobby to the stairs and reached the second-floor balcony.

"He's in the courtyard," Oleg said. "Over."

Levi knelt and slowly eased his head over the balcony railing. Sure enough, Dooley stood alone, seemingly listening to or studying the buildings. It was impossible for Levi not to smile. How mysterious everything must seem to Dooley. No one was sweeping the concrete. Children weren't playing in the new sandbox. Fishermen weren't coming from or going to the bay. Only the morning breeze whispered past the buildings and shifted trash on the ground that had blown in overnight.

Dooley faced west and Levi ducked out of sight. The infiltrator was probably noticing that the clothes lines between the buildings were empty and no one was on the balconies tending to garden pots or shaking out laundry. No voices or singing or infants crying.

"Okay, he's going to ELM's front door," Oleg reported. "Make yourself scarce. Over."

"Copy."

Dashing from the balcony, Levi reached the stairwell to watch from the corner. Sure enough, Dooley hesitantly entered the front door from where he surveyed the empty goat pens and milking stations. After a moment, he walked to the open elevator shaft and looked up. The sound of him yanking on the cables reached Levi, but he knew he had effectively disabled the three dollies in their respective stages.

When Dooley glanced about for the stairs, Levi ascended to the next landing to watch from around the corner. Reaching the first balcony, Dooley spent a moment observing the courtyard outside, even leaning far over the rail to search for any sign of anyone.

Leaving the balcony, Dooley continued upstairs. Levi remained against the wall at least a flight and a half above him—and trusted his ears when to move in unison.

On the third floor, Dooley left the stairs and Levi prowled closer to watch. The man checked the four apartments on that floor, all vacant and abandoned since Pan-Day, though they still had some furniture. No one lived in the ELM building lower than the fifteenth floor, so Levi hoped Dooley would get tired and just go away.

But this was a man committed to either uncovering the mystery of everyone's disappearance or discovering what he might take. As yet, Dooley hadn't emerged with anything from any apartment, and Levi couldn't see any weapon on the intruder, either.

Dooley continued to the fifth and sixth floors, checking each apartment in turn. Levi was just falling into the man's pattern when Dooley skipped four floors and climbed rapidly to the eleventh.

"You good, Levi?" Oleg called. "Over."

He was too close while spying on Dooley to answer verbally, so he responded with three clicks on the radio.

"Fran is outside calling for Dooley," Oleg said. "She's going into the Hopefuls' building. She looks nervous since no one's around. Okay, she's inside now. Over."

Again, Levi clicked three times, then ascended another story as Dooley returned to the stairwell. But instead of climbing the stairs, Dooley stood very still on the eleventh-floor landing. Levi knew he was listening for sounds of life. It was tempting to give Dooley something to chase, but this wasn't a game, even if Levi was enjoying being the mouse for the cat.

Suddenly, Dooley descended the stairs all the way to the first floor and walked out the front door.

"Okay, he's leaving the ELM building," Levi said. "Over."

"Fran is still in the Hopefuls' building. It may be time to divide and conquer. Over."

"Copy."

Levi watched the courtyard from the second-floor balcony. Dooley returned to the Overcomers' building, seeming to search for Fran where they'd been housed on the tenth floor. It would take Dooley five minutes to reach their apartment, then another four perhaps to descend once he didn't find her.

After setting his watch to track the time, Levi ran down the stairs and out the front door of the ELM building. As he approached the Hopefuls' building, he drew his silenced handgun, a twenty-two caliber, and entered the open door. His eyes adjusted to the dimness as his ears listened for Fran.

Yes! He heard a little clatter on the floor above. The Hopefuls had been housed two months earlier beginning on the third floor. They had rapidly accumulated property from so much in the city that had been left behind. It was these possessions that Fran was picking through when Levi came upon her in apartment four on the third floor.

She was bent over and rummaging through a cluttered closet when Levi stepped into the kitchen to wait. Dooley and his gang had murdered and pillaged their way through San Diego's eastern suburbs, so Levi knew this woman was probably at home picking through someone else's belongings.

Fran backed out of the closet with a plastic bin full of miscellaneous items belonging to a current or past resident. She tugged off the lid and must've sensed the figure standing at the hallway entrance.

Firing a tranquilizer from his silenced pistol, Levi struck her thigh before she'd fully turned to confront him. She collapsed on the carpet, a handgun half-drawn from her waistband. Kneeling over her, Levi checked her for additional weapons, found none, then unloaded the handgun.

"I've got her," he announced to Oleg. "No problem. Over."

"Go ahead. It's still clear. Over."

Fran weighed less than one hundred and thirty pounds, so Levi easily drew her over one shoulder and kept one hand free for his weapon. After descending to the ground floor, he emerged from the Hopefuls' building at a quick walk. He hustled across the courtyard, beyond the Overcomers' building, and reached the fourth apartment building where Oleg was hiding somewhere above.

Inside the front door, which hadn't been repaired since Pan-Day, Levi laid her on the floor and tightened plastic zip-ties around her wrists and ankles.

"She's all yours," Levi said, then sprinted back across the courtyard to reach the cover of the ELM building. "Go ahead. I'm safe. She's there. Over."

"Copy."

Winded, Levi sat down on the second-floor balcony and waited. He imagined Oleg descending the stairs to tend to his prisoner—the first of several if Levi and Wes had presumed correctly. Fran would be kept by Oleg in safety and secret for the coming hours.

"Fran!" shouted Dooley in the courtyard.

Patiently, Levi kept from peeking over the balcony rail right away. Their plan was working. Dooley was losing his grip as he realized he wasn't in control.

"Fraaan!"

Only silence answered Dooley's calls. Minutes passed as he stomped left and right, calling for his girlfriend. Licking his lips, Levi wished he could read Dooley's mind right then. The sheer magnitude of apartments to search in the buildings must've been overwhelming for him to consider. Fran could be anywhere. Levi was counting on Dooley not searching the fourth building inside the southern part of the perimeter—where no one obviously lived. But if he did, Oleg would be ready.

Levi unwrapped one of the goat milk bars his mother had begun experimenting with. They weren't popular on account of their bland flavor, but they were convenient and rich in protein. He was ready to wait out Dooley for as long as it took!

Sergeant Dom Lesage sat on a chunk of concrete rubble to peer out a window with no glass. The building that he, Noah O'Shea, and Brand Windfield had chosen for refuge had collapsed after being partially burned. Rebar jabbed Dom in the shoulder when he leaned over to gaze down the street, but he didn't reposition himself. He was learning quickly that pretending to be a Caspertein involved a lot of discomfort since the Christian code was all about putting others first. The sergeant had even considered spray-painting the ELM tree symbol on the wall of the building in which they hid—if he'd had any paint.

"Any movement?" Brand knelt next to Dom, who'd been on watch most of the morning while Brand and Noah had rested. "Sounds quiet."

"I haven't seen or heard anything for half an hour." Dom gestured down the street. "Except for smoke from the fires, there's no sign of life left here."

The day before, the rescue party of three had left O'Shea's attic and come upon a PSDF unit with a dozen fighters who had attacked a local stronghold. The previous day and through the night, the three had decided to hide inside a sports memorabilia shop. Since they were so close to the school where the bandits were calling home, Brand hadn't been willing to instruct Dizzy to lead them around the urban battle. Throughout their waiting, O'Shea had been the picture of restlessness about finding his kids.

A day earlier, Dom had used binoculars to study the PSDF troops who'd surrounded the local holdouts. He'd recognized a few senior soldiers, but it was Kip Brogdon who had made Dom curse under his breath. Looking around, he'd made sure Noah and Brand weren't nearby to hear him. After all, Dom knew that Christians didn't use foul language. Nevertheless, he held bitterness in his heart for the general's uncouth son who was interfering with Dom's current mission and straining his cover.

Dizzy wandered into view as she sniffed at the wheels of abandoned cars across the street. Dom envied the dog's freedom. She'd been the only one in their party at liberty to run around the past twenty-four hours. If the PSDF or locals had tried to shoot at the dog to make a meal out of her, she certainly wasn't acting too skittish about it. When Dom had asked Noah about it during the night, he'd said that the vest Dizzy wore showed locals that she belonged to someone in the vicinity, and no one was willing to reveal their hideout with a rifle shot.

Brand notified Noah that they were ready to leave. They bundled up their light blankets and buried food wrappers under the building's rubble. Dom's own food was nearly depleted after hunkering down with the two men for the day and night, but it'd been worth it. They'd become better acquainted as they'd shared food and conversation. Though Dom had mostly kept his mouth shut while they'd waited for the siege and battle to end, he believed he'd earned the respect of the other two simply because he hadn't complained once about their circumstances or unexpected detour. Indeed, he was acting like a true Caspertein!

"It's only three blocks from here, you say?" Noah asked Brand for the tenth time since they'd been hiding there. His fatherly concern was tangible.

"About that." Brand whistled to recall Dizzy to the building. She hopped through the window frame nearest Dom and accepted her master's affections. "You ready, girl? Let's go!"

Spinning in two tight circles, Dizzy then leaped out the window and bolted away—like she knew exactly where they were going. Dom was impressed with Brand's knowledge of every street, neighborhood, and landmark. The man must've had extensive knowledge of other stashes of provisions, but he hadn't seemed familiar with the residents who'd fought the PSDF overnight. Or he'd just been unwilling to interfere.

Following Dizzy, Brand led the men, trailed by Dom, then Noah. Though Brand was armed with his sidearm, he kept it holstered. Dom resisted the urge to draw his shotgun, even when armed locals were glimpsed in nearby buildings. They trusted Dizzy's ability to warn them of actual threats, though Dom would've preferred to trust with a rifle in his hands. But his prayer with Noah the morning before was also nudging his soul, inclining him to wonder more seriously about trusting God and how He works. After all, God had moved in favor of the Casperteins in a dozen situations that Dom knew of personally.

The three skirted the destroyed residence where the locals had made their stand. Dom guessed the PSDF hadn't taken many spoils since the house had been riddled with bullets and demolished by RPGs. Kip could always be counted on to cause more damage than necessary. Though the youngster was still a teen, no PSDF soldier except Dom dared oppose the general's son, and Dom hadn't been there to temper the youth's bloodlust.

Several winding blocks later, Brand whistled for Dizzy to join his side. The three men crouched at the corner of a building that had been under construction when Pan-Day had occurred. A discarded tool belt, shovel, and wheelbarrow still lay nearby.

"That's the school." Brand pointed at a single-story, red brick complex across a wide avenue. "Dizzy and I have scouted it at night. There's a door there and at both ends. They're in there. About ten of them."

Nodding, Dom felt the men's eyes and pressure to perform as he'd claimed. Casperteins helped people because God helped the Casperteins. To them, every life mattered, so Dom needed to fulfill his role, even if it were one he'd lied his way into. Being found out now to be a PSDF officer could have fatal consequences. Noah wasn't a killer, but Dom had seen how Brand moved—like a predator. The man was hard to read. And Dizzy would surely come to Brand's aid if a scuffle started.

It was almost possible, Dom hoped desperately, that the God of the Casperteins might actually give him an edge against the kidnappers.

"What's your plan?" Noah asked. "You've done this sort of thing before, Brand says."

"Of course," Dom lied. "I'll go in the front door there. I see no sentries keeping watch. Most criminals nowadays aren't too disciplined or vigilant. You two go in the other entrances on the ends, and then we can—"

"Wait." Brand held up his hand. Dizzy tensed, perhaps wondering if he were signaling her. "I'm not going in. This is your show, Dom. Dizzy and I did our job. We got you here. I'm not picking a fight with anyone I don't have to when I have my own troubles to see to."

Dom bit his tongue rather than call the scout a coward. He thought Brand was a friend of the O'Sheas! Where was the loyalty?

"I'll go." Noah gripped and regripped his rifle. His eyes twitched and his shoulders rose and fell with near-hyperventilating speed. "They're my kids. And I'll . . . back you up. Yes, I can do this."

"No," Dom said after a moment, then set a hand on the frightened father's arm. "Wait here and cover me when I come out. I'll go in alone."

The last thing Dom needed was an inexperienced shooter backing him up. Noah was a Christian and a family man, a civilian, not a soldier or killer. Whatever happened in the school, only a person with experience and battle-hardened nerves would prevail—maybe with a little favor thrown in from the Caspertein God.

"Just be ready to go when I get back," Dom ordered in the voice of the commander he was used to being, to which Brand scoffed and raised his eyebrows. "Something funny to you, Brand? Those are his kids in there!"

"Hey, you're the two who claim God is watching over your families. I'm here to witness a miracle, not get shot in the crossfire. Dizzy and I will be ready to move when you come out. *If* you come out."

Dom nearly cursed and backhanded the man, but instead he turned his gaze again to the layout of the school. How was he supposed to do this? How would the Casperteins attempt such a rescue? They were the true deliverers in the area.

The sun was high, nearly noon. No clouds. Nothing moved on the avenue except a little trash rustling in the wind.

An idea suddenly came to Dom and he licked his lips. Was it an idea from God? He wasn't sure. Maybe it was just his own creative imagination, but maybe not. He'd never moved against hostiles on his own before, so he wasn't sure where his natural soldiering ended and something supernatural might begin.

"I'm leaving my pack here." He set it against the wall, but retrieved a bottle of lighter fluid from the front pouch. "Take it with you if you move."

"No problem," Brand agreed. "Anything else? That's all you want? A little fire-starter?"

"It ain't easy keeping things simple, is it?" Dom said, recalling Levi's sense of humor that diffused every tense moment. "I'll be back in a little while."

"Go with God!" Noah called in a whisper as Dom jogged across the avenue.

He veered to the right end of the expansive building. With concern, he watched the many classroom windows, most of them intact and dark inside. An army could hide inside such a complex!

Crossing an empty parking lot seemed like a mile of desert exposure, but he finally reached the end entrance Brand had told him about. Stooping as he approached the building, he collected handfuls of flammable trash—an armful by the time he reached the doors. The doors had no glass in them. He stepped on crunchy shards inside the entrance and peered up a long, dark hallway with lockers on both sides.

There, he set his garbage in a wrinkled pile, then squirted lighter fluid on the trash. His lighter sparked and caught the papers in flame immediately. The breeze through the school was perfect! Smoke drifted into the hallway rather than outside.

Dom backed out of the school and ran excitedly around the back of the building. If Levi could only see him now! Risking his life for two kids, braving danger for good as a believer of Jesus would do. Such behavior had always disgusted Dom. But not today.

"Don't fail me now!" Dom panted to God, if He were really there.

After all, he had no plan and he hoped God would give him more good ideas like using the fire as a distraction.

He stopped at a broken-out classroom window and climbed through. He tumbled onto the floor and bumped into desks that cluttered a room in disarray rather than perfect rows. No doubt scavengers had searched the school for valuables many times since Pan-Day. Wall posters, some of them hanging loosely from weathered tape or tacks, depicted algebra equations, geometry formulas, and scientific calculator keys. It seemed to be a high school.

Wading through the desks, he reached the closed door to the hallway. He opened it slowly and listened. Nothing. The bandits may have relocated since Brand had last located them.

Easing into the hallway, he checked left. His fire had caught onto other trash on the floor. The smoke rolled into the hallway along the ceiling, reaching like fingers into every room. Without waiting to be discovered, Dom ran straight up the littered tiles, past many open lockers, and turned left into a side hall of administration offices. He dove over a counter just as he heard voices and several shouts.

Once he righted himself, he peered over the counter to see no more than five young men and one girl hurrying up the hallway toward the fire. They carried baseball bats, homemade swords, and a crowbar. The males' hair looked shaggy and unwashed. The female wore trousers and a tank top.

With no time to spare, if he wanted to utilize his distraction, Dom scrambled back over the counter and turned up the hallway in the opposite direction. Where had the bandits made their home? Which classroom?

Judging by the amount of trash on the floor outside one doorway, Dom slid to a stop and crept into an auditorium. Chairs had been heaped by the hundreds in rows, offering lanes between and space to sleep on the floor. Wrestling mats and blankets lay on the auditorium floor. But that wasn't all. Inside one four-foot-high barrier of chairs were several imprisoned youths.

Only one young man sat guard on a soft chair, which had probably come from the teachers' lounge. He'd placed the chair in front of a single gap in the circle of chairs and was cradling a metal baseball bat on his lap. His feet were kicked up on another chair.

Dom approached him from a side angle and slightly behind. With vigorous strength, Dom forced the soft chair backwards and spilled the young hoodlum onto the floor. As he tumbled free from the chair, his limbs flailed, swinging the bat at the air. Effortlessly, Dom caught the bat and yanked it from the young man's hands. He'd physically handled many soldiers this age on the island, literally whipping them into compliance in some cases.

The bandit rolled to his haunches and stared wide-eyed up at Dom, who now wielded his bat overhead. After slipping twice on the floor, the thug scrambled aside in retreat, reached the door, and ran down the hall.

"Mae! Isaac!" Dom called to three youths inside the corral. All three were on their feet. The girl had dark red hair, and Dom saw one of the boys had a lighter tint of red on his head, much like his father. The third teen was a mystery. "Noah O'Shea sent me. Come on. We don't have much time!"

The third teen was a lanky, dark-haired boy of perhaps fifteen.

"They said they killed Dad," Isaac said, emerging from the makeshift cage, yet keeping his sister protectively behind him. "He's alive?"

"Yes, he's outside with Dizzy and Brand. Let's go!"

Giving the kids a quick look over, Dom found they were seemingly unharmed, though clearly disheveled from their living environment. They'd been given sleeping mats, but Dom saw no blankets.

He started toward the door with his recovered prisoners, yet he knew time had run out. Not surprisingly, six young men in their late teens or early twenties filed through the door and spread out to block their escape. The young lady entered last, clearly older. All were brandishing weapons except for the youth Dom had disarmed.

Thirty feet from the wall of hoodlums, Dom stopped and measured his chances against such a force. He could take maybe two on at once, but not all six—or seven if the woman jumped in. And one had a handgun tucked in his belt.

"You'll move aside now," Dom declared, pointing with his bat. "I'm taking these kids out of here."

"There's nowhere for them to go," said the one with the pistol. He stood in the center of the thugs. His chest was ornamented with a chain bandolier. Besides the handgun, he held a length of sharpened metal like a sword in length, its hilt fashioned with layers of tape. "They're orphans and they belong here now, with us."

Dom recalled what Brand had said about the gang probably recruiting other youths. Such compelling tactics had been used to force children to act as soldiers all over the world. Once isolated, the kids were brainwashed and intimidated to act as they were instructed. Those who resisted were usually killed.

"They aren't orphans. Their father is outside." He rested the bat over his shoulder like he'd seen Titus do with the paddle two months earlier, but he wasn't sure these were the same youths. "Maybe you'd like to meet Noah O'Shea. He's across the street right now."

"You can't just come in here and trespass—and take what isn't yours!" said the lead thug. "We don't care who's outside. These three aren't leaving. Ask them. They're with us now. They want to stay. We have plans for them. We'll keep them safe. They'll be better off with us than with anyone else out there."

Glancing at the three, Dom saw they seemed frozen in fear—except for Mae, who met his eyes. She subtly shook her head. Though Dom was alone, she was trusting him to keep her from being harmed by these predators. With shame deep inside, Dom admitted to himself that he'd done everything but protect civilians for months now. Once, he'd even made one of Kip's kidnapped girlfriends disappear to spare the general the rumors of his son's crimes against her family.

But that was the old Dom, he realized. Something had happened to him, something he couldn't explain. Pretending to be a Caspertein had affected him deeper than a surface impersonation. He stood taller, found resolve in his righteous goal, and felt as if God Himself was inspiring him to play out his Caspertein role.

"Maybe you want to talk to Titus Caspertein, my cousin?" he offered. "Maybe we should ask Titus Caspertein what he thinks about you keeping these kids from their families?"

The bandits shrunk away so obviously that Dom knew immediately that at least some of those present were among the four Titus had disciplined with the spanking paddle.

"Titus Caspertein is here?" The leader's eyes took in every inch of the auditorium, searching for other threats. "Where is he?"

"He's not far away." Dom knew he had them now. They drew even closer to each other as they cowered. "He'd be disappointed that you've kidnapped people again. He may not be here, but I am. I'm Dom Caspertein."

Two of the young men turned and fled—right out the door and down the hall. Those who remained, huddled together and exchanged a few whispered words. Dom saw their fear. Titus' paddle session weeks earlier had indeed left an impression.

"You can leave," the leader finally said.

The youth tossed his sword onto the floor. The others' weapons clattered loudly as they dropped them as well.

"Yeah, I know I can leave," Dom said.

"Go ahead. We won't do anything." The bandit leader drew his companions aside. "Take them. Go. You Casperteins are crazy. We don't want any trouble. That's why we left the city. How'd you find us down here?"

"I follow God," Dom stated, "and God sees everything. Don't make me come down here again!"

"We won't."

"Next time, I'll bring the rest of my family."

The gang continued to back away from the door, hands empty and raised.

"Let's go," Dom said to the three behind him. "You're safe now."

He walked slowly, keeping himself between the bandits and the kids. Finally, they were in the hallway. As tempted as he was to run outside, Dom walked to the front entrance, his head swiveling to spot dangers, ready to strike with the bat.

"We thought Dad was really dead," Isaac said. He'd started to grow a thin, red beard like his father. "That's what they kept telling us."

"Nah, your dad's too tough to die by their hands." Dom scoffed. "God's definitely with your family. I didn't know what kind of shape we'd find you both in, but you look fine to me."

"They wanted us to join a scavenger team with them," Mae said. "We just kept praying. Then God sent you. A Caspertein! You're an answer to prayer, Mr. Caspertein!"

Outside, Noah revealed himself across the avenue, and the kids ran to him. The lanky youngster with them ran as well. Dom hadn't asked who he was, but he figured the O'Sheas or Brand would look after him.

Dom stood in the middle of the street as the family was reunited. Dizzy spun around, ran in circles, and jumped onto the teens for their attention. Brand emerged from his cover and stood next to the building under construction. He stared in Dom's direction, but Dom didn't go to them. None of this was right.

How could he ever be a Caspertein? Now he had to return to Coronado. How was his life ever going to be the same? There was no way he could return to those streets as part of a patrol and confiscate goods from civilians. He might run into Brand—or one of the houses where Brand had installed countermeasures! General Brogdon would expect him to be the same brutal officer he'd been— challenging the regular troops to join his elite soldiers for bloody assignments in the field.

Dizzy trotted up to him, then looked back at Brand. The others were ready to leave and start back to their home and attic, but Dom didn't move.

"Go on," Dom gestured to Dizzy.

Brand seemed to understand, waved casually from a distance, then dropped Dom's pack on the side of the street. Mae waved her thanks to him, but then they moved on down the avenue, Dizzy leading them north. They weren't his people. He didn't belong with them. Loneliness swept over him like he'd never known before.

Though he'd find his own way back to Coronado Island in a few days, he knew that he didn't belong there, either. God had pierced something deep inside him. He belonged now with the Casperteins, but with his past, he couldn't imagine how that could ever become a reality.

Sandy-haired Neil Dooley blinked up at the quiet balconies above him. He may as well have been screaming at any of the other empty buildings in the city. No one was there to answer him. Not even Fran.

As he stood in the courtyard, his thoughts began to trouble him. Maybe Fran had finally left him. She'd threatened to leave before—during some of her bouts of criticism and moodiness. But that was just Fran. Surely, she wouldn't leave him like this in the middle of claiming their biggest prize, would she?

The mystery of her own sudden disappearance was compounded by the absence of all the people who'd lived in the three apartment buildings—as recently as the evening before. He knew he wasn't imagining it. Through the night he'd fantasized about taking control, ruling on high, using whomever he didn't want to kill—to gratify his own existence in the city.

The shoe and boot prints in the thin layer of dust in the courtyard didn't help him. He'd never been too good at reading sign. But the footprints did confirm that people had been there quite recently. They hadn't been ghosts who'd welcomed him and Fran the morning before.

Fear of the unknown gripped him. Strange forces could be at work. The Meridia Virus had killed tens of millions. Maybe other . . . things had come to play havoc with the remaining humans. Maybe biblical things. Or alien beings. How else could so many people just disappear unless the supernatural or extraterrestrial were involved?

Dooley recalled his search of the ELM building and its lowest apartments. Doors had been left open. Even the goat pens had been empty! Whatever had taken Fran and the people had an appetite for goat meat as well!

He scoffed at himself. This wasn't rational. Someone had to be messing with him. After all, during his fruitless search of the ELM apartments, he'd sensed whispers of movement not far behind him, or an occasional soft footfall in the stairwell. But those could've been echoes from his own noises.

Fran had had their only handgun, so Dooley accepted the fact that he was unarmed until Kid and the others arrived. No one messed with Kid Irling. The guy even kept a list of enemies he hoped to kill one day. His long-haired hippy look had sometimes caused people to misread him—until he fired his assault rifle. Kid had probably killed more people the last six months than Dooley, and that was saying something!

Leaving the courtyard, Dooley walked to the eastern perimeter where the gap in the vehicles had allowed his entry twenty-four hours earlier. As expected, there was no sentry seated on the bench under the bell. He weaved through the vehicles to stand outside the perimeter and gazed east. Far up the street, a lone figure approached. Right on schedule. Dooley mentally rehearsed his explanation for Kid—so he wouldn't sound like a crazy person. Kid would make sense of this mess.

His confidence grew the closer Kid drew until he smiled and waved.

"Been waiting for you."

Kid marched right up to him, his .223 rifle in his hands and a pack on his back. Like Dooley and Fran, Kid had arrived with gear that appeared to have been through miles of travels—instead of only a three-hour hike from Pepper Park.

"This wasn't the plan." Kid's eyes narrowed at the looming buildings nearby. His thin, blond mustache and goatee showed remnants of the thirty-five-year-old's morning oatmeal. Kid loved oatmeal. "The guys are waiting three blocks away for my signal. Is this the right place?"

"Yeah, this is it." Dooley turned to stand beside him and gaze up at the towering buildings. "But something weird is happening. All these people were here yesterday, welcoming me and Fran, giving us the tour, giving us food. And overnight—poof! They've all left!"

"They *left?* Where'd they go?"

"Almost a hundred people just . . . disappeared. I mean, *gone*. I've searched the buildings. The doors are all unlocked and open. The beds still have sheets and blankets. It's like they all just left in the middle of the night, even the people in my own building. But they left me and Fran behind."

"So what?" Kid shrugged. "So, they figured out who you are and they ran off without a fight. That works for us."

"Not these people." Dooley shook his head. "No way. You should've seen their weapons. I mean, not everyone was armed, but the ELM people were, the ones in charge. Fran thought they looked weak. I guess I did, too. We planned to take over with your help today, as soon as the others arrived. Now, I don't know what to do. There's no one here to take anything from!"

"You're losing it, man." Kid cursed. "We can move into what they left behind. They must have fresh water, right? What's Fran think of all this? She usually has an opinion about everything."

When Dooley had been in college, gradually studying to take the bar exam, he'd prided himself on being mentally quick on his feet. A lawyer had to have a response or defense—always. But right now, he didn't want to tell even his closest soldier the truth. Yet how could he hide it?

"I told you it was weird, right?" Dooley scoffed at himself. "Now I can't find Fran and she has our only gun."

"Well, I've got an extra for you." Kid took off his pack and drew a nine-millimeter plus a shoulder holster from a pouch. "Feel better?"

"It's a start." Dooley fit the straps over his shoulders and across his back. "Both of us together can tear this place apart. And keep your eye out for another inhaler for me besides searching for Fran."

"You got it. No one could take Fran without a fight. There has to be some sign of something."

Together, the pair returned to the courtyard and Dooley told him where he'd searched already—in his own Overcomers' building and up to the eleventh floor in the ELM building.

"That's a lot of stairs to climb since the dollies don't work. There were people here who kept things running, but without them, this place may as well be like anywhere else—dead."

"What about the military?" Kid pointed west. "They're just across the bay, right? Maybe they came in during the night? That General Brogdon guy is unhinged. He has a reputation."

"Okay, but without a shot fired?"

"So you really heard nothing?"

"Do I look like I'm in the pranking mood?"

Kid frowned and gazed up at the ELM structure.

"You only went up to the eleventh floor. This is their headquarters building, you said. They have to have something in there. Are those plants on the balconies?"

"Gardens. They have flower pots and containers made out of everything, even dresser drawers, holding dirt to grow vegetables and stuff. Onions, tomatoes, cucumbers, lettuce, and all kinds of herbs. Someone in my building said that there's even plans to build a root cellar in the spring. All they need is something to dig a hole in the ground. This is no small enterprise, Kid. They have a whole fishing crew that rotates or something, catching all kinds of fish."

"Did you go to the bay?"

"Hey, we're already flirting with disaster being this close to the PSDF. I'm not trying to be too visible."

"I say we search that whole ELM building." Kid tied his long hair back. "Stairs or no stairs, we need to search more. There's two of us now. We can cover more ground."

"We came here to be kings." Dooley swore and wrinkled his face. "Can you believe this? Do we look like detectives?"

"Hey, if worse comes to worst, we steal some tomato plants and go back to Pepper Park. I could do a lot with fresh tomatoes."

"They don't go in oatmeal."

"You don't know that."

Dooley was about to laugh, but Kid's face revealed that he was serious.

"Well, I'm not leaving without Fran."

"Bro, no offense." Kid leaned closer. "You could do better than her."

"I don't want to do better!" He shoved Kid and walked away. "Come on."

Inside the door of the ELM building, Dooley pointed out the empty goat pens with fresh droppings inside. They moved to the stairs and started climbing, Dooley in the lead, though winded, wishing he were in better shape with a few extra inhalers. His whole gang, including Kid, partied too much on homemade wine when they couldn't find factory booze, but Kid was in better physical shape altogether.

"Wait!" Kid grabbed at Dooley's shirt, then whispered, "I thought I heard something up there!"

Leaning over the stair railing, Dooley looked up into infinity.

"They could hide a battalion up there and we'd never know it down here."

"No way." Kid whispered. "Over a hundred people hiding in here? We could totally find them."

On the twelfth floor, they left the stairwell for the apartment hall.

"Four apartments on each floor." Dooley pointed. "The suites are huge. Rich folks definitely lived here. Some furniture is still here, mostly wooden stuff we'd usually burn, but it gives you the impression—they were rich people."

"Sounds quiet." Kid gestured to the right. "I'll take one. You take the next. Search everything. Call out if you hear or see anything suspicious. I'll come running."

"I just want some answers."

"Stay sharp." Kid nodded resolutely.

Dooley nodded back, then rested his hand on his holstered gun. Anyone would be stupid to try something now—with him and Kid together!

As on the other floors, the front door to the next apartment was open. Dooley pushed it wide as Kid entered the one next door.

"No one's here," Dooley said.

Kid returned to the doorway.

"Just look, Dooley. They can't all be empty. Those people you saw were living somewhere. They didn't just disappear."

Sighing, Dooley entered. He sure wasn't feeling like the leader of his gang. Nothing about this felt right. In the past, he'd killed and stolen on impulse to stay alive. But here, there was no one to kill and there seemed to be too much to take, even though *everything* was there for the taking!

He opened bathroom doors, wandered through bedrooms, and checked the kitchen cupboards. The place had been cleaned, but it was still fully furnished—crystal in a glass display, a huge windup clock ticking away. Pan-

Day looters hadn't even bothered to climb the stairs this high.

On the balcony, Dooley picked a ripe tomato. Other plant leaves in flower pots weren't ready to harvest yet—squash or something. The tomato dripped down his chin as he chomped. At least he'd get some vitamin C while he wandered around.

Returning to the corridor, he called out to Kid.

"I told you, there's no one here." Dooley listened. "Kid? Kid!"

Drawing his sidearm, he aimed it at the stairwell door. Had the door just clicked closed? Kid would never abandon him. Licking his lips, Dooley edged into the apartment that Kid had been searching. No signs of a struggle. The sliding glass door to the balcony was closed. The bedroom and bathroom doors stood ajar.

Suddenly, Dooley ran out of the suite and lunged for the stairwell door. He threw it open and dove onto the floor landing. His gun was leveled. His ears were alert. Silence. No one was there.

But there had to be! Stubbornly, Dooley waited, his gun wavering. The minutes passed. Kid had known the score. He'd been prepared for anything, anyone. The Dooley Gang were predators, killers across every San Diego neighborhood. Who could possibly take them down without a sound? *This wasn't possible!*

After ten minutes, Dooley rested his back against the wall, but he didn't holster his weapon. They wouldn't take him without a fight. He wouldn't go without a shot fired. This wasn't how he'd planned his takeover!

He'd had enough of this building. No way was he going to the top floor for nothing at all. Or to be captured. This wasn't worth the hassle. Or the terror. Nobody was this quiet. This was unearthly!

While stopping often to listen along the way, he finally reached the ground floor, then walked out to the courtyard. *People!* But then he realized it was just three young men, all ex-convicts, from his own gang. They'd grown worried and come on their own accord to investigate, to reap the spoils, or move into a post-apocalyptic paradise—compared to what the rest of the city had become.

They listened curiously as Dooley explained the morning's events. But their curiosity turned into concern and then downright fear.

"This should've been an easy job: kill the leaders and assume control. Everything could've kept running. But this isn't natural. It's *supernatural!*"

"Spirits?" asked one gunman, a machete his preferred weapon. "Or demons?"

"I always thought of ourselves as the demons." Dooley lowered his head. "We have to get out of here. Kid and Fran disappeared somewhere. Or worse, they've been taken captive. I've searched all these buildings. There's no one here."

"It's haunted." Another man shivered, his grip on his shotgun apparently giving him no confidence. "I knew we should've never left Pepper Park. We have enough pretzels to eat back home."

Under other circumstances, Dooley would've punched the youth for his insolence, but today, he agreed.

Walking out of the ELM perimeter, they hoped to run into the rest of the gang on the way—and warn them away from downtown. Fran and Kid were lost, and the mystery of their disappearance wasn't worth it to Dooley to risk himself being killed as well.

✝

Milli Lusis played with her hair as she watched Mayor Ridley Malden in the Garden. He was everything Oliver hadn't been—confident, decisive, passionate, dominant, and beautiful. Of course, she appreciated Oliver's attempt to keep her alive the last few months, but it had all been a weak and beggarly effort. Yet here . . . was a man who knew what he wanted and how to rule.

At that instant, Malden smiled at her from where he stood on the flower path below the bridge. Dr. Ferguson was with him, speaking in hushed tones, but Malden had assured Milli that the doctor was merely his advisor and close friend. Milli was the only one for him, he'd said. He'd even hinted at the prospect of having a baby with her, a baby that would be worthy of him, the Garden, and their future together. Oliver and Rory were in the past. Malden and the Garden were future.

Muscled and fierce Sazon returned sweaty with two other men, handguns on their hips, which were mostly concealed by their polo shirts. Everyone around Milli seemed to gasp at the return of Sazon. They'd all heard the gunshots through the orchard, but it seemed Oliver and Rory had escaped. Yet that failure wouldn't detract from the residents' fascination with the mighty man who'd been resurrected from the dead. Milli herself had seen Sazon lying dead on the path, shot by that terrible, blond man who'd been with the disgusting, crippled lady in the wheelchair. She thought of them as such refuse because Malden had called them that—terrible and disgusting. They defied the compassionate CARE Protocol of the Garden, and anyone who defied what was pure and good for humanity was worthy of disdain and death.

"Please, my family, come near," Mayor Malden called to the residents. "We're all together now. Let me speak on what has happened this afternoon. You have seen for yourselves the violence with which those outside the Garden are willing to spread. Oliver has joined that killer because he was never really with us. Emily as well has taken her place in the world of disaster, disease, and disgrace.

"But we won't be intimidated! Our cause is righteous. Our cause is just. Our cause preserves life and restores us to our destined future. The Garden is the answer to humanity's needs, and we have all agreed that the solution to the problem outside our walls is to take our CARE Protocol beyond the Garden."

"Beyond the Garden," the residents repeated, Millie with them. Their cause was now her cause. She was one of them. This was her family. Malden was now her world, her lord.

"Now, we have to be the savior of all who want life," Malden continued, his face radiant with enlightenment. "We have plenty, so we must take our plenty to those who may be saved by our three *Rs:* Recover humanity, Restore health, and Return honor. *Beyond the Garden!"*

"Beyond the Garden," they droned.

"We can grow in influence and spread our message by way of our excess of produce. Our fruit and vegetables here aren't ours alone. Using baskets, we can carry them outside. This will be our mission. By this method of sharing what we have, we will cleanse and restore and gain. Doctor?"

The tall woman smiled down at the Garden residents. Milli felt her love, her personal care. After all, Dr. Ferguson was one in purpose with Malden.

"My brothers and sisters," she began with a voice almost as deep as a man's, "nature itself identifies for us those who should remain and those who should be removed. The health of any people group has always depended upon their willingness to set aside the ill and diseased from among them. Our strength builds as weakness is expelled. It is pure and basic science."

"It's just science!" Malden laughed as if any other concept would be too foolish to entertain.

Milli accepted the science they offered.

"I have developed a new cleansing agent." Dr. Ferguson opened a silver case and offered its contents to her observers. "Each of these syringes contains a highly lethal dose, not unlike cyanide, that will compassionately remove the burdens from the people beyond the Garden."

"Beyond the Garden."

"This toxin is set in microscopic capsules meant to be effective on a time delay of twenty-four hours or less after injected into the bloodstream. Those of you who leave the Garden from now on will carry one of these syringes. Share your fruit. Distribute our vegetables. Care for the people everywhere. But for the purpose of restoring humanity, show your compassion by injecting the mentally ill, the elderly, and the disabled. It's not necessary to ask for their permission. Tell them it's a blend of nutrients or a health vaccine. However you administer the shot, don't delay. After all, their weakness diminishes our strength as a people."

"Thank you, Doctor." Malden took her hand at her side. "My family, my children, I didn't realize this urgent call for compassion until our brother Sazon was murdered. But the grave rejected this perfect specimen of health and strength, so that he would remain among us. In your mission of mercy, whoever volunteers to share what we have with the communities around us—you will be protected as well. Fear no one. Love everyone. Cleanse all. Restore everything. This is our CARE Protocol for the world. Sazon?"

"We'll leave immediately." Sazon's voice was as fierce as his appearance. "Gather fruit and vegetables tonight, and tomorrow, we will leave in three groups of three to disperse our first gifts to the people. I will lead one group myself. All who want to go will get a chance in the coming days, but we must continue to cultivate what we have here in the Garden. In the months to come, it is worth imagining other Gardens being propagated all over the city and spreading into the rest of the state and country. By going beyond the Garden, we will restore everything."

"Beyond the Garden."

Milli folded her hands and bowed her head. Yes, she knew this was her purpose in life—to serve Malden, to bear his children, to further the health and purity of all humanity. Never again would the Meridia Virus sweep across the nation. Health and science and compassion would govern them through nature.

After the meeting, she went to Malden's side and kissed him.

"Please, I want to volunteer tomorrow," she said, "to help restore everything."

"Are you sure? Milli, you just arrived."

"I don't care. I know this is where I belong. I want to share what we have—and be a messenger of the CARE truth."

He took her hands in his own and gazed into her eyes.

"You understand, Milli, that we will need to cleanse Oliver for the good of everyone. Otherwise, he'll spread his lies about our purpose. We'll need to find him and those who harbor him, and cleanse them all."

"Yes, I understand." Milli's eyes filled with tears—tears of joy. "I'll cleanse him myself if I ever see him again, if I can get close to him."

"And you may be just the one to do it." He took her face in his hands and kissed her. "I'll send you with Sazon tomorrow morning. That way, I'll know you'll remain safe. But tonight, we'll celebrate together, just me and you. How's that sound? A nice dinner!"

"Malden, I'm completely yours. Completely!"

She embraced him and felt his strength pull her into him.

"I ask nothing else from you." He kissed the top of her head. "You are perfect."

✝

Somewhere near Paradise Hills west of Bonita, Titus strolled up a four-lane street next to Emily Pickford as she pushed her wheelchair. Unlike ghost communities he'd walked through, this one was populated by families outside their homes and on the street. Only thirty minutes earlier, they'd fled the Garden with Dusty in tow, yet here was another pocket of civilization so close to ELM.

"They must have good water somewhere nearby," Emily stated as she rolled next to Titus. "Should I ask them? Or warn them of the Garden?"

Titus noticed men, women, and children trekking with empty water jugs toward a single-story factory building, then exiting with full containers. The only weapons anyone in sight seemed to have were held by two men at the factory door. They were monitoring the traffic in and out.

"Everyone here seems pretty peaceful." Titus nodded to a father of a family of three, maybe Middle Eastern judging by the *hijab* the mother wore. The young girl who walked hand in hand between her parents boldly greeted Titus in Arabic, and offered a smile. Though Titus responded in kind, the parents hushed the girl and they hurried toward the factory with their containers. "Well, whoever we ask for water might be the same people we ask for a place to stay for the night. We don't need to hurry home."

"That girl spoke another language to you." Emily paused in an intersection and looked back. "What was it?"

"Arabic." Titus stopped with her and noted that Dusty was about forty yards back, covering them as they walked. "Seems strange that this many people are out all at once. They must have an appointed time to come out and fill their containers. It's very organized."

"Should we try, too?" Emily gestured at the factory. "It doesn't look like they're charging anything. You want me to ask? My bottle could use a refill."

Far up one street, civilians suddenly scattered and scrambled for cover in buildings, driveways, and alleys.

"Not just yet." Titus flicked off the safety of his battle rifle as panic spread up the street. "I think we're about to find out why all these people came out together or not at all. Dusty, come in. Looks like trouble. Over."

"Copy. I'll hold here. Over."

"What's happening?" Emily pushed her chair closer to Titus as families sprinted left and right, many of them shrieking in fear, to reach shelter. Some even abandoned their heavy water containers to reach cover faster. "Titus?"

The Middle Eastern family returned up the street at a jog, their empty water jugs jostling since they hadn't reached the factory before some alarm had been sounded. Sure enough, the factory had been shuttered and the two gunmen were no longer standing outside.

"May we stay with you, please?" Titus spoke in Arabic to the father as the family of three passed.

The frightened father dropped a large water jug on the dusty pavement to pick up his daughter and continue faster toward a row of duplexes.

"We don't want any trouble!" the man responded—his accent identifying him as Syrian.

Titus scooped up the dropped container and jogged after the family. Emily had no problem pushing her sporty chair a little faster to keep up. They were among the last on the street.

That's when Titus saw them.

Far up the avenue where the panic had first begun, a cluster of cyclists slowly peddled their mountain bikes into the neighborhood. They appeared to be predominately men, numbering about thirty. Their weapons seemed limited to clubs and swords, but no doubt some had firearms.

"How do you know Arabic?" Emily panted beside him. "I knew you were some kind of soldier."

"Not quite. I was some kind of criminal. The God of the Bible rescued me from all that. Get up there, Em. We don't want to slow them down from getting inside."

Emily sped ahead, her mag wheels spinning faster than Titus' legs were churning, but he wasn't about to dump his heavy pack or drop the water container that belonged to the father. It just might be their ticket into gaining the man's trust—if they could keep up with him.

The family ahead cut through a hedge and climbed a straight flight of wooden stairs to an apartment above.

"Just carry me up!" Emily stopped at the bottom of the stairs and raised her arms to him. "Leave my chair here."

"Not a chance!" Titus tossed the jug onto her lap. "Hold on!"

With his rifle hanging on the sling, his hands were free to bend over Emily and grip her seat back and the front of her chair frame. He picked her up, chair and all, and shifted her to his side so he could climb the stairs. If he were alone as Dusty was, he might've stood his ground outside and greeted the cyclists who clearly terrorized the community. But not with Emily to care for.

Breathlessly, he reached the top of the stairs as the father slammed a heavy door, perhaps reinforced on the inside.

"Please, let us in!" Titus begged in Arabic. He glanced back at the street. Several cyclists had spotted them and were turning into the lane. "I have your water container. Be merciful!"

Dusty was nowhere in sight, but Titus wasn't worried about the young man. For more than two months, he'd been sneaking around San Diego with Levi, and before Dusty had joined ELM, he'd been a crafty scavenger and thief. If he happened to perish now, Dusty was at least a believer in Jesus' gift of salvation. He was safe in God's hands.

The door opened six inches.

"Hurry!" urged the father, then noticed the cyclists racing toward the row of duplexes. "They're coming!"

He started to pull the door closed, but Titus stuck the toe of his boot inside the door and forced it wider. Using Emily and her chair as a ram, Titus forced his way into the room. Roughly, he set Emily on a carpeted floor, then turned and slammed the door. The man of the house joined him, fumbling with a series of dead bolts and a heavy brace across the width of the door.

Whoops and hollers from outside indicated they'd definitely been discovered, but Titus gasped for breath and relief. The reinforced door would at least buy him some time.

"Thank you." He set a hand on the father's shoulder. "I am in your debt."

"You cannot stay here!" The man threw off Titus' hand and backed away to guard his family. His small daughter of about seven peered around his leg to study Emily and her wheelchair. "You've endangered us all!"

"Yasif!" his wife scolded. "They are guests."

Titus didn't feel it necessary to translate their concern for Emily. The young family was clearly uncomfortable with visitors—and Titus understood he had indeed put them all in a predicament.

"I remind you, we're vulnerable here!" Yasif fired back at his wife. "We're only safe if we can hide. Now we're not hidden!"

"Your door is secure." Titus touched the bolts and brace. "This is well-done. They can't break through here."

Heavy boots thudded on the wooden stairs up to the apartment. It sounded like three or four people. Titus went to the front window and gazed at an angle to see about fifteen bikes had been abandoned in the empty driveway as the riders scouted around the duplex and others nearby.

"You must go!" Yasif insisted with a hushed voice. "We have nothing to give to you or to them."

"It ain't easy being hospitable sometimes." Titus left the window and took off his pack. "But we're not here to take anything from you. I'm here to give."

A heavy fist pounded on the door.

"We know you're in there!" shouted a man with a young voice. "We saw you close the door. And you have women."

Titus placed his palm against the door. It would definitely stop a small caliber bullet.

"Titus!" Emily's face was filled with terror.

He held up a finger for her to remain quiet and to give him a moment to think.

"The family that lives here," Titus said loudly to the door, "doesn't have anything to spare. We thank you for your company, but we cannot give you provisions we don't have."

"Ah, we don't want provisions." The men at the door sniggered together. "Send out one woman and we'll call it even. That's all we want."

Behind Titus, Yasif softly translated for his wife, indicating he spoke English but she didn't.

Leaning against the door, Titus considered a response. He understood Emily and the family's fear, but he'd been in tighter spots.

"Dusty, what's your twenty?" Titus asked his location on his comm. "Over."

"I'm in someone's back yard," Dusty said. "But I didn't see where you went. Over."

"Can you see the street we were on? What do you see? Over."

"Yeah, I see a gas station on the street, and next to me there's some blue apartments, single and two-story. Over."

"Okay, I think you're two lots away from me. Can you get onto the roofs of the blue apartment buildings? Over."

"Maybe. I see a fire escape I can climb. Yeah, I can get up to the roof there. Over."

"Perfect. I'm probably going to need you up there for cover. These bikers have me and Emily cornered in an upstairs apartment. And they're not friendly. Over."

"Copy that. I'm moving now."

Titus sighed and knocked on the door.

"You still there?" Titus shouted.

"We're not going anywhere." Two cackled with the speaker. "I told you already, I'll go away as soon as you send out a pretty date for me for tonight."

The light was indeed fading outside. Titus knew darkness wasn't an asset for him or Dusty. Their superior firepower was useless if they couldn't see.

"No one's leaving this apartment tonight," Titus said, "so you might as well keep moving."

"If you don't want to come out, then we'll come in. Or we'll get a fire started downstairs. Maybe a little heat will warm you to the idea of sharing your female company."

"These guys just aren't getting the message." Titus frowned at Emily. "How're we supposed to get to know our new friends here with all this ruckus outside?"

"What?" Emily's eyes widened. "How can you be so nonchalant?"

"The Lord hasn't abandoned us, Emily." Titus went again to the window. "We can trust God to watch over our souls, even if the worst happens to our bodies. You might want to learn to rely on Him."

"The Garden had enough crazy in it to scare me straight from any more cults. No thanks, Titus. Sorry."

"Trusting in Jesus as your Savior isn't a cult. Cults bring bondage. Christ offers freedom. You've known me for a few hours. Do I seem to be free or a slave? Bummer. I can't get to the roof from this window."

"Why do you want to get to the roof?" Yasif asked. "Stay away from the window. They'll see you!"

Returning to the door, Titus knocked loudly.

"Hey, out there! You promise to leave us alone if we send someone out?"

"We promise!" More laughter. "We promise!"

"Okay, give us another minute." Titus touched his transmitter. "Dusty, you on the roof yet? Over."

"Who is he speaking to?" Yasif asked Emily.

"Yeah," Dusty said, "but I can't see much. I see a bunch of bikes and a few guys in someone's driveway. Over."

"That's where I am. When I tell you to, open fire on those cyclists. Copy?"

"Copy."

Titus waved Emily and the host family to his left so they would be fully protected by the door. Then he began to remove the bar and locks.

"Stop!" Yasif gasped. *"They'll get in!"*

"Stay back!" Titus waved his hand, then paused at the final deadbolt. His other hand drew his silenced handgun and mentally rehearsed the angle he'd need to hold and fire. "No one's getting in. But I'm going out."

"Let him do his thing," Emily pleaded with Yasif. "I trust him, even if I'm scared, too."

"Now, Dusty!" Titus said, and threw the last lock.

Somewhere above, Dusty's rifle boomed. Titus could only imagine the terror it would send into the hearts of the cyclists who had no such rifle. They were probably familiar only with handguns and panicked victims.

At that instant, Titus opened the door two inches—wide enough to slip his muzzle into the crack as well as wide enough to see the four men on the landing mere feet away. As planned, the attention of the four had been drawn to those below who were under attack from a mysterious sniper.

Titus fired into their midsections. Three went down. The fourth scrambled for the stairs. Widening the door, Titus shoved his arm outside and more carefully fired at the fourth, dropping him hard on the stairs.

Dusty had already tranquilized several of the cyclists below, but the rest had leapt for cover. When Titus stepped onto the stair landing, his elevated position gave him full command of the driveway and yard from a fresh angle. He holstered his handgun and raised his rifle. The cyclists' demands and threats still rang in his ears as his weapon thundered. They certainly believed they were dying as he easily targeted them one at a time.

Then, nothing moved. Titus counted the bikes and compared that count with the unconscious aggressors lying below. He remembered seeing more cyclists on the main street, so others weren't far away, but everyone at the apartments had been put down temporarily.

"Yasif, come help me," Titus said in Arabic. "Let's go. Quickly!"

The man hesitantly joined Titus on the landing, glancing often back at his wife and daughter.

"I am not a killer," Yasif stated, his head bowed.

"Neither am I." Titus reloaded his rifle and handgun, then freed his hands by hanging the rifle on his harness. "I've only tranquilized them. Help me collect their weapons. Emily, stay with his wife and daughter." Then on his radio, "Dusty, watch that front street for more cyclists. Over."

Following Titus down to the driveway, Yasif collected weapons as they went. Once they had all the weapons, Yasif took them up to his apartment to stash them. Meanwhile, Titus wheeled their bikes two at a time out to the street. There, he slashed their tires and stomped out their spoked wheels.

Standing over the wreckage of bikes, Titus studied the neighborhood. The other half of the cyclists were nowhere to be found. Nothing else was moving, which impressed him since he knew how many dozens of people lived within earshot of the recent gunfire. These were people familiar with hiding and secrecy. Their source of water alone proved they knew how to cooperate to some degree, but they'd lacked the courage or creativity to dispose of the cyclist threat.

Titus returned to the apartment driveway where Yasif was searching the packs and saddlebags of the cyclists. He looked up at Titus.

"The spoils of war," said the Syrian as he continued. "You disapprove?"

"Oh, I never disapprove of what may humble wicked hearts. Just hurry." Titus signaled Dusty and spoke in English. "Join us inside, Dusty. We can watch from the window upstairs to keep guard through the night."

"I think I got five." Dusty stood on the edge of the nearby roof and admired the scene of the fallen. "Is everyone inside okay?"

"Yes, they are. The fact that you even asked confirms that you're the right man for this work. Come on down."

Yasif filled one cyclist's pack with water bottles and food, then labored carefully up to his apartment with his acquired stash. Dusty joined Titus to carry the four from the landing and leave them among their comrades. Finally, they joined Yasif's family upstairs, and Titus secured the door.

"This is so unhealthy." Emily grinned past a mouthful of rice crispy bar salvaged from some vending machine. She handed Titus the second half. "But it's delicious."

Titus popped it into his mouth as Yasif offered Dusty more scavenged treats while he sat at the window. Yasif's wife and daughter ate what he'd given them—as if they hadn't eaten well in days.

"Slowly, Yasif," Titus said. "They'll get sick from this packaged food if they're not used to it."

Gazing at his family, Yasif's own mouth was too full to speak for a few seconds.

"That's enough, Majeda," he told his daughter. "Save the rest for later."

Her mother took the leftovers from her and wrapped their treats for leaner times. Yasif stashed the sweet spoils into a high cupboard in the kitchen, then returned to the living room. The sky was growing dark, so he lit a candle, then covered it with fogged glass that allowed the barest hint of light to shine out.

"Now they know where we live," Yasif said as if the villains were still lurking outside the door. "You've endangered us all. There's nowhere safe for us to go."

"Okay, they're waking up out there," Dusty said. "I can kind of see them moving around."

"Since we won't let them in, they'll start fires downstairs," said Yasif. "We've heard of it before."

"They probably won't do anything else tonight." Titus opened a bedroom door and noted another window that faced their back yard—a secondary escape route by rope could be fashioned. "I'm sure they're confused, weaponless, and without transportation. That makes them more vulnerable than us. Just because an enemy is ruthless doesn't mean they're stupid. But they'll leave until they come up with a new plan."

"Wow, they were definitely surprised by your guns." Emily grinned. "The whole neighborhood heard those!"

Little Majeda eased out of her mother's arms to pet Emily's wheelchair as if it were a shy animal.

Titus lifted the curious girl and set her on Emily's lap before her parents could object. Her mother opened her mouth then glanced at Yasif, perhaps only now considering the ongoing Meridia threat. But Yasif said nothing as Titus crouched next to where Yasif sat on a sofa cushion on the floor. The sofa frame had long been removed, maybe burned for fuel.

"You've done a good job protecting your family," Titus said in Arabic for Yasif and his wife to hear together. "But it's time to leave. My name is Titus Caspertein, and I invite you to come live with us downtown where many other families now live and work and play."

"But how will we fit in?" Yasif looked at his wife. "Gizem speaks no English. Perhaps America was once more hospitable, but we are foreigners here. I have never heard anyone in California speak Arabic as well as you do."

"For about twenty years, I lived around North Africa and the Middle East," Titus said. "Fear may have stopped American hospitality in most places, but I'm first a follower of Jesus the Messiah, or Isa as you've heard Him called. It pleases Him that I welcome you to live within my protection, with my wife, son—and sister, Wynter, who teaches the children grammar and mathematics lessons. Her husband is named Wes, and he is a language expert."

"Your sister teaches school?" Yasif's head lifted. "It's one of the reasons we left Syria. We want Majeda to receive an education without being threatened as a girl."

"Well, Majeda has no shortage of curiosity." Titus chuckled as the girl fingered Emily's necklace—a piece of metal on a thin, silver chain. "She'll fit right in with the other kids. We even have a giant sandbox outside!"

"But we are not . . . followers of Jesus." Yasif shook his head. "I am sorry, but I believe He is a false God."

"I won't tell you what to believe, my friend. I ask only that you judge our Lord and Savior by the love He inspires us to share with you. My blood brother is named Rudy. He lives far away in Colorado, so I have room in my heart here for another brother. My family has just grown by three more members, if you will accept my invitation."

"As . . . your brother?" Yasif's chin trembled as he met Titus' gaze in the dim lighting. "Not even in Syria did my own neighbors show me such kindness when ISIS came and ruined our homes. You cannot be rich since no one is rich today, but you are rich in other ways. Your man at the window and the young woman in the wheelchair are evidence that your closest companions trust you."

"Then you accept?" Titus offered his hand.

"Yes, I accept that I have not been told the truth about you Christians." Yasif accepted Titus' hand. "And I accept your brotherhood."

"Good!" Titus laughed and clapped Yasif on the shoulder. He drew out a flashlight and handed it to Emily.

"Em, the room is dark back there. Help them pack to leave with us early in the morning."

"Me?" Emily tested the light against Majeda, who giggled. "I don't speak their language."

"You know the only language worth speaking tonight." Then to Gizam, he said, "Little sister, Emily will hold the light for you as you pack clothes for yourself and Majeda, if your husband approves. Take only what you can carry. Nothing more. We have several hours of walking tomorrow."

Emily gave the child a ride into the bedroom, and the mother could be heard opening drawers and giving the girl instructions. Yasif joined his wife in preparation.

At the front window, Titus peered out at the front yard and the street beyond.

"Any movement?"

"Once they realized their bikes were busted," Dusty said, "they walked out to the street and turned right. We're really gonna take these people home with us?"

"Every life matters."

"What if they spread their religion?"

"False religions will always be in the world, Dusty. It's our job as Christians to show that faith in Jesus is the only valid belief system worth having. The best way to shut down lies is by living out the truth. There's nothing like Christ's love that can shine on hearts to discourage people from chasing after empty religious promises or false gods. We don't approve of Yasif's current religion, but we're confident that by living boldly for him to witness Christ in us—he'll be won naturally."

"I guess that's how Levi won me." Dusty grunted. "No one ever treated me like you guys did—do. Like family."

"And now look at you—standing guard over people who're at the threshold of learning the same lesson. The same thing happened to me. I saw what I was missing when a man named Corban Dowler valued me as God does. Accompany that kindness with the Gospel message, and people are ripe for citizenship in heaven."

They watched the darkness for a few minutes.

"It'll be slower and more work for us with three more people tomorrow." Dusty said. "Who knows what's between us and downtown? We must still be about seven miles out."

"We're not in a hurry. Levi and Oleg are dealing with Dooley at ELM. God never stops teaching us to trust Him. You up for the job?"

"Oh, I wouldn't miss it!" Dusty grinned. "I just wish Levi were here to share some of the fun!"

Chapter Five

Fran Garrick blinked awake. She sat up on a flowery sofa in a carpeted living room. Two candles were burning on stands against the wall in front of her, and the room smelled like . . . *warm bread?*

Her memory was a little foggy. She'd been with Dooley, searching the ELM apartments, and then, nothing. Rising slowly, she felt soreness in her right thigh. With her hand, she pressed on the flesh. Just a bruise. Maybe she'd fallen, or— No, it was the same kind of bruise she'd felt after being shot by that young blond's tranquilizer gun weeks earlier!

Voices drew her from the living room to a dining room and kitchen. A tall, brunette woman was running water at a sink and a rugged-looking, young, blond man sat at the dining table peeling potatoes. Chopped carrots sat in another bowl at his elbow. His hair was a little shaggier than she remembered, but it was him—the one who'd tranquilized her two months earlier!

"I'm just saying, Mom," the young man stated, "that if we could find some cattle, they'd be worth the effort to keep alive. Beef stew has got to be better than fish stew."

"You haven't tried my fish stew, Levi," the woman chided. "Besides, where would we keep a herd of cattle? On the roof with the chickens?"

The sliding glass door next to the kitchen counter led to a balcony, Fran noticed, but the balcony seemed to be very far from the ground. And the sky was dark outside. How long had she been asleep?

"Hey, you're awake." Levi glanced casually at Fran. "You have a good nap? So, you're not going to make me peel all these potatoes by myself, are you?"

He offered a silver peeler and shifted the bowl of potatoes into the center of the table. Bewildered, she sat opposite him, still trying to track how she'd arrived there.

"Fran," the woman said as she approached the table, "don't let Levi pawn off his chores on you. How're you feeling? You want a glass of milk? How about some nut bread? It's still warm."

She nodded slightly as the woman set a plate of buttered nut bread before her—*and a glass of milk!* Fran's hand trembled as she reached for the glass. The woman returned to the kitchen counter. The milk was even chilled. After sniffing it, Fran took a swallow. *So sweet!* Never had she tasted such delicious milk. Powdered milk the last few months hadn't tasted the same as real milk, or worth the bother most days.

The buttered nut bread seemed to melt in her mouth. She closed her eyes as her whole body relaxed to the smells, tastes, and comfort of the room. Dooley and the gang were good at stealing whatever they needed, but what these people had . . .

Tears rolled halfway down her cheeks before she wiped at them in frustration. No, this was a trap! The man across from her was an enemy. He'd stolen more than half of the horse meat from Dooley and he'd tranquilized her! And where was Maddix Striber?

"What would you prefer, Fran?" Levi tossed another peeled potato into the next bowl. "Beef or fish?"

"It's all in the preparation and seasoning, Levi!" The woman laughed as she argued without really arguing. Fran could tell mother and son were close, even though he teased her about her cooking. "Wait till tomorrow night. You'll see."

"How do you know my name?" Fran asked and touched her hair, guessing she looked a fright after sleeping on it. "I don't have any identification."

"Oh, come on." He frowned. "We met weeks ago. I'm Levi. This is my mom, Annette. And you're Fran."

"Weeks ago?" She stiffened. "Oh, you mean with the horse meat. And the grill. You remember me."

"You were very kind to share what you had with the town." He winked. "That was some pretty good horse meat."

"The way I remember it," Fran said, "you shot me and stole the meat from us."

"No, no." He chuckled. "That was Sergeant Lesage who shot you."

"Sergeant Lesage?" Fran winced, trying to remember more. "Who's that?"

"The man who was with me that day. He's a sergeant in the PSDF. I was escorting him home after he was wounded up in the hills. His gun went off accidently when the door hit his elbow and you were struck. Thankfully, our weapons are loaded only with tranquilizers, so you were unharmed, right?"

"But you stole our meat."

"Actually, I confiscated about half of the horse meat after Dooley shot Conrad's riding horse out from under him. And you guys almost killed Conrad. He's still not right in the head."

Fran glared at him with old hatred she'd carried for weeks. After burning neighborhoods and killing civilians, searching for Maddix Striber and hunting down this kid, it couldn't have happened by accident like he said. *An accidental shooting?* And Dooley was at fault? She fought to hang onto the bitterness she'd become so acquainted with even as her hatred melted away as fast as the butter on the warm bread in her hand.

"But all that's in the past, right?" Annette brought over a bowl of celery for Levi to chop. "We can all move forward as friends now."

Friends? Fran looked away from Levi as he finished the potatoes and started dicing the celery. Stew did sound pretty good. She couldn't remember the last time she'd eaten fresh stew. If Annette's stew was anywhere close to her nut bread . . .

"Where's Dooley?" she blurted the instant he came to mind, but regretted it an instant later. "I mean, Neil . . ."

"He left early this morning," Levi said. "Walked right out through the perimeter heading east."

"No, he wouldn't leave me."

"Well, I watched him from the balcony." Levi nodded at the sliding door. "I can see for miles on a clear day, especially with my telescope. Dooley met up with some others and they all moved southeast."

She cursed and scowled at the table cloth. Dooley never did have the backbone to finish a job the right way! Now, he'd abandoned her. But *here?*

Nothing was making sense. Her lover had left her with her enemies who were . . . feeding her?

The milk and bread were gone. Levi set a paring knife in front of her and shared his bowl of celery. Annette brought over an additional cutting board and a bowl of carrots, and left both in place of the empty milk glass and plate. Fran picked up the knife and checked the blade's edge. If these people knew how many she'd hurt with knives and guns, they wouldn't let her within an arm's reach of a weapon!

Taking a carrot, she slowly chopped it in sections like Levi was doing with the celery. No, this definitely wasn't normal. Dooley had vowed vengeance against this young man—who couldn't have been older than twenty-five. She'd fallen asleep in past nights imagining what she'd do to the man who'd tranquilized her. *Yet now she was fixing dinner with them?*

It was hard to hate an enemy who showed understanding and mercy. But that was just part of her frustration. Dooley had really abandoned her! With embarrassment, she admitted to herself that she believed Levi, that Dooley had rejoined his gang and gone south. That proved who she was to her former lover—and that truth hurt her less than expected. Sure, she'd criticized him a lot on slow days, but only because she knew she'd make a better leader than he was.

"You can stay here," Levi said suddenly, as if he could read her thoughts. "With conditions."

She stopped dicing and looked up. There was nothing but contentment and confidence, even patience, on his young face.

Of course, Dooley's gang was his own. Without him, what was she? Where could she go? She had no one. Maybe there would be more people out there somewhere she could find to live with, but she and Dooley had killed so many—especially competing scavengers. The power she'd felt having shed so much blood didn't seem so relevant right now.

"What conditions?"

"Agree to be neighborly." Levi scraped his cutting board full of celery into the potato bowl. "And you find a job. Something to contribute to the community that cares for you."

"That's it?" She eyed Annette whose back was to them. "No . . . probation or whatever?"

"Would you feel more comfortable on probation?" Levi raised his eyebrows. "We can put you on probation if you'd prefer that."

"No, it's just that . . ." She swallowed. "I think you know . . . what we've been doing. You know, in society. The Dooley Gang?"

"The PSDF runs the government in this area," Levi said. "We submit to their authority, but we don't do their job. My dad might discipline criminals when they need it, but we're Christians. We're more inclined to seek reconciliation than hold people under accusation. But some people prefer accusation rather than reconciliation. It's your choice."

"What's reconciliation mean, exactly?" she asked.

"Reconciliation happens when someone offers mercy to an enemy in order to become a friend," Annette said as she retrieved the bowl of vegetables to add them to a huge pot on the stove. "One party extends the hand of peace—that's us. And the other party—that's you—accepts or rejects the hand of peace."

"Well, I'm not saying that doesn't sound nice," Fran said, "but I don't exactly see how you think I deserve, you know, what you're offering. It feels like a trick."

"It's not about what you *deserve*, Fran," Annette said. "It's about what you *need*. We all have to learn this lesson from God. In our sin, we offended Him. But He offered us peace. That's who He is. His people offer the same to others. That's one reason why my son uses tranquilizer rounds in his weapon. We leave room for reconciliation."

Fran stared at the knife in her hand. This was unthinkable. They were offering her a life again? Could a pardon from her recent past be possible?

"What job would I have?"

"I can show you around tomorrow," Annette said from the kitchen. "You'll stay next door with Carla. She works with the laundry and gardening. There's plenty of that work to do, or you could join Levi at the boats."

"Fishing." Levi nodded. "It's pretty fun landing a forty-pound rockfish."

"Then there's the goats, janitorial, teaching kids if you have a skill," Annette continued, "or mechanic apprenticing with Chevy. What'd you do before Pan-Day?"

"Um, I worked at the Pretzel Factory in National City. Quality control. I wasn't management, but I was a good worker." Fran sighed, surprised but resigned to the fact that she wanted their approval and acceptance. Who else was offering her anything? "I guess I could do something with food preparation? Or the fishing. But I'm not really into catching fish."

"I could teach you how to make goat cheese," Annette said.

"It ain't easy calling that cheese, Mom." Levi shuddered, then winked at Fran.

"Well, I'm just saying you have options," Annette said. "No need to decide tonight. Sleep on it and see what else we have around here tomorrow."

Fran was shown next door to meet her new roommate, Carla, a forty-something woman with ugly scars on the right side of her scalp and face. But instead of hiding her disfigurement, she whisked Fran away from Levi and into the apartment.

"Annette told me your size." Carla stopped at their dining table piled with folded clothes. "I'm sort of in charge of laundry here at ELM, so I found some things that'll fit you. Oh, and I made up your bed in your room here. My room's over there. And look—our balcony! We face east, so we have these amazing sunrises over the city!"

Carla continued to point out the apartment's highlights as Fran struggled to take it all in. Even under Dooley's ruthless leadership and efforts to steal, she hadn't experienced hot water and electricity since Pan-Day.

Finally, Carla helped her move her new clothes into her room, tucked them into drawers or hung them on hangers in a sizeable closet. The older woman embraced Fran, then held her at arm's length.

"It's weird, huh?" Carla smiled. "The way the Casperteins do things isn't ordinary, but they're good people."

"Yeah. I was sort of thinking they're aliens." Fran scoffed. "I actually ran into Levi a couple months ago, and I've hated him ever since. Trying to find him became my life ambition—to make him pay. Now, I'm not exactly sure what to think."

"Well, you're here now." Carla walked to the bedroom door. "It sounds like Annette will give you the tour tomorrow, so you'll want to get some sleep. The Casperteins are early risers."

A few minutes later, Fran heard Carla close her bedroom door. A lamp remained flickering in Fran's room, but the rest of the apartment was dark. Her whirlwind welcome seemed to be over, but instead of feeling weary, she was wide awake. Why had Dooley fled so quickly, abandoning so much wealth and her with it all?

Through the sliding glass, she reached the balcony and stared at the dark expanse of the city to the southeast. Just barely between the buildings she could see an overpass a mile or so away. The overpass was only visible by the light of the moon. Maybe Dooley and the others had already reached Pepper Park. They'd continue to loot, pillage, and kill, but now they'd do it without her. The family that had thrown her away had been replaced by another—the Caspertein family.

She realized now that she'd been tranquilized, maybe multiple times for the last few hours—before waking up in the Caspertein apartment. The bruise on her leg was no mystery and Levi hadn't denied that he'd tranquilized her. By isolating her, even kidnapping her from Dooley, they'd given her a life she hadn't imagined was possible again. But her past and her future couldn't have been more opposite!

Inside the apartment, she wandered around in the dimness, appreciating being alone and safe. From her bedroom lantern, she lit a lamp to carry it with her as she went to the front door and found it locked—from the inside. They weren't trying to keep her in, even though she'd been complicit with Dooley to kill everyone at ELM. No, Carla had locked the door to keep out everyone else.

Opening the door, she listened to the hallway. The Casperteins' doors were closed. Leaving her door open, she walked to the elevator shaft where she shined her lamp on the cable and pulley system until she understood how it worked. After setting the lamp on the floor, she tugged on heavy gloves and pulled on the brake lever. Hand over hand, she lowered the dolly. The cable wheels squeaked just slightly above until she'd reached floor twenty-eight. Fascinating!

Exploring next through the stairwell, she wondered why the dolly had stopped until she found another operable one on floor twenty-six. And again, on floor fourteen to the fourth floor. For security, she guessed, the Casperteins had made a maze of their elevator shafts. No wonder Dooley hadn't taken over this place. The Casperteins were too smart for some two-bit thug.

It all seemed pretty foolish now—the whole notion of trying to replace the ELM people to assume leadership and reap what they hadn't sown. Dooley had burned down houses with people in them when they hadn't opened their doors to his gang. But how could Dooley retaliate here? The buildings were concrete, steel, and glass. Annette and Carla had both kept heavy caliber rifles by their doors. Everything about ELM, seeing them from the inside, made them seem invincible.

On the first floor, several lamps were lit to illuminate the animal pens. Goats. Now the cheese and sweet milk made sense.

When she found a metal door, she turned the wheel to slide the bar away. The air outside was cool and the stars were bright so she left the lantern inside.

In the courtyard between the buildings, she turned in every direction, listening, wondering if she could indeed start over in this strange place with weird people.

A man laughed somewhere above in the Hopefuls' building. Someone hushed him and a light went out.

Walking softly west, retracing her steps from the day before, she reached the east perimeter. A single man occupied the stool and checkpoint where he was reading a book by lantern light. He nodded at her, then returned to his book. The gap between vehicles stood ungated. Someone could arrive or she could depart—in relative safety, it seemed. For whatever reason Dooley had given up and left—she was glad. This place carried a taste of their early days together, yet there was something more. A closeness. A familiarity and sense of community that had been lost long before Pan-Day. Somehow, the Casperteins had revived it. Though she couldn't deny the rush of excitement in her violent past, this place offered much more: a refuge, a break from all the turmoil and bloodshed and—

"*Fran!* You're alive!"

She spun around to find Kid Irling emerge from the night shadows of the Hopefuls' building. His long hair was loose as he ran up and grasped her by the shoulders.

"Of course, I'm alive." She embraced him briefly. "I thought you'd left with the others."

"Others?" He backed up a step. "What others? Dooley's gone?"

"He left this morning."

"Why didn't you go with him?"

"I . . . probably would have." Fran licked her lips. "But he left without me. He didn't even wait to see if I was alive or dead."

"You can't blame him for saving himself. This Russian guy held me prisoner upstairs for hours. I fell asleep and when I woke up, he was gone. Now I just want to get out of here. These people were lying wait for us! There was no one here this morning, and now there are tons of people. Man, I don't get it. There's no way we can take over this place."

"They seem . . . okay to me."

"Okay?" Kid swore. "What's wrong with you? You hate people like this. So, what do you think?"

"About what?"

"That." He gestured at the gap between the vehicles. "It seems darker out there. You think it's a trap? There's only this one guy who guards the way out. We can probably take him out if we work together."

"Him? He's not keeping us in here. There's no trap, Kid." She almost laughed, then realized how serious he was. His experience with ELM had apparently been much different the last couple of hours. "There's no one waiting for you out there in the darkness. If you want to go, then go. No one will stop you."

"I don't know. They took my gun. And my pack."

"It's only a couple hours back to Pepper Park."

"So why are you waiting? I saw you hesitate, too."

"Kid, I'm not leaving. I just came to— I don't know. To say goodbye, I guess."

"Goodbye to whom? You said you didn't know I was here." He cackled softly. "Fran, you're not making any sense."

"Leave if you want. No one's stopping you. I'm staying here, Kid."

"What? I'm not leaving without you. Dooley would kill me if I showed up without you! He was searching for you. We didn't know what happened, but he'll want to know what happened to you."

"Then tell him what happened. I'm good here."

"Fran, you can't stay here! You don't belong. These people are trying to resurrect everything we hate. We're anarchists! Don't let them cage you. You're not yourself right now."

"They're not trying to cage me. They . . . want to give me a job."

"A job?" Kid stared at her in the nearby lantern light from the gate. Suddenly, he grabbed her arm with one

hand and her neck with the other. "You're coming with me. They're messing with your head!"

"Kid, no! Let me go!"

She fought off one hand, but he got behind her and put her in a choke hold.

"Don't fight it," he whispered in her ear as he dragged her toward the gap in the perimeter. "I'm taking you back to Dooley. Things will be just like they always were."

She clawed at his arm as her vision faded.

Boom!

Fran dropped to her knees, her ears ringing from a nearby gunshot. She rolled over and kicked frantically away from Kid's body. Gasping, she clutched her bruised neck and wept. *How dare he try to force her to leave!*

"You okay, Fran?"

Panting, she looked up at Levi as he came closer. She'd already learned his voice. He pulled her up and steadied her on shaky legs.

"He was . . . trying to make me leave with him."

Levi let her stand alone as he crouched over Kid and checked his pulse, then moved Kid's head so he could sleep more comfortably.

"Oleg said he resisted any offers to join our little community here." He rose and stood next to her, his rifle between them. "You know you can leave if you want to, right?"

"Yeah, I know. That's what I told Kid. I'd just come out here, I guess, to leave it all—my past—behind. For good. I'm done with Dooley."

"Well, Kid can sleep it off out here." Levi nudged Kid with his boot. "If you're okay, I'm going back inside. You staying out here a little longer?"

"No, I'll go in with you." She walked beside him toward the front of ELM. "How'd you know I was out here? I thought you'd all gone to bed."

"My dad's gone right now. I feel like I need to keep an eye on everyone. Besides, I'm a light sleeper. I heard the dolly wheels when you started down."

"That guy guarding the gate doesn't have any weapons. If you hadn't shown up, Kid would've taken me right back to Dooley—by force."

"Well, that won't happen again, not on my watch." Levi offered with his hand for her to enter the building first. "Remember, I told you I'd keep you safe. You're with us now. Family isn't something we take too lightly around here."

Fran was silent as Levi drew on the cable and raised the dolly for them both. She felt alive from a haze she'd been wandering in for months. There was no going back from this. There was no denying what she'd found—her new home.

†

Sazon smiled as he knelt in the dusty road. The footprints of a man and small child emerged from a field above Stillwater River. The tracks were heading north. It had to be Oliver and his son, Rory. Mayor Malden had said he wanted the boy back at the Garden, if possible, but Oliver needed to be eliminated. Anyone who had come inside the Garden and had left in disagreement with its policies were clearly enemies of humanity. That included wheelchair-bound Emily Pickford.

The chants of the Garden residents still rang in Sazon's ears. *Beyond the Garden!* Yes, he would gladly take their quality-of-life measures beyond the Garden's walls and into the world. Most of his adult life he'd been a day laborer, usually as a forklift driver in a warehouse or shipping yard. He'd never given much thought to population control or euthanasia, but now that resources were short in the world, it made sense to decide who deserved those resources. Those with diminished abilities needed to be removed. The elderly, mentally ill, and disabled needed to be culled from among the productive and healthy. It was science. It was natural. The earth required it. And the continuation of the human species demanded that Sazon do his part.

"This way!" he yelled back at Milli Lusis and Leo Busche. Both had syringe pouches on their hips with an extra vial of Dr. Ferguson's sympathetic toxin. "Keep up!"

Preferring to work alone, Sazon had prowled outside the Garden's walls before, but never with anyone else. Now he had to escort Milli and Leo into the community. Neither person was adept at keeping a hardy walking pace. Milli was a cute redhead who'd caught the mayor's eye, but she was hardly a symbol of fitness. She'd probably been hiding in a house for the last few months, exercising little.

Leo Busche had been a Garden resident since the beginning. Though the forty-year-old French man was healthy, he hadn't originally shared Sazon's zeal to make known and enforce the Garden's doctrine abroad. Mayor Malden had interviewed all the residents of the Garden in the early days, and Leo had admitted to being an illegal immigrant from Mexico, an ex-con with a quick smile and even quicker fraud schemes. But the crooked path for the Frenchman had come to an end, Malden had told him, because Leo was needed at the Garden to help maintain the property's irrigation system.

"What a beautiful day!" Milli's face glowed in the morning sunshine, regardless of the heavy bag of vegetables over her shoulder in a tote bag. She passed Sazon where he stood over Oliver and Rory's footprints. "You think we'll find anyone?"

"There's got to be people here," Leo said as he walked beside her. He carried a similar tote bag, but his was filled with fruit. "See that water tower up there? Definitely people living here."

Sazon watched them continue ahead. True, they weren't physically superior as he was, but he didn't doubt they'd use their syringes as soon as they found someone ill or old. Milli's complete submission to Malden's affections and dogma surprised Sazon. Theirs was religious fervor, but Sazon simply saw the practical value of removing the lives that burdened this struggling society.

Continuing after the pair, Sazon kept a wary eye on their surroundings as well as on the footprints in the dust. And he was under no illusion that he'd actually been resurrected from the dead. The bruise he'd received from some bullet from Titus Caspertein's rifle was evidence that he'd been tranquilized and not killed. But the resurrection theory worked for Malden's cause, so Sazon hadn't spoken against everyone's awe. After all, who else was such a specimen of strength in the Garden? His biceps that morning bulged from the sleeveless green plaid shirt he wore. He was born for this!

However, he still remembered how Titus had so boldly entered the Garden—just to recover Emily's wheelchair and to confront Malden! A man with no fear was a man no one could control. To make matters worse, Titus had appeared to be an example of health and strength himself, and he'd readily shown approval of people like Emily living among them—as if her very disabled existence wouldn't burden everyone around her. Such an attitude was a threat to the Garden's message. But that didn't mean Sazon was in a hurry to be the one who faced Titus again.

Hopefully, Titus and Emily had returned to their downtown location. The Garden's Sympathy Agents would find their way down there eventually. After all, the Garden was just at the beginning of their community campaign and outreach work.

Ten minutes later, Sazon joined his partners as they entered a small community of survivors. The footprints of Oliver and Rory mingled with the prints of locals, but Sazon was confident that Oliver was taking his son downtown to join the Casperteins.

With a friendly wave, Milli greeted a child with her parents as they emerged from an alley. After noticing the three strangers, the family backed into the shadows until Sazon had passed. On the other side of the street, two middle-aged men stood and watched the newcomers. One cradled a red toolbox like it was an infant, and his friend held an old hunting rifle. Sazon made an effort to nod a greeting to them, but they didn't return the gesture.

"Over there!" Milli pointed at a type of farmer's market in a parking lot of a mall. About forty people were visible.

"This is a good place to begin," Sazon said, then urged Leo and Milli to go ahead and meet people at the market with its few tables and carts of meager products or supplies to trade.

Sazon kept his distance, ready to draw his sidearm if Milli or Leo needed defending. Malden wanted Milli to exercise CARE oversight, but he wanted her kept safe. Instead of trading with the locals, Milli approached a young family with two children and gave them each a vegetable. Her compassion seemed genuine as she so sweetly greeted each person, then kept moving.

Leo followed Milli's lead and offered his fresh fruit to those who'd accepted the vegetables. Others in the market realized what was happening and they made their way closer to receive handouts as well. Milli was a natural, Sazon thought—a pure angel in the midst of many of these unwashed, useless eaters. He could see several elderly who quite plainly shuffled on their feet with difficulty. These needed a sympathy ending.

When Milli and Leo's tote bags were empty, they circled back to introduce themselves and accept the gratitude of the locals. More people gathered from an adjoining street where a train depot seemed to house several families.

"Oh, we'll come back again," Milli promised meekly. "We just want to share from our abundance. And we want to teach you all how we came to have so much."

Milli was a regular missionary of mercy, and she was so accepted by the strangers that Sazon relaxed and studied their surroundings a little closer. Dark business buildings appeared to have been looted and destroyed along the street, but farther back, apartments and small residences seemed to house many of the locals. Sazon was one of the few from the Garden who'd ventured into the outside world, so he wasn't surprised to find people surviving on scraps—and pulling together for protection. But their existence was shameful compared to what excess the Garden possessed.

Sazon noticed a solitary man leaning on a wooden cane at a street corner. The man appeared to be in his seventies, his clothing drab and wrinkled, seemingly unwashed.

"The times are difficult," Sazon said sympathetically as he came to stand beside the old timer. "How are you making out?"

"Barely." The local eyed Sazon suspiciously. "Your skin looks clear, but my eyes aren't as good as they once were. You have any symptoms?"

"No." Sazon watched Milli work her way to an elderly woman in a wheelchair who was tended to by a teen girl. "I have no virus symptoms. We at the Garden have been secluded for months as things settle down out here."

"You're lucky you had some place to hide." The old man cursed. "I'm from Los Angeles. My grandkids ran off around Pan-Day so I was left to fend for myself. My clothes hang off me now like window drapes."

"My people have developed a . . . vaccine," Sazon said carefully. "It offers a long-term solution to our local health challenges. I believe it'll end your suffering, sir, and improve the lives of those around you."

"A vaccine, huh? Like a serum? How much?"

"It's free." Sazon opened the pouch on his belt and drew out the syringe. "One shot and you'll find your escape from life's burdens within twenty-four hours."

"Sounds too good to be true." The man frowned. "I remember the vaccine promises of the past. How do I know this one will really work?"

"Actually, it works best with those who are immune compromised or experiencing preexisting health conditions. I've seen it work and I've seen the benefits it brings. You'll need only one shot. Here, you don't even have to roll up your sleeve."

Sazon smoothly jabbed the needle into the old man's shoulder.

"Ouch! That's some needle!"

"That's it. It's over." Sazon smiled and gently rubbed the injection site. "Find a quiet place to rest as this solution takes effect, especially tomorrow morning about this time."

"Oh, that won't be a problem." The man cursed again. "I live alone in a grocery store bathroom where I sleep on the floor in there on a mattress. At least the plumbing doesn't back up."

"Your days of suffering are certainly about to change." Sazon refilled the syringe, then pouched it. "Enjoy the day, sir. You never know when it could be your last."

Walking toward the market, Sazon felt quite satisfied with the successful injection. Those he'd injected at the Garden had usually been taken by force, even if they'd once subscribed to the Garden's philosophy. But misleading people was much easier!

He'd be gone and forgotten by the townspeople when the toxin took effect.

Milli jogged over to him, her face more radiant than ever.

"I gave two people the shot! I told them what Malden said to say, that this is a vitamin mixture that'll help their troubles, aches, and pains go away."

Leo arrived as he refilled his syringe with an extra vial of toxin.

"Nice people," Leo said. "I found a woman sitting by the wall on a milk crate. She was talking to herself, clearly deranged."

"We've done this neighborhood a service today." Sazon nodded at his companions, surprised at their ability to kill the afflicted without a single qualm. "Let's return to the Garden to share what we've accomplished. The other teams will probably return soon as well."

Walking side by side, Milli and Leo headed south. Sazon watched the market lot for a few seconds more. Some nodded their appreciation or shyly waved at him, perhaps thanking him for the gifts his friends had brought. They thanked him now, but he hoped they understood how he was really rescuing them from the burdens that their loved ones had become. They needed to understand the service the Garden offered.

He turned to gaze at the tall, downtown buildings in the distance. Titus Caspertein was a threat to the Garden, but today wasn't the day to kill him. When no one was accompanying him, Sazon guessed he'd be able to travel much farther and faster to complete even the sympathy cleansing of Emily Pickford. She didn't need to go on suffering as a crippled woman—drawing from others of their valued resources.

Killing Titus Caspertein would be a bonus for the Garden. Sazon certainly wouldn't mind a little vengeance against the bold rifleman.

†

Levi stood aside on the dock as his fishermen hopped aboard the sailboat. A young captain stood at the helm of the thirty-nine-foot, single mast. The captain's name was Raymond Weaver, a curly-haired, quiet man who continued to impress Levi with his knowledge of fish and currents around the bay.

Seven ELM fishermen jostled for prime deck positions as seven other fishermen climbed aboard an adjacent sailboat, piloted by Pepper Scaggs. Levi had noticed that she filled the role of Raymond's older sister. Pepper had several blackened, dead teeth from being abused by a prior boyfriend, according to Raymond. The ELM fishermen who were women usually boarded Pepper's boat, though Pepper sailed only according to Raymond's navigation when out at sea.

As excited as everyone was to get back to fishing and providing for ELM residents, Levi wasn't convinced that they were past the danger of Dooley, even though Fran had moved in with Carla on the fortieth floor. After all, Titus hadn't returned with Dusty yet. Levi craved action where he felt he was most useful, but the fishing industry was his endeavor. With so many living within the ELM perimeter now, fish had become a major staple for its residents.

Everyone was finally aboard the two sailboats. Raymond signaled for Levi to cast off the stern line when Levi's radio squelched.

"Levi, come in."

It was one-eyed Wes Trimble's voice.

"This is Levi. I hear you. Over."

The fishermen on both boats watched Levi as he held up his hand. He saw the concern on their faces. They were eager to go fishing since the ELM food supply needed to be supplemented with a daily catch, and most of them had family members back at ELM. It was rare for ELM to contact Levi while he was on the bay. Surely, they would think it could only mean danger or a problem had arisen.

"Levi, two new arrivals just came in," Wes said. "They have news of your dad. I think you should get back here. Over."

"Is there an immediate threat to ELM? Over."

"Negative. Can the halibut hunters do without you today? Over."

"On my way back. Over." Levi cast off the stern line and handed his radio to someone else on deck. "I'll go check it out and call you if it's anything important. Be safe, everyone."

Standing on the dock, Levi waved his goodbyes to the fishing crew. They'd fish until noon, then return to shore to clean, fillet, and package their catch. It was a smelly job, and Levi hadn't missed the stench during the few days ELM had been on alert from the Dooley threat.

As soon as the pair of vessels were safely headed out of Harbor Island Marina, Levi hustled ashore to reach North Harbor Drive. A few locals were about, some who'd found shelter up at the airport or on the west peninsula of Harbor Island. They acknowledged Levi from a distance as he marched east along the shore toward downtown. He'd met most of them with Dusty at his side, introducing them to Jesus Christ as well as offering ELM's developing commerce.

Because of this contact, locals that weren't living at ELM were now involved in the trades at ELM. Chevy had expressed his excitement over their ability to provide for so many, even the military on Coronado Island, since such bartering and trade made the spread of the Gospel more natural. Not all the Hopefuls were believers, but many had joined Chevy's discipleship classes or Annette's ladies group that met twice a week to discuss Scripture, housekeeping, and gardening.

Ten minutes later, Levi jogged into the ELM courtyard, his rifle still over his shoulder, but he'd practiced flipping it into readiness in a split second if it seemed necessary.

Someone had found and set up lawn and patio chairs beside the sandbox in the shade of the apartment high-rises. This was where Levi found Wes, his wife Wynter, and a familiar-looking young man whose name Levi didn't know.

However, the young man, wearing a tattered blue suit, smiled broadly as he walked forward to meet Levi. An unfamiliar little boy of about six remained next to Wynter where she knelt and spoke to the child who was gripping a thin, wooden, checkered box.

"Levi Caspertein!" The young man and apparent father shook Levi's hand with tears in his eyes. "You may not remember me, but you changed my life!"

"Yes, I do remember you!" Levi clapped him on the shoulder. "I always regretted not asking for your name a few months ago. It seems God meant for us to meet again just so I could learn it."

"Oliver Gleason. And my son, Rory."

"It's a pleasure once again, Oliver." Levi walked him back to join Wes. "I'm guessing those fires last week went through your neighborhood."

"Yeah. Everything fell apart after that." Oliver shook his head, the joyful reunion suddenly fading. "My girlfriend, Milli, and I took Rory and left with nothing the night of the fire. We were on our way here when we met someone named Sazon—a big, muscled guy who took us to a place called the Garden."

"Has Dad mentioned hearing on the radio anything about a place called the Garden?" Levi asked Wes. Levi knew if anyone in ELM knew of a threat beyond the perimeter, it would be Wes since he'd been an intelligence officer prior to Pan-Day.

"I've never heard it mentioned," Wes said, then to Oliver, "Go ahead. Tell him what you told us, Oliver."

"The Garden felt wrong from the start. The way they looked at Rory, like he was, well, it seemed weird. But Milli fell in love with the place and the people almost immediately. They have gardens and flowers everywhere. Fruit and vegetables to spare. The day we showed up, they were having a funeral for one of their own. Then the next day, another one. People don't die that fast in a healthy place like that."

"They were killing their own people," Wes explained. "Quality-of-lifers."

"*Quality-of-lifers?*" Levi shook his head. "Fill me in."

"Before Pan-Day," Wes said, "there was a movement to promote population control. Some said that's what the Meridia Virus was meant to do—to diminish the world's population. But quality-of-lifers, or QOLs, were people who stood for a type of social justice that believed sympathy killing was justified. If someone's life didn't match the majority of society's opinion of a quality life, they made laws to have them compassionately executed. Nations worldwide, especially in the West, practiced it, calling it compassion."

"QOLs." Levi frowned. "Sounds messed up. What's this have to do with my dad?"

"At one of the funerals, the leader named Mayor Malden told me he was taking Milli for his own woman. I knew I had to get Rory out of there, but they'd already adopted him into their children's classes. That's when Titus Caspertein showed up with a woman in a wheelchair."

"A woman in a wheelchair?" Levi chuckled. "I'm guessing a QOL cult wouldn't like her too much!"

"Titus said he came to confront Mayor Malden specifically." Oliver sighed. "It was tense for a few minutes. Then Titus left, but Sazon tried to stop him. That's when Titus shot Sazon. I didn't realize until later that it was just a tranquilizer. Mayor Malden said Sazon was resurrected to go out and promote the Garden's message. Rory and I barely escaped. I . . . . think they followed us partway here."

"The Garden QOLs aren't staying in their Garden any longer," Wes said to Levi. "Titus and Dusty should've been back by now."

"I learned that Sazon keeps a black pouch and syringe on his belt," Oliver said. "Titus broke his syringe. That's what he used to kill people for the Garden, I think."

"We need to let everyone know," Levi said, "to avoid anyone who comes from the Garden. Our perimeter guards should be warned, especially."

"And the disabled and elderly people," Oliver said. "I think they're in the most danger."

"They think they're helping society," Wes said, "but they're just assassins."

Levi took a deep breath and prayed for wisdom. When he'd craved action rather than fishing that morning, he hadn't imagined something so dark and sinister would require his attention.

"This makes Dooley and his buddies seem not so scary," Levi said to Wes. "What do you think we should do?"

"You guys work it out," Wynter said, her hand on young Rory's head, "but these two are going to get washed up, fed, and settled in. When was the last time you took a bath, huh, Rory?"

Rory's eyes widened. He glanced at his father then back at Wynter.

"The Garden lady made me take a bath with a bunch of flowers and floating fruit. Do I have to take a bath with flowers and fruit?"

"Absolutely not! That's disgusting!" Wynter wrinkled her nose. "How about a hot bath with no flowers or fruit? And Oliver, we've got an apartment for you. Come with me, huh?"

After shaking the young father's hand again, Levi then turned to stand with Wes in the courtyard to watch the people, including the kids playing in the sandbox. Oleg stood on the balcony above, his rifle clipped to his chest. Conrad Prosky followed the Down syndrome child, Gabby, across the expanse. He stooped to pick up trash when Gabby ordered him to. Several ELM residents arrived back from outside the perimeter, their carts full of tree branches and twigs for Gustavo's milk goats.

"We can't spare anyone," Wes said as if reading Levi's thoughts. "Your dad's not answering the radio, which means he's around too many buildings or he turned off his radio to conserve power. And he may not want to light a signal fire for us to see, if he has QOLs hunting him down. He'll want to keep the wheelchair lady safe."

"So, I'll go out alone," Levi said. "Do some recon. That's the direction Oleg and I were when I met Oliver. If Dad's in trouble, there'll be gunfire. I might make radio contact with him, too."

"Going out alone?" Wes lowered his head, his one eye showing his amusement. "Wynter will tell your mother, you know. Well, I suppose if you're going, you'd better head out right now before there's a ruckus."

"I'm not afraid of Mom." Levi chuckled, then his humor faded. "Actually, you're right. I'd better take off. You can bear the brunt of Mom's wrath."

"Hey, wait a minute!" Wes gasped playfully. "That's not what I had in mind!"

"It ain't easy facing down Mama Bear." Levi laughed at his friend's mock panic as he headed into the ELM building.

Upstairs, he packed lightly for a couple days abroad. Carla entered as he drew dried foods and jerky from his pantry—the refrigerator that wasn't plugged in.

"You're going somewhere?" Carla folded her arms. The forty-year-old had tucked her gardening gloves into her waistband, having recently returned from the balcony planters on some floor. "Let me guess—it's your dad?"

"He should've been back in radio range by now."

"When you've been overdue, your dad trusts you," Carla said. "I don't think you have to go out there. You're choosing to place yourself in danger. Again."

"I know the neighborhoods." Levi swung his pack over one shoulder and checked his rifle magazines. "Besides, there's a new threat out there we haven't faced before. Dad might need my help."

"More dangerous than Brogdon's military or the Meridia Virus?" She scoffed. "What is it now?"

"Assassins. They come from a place called the Garden."

Carla was speechless as he moved for the door and dolly.

"Who's going with you?" she asked as he pulled on gloves to lower the platform. She climbed on with him to bring the dolly back up. "You're going alone, aren't you?"

"Wes doesn't want to leave ELM short-handed if something happens around here." As he lowered the platform, Carla steadied herself with a hand on his arm. "If Dad sees danger coming, he'll hole up somewhere. He's probably waiting for me. I'll get him on the radio and figure it out."

"And what if he doesn't see these assassins coming?"

They reached the twenty-eighth floor and Levi disembarked. He took off the gloves and gave them to her.

"Dad's not easily duped," Levi said. "I'm just going as backup. Tell Mom I'll be back in a day or two. She can try to warn him on the radio, but Wes thinks he might have his radio off."

"You haven't told Annette you're leaving?" Carla blinked. "Levi, she'll be furious!"

"She'll understand. She wouldn't rather lose Dad. Tell her that."

Carla embraced him and touched his cheek with her hand.

"Oh, you Casperteins are so reckless! You still think your God will protect you."

"Not protect me." He backed toward the stairwell. "But I know He'll hold me true through the fire. And by the way, He's your God, too."

"I'm not convinced of that."

Levi let her have the final word, then he descended the stairs to the next dolly stage. Wes and Oleg waited at the second-floor balcony. Both had their rifles.

"Chevy and Wynter will let people know to watch out for QOLs from the Garden," Wes said, shaking Levi's hand. "I'd tell you to be careful out there, but you're too much like your dad to think about caution."

"Titus would say he's too ugly for danger to approach him," Oleg said. "I partly agree with him, but what can you say, Levi?"

"Uh, like father, like son?" Levi laughed with them. "But I'd welcome some prayer all the same."

The three stood together as Wes prayed for Levi and Titus' effectiveness for Jesus in the midst of the rising threats.

Heading east, Levi walked briskly past the perimeter post and through the vehicles. Another adventure! There'd been no sign of Dooley or his gang since they'd been scared off. And with Fran staying behind, having turned her back on Dooley, Levi guessed the gangster wouldn't let himself be seen around ELM again. But Levi wouldn't mind crossing the villain who'd burned dozens of houses on a path all the way to Pepper Park, which was Dooley's home base according to Fran.

"Levi, come in." It was Annette.

He stopped walking. The interstate wasn't far ahead. Once he passed I-5, the CB frequency range would weaken.

"Yeah, Mom, I hear you. Go ahead. Over."

Seconds passed. He sensed her grief—and her pending wrath for his leaving without hearing her out. She'd ask him to stay, he guessed. Or return now. But he couldn't. The danger didn't outweigh the possibility of helping his father.

"Bring your dad home, Levi. Over."

He sighed, his heart filled with emotion at her choice of words—encouraging instead of demanding or worrying.

"I will, Mom. Out."

With a deep breath, he walked under the interstate.

It was Titus' decision to stay the night only a couple miles from where the Husseini family had lived. And here, they were among new friends. They'd come upon a farmer's market, and deciding to visit with the locals, Titus had lost track of time. Dusty reminded him of the late hour as the sun set on another day abroad.

As Titus had visited with the locals and even traded some .308 rifle rounds for food for his companions, Emily remained close to his side, though quiet unless spoken to. Titus sensed her timidity, which wasn't surprising since she'd spent several months inside the Garden's death cult, cut off from normal society.

Similarly, Dusty remained aloof and on the fringes of wherever Titus found people to visit and entertain. No one bothered Dusty or mistook him for an aggressor, Titus noticed, since he and Dusty carried the same unique rifle and wore the same kind of ammo vest.

Titus told the locals of ELM's calling for God downtown, and one local stepped forward to welcome Yasif Husseini and his family, who were given residence for the night in a nearby furniture store—a shelter for many who attended the market. But Yasif was very adamant before he took his family to the furniture store that he wasn't staying in that town. In Syrian Arabic, he reminded Titus that they were brothers, and they weren't to remain separated come morning. Titus assured his new friend that he wouldn't leave without him.

While the sun set, Titus and Emily were welcomed into the upstairs loft of an elderly married couple. The downstairs was left intentionally as a looted and smashed electronics store. The staircase to the upstairs, which Titus used to carry Emily up, was disguised and hidden behind two soda vending machines.

"Say, I'd rather stay down here," Dusty said privately to Titus when he returned downstairs to check on his partner. "I'll keep an eye on things."

"There's room to lie down upstairs," Titus said. "Get some rest. Relax a little. There doesn't seem to be much danger around here."

"That could change fast." Dusty seemed to relish his job as a stoic guardian, something Titus knew the new believer had learned from Levi. "I'll be okay. Maybe I'll find a car to sleep in or something."

"You're a good man, Dusty." Titus shook his hand. "I'm glad to have you along. The Lord is building you into a fine shepherd. That's the best compliment I can think of to pay you in this broken world."

"Thank you, Titus. I almost wish we weren't going home tomorrow, except Levi makes me laugh."

Dusty left the electronics store and Titus returned upstairs to make sure Emily was comfortable. As a paraplegic who couldn't feel half her body, pressure sores were a constant concern, so he made sure she had a soft mattress, then settled onto an inflatable mattress on the floor for himself. Bed frames had generally been burned for fuel in the early days, but Titus had slept in much more uncomfortable environments.

By candlelight, he opened his tattered Bible on his mattress so God's Word would be the last thing on his mind before he slept.

"We're atheists," said elderly James Walden in a grave but not unkind voice. To prepare the loft for night, James pulled on a rope attached to the stairs below. "Not much use for God these days."

Titus leapt up to help the man, but then realized the stairwell and rope assembly was engineered with a counterweight. Anyone who entered the store on the first floor would find the loft fifteen feet out of reach.

"Sometimes our use for God is discovered only by realizing our need of Him," Titus said softly, noticing that

Emily and James' wife, Katherine, were listening from their beds. "Whatever your experience, my friend, don't dismiss God based on your dissatisfaction with people."

James' eyes were mere slits on his wrinkled face, but Titus could still see him staring at him.

"People haven't made me turn from God," James finally said. "God has inclined me to turn from Him. He isn't real. If He were, He would provide for His people. No, we're alone on this blue rock, young man. We take care of ourselves. Like we always have."

"And fine care that has been." Titus sighed heavily, missing Annette and his like-minded companions back at ELM. "I believe God intends for us to realize our need of Him through our hopelessness in ourselves."

"Speak for yourself. Just this morning, I was given a vaccine against coming disease. Next time it's available, I'll make sure Katherine receives the inoculation as well. She was here in the loft when those visitors came. That didn't come from God. It came from a man who gave us hope for a better future. I believe society is on the mend. God isn't necessary."

"A vaccine against coming disease?" Titus felt a cold chill. "Were they from a place called the Garden?"

"Yes, and they came with fruit and vegetables. I never saw such bounty even in the years before Pan-Day, what with the shortages back then and all."

"Who among you were given this vaccine shot?" Titus asked.

"Four of us on the downhill side of life. They'll be back." James patted Titus on the arm. "Yes, they'll be back. We'll see more of their kind of hope from the Garden. You'll see. We don't need God anymore."

Titus returned to his mattress and candle. He desperately wanted to discuss this news with someone, but Emily seemed to be asleep already. The Garden was giving shots to the elderly, so how were the elderly still alive? Something was wrong with a lot more than James' confidence in humanity's miracle medicine. The Garden had wasted no time in reaching out to the nearby communities!

In the morning, Titus blinked awake from his troubled rest to the sliver of sunlight coming through an otherwise curtained window.

"Hey, Titus," Emily whispered, then nodded toward James and Katherine's bed against the opposite wall. "I think he died in his sleep."

Quietly, Katherine tried to wake her husband.

"Jimmy? Talk to me," she pleaded. "Honey, wake up."

Lacing up his boots, Titus prayed for how best to communicate the truth to these people. James had said that four of them had received some sort of vaccine. Apparently, as suspected, it was indeed a vaccine—against living! But it had some sort of time delay. The Garden's murderers had safely made their getaway, yet the death they desired to spread had remained.

After lowering the stairway, Titus insisted on checking the street before returning for Emily. He then carried her down to the electronics store, sharing his dread with her about the Garden visitors. Upstairs, Katherine was still trying to wake her husband.

"It had to be Sazon," Emily said. "Maybe some others. They're coming for all of us. Especially me! But James was fine last night."

"The new toxin mixture must be on a time delay so the Sympathy Agents can make their getaway." Titus helped Emily situate her backpack on her seat back, ready for travel. "Emily, we can't foresee every form of evil in this world. We can only trust God in His timing and protection until He calls for our departure to face judgment."

"That's pretty bleak." Emily followed him to the storefront.

"It's only bleak if judgment holds a fearful expectation for you." Titus eased his rifle muzzle out the front door, its glass crunching underfoot. "I assure you, after trusting in God's loving gift, a judgment could await you that offers only rewards and not wrath. It's your choice. I feel no terror about the Bible's prophecies coming to pass—because I've received the gift of Jesus' life for me on the cross."

"A man was just killed upstairs while we slept, Titus, and you're still talking about some gift of life? Tell that to Katherine."

Realizing that she needed more time—and gentle sowing—Titus didn't respond. He stood on the sidewalk in front of the store. Sure enough, Dusty waved casually from the back seat of a parked car across the street. But all wasn't quiet in the community. A gathering had materialized down the block at the open lot where the farmer's market had been the day before. Their voices rose as Titus walked closer, and when he walked into the lot, angry faces turned toward him.

"Everything was peaceful here yesterday," accused a man shaking a sidearm in his fist. "And then you showed up!"

The Husseini family was there as well. Poor Yasif pulled his wife and daughter away from the incensed people. Titus gestured to Yasif to join Dusty behind them, then he moved in front of Emily as she backed away in her chair. Dusty remained at a distance, his battle rifle half-raised, but Titus hoped the young guardian didn't start anything that might be settled with words.

"What's happened?" Titus gripped his rifle with his right hand, but he raised his left, open palm toward the angry mob. "I brought you nothing but well-wishes from ELM and the God we serve."

"Three of us are dead!" shouted the gun wielder.

The hammer on the townsman's pistol wasn't pulled back, or Titus would've been more concerned. It was possible he had the weapon for threatening purposes only since ammunition was so scarce.

"I haven't killed anyone," Titus said.

"You and your God-talk—it's brought us a curse! Get out of here and let us bury our dead. Go!"

"It wasn't us." Titus didn't move. "The people who came from the Garden poisoned four of your people. Remember the syringe that—"

"That Garden visited us with food!" The man pulled back the hammer on his pistol and Titus wondered if he should tranq the man then and there. "Nobody that nice would kill us. No, these people died on your watch!"

"Don't let them near you," Titus said louder for all the people. "The people of the Garden will kill you all, one visit at a time."

"He's telling you the truth!" Emily insisted.

"Wait, four of us received the shot!" shouted a woman from the crowd. "James Walden's dead, too? You stayed the night with him!"

"What'd you do to James?" The gunman aimed his sidearm directly at Titus' face. "He'd better be alive or you're dead!"

The crowd surged in two directions, toward the electronics store and toward Titus. He stayed ahead of their march by skipping backwards. His cries of, "It wasn't us!" were drowned out by louder voices of blame and threats.

Titus knew he had only a few seconds. The first few men were already reaching the electronics store. He gestured to Dusty to pull back with the Husseinis rather than escalate the situation. Several in the crowd held knives, baseball bats, and even a javelin—possibly from a high school track and field locker.

"Don't let them get away!" shouted a man.

The marching crowd rushed Titus and Emily. Titus' first concern was for Emily, so he placed himself in their path. She was quick in her wheelchair, but not faster than an able-bodied runner.

A handgun fired, sounding like a balloon popping since it was a small caliber. Suddenly, more sidearms materialized from beneath jackets and hidden holsters. Titus saw their crazed faces and knew there was no reason left in them.

He fired into the press of bodies mere yards away. Dusty's weapon thundered on Titus' right. Emily was pushing herself as fast as she could, but the street wasn't swept or clear of debris, so she had to weave left and right to avoid the litter.

Gunfire blasted so directly at Titus that he was surprised he and Emily weren't struck. But such was the haste, fear, and aggression of the crowd that they lacked precision.

Titus focused his rounds on those with guns first. Their tranquilized bodies fell, hardly checking the momentum of the crowd. Dusty had been trained by Levi, but he had less experience. He tripped backwards over a bicycle on the curb and the mob was upon him. Knives, boots, and clubs descended. The Husseinis ran ahead, safely beyond the mindless mob.

In an attempt to defend his partner and take back some ground, Titus switched his rifle to fully automatic and sprayed the nearest aggressors with tranquilizers. Townspeople fell and others backed off enough for Titus to stoop and drag away Dusty by the collar of his ammo vest.

When he had twenty yards of free space, Titus stopped and knelt over Dusty's head. He kept his rifle aimed at the snarling crowd, who seemed more like thoughtless zombies than humans with reason or intellect.

"Tell Levi—" Dusty gasped. His throat was torn and blood oozed from a half-dozen wounds in his chest and torso. "Tell Levi . . ."

"Yes, I will." Titus touched the side of Dusty's head to assure him. There was nowhere else to touch him that didn't seem battered and wounded. "I'll tell him, Dusty. You go with God now. Go in peace, little brother. In peace. I'll see you soon. It's okay. You did well."

Dusty's mouth opened and his eyes widened on Titus. Then he was still. Titus closed Dusty's eyes. His adopted son was gone.

"They killed James!" yelled a man from the front of the electronics store. "We just checked. James is dead!"

Calmly, Titus replaced his empty magazine as the remainder of the crowd surged—about a dozen people. Some of them had picked up dropped handguns from the fallen.

From his kneeling position over Dusty, Titus fired methodically until the street was a blanket of tranquilized men and women. Only a few far up the street near the store and market stood still and witnessed that which they surely thought was the massacre of their neighbors.

No one else approached, but Titus knew this was no victory. It was a disaster. The Garden was only partially to blame. For a long time, the people had lived on the edge of panic over uncertain circumstances and the suspicion of strangers. Without God's gentle voice in their lives, they couldn't moderate their terror about the world or its future.

Looking back, Titus saw that Emily and the Husseinis had stopped a block and a half away and were waiting for him. With some effort, he drew Dusty over his left shoulder. The thirty-five-year-old wasn't a big man, but Titus knew he'd need to find a different way to get Dusty home besides carrying him the last few miles.

"Is he dead?" Emily asked.

Titus didn't think he needed to answer. His entire left side ran red from Dusty's wounds.

Stepping forward, Yasif helped Titus ease Dusty's body to the pavement.

"He saved our lives," Yasif said in Arabic. "I've seen this madness before in Syria. You paid them only kindness. Their rage was misplaced. They have destroyed much this day."

"I have lost a brother," Titus said solemnly, "but my Lord in heaven has gained a son."

"Yes, if his deeds were enough," Yasif voiced from his Muslim perspective.

"No, because he chose to trust in Jesus the Savior," Titus corrected, "the only payment for us sinners. None of us are worthy, my new brother, but mercy is shown by God toward those with faith in the deeds of Jesus."

Yasif only bowed his head, though Titus was ready to speak further if necessary. He knew well the flaws of many religions that held to varied forms of works-based salvation. Because he cared, he couldn't but correct such confusion about God's method of salvation by grace through faith.

Young Majeda wept as she clung to her mother. Dusty hadn't known their language, but his actions had proven his compassion for them. They'd known his shepherding hand.

"Could you please carry these, Yasif?" Titus unclipped Dusty's rifle and unzipped his ammo vest. "You don't have to use them, but—"

The man accepted the rifle and vest, chambered a round in the weapon, and switched on the safety like he knew rifles—as most Syrians did who were born into conflict. He fit on the torn and stained vest and nodded resolutely at Titus, who nodded back, then pulled Dusty over his shoulder again.

Yes, he would tell Levi of his friend and brother's faithful sacrifice.

Chapter Six

Seven blocks southeast of ELM, Dooley and ten of his men stood on the roof of an office building. He held binoculars to his eyes for five minutes before he reached for his inhaler. After shaking it, he inhaled deeply through the sprays. It was nearly empty.

He could hear his men whispering. They had reason to. Fran was alive and she'd remained behind at ELM. Kid had told them so. Oh, how he hated the Casperteins even more. They possessed such order and authority—two things he despised. But they'd tricked him by abducting Fran and then Kid; they'd confused him and caused his men to doubt his abilities.

ELM was wealthy. He knew that very well now. Their food was plentiful, partially because of the manpower they'd welcomed into their perimeter. But they had much because they'd prepared. They must have put away stocks and provisions for weeks prior to Pan-Day to be this organized so soon after destruction had swept the country.

Destruction? Dooley had never wanted to destroy anything as badly as he wanted to destroy ELM. First, they'd stolen his horse meat, then they'd stolen his pride by taking Fran from him.

How could she? What had they promised her? He'd rehearsed their last times together, and he couldn't recall pushing her away. As usual, she'd been critical of him. How could she be happy with anyone else? After all, she loved anarchy and crisis as much as he did!

"We've been here for over a day now," Kid suddenly said at his side. "Our food and water are pretty low."

After gazing at the ELM buildings, Dooley lowered the binoculars. Only Kid dared approach him at a time like this. Maybe the others sensed his temperament. Wise, since he didn't trust himself not to throw them off the six-story building if they brought up his recent failures. But Kid was his coldest soldier, someone who Dooley appreciated since the long-haired man valued chaos before consideration.

"I'm not willing to concede this round," Dooley said quietly. "They have Fran."

Kid fiddled with his rifle, which had been brought to him with his other gear by the rest of the men since he'd entered ELM undercover.

"Dooley, we're with you," Kid said. "You know that. Tell us the plan and we'll get to it. I'll even lead the way you point out. That's worked for months. But we need to eat."

Hating to be pitied, Dooley growled under his breath. But he knew the men were aware of his defeats. And those losses were like a fog on his brain. The rage he now carried wasn't being channeled to aid his recovery. If he didn't think of something soon, the men would turn on him or scatter. Maybe they'd turn to Kid for leadership. They were all a bunch of cutthroats, but they were followers—and they were *his* cutthroats.

A rumbling rifle shot shook the air to the east. Dooley ran to the edge of the roof with his men and searched the street. The gun report had been low and sharp, a heavy caliber, but definitely a rifle.

"There!" Kid pointed two blocks away. "They shot someone."

Lifting his binoculars to his eyes, Dooley could see a small band of civilians huddled around something in the middle of a street.

"It's a deer," Dooley reported. "They shot a deer."

"There's our food!" Kid nudged Dooley's side. "Huh, Dooley?"

"Wait a minute." Dooley licked his lips. "That looks like Levi Caspertein! Or . . . maybe not. This guy's older, but the same hair and build. And the same rifle. They're ELM! It's got to be the father, Titus Caspertein. Someone said he was out scouting for us or something."

"Who's with him?" Kid asked.

"Looks like . . . some lady in a wheelchair and a man and woman with a kid. And they have backpacks."

"Ambush?" Kid raised his eyebrows. "It doesn't get any sweeter than this!"

"And we'll get the deer meat after they butcher it." Dooley lowered the field glasses. "Go on. Both sides of the street. Use our elevation. Wait for me to shoot first. Go!"

Kid and the other nine scrambled for the roof access door. They'd done this before, especially at the beginning of Pan-Day. Ambushing travelers and living off their kills was in their blood. It was that much sweeter, however, since Titus Caspertein was with them. And the man was about to die.

Dooley walked to the stair access without haste. They had time to get into position. His men would wait for his signal. Titus would need twenty or thirty minutes to butcher and maybe quarter the animal. Then they'd continue home toward ELM. The street below would be the last street they'd ever see . . .

On the third floor, Dooley found a tall window in an office break room that overlooked the street below. He broke out the glass of the window and swept all the shards outside. In the quiet that followed, he heard his men making similar arrangements in their own perches. Soon, Caspertein and his party would wander unsuspectingly closer, and the ambushers would be completely silent. They knew their jobs. And they all needed a win.

After setting down his rifle, Dooley turned over a metal vending machine with a crash, hoping to stop any bullets that Caspertein might fire. Of course, the man probably used tranquilizers like the rest of ELM, but the vending machine would easily stop those rounds.

Taking up his rifle again, he rested it over the vending machine. He guessed he was nearly invisible from the street below since he was elevated and a few feet inside a shaded window. The sun was just right. If all went as Dooley expected, Caspertein would be dead before the man even fired a shot.

Ambush waiting was always a tense time. Dooley wiped his brow and watched the littered street below. The targets would wander past several abandoned cars, cross a dusty intersection, pass a fallen construction crane, and move into the kill zone. The deer meat would be quite a prize, but getting his hands on one of those battle rifles— Dooley nearly salivated at the thought of such a powerful weapon in his hands!

He stretched and cracked his neck, then used his inhaler. The fight would be over quickly once it started. Nothing could go wrong. ELM had made a fool of him more than once, and they'd taken Fran from him. Though he'd never met Titus specifically, Dooley figured Levi would suspect it was him getting some payback. Nobody messed with the Dooley Gang! If Levi wanted to retaliate, then Dooley would oblige. His headquarters at Pepper Park was well-manned and defended.

There was movement on the street! Titus was out in front, rifle in one hand. With the other hand, he pulled a grocery cart . . . with the deer in it? No, there was a partially covered body in the cart. A man's hand was exposed from under a blanket. So, where was the deer meat?

The woman in the wheelchair followed Titus. She had broad shoulders for a slender woman, probably because she'd pushed herself for a while. Her backpack looked like it was on the back of her chair, but the pack wasn't bulky enough to contain a quartered deer.

Behind the disabled woman walked a woman who wore a Muslim covering on her head, but her face was exposed. Beside her was a child, a girl. And behind them—a man was pushing another grocery cart. Ah, the deer meat!

But this last man had another rifle! Two rifles. Dooley's heart skipped a beat. But it didn't matter that they had two weapons. He and his men totaled eleven experienced ambushers.

Titus stopped in the intersection to kick aside a plastic bag full of garbage. He was eighty yards away from Dooley, too far for a precision shot with Dooley's assault rifles and his gang's skills. Dooley liked them nice and close . . .

In the rear, the presumed Muslim man wrestled his heavy cart through the debris in the intersection to park it next to Titus. The grocery carts had become invaluable in those days. Even Dooley had oiled the squeaky wheels of old metal carts to transport loot back to Pepper Park.

"Any second now," Dooley whispered, his finger already on the rifle trigger. "Just a little closer."

Kneeling in the intersection, Titus examined the ground. Dooley smiled. The man could look for tracks all he wanted. He and his men hadn't crossed in that spot to reach the building and its roof the day before.

Then Titus raised his rifle and used the scope to examine the street ahead, even the buildings. Dooley didn't move. He hardly breathed. His men had better not be visible!

Wincing, Dooley wondered if the broken-out windows at intervals were a giveaway that an ambush awaited him. He cursed and realized they should've left the glass in place—to break it at the last instant when ready to shoot through the windows. These Casperteins were too cautious for a commonplace ambush.

With breathless amazement, Dooley watched Titus direct his party to the left down a different avenue. They were going around the building! Dooley was furious, because this meant someone had given away their position. But he was too bloodthirsty to give up yet. He ran from the break room and charged up a hallway past office doors and conference rooms. Huge copiers, useless tablets, and scattered paper littered the floor, making it somewhat slippery.

Maybe Titus could avoid one trap, but he couldn't avoid every street to reach the ELM compound. Dooley knew exactly where Titus was going, and the other side of the building would offer the same advantage to overlook the next street.

Titus Caspertein and his friends were about to die.

Dooley reached the other side of the office building, but came upon a maintenance room that had no windows. The floor above or below had to be better! He dashed for the stairs to descend one floor for the same shooting advantage. Imagining Titus reaching the next street that very second, Dooley had no time to spare. Hopefully, his men were relocating as well—above, before, and behind Titus.

Throwing open the door to the stairs, Dooley plowed into darkness. Instead of finding a solid landing or stairs underfoot, Dooley flailed his arms as his momentum sent him into empty air. *What had happened to the stairs?* The stairwell had no windows, so he couldn't see what might have been below, rushing up at him. The fear of the unknown and a catastrophic injury where no doctors could help him plunged his mind into desperate panic.

He screamed an instant before he collided into the second-floor stairwell landing. As consciousness faded, he acknowledged his bruised limbs and head, but very little pain. With hate in his heart, he realized Titus might actually get away. After all, his men wouldn't initiate the ambush. They would be waiting for him to fire the first shot . . .

Sazon left the Garden early and alone. The day before had been a great success in nearby communities. Each team had reported back to the residents about the impact they'd made with local strangers. They'd given them fruit and vegetables, and then compassionately released the elderly or disabled from their diminished quality of life.

But Mayor Malden wanted more. He wanted them to go farther with the Garden's message and rescue other pockets of Pan-Day survivors from disease and disgrace.

This was the way Sazon preferred it—prowling the streets alone, with his nine-millimeter on one hip and the syringe on the other. He'd come a long way from being a day laborer and forklift driver. Now, he was restoring humanity to meet her social potential like never before. It was an added perk that the Garden residents had begun to worship him as the "Resurrected One"—thanks to Titus Caspertein's tranquilizer.

It took Sazon only an hour that morning to reach the location of the farmer's market. While still a few blocks away, he heard with astonishment a raging gun battle that was taking place. Instead of investigating its cause, he went around the community that was certain to be already benefiting from the useless eaters who'd received the toxin the morning before.

On the far side of the community, he picked up familiar tracks in the dust: a wheelchair and a small group of people on foot. It had to be Emily and Titus Caspertein, plus two more adults and maybe a child.

He wasn't surprised to find that the tracks he now followed angled toward the downtown area. Titus was returning to his base of operation, and he was taking Emily with him. It was so sad, Sazon thought, that an otherwise strong person like Titus would burden himself and others with Emily's debilitating physical condition. How could they or anyone else restore humanity to excellence when acts of charity were exercised before compassionate killing? Didn't they put down sick and suffering animals? People didn't understand how much they were harming themselves by keeping alive those already miserable or permanently weakened by physical ailments.

Moving faster than the party in front of him, Sazon easily overtook and came within a block of Titus' party. He backed off and chose a parallel street east of Titus' heading. Though he knew Titus would never let him approach his people, this day was about recon—so that others from the Garden could covertly implement the CARE Protocol. Cleansing All, Restoring Everything, would someday be the whole world's mantra. Mayor Malden would lead them to that precipice, and Sazon wanted to be the tip of that spear as strength and health became the foundation for rebuilding.

Weary of Titus and Emily's slow pace, Sazon hurried ahead to survey streets he hadn't seen since before Pan-Day. Mostly, every road, highway, and avenue looked like another—abandoned vehicles, trash, and the occasional corpse picked clean by bandits or wild animals.

Almost too late, Sazon noticed a band of gunmen, about ten strong, on the roof edge of an office building. They were peering down the very street that Titus was approaching and from where a single rifle shot rumbled.

Fascinated with the gunmen's strategy, Sazon skulked closer and scooted on his belly underneath a delivery truck to watch the ambush unfold from his cover. Just the way these men disappeared one minute and carefully broke out certain building windows—it was obvious that they were skilled at hunting prey. Titus didn't stand a chance against this elevated and superior force!

Smiling, Sazon relished in the Garden's good luck. Yes, fate wanted their message spread, and Titus' demise would make that easier. Milli and the other ambassadors of restoration would move unrestricted into downtown, maybe even all the way to Coronado Island where Malden had aspirations to join his vision with General Brogdon's efforts.

In minutes, Titus drew closer to the anticipated ambush. But then he stopped at the nearest intersection. Sazon glanced from the ambushers' windows to Titus, who was clearly concerned about a possible ambush. No, Sazon realized, Titus had actually been alerted to some danger ahead! It was then that Sazon understood that Titus was speaking on some sort of radio. His left hand pressed down on a transmitter button as his head tilted just so and his mouth moved almost imperceptibly. Anyone farther away than Sazon's position would probably not even see Titus' small gestures.

Titus and his party then turned left at the intersection!

Sazon emerged from his hiding place and quietly entered the nearest office building. Titus would still be taken out, he expected, but he wasn't going to make it easy for the ambushers. Someone else was helping him, someone nearby. Out of curiosity, Sazon picked his way through the first floor of the building, past a dry water fountain, beyond a reception desk, and over scattered pieces of a fallen chandelier. Though he expected gunfire to break out long before he reached the west entrance, instead, he froze and watched Titus and his people walk safely down the street. Barely breathing, Sazon hoped Titus' party didn't look to the right into the building's empty windows and door frames. If they did, they would've seen him.

Seconds later, they were past. Almost disappointedly, Sazon wondered why the ambushers upstairs hadn't taken advantage of the travelers. Titus and his few companions clearly had quite a few provisions for such a small party.

A low groan came from the stairwell on Sazon's left— was it a human or an animal? He drew his sidearm to investigate. After propping open the stairwell door to allow daylight in, he found a slender man with sandy-colored hair lying on the second story landing. And no wonder—the stairs above had partially collapsed. The charred walls revealed that an old fire had spread through the building before it must have burned itself out.

Picking up the man's rifle, Sazon checked it to see that it seemed to be in good working order. The Garden had a small armory, but Malden had insisted that their weapons remain more subtle and quiet than mere firearms. Nevertheless, Sazon took the rifle with him as he avoided the collapsed section of stairs by leaping to the next landing and climbing up the rail.

Safely on the scorched second floor, Sazon moved to the west wall of windows—where the glass had been blown out by the fire—and saw Titus and Emily to the far right. Just to use the scope, Sazon raised the rifle to gaze after Titus. *Lucky man.* The one who'd fallen down the stairs must've been the shot-caller, literally. Therefore, the ambushers had let Titus pass. The dying gunman in the stairwell had saved Titus, but Titus would never know.

A sharp whistle caused Sazon to lift his head. Suddenly, he was staring straight into the big bore muzzle and scope of a rifle aimed right at him from directly across the street. In that second, he knew he was going to die. He didn't have time to explain who he was or the righteous mission he was on. But it dawned on him that this new adversary was probably the one who'd alerted Titus on the radio that an ambush was imminent.

The muzzle flashed and Sazon knew he was finished. But he froze, too startled to react. The round slammed into him with familiar force. *Familiar?* He looked down at his chest, expecting to see crimson coloring his green, plaid shirt. Instead, he felt breathlessness and saw a wet mark on his shirt. *Not another tranquilizer!*

His eyes closed as he tumbled forward out of the window. Where were the ambushers? How had Titus placed someone so perfectly in the building across from the ambushers? No one could be this protected, not even accidentally.

Waking with a start, he found he was next to a low-burning fire inside a building. A young man sat across the fire from him, a man who could've been Titus' twin except this one was maybe twenty years younger.

Sazon closed his eyes at his throbbing head and spinning vision. *His vision!* He lifted his hand to find that his whole head and right eye were covered with bandages.

"God allowed you to live," the young man said. "You fell out of the second story window. The Lord must not be done with you yet to keep you alive. Careful, don't get up. When you went into shock, I started a fire to keep you warm. A fire hydrant broke your fall, so to speak. Crushed your eye socket pretty bad. I dragged you in here to sit with you until you died or woke up."

"How long ago?" Sazon gently felt the bandage, pressing where he knew his eye should be. "A fire hydrant, huh?"

"It ain't easy using your head like that." The man chuckled. "The name's Levi Caspertein. Uh, I tranquilized you about three hours ago. I live a few blocks away at the ELM building."

"You Casperteins . . ." Sazon cursed. *"You blinded me!"*

"Just one eye. You've got another one. So, you've heard of my family? Take your time. Here's a little water. You lost some blood, so you need to start replacing it."

"The ambush . . ." Sazon sipped from a green water bottle. "What happened?"

"Dooley and your buddies are gone now. They looked around a little, but they didn't come down here. I saw their ambush and called Dad on the radio. You'll have to find another way to kill him, but it won't be easy. He's supernaturally protected until God wants to take him home."

"Those guys weren't my buddies." Sazon swore again. "But I figured someone must've warned Titus. I was . . . just following him, just watching. *Oh, my head . . .*"

"Sure. You were just watching."

"Yeah, I'm from a place called the Garden. I wasn't with those Dooley people."

"The Garden?" Levi's eyes narrowed. "I've heard of the Garden. And the things I've heard haven't been good. But I guess that explains the syringe on your belt."

Sazon closed his eye. He'd never had a headache like this. There was no way he could stand let alone defend himself against this foe.

"Oliver must've reached you," Sazon acknowledged without opening his eye. "He told you about us. I should've known."

"And that would make you—?"

"I'm Sazon." He didn't offer his hand. There was no kindness in his heart for a man who'd tranquilized him—again. "What're you going to do to me?"

"*Do* to you?" Levi sighed. "I think you'd only ask that from a guilty conscience, because maybe you expect some punishment. Sazon, I'm not your enemy or your punisher. My dad's not even your enemy."

"You both shot me."

"We both tranquilized you. Oliver told me what happened at the Garden. And now I've bandaged you up to keep you alive. I'm not sure what inclined you to lunge out the window, but that was all you, pal. I only tranqed you. You want to eat a little something?"

"No." Sazon passed back the water bottle. "Oliver's staying with you now? With Rory?"

"Yes, Oliver and his son are under ELM protection. They're already learning about God's love, not a murdering protocol. There'd better not be any Garden people up here. We know what to look for now."

Sazon wasn't looking forward to hearing the disappointment in Malden's voice when he found out that the Garden's Sympathy Agents would meet such local resistance.

"You can't stop us."

"Maybe." Levi added a two-by-four to the fire. "But we can stand against you and warn people about the wolves who come offering food for their souls. We'll keep offering people the good news about the mercy of Jesus. That's more powerful, but people will be responsible for choosing what they want more: your protocol or the Gospel."

"The Gospel? You can't care for everyone who's diseased. Nobody can. More unhealthy people need to die so the healthy can live."

"That's not your call," Levi said. "The God who created the heavens and the earth gave you life and cares for you. He cares for everyone who has life, no matter the quality of that life that you assign to it. God's view is the only one I've learned to care about. And that's why you're still alive, Sazon. Your life matters."

"There will never be a day that your foolishness succeeds," Sazon said. "There are too many people and not enough resources. Such foolishness will kill us all unless the Garden succeeds."

"And that's where you're wrong, my big friend. God regularly uses the foolish things of the world to put the self-professing wise in their place. If I'm foolish, then you may consider yourself so placed."

"You're pretty clever for a kid." Sazon took a deep breath. It was at least a couple hours of walking back to the Garden. Bandits were everywhere, like those who had nearly ambushed Titus. And now he had no vision in his right eye? "I'm leaving. You won't try to stop me, will you?"

"No. You were never my prisoner, only my patient." Levi gestured with one hand at the afternoon light. "I suppose you want this back."

The young man offered a sidearm, and Sazon realized it was his own. After accepting it, he tested its weight, then ejected the magazine to find no bullets remained. He holstered the weapon on his left hip, then rocked sideways to get up on one knee.

Levi reached over the fire to steady Sazon before he fell into the flames. Then he helped him rise to his feet.

"My equilibrium is all off." Sazon wished he didn't need to lean on this enemy of his, but strangely, Levi seemed there to help him instead of harm him. "I'm fine. Let me go."

"You should come back to ELM," Levi said. "Let my mom look at that eye. I'm no doctor, but you've probably lost it for good."

"For *good?*" Sazon pushed off Levi's shoulder. "There's nothing *good* about today. If you cost me my eye, I'll come back and kill you."

"Um, you're in no condition to make threats like that. Are you going back to the Garden now?"

"That's my home." Sazon attempted a step away from the fire but staggered sideways. Everything was spinning around him. "I'll be fine there. We have everything we need."

"Maybe I should walk with you, at least halfway. I don't mind."

"Walk with me? For what?" Sazon waved his hand dismissively. "Leave me alone. You and your dad have done enough damage. You'll pay for this. Mayor Malden won't tolerate you harboring Oliver and Emily."

"I don't know who Emily is," Levi said, "but it's not you or your mayor's decision who we help. We help whoever's in need. Today, that happens to be you."

"You can't help me!"

"God's trying to open your eyes to the fact that I have," Levi said, "by taking one of your eyes."

"*God!*" Sazon cursed and kept walking. He used a building wall to lean against. At the next corner, he looked back. Levi was standing next to the fire, watching him leave.

Only religious fanatics talked about God like that, Sazon considered. He was Sazon, the Resurrected One! He had no use and no need for anyone else. In the Garden, he was the perfect picture of health. Who else could claim to have been resurrected two days earlier? Or at least that was the mayor's story for the people.

The farther Sazon walked, the better he felt. Of course, he'd feel safer if he had bullets for his gun! And now that he felt the pouch on his other hip, he found that the syringe was gone, too. Fulfilling his mission for the Garden was still his vision. This was only a minor setback. After a good night of sleep and a fresh syringe of toxin, he'd come right back here and face ELM openly. No one would stand against him. He was Sazon of the Garden, the Resurrected One, the Sympathy Agent. His calling was a righteous one.

With some frustration at having only his left eye, he recognized neighborhoods and communities where people sheltered in hiding. Other Garden Sympathy Agents would pay them visits in the weeks to come, but his personal focus would be on ELM. It was likely if they'd taken in Emily, then they harbored other disabled people as well, maybe even the mentally disabled. Eventually, he'd find a way to reach them. Anyone diminished in ability or burdensome to the community needed to die. Their reduced quality of life demanded it!

Beyond the interstate, he came upon a family of four dragging a pine tree in the other direction. Sazon couldn't imagine how far they'd gone to find a standing tree, but people were desperate. They moved to the far side of their tree on a rope tether until he passed. His head throbbed with every step, so he didn't slow down; he was in no condition to try to talk to anyone. If he had felt like it, he would've at least learned where they were living, so he could return someday to share the CARE Protocol with them. And if they had any debilitated civilians living with them, he would compassionately remove them for everyone's good.

The Garden gate finally came into sight. He trudged almost frantically forward and fell against the cold iron. With his heavy fist, he pounded on the gate until one of the sentries peeked over the wall from a platform on the inside.

"It's me, you fool!" Sazon cursed the man as the bars inside were lifted.

He pushed through the opening gate and ignored the shock of the sentry at his bloodied and bandaged appearance. Once over the bridge, he noticed several residents among the rows of plants.

"Where's Dr. Ferguson?" he demanded.

When he heard she was at her villa apartment, he marched straight to the chapel flower gardens then on to her apartment. He felt the eyes of the residents on him. Sazon the Invincible had been injured somewhere beyond the Garden wall. It infuriated him that he'd need to explain his injury to Mayor Malden, who would need to put it in perspective for the Garden residents. People, especially Sympathy Agents, would need to be reassured that it was still safe and necessary to venture beyond the wall.

Doctor Ferguson opened her door after two knocks.

"Sazon!" She reached for his head, then withdrew her hand. "What happened? Come in!"

She seated him on an exam table curtained off from her living quarters, then he allowed her to unwrap the bandage.

"What'd you use?" She held up a bloody strip of cloth. "This looks like a torn shirt."

"I didn't wrap it. Titus Caspertein has a son named Levi. He shot me then felt bad and tried to fix me up."

The doctor tossed aside the last wrap.

"This doesn't look like a gunshot wound." She used a sterile gauze to dab at his brow, which he couldn't completely feel. "Sazon, your eye socket has been crushed. I see bone floating free. And if I'm not mistaken, your eyeball is . . . detached."

"*Detached?* What do you mean? Reattach it! I'll be fine. I walked all the way back here, didn't I?"

"Are you in pain?" she asked.

"Just my head. It's like a freight train is roaring through it."

Stepping back, she studied him for a long moment. If anyone had inspired Malden to enforce the CARE Protocol, it was this sometimes-methodical scientist. For months, she'd been Malden's lover, and Sazon guessed she still was, even though Malden wanted to have a child with Milli. Milli was nothing to Malden except a delivery system to secure another generation with the Garden's policies intact.

"Let me get you some antibiotics." Ferguson turned away. "And something for the pain."

Sazon closed his good eye as the doctor sorted through vials at the cabinet against the wall.

"The Casperteins have declared war against us here," he said softly. "In a matter of days, we need to get Sympathy Agents downtown to give food away. Whatever influence Titus and Levi have there, we'll undermine it and instill CARE Protocols with any survivors."

"Sounds like a good plan." She returned to the exam table. "I'll definitely tell Malden."

Something in her voice alerted Sazon. His eye flashed open and he caught her wrist as she lowered a syringe toward his shoulder. He recognized the syringe and its contents, then twisted it out of her fingers.

"What is this?" He shook the syringe in front of her face, still holding her wrist. "Me? You use this on *me?* Do I look like an invalid?"

He backhanded her. She was a healthy, big-boned woman, but Sazon's force was supported by heavy muscle and years of experienced labor. Ferguson crashed over a metal table and rolled against the cabinet. Finally, she sat up, holding her cheek.

Standing shakily, Sazon grabbed up a roll of gauze off the floor. She'd just tried to remove him through a sympathetic killing! Sympathy for him? He wound the gauze around his head, daring Ferguson with a glare to try to inject him again.

"You agreed to the protocol." Slowly, she stood but didn't advance, her hand still holding her reddening jaw. "Sazon, you have to be cleansed. Everyone will know if we let you escape. Now you have only one eye."

"I'm not . . . diminished!" Sazon shook with fury. "How dare you kill me for this! I can live just fine with one eye! This isn't something I did to myself. I'm not some sick animal who needs to be put down!"

"But your quality of life is already—"

She stopped talking as he lifted his fist. Even though he was several feet away, his threat was enough to silence her. But it wasn't enough to silence his own realization. He'd just made the same argument that many others had made to him about themselves, right before he'd killed them!

Sazon looked down at his fist. No, this was all wrong. He didn't deserve to die just because his body was wounded. Who was Dr. Ferguson to say he should die? Or that anyone else should die?

He didn't know how to resolve the meager supply issue for so many people, if no one should die so others could live. But now he understood that he'd murdered in ignorance. Others had begged for their lives and he had overpowered them. It all made sense now—the wrong thinking he'd applied to the world's problems.

"What are you going to do?" Ferguson asked. "You can't stop us all, Sazon. We'll get you. We'll get everyone who needs to be cleansed."

Numb from his realizations, he picked up his jacket and empty pistol. Maybe he could find cartridges somewhere else, but the Garden wasn't his home any longer. Mayor Malden would kill him if he stayed here, and there were dozens of residents already brainwashed as he had been who would try to inject him as quickly as they could.

Ferguson followed him cautiously as he moved to the front door and left her apartment. From her doorstep, he surveyed the Garden. The fruit trees, the rows of vegetables, the flowers around the chapel—he'd planted and cultivated every inch of the habitat for months. How would he even eat outside of the plenty in this Eden? Where was there fresh water or food to be had? Even though he knew how to garden, it would be months before a new garden could produce like this if he got started somewhere else.

For weeks, he'd been quietly killing people to preserve the stability in the Garden. It now seemed reasonable that he would kill others outside the Garden so he could eat and drink to stay alive. But again, who was he to say who died so another could live?

The weight of the sidearm in his hand felt unbelievably heavy. He looked at it like it were a dead snake. With a flick of his arm, he tossed the weapon into the rose bushes beside the path. That was it. No more killing. Even if Malden himself came after him. And he certainly would. Ferguson had said it herself. They couldn't let him live any more than they could allow Oliver or Emily to remain alive.

Nothing was the same any longer, he thought as he walked up the path toward the bridge. Since Pan-Day, he'd been at the top of the food chain. But the loss of his eye changed all that, at least according to Garden philosophy.

He reached the bridge and looked into the slow-moving water. This wasn't fair, not after all the good he'd done for the Garden residents. *Good?* Maybe it wasn't good at all. No, he decided he couldn't call it good now. All the death tainted everything he thought he'd been accomplishing with Malden.

The words of young Levi Caspertein floated through his thoughts of self-pity and despair. *His eye injury had helped him?* Yes, his eyes were open, so to speak. But was it really possible that God had orchestrated all this? Was this the way God worked—through irony and coincidence and enemies to tear down pride and prejudice? Such questions now haunted him. And he could no longer live without the answers!

The residents materialized from all over the Garden. From his elevated view on the bridge, Sazon turned left and right, but the residents were there, emerging from the orchard villas and crops. Many of them held syringes in their hands. Somehow, Dr. Ferguson had gotten the word out. The mayor's army of sympathy killers was committed to their cause. All they needed was the proper stimulus: a target. Sazon had played his role to train them, and now they were ready to show him what they'd learned.

Farther up the path, Malden and Ferguson watched the horde close on the bridge. Those without syringes held their arms wide, like they were corralling loose livestock.

Milli was in the front of the group that approached from the chapel. She, of course, was already experienced at this part. She'd tasted the sick power of taking a life, and her eyes showed she was drunk with fanaticism and zeal. As Malden's puppet, she was a victim of her own pursuit for meaning in this tragic world.

At the last second, before outstretched hands grabbed at his clothing, Sazon attempted to lunge over the bridge rampart and fall into the shallow water. Maybe he'd survive the swim and find a way out of the Garden. Somehow, Emily had done it. And Oliver and Rory had done it, too!

But they caught at his clothes and dragged him back from the edge. Hands grappled with his powerful arms and legs, pinning him to the bridge stone. There were too many to fight, though he did try to kick and wrestle them off.

A needle plunged, then another. He felt their subtle pinches. Milli was the second to inject him. Her face was close to his. He saw the relish in her eyes.

Then, as a single organism, everyone withdrew, as if he carried a contagion like Meridia. He sat up and stared at his wrists. Although everyone had backed away, handcuffs had been clasped around his wrists, one pair on each thick wrist. The metal dug into his flesh, but that wasn't the worst part. Each of the handcuffs was attached to a carabiner and a length of nylon rope held by three or four people on each side.

A figure stepped through the ring of people. Malden's face was calm, even compassionate. In contrast, Sazon felt that his head gauze had slipped aside a little, and the violence had started his eye socket to bleed again.

"You have twenty-four hours, Sazon," the mayor said softly, but the Garden was so still that Sazon could hear him clearly. "If we were to let you leave the Garden, you could do a lot of damage to us in that amount of time. So, you'll stay with us here. We'll make sure you're comfortable to the end. When it's time, you'll go quietly."

Sazon glanced at the two injection sites, one on his thigh and the other in his arm. He doubted even Ferguson knew what two injections of the toxin would do to him. Maybe he didn't have twenty-four hours. Maybe two injections worked faster.

"Murderers!" Sazon pulled against the cuffs and ropes that held his arms apart. Because of his strength, those who held the ropes stumbled forward initially, but then they recovered and held him more securely. "I didn't have to die!"

Malden lay a hand on Sazon's head, even drawing his long hair away from his damaged face. His touch was tender, but Sazon wasn't fooled. Milli was a petite young lady, but her jab with a syringe was just as deadly.

"Oh, Sazon, we're not murderers." Malden shook his head. "No. If you could see yourself, you'd know this is for the best. Sometimes one must die for what's best for the people. It's what you agreed to. No one with a diminished quality of life can be allowed to live. Otherwise, weakness will spread. You know this is how restoration must occur."

Those who held the ropes pulled him back toward the chapel. To follow them, he was forced to his feet. His strength was sapped. The day had exhausted him. His losses and confusion and pain stole his willingness to fight.

He submitted as they led him off the path, behind one of the villas, to the grass between two sturdy and mature orange trees. Tombstones stood nearby as testaments of other deceased residents—Sazon's own victims, each of them. There, they fastened the ropes to the trees on either side of him. There was some slack so he could kneel down on the grass, though with his arms spread wide.

The people watched him and he looked back for a moment. Then he lowered his eyes. This was the end. He'd literally been led out to pasture—to die.

The residents dispersed. Malden walked away beside Ferguson. Milli was one of the last to leave. There was pride instead of pity in her eyes.

Alone in the Garden, he lifted his head and watched the sky. How could Levi be so sure there was a God? Would God show him compassion, even after all the things he'd done for Malden? Would God find him acceptable now that he understood his many wrongs? Was there still hope for him?

"God?" His eye flooded with tears and his body shook with sobs. "I don't want to die like this. Can You . . . do something? Maybe send an angel or something? I'm open to anything. I'm lost unless You do something. That's just where I am now. My eyes are open, like Levi said. Is he one of Yours? How can I die after finally understanding everything? *Please* . . ."

Levi took his time returning to ELM. Having crossed Dooley and his gang, and then Sazon from the Garden, the world seemed like a much more dangerous place than it had been just a week earlier. The existence of ELM and its important work in the city had seemed complicated enough dealing with rogue bandits and Coronado's soldiers. Now there was a gang with a grudge against the Casperteins and a Garden of assassins hoping to execute anyone who revealed human weakness.

He entered the east perimeter access and offered a greeting to the sentry who sat on the stool there, the man with the withered leg. Everyone able to work in the perimeter was encouraged to contribute—for the safety and dignity of all. Despite the difficulties, there was an air of optimism and satisfaction inside the perimeter.

Farther into the courtyard, Levi stopped to watch the comings and goings of the people. Everything seemed normal at that noon hour. Gabby was ordering Conrad around as they picked up wind-blown trash. Children were playing in the sandbox or drawing hopscotch with chalk on the concrete. Women had set out chairs and a folding table where they peeled tubers and fanned themselves against the rising heat and humidity. Gus had allowed a couple of older youths to take two goats at a time out of the ELM building for sunshine and exercise. And higher up, residents helped neighbors on their balconies, watering and weeding potted gardens that Chevy, Carla, and Annette had helped install. But Levi remembered being the one who'd carried the soil up to those elevations.

Their bliss was only possible, Levi realized, because he didn't shout aloud the escalating threats against them.

Oleg appeared on the second-floor balcony of ELM, his battle rifle in hand. And he wasn't alone. Pregnant Wynter stood with her back to the railing, a water bottle on a sling over her shoulder. It was almost unfathomable that a child would soon be born among them, in this volatile city. Aunt Wynter seemed at ease with stout Oleg since he was one of her brother's oldest friends, but Levi knew Oleg didn't mingle too much with his ELM neighbors. Except for Carla. The two seemed to be taking a lot of meals together lately.

Carla had been spending her evenings down on the twenty-seventh floor rather than eating at the Caspertein table upstairs. Levi didn't mind that her affections were finally directed elsewhere. He was half her age and too focused on security and fishing to think seriously about romance. If he were to think of anyone that way, it would be Jenna Dowler, but she was far away in New York.

ELM's front door opened and a small procession emerged—Titus and Annette, then Fran and Carla. Chevy helped lift a cart over the threshold and stabilized it on the sidewalk pavement. It was a multipurpose cart that was used for everything from carrying away trash to bringing in feed for the goats. Today, it was loaded with a body.

Someone had died.

Starting forward, Levi wanted to see who of the Hopefuls had passed away. Just then, a man in his late thirties helped a woman in a wheelchair over the threshold to join the funeral procession.

The cart reached Levi and stopped when he didn't move aside. Dusty was in the cart, his light brown hair clipped and combed in a way Dusty would've never tolerated if alive. Annette had probably done it to prepare him—a mother's touch on a man whom they'd known only a couple of months.

Startled at finding Dusty in the cart, Levi reached out and touched his roommate's shoulder. This was real. He could almost feel the clammy coldness of the corpse through the collared shirt he'd been dressed in.

"What happened?" He raised his eyes to his father. "No one said anything on the radio. It seemed like he'd learned to keep his head down and not make a target of himself."

"We were chased out of a neighborhood," Titus said. "Dusty took on fire so others could live."

Levi fought back tears. He acknowledged the Middle Eastern family and the woman in the wheelchair. They were strangers, yet their faces were somber, not meeting his eyes. They must've returned with Titus, maybe meeting Dusty on the way back.

"He was pretty selfish in life," Levi said, "but I'm glad his death meant something to others. May I help?"

Titus moved aside so Levi could push the cart himself. Dusty hadn't been a popular ELM resident, most often shadowing Levi without saying much to anyone, so Levi wasn't surprised that so few were attending his funeral.

"I'm sorry." Carla touched Levi's arm as he led the procession with the cart. "He was a good man."

"Only for a little while." Levi chuckled and sniffed. "I'm glad you're here. The two of us probably knew him best."

Though Carla was still not a believer, Levi knew she was learning from his family to see the world as God saw it. She was beginning to see people in their human need instead of through their failures of the past.

Up at the ELM cemetery amongst the trees, where Dusty had dug many graves for others, Titus helped Levi dig as the rest stood in silence. Then, Levi stood at the head of the hole and rehearsed Dusty's life, as Levi had known it after meeting him in the desolate wilderness to the east.

"He'd come to believe in Jesus after a while," Levi said, "so I'm not surprised he died like his Lord—serving others. I just wish I'd been there."

They covered Dusty slowly, then without further words, they filed out from the trees, down the streets, and back to ELM. Once they reached the courtyard, Chevy jogged up to the woman in the wheelchair to explain to her about some contraption Levi had noticed on the side of the ELM building.

"That's Emily," Titus introduced as he walked alone with Levi. "She escaped the Garden, just barely. Chevy's obviously got a new elevator idea for her. She'll live on the fourth floor, apartment three."

"Alone?"

"She's quite independent." Titus shrugged. "And my new Syrian friends, the Husseini family—Yasif, Gizem, and Majeda. Dusty saved their lives. My life, too."

"Upstairs won't be the same without him."

"You still have Conrad." Titus clapped Levi on the shoulder. "He's good for you."

"Yeah." Levi scoffed, but not with discontentment. Conrad's head injury made him reliant on others for meals and cleanliness. "We're good for each other, I guess."

He shared what had happened a few blocks away, interrupting the ambush and caring for Sazon after he'd fallen from the building.

"I crossed that giant in the Garden," Titus said. "It's a bummer you couldn't win him over. He's their number one assassin, I think."

"Maybe not with only one eye, now." Levi winced. "They might even try to kill him since he's no longer a complete man, in their eyes."

"You're right. The Garden doesn't tolerate weakness, or what they think is weakness. Emily has explained to me about their CARE Protocols for sympathetically murdering people. It's the same euthanasia and population control efforts we saw rising in Canada and here before the pandemic. People grasp for meaning, order, and preservation. In their desperation, they grab onto man's twisted philosophies instead of God's promises. You know the rest."

"We need to think about a permanent guard around ELM," Levi suggested. "At the beginning, it seemed we were always vigilant. I think we need an armed lookout at least. Dooley's still out there, and now these Garden people know where we are, too."

"Well, I'd say we have enough people for around-the-clock security at all three gates." Titus shielded his eyes from the sun as he studied the buildings above. "But ELM is our motto. It'd be real easy to get caught up in self-preservation, Levi. Sure, we all want to be safe, but our efforts should continue to be about God's priorities. If a threat arises again, we'll try to head it off. Living by faith isn't always safe. You know that better than anyone. A strong presence for Christ and caring for our neighbors—that remains our best defense."

"Contend *for* the faith," Levi recited from the Book of Jude, "instead of contending *against* our enemies?"

"That's Christ's way, but it wasn't too popular in America or anywhere else in the world." Titus was silent for a few minutes. "The others will need help understanding. Can you stand with me on this—if you see it as standing for Jesus as I do?"

"Yes, I can." Levi stood up straighter, realizing he was receiving a proposal and not an order. "I will, Dad. Even though it's the hazardous path."

"And the unpopular one, no doubt."

The two watched as Oliver and his son Rory wandered through the courtyard. Oliver urged his son to go play with the other kids in the sandbox, but the youngster only sat on the containment wall of sand and set up his board game to play alone.

Oliver spotted Titus and waved, then approached.

"All settled?" Titus shook the young father's hand. "Levi and I were just talking about trusting God for our safety. You've faced a lot lately, Oliver, you and your family. ELM needs good men who've walked through the fire yet still find their hearts settled on Jesus Christ."

"I'm still reading the Bible and figuring things out," Oliver said, "but I believe what Jesus did. Yeah, I'm here to stay. I'd be pretty dumb to come through everything lately and think it was just by chance—like meeting Levi weeks ago. God is real, I know, and I owe you two for that."

"The only thing we want from you is for you to follow Jesus with us," Titus said, "and to be a good father to Rory. The rest will come naturally."

"What about being a good husband?" Oliver wagged his head. "Milli and I weren't even married, but I can't help but see her every time I look at Rory. Those people just got into her head. I know it. She's got to come around sometime, but now she's a whole day's walk away."

"You know her best," Titus said. "Do you really think she could come around? Would she even want to?"

"If my love for her is real, then I have to hold out hope, don't I?"

Levi listened to his father thoughtfully consider Oliver's concern for Milli. Though Levi had never met the woman, Oliver was with them now. The Caspertein way was to care for those in their fold. He had learned that was only the Caspertein way because it was Christ's way.

"It's the valley of the shadow of death out there." Titus frowned at Levi. "How do you feel about taking him back to get Milli? One more try? I can't go this time. I've been gone long enough."

"For you, Oliver, if that's what you feel you need to do." Levi nodded. "It ain't easy walking back into the assassins' lair."

"Well, I'm a pretty good shot." Oliver gestured at Levi's weapon. "I had more practice after the first time we met, but the Garden took my rifle."

"Give him a battle rifle," Titus said. "I've been in the Garden, so I can draw you a map how to get in and out without detection. But you might want to talk to Emily for more intel."

"Do I tranq Milli and haul her out?" Levi asked, realizing too late that he was being insensitive in front of Oliver. "I mean, what's our real goal here?"

"I say this to you both," Titus answered, "that she has to come willingly. The battlefield requires some extreme measures sometimes, but we can't kidnap her and hold her here. If the draw of Oliver's love for her or her love for Rory isn't enough, you might have to walk away from her, maybe forever."

"If I can talk to her alone," Oliver said, "I think I can convince her."

"When do you want to leave?" Titus asked Levi.

In the past, his father had arranged such departure times and events. Levi felt the honor of responsibility, even though he was younger than Oliver.

"Tomorrow morning," Levi said to Oliver. "Early."

"Leave Rory with us." Titus rested a hand on Oliver's shoulder. "We'll take care of him like he was our own. And God will take care of you guys."

✝

Dooley woke in semidarkness. Panic gripped him as he struggled to remember where he was—and why his whole body throbbed with pain. *This had to be hell.* Surely, he reasoned with great despair, he'd been killed and this dark void and misery was now his reality.

Tenderly, he felt around where he lay awkwardly on concrete rubble. His hand brushed over jagged rebar and broken fragments of building materials. Slowly, his memory returned before his senses could discern his surroundings. That was it! He'd run headlong into the emptiness of a collapsed stairwell!

Caspertein!

He sat up and searched in the darkness across the fragmented construction material for his rifle. It had to be there. His men were waiting for him to fire the first shot to start the ambush. The Casperteins had tried to destroy him, but he would instead destroy them!

His lungs rattled. From his breast pocket, he drew his inhaler and shook it. It wouldn't last more than two more days. One squirt and inhale was all he dared for now.

The rifle was nowhere to be found, and there wasn't enough light in the stairwell to search farther. At least he still had his sidearm in its shoulder holster. With difficulty, he reached overhead and grasped a broken handrail to pull himself up to the next landing. Finally on a level surface, he limped across an office floor, past metal desks and cabinets, and reached the window that overlooked the street. Nothing moved below except trash that blew in the afternoon breeze.

Afternoon? His eyes widened at the shadows and placement of the sun. He'd been unconscious for hours! No wonder the windows across the street were empty of his men's muzzles. Titus Caspertein was long gone. Since he hadn't initiated the ambush with the first shot, Dooley doubted the ambush had ever happened at all.

The mystery that was Maddix Striber and the crimes of the Casperteins remained unresolved.

Back on street level, Dooley limped southeast, disdaining the feeling of defeat with every step away from ELM and Fran, wherever she was.

Beyond the interstate, he entered a lot filled with lawn maintenance equipment. Lawn mowers and small tractors sat collecting dust. Not surprising to Dooley, some lawnmowers had been tipped over and the blades removed, probably to be used as weapons.

The thought of scavengers and bandits in the area made him draw his sidearm and walk with it at his side. The Dooley Gang had often crossed competing scavengers and anarchists. In those instances, Dooley had used his superior numbers and weapons to intimidate, kill, or recruit. But now, Dooley was wounded, alone, and carried only a handgun.

Beside the wreckage of a garbage truck mangled with a fire truck, Dooley sparingly used his inhaler again. He cursed himself for being asthmatic. It wasn't fair. But he was determined not to let it beat him. If only he could find—

He suddenly spied an elderly man two blocks away. The stranger's frame was bent, betraying his frailty, yet he still walked with purpose and speed, even with a bag over one shoulder.

After glancing left and right, Dooley lowered his head like the predator he knew he was, and climbed beyond the wreckage. In minutes, he'd caught up to the old man, yet stayed beyond speaking distance and kept abandoned cars between him and his target.

The local cut through a yard, opened a residential gate, then disappeared. Dooley crept up to the mailbox as a back door thudded closed. This was almost too easy. An aged survivor like this man—Dooley had often killed such men for their stash of provisions. And inhalers were sometimes found in their possession!

Dooley let himself through the gate and entered the back yard. There he found a large tarp covering a . . . vehicle? He lifted the corner of the tarp enough to see the bumper and front tire of an SUV—probably a working one!

Voices were coming from inside the residence! Dooley ducked behind the SUV. The elderly man wasn't alone. Isolated all these months, whoever lived there had become careless. How easily Dooley had found them! But if they had a functioning SUV, they might have a firearm or two as well. He'd need to be very careful.

Cautiously, he approached the back door. It appeared to be of sturdy wood, but the frame was beginning to rot under the old paint. Dooley holstered his weapon and drew his knife. His victims numbered in the hundreds from tactics such as this, especially in the first weeks after Pan-Day. It had only been him and Fran back then—killing and stealing to stay alive.

The blade fit into the rotting wood. With a twist, he forced the lever out of the socket. The door opened on old but squeak-free hinges. He sheathed the knife and drew his sidearm to enter a cluttered hallway. There were no lamps and the windows were covered, so he left the door cracked to offer some light.

The clutter he passed in the hallway wasn't trash as he'd expected, but food supplies. *Food!* The stacked row of cartons and cans wrapped in plastic could feed the Dooley Gang for weeks. Or a couple people for perhaps a year. The operable SUV outside was too dangerous to drive since the Pacific States Defense Forces were always on the move, but this much food could be carried or carted back to Pepper Park.

Edging deeper into the house, Dooley approached a doorway to the right and an archway to the left. A staircase led upstairs. He peeked around the corner of the doorway on the right. An office, untidy as well, had a radio on the far shelf. The elderly man sat there, his back to Dooley. It seemed impossible that he hadn't heard him breaking into the house—unless the man's hearing was lacking.

Rushing into the room, Dooley pressed his gun muzzle to the back of the man's neck. His clothes were clean, and his skin and sparse white hair appeared to be washed. So, there seemed to be a good source of water there as well!

"Turn around, slowly," Dooley ordered quietly, aware that there was someone else in the house. But when the man didn't move, Dooley spoke louder. "Turn around!"

Taking a step back, he allowed the old man to swivel in his office chair to face him. His white mustache was trimmed and his gray eyes were rimmed by thick glasses. Dooley continued to aim his gun at the man's chest. There was no fear in his eyes, only weariness, and his hands remained on the armrests.

"I need an inhaler," Dooley said. "You know, albuterol or salmeterol."

"What?" The man tilted his head. "Eh?"

"An inhaler. I need one. Do you have any bronchodilators?" Dooley used his left hand to fish out his inhaler and shook it. "Do you have any canisters?"

The old man's eyes twitched, and Dooley realized his error too late. A large gun barrel pressed in the middle of his back. He straightened, hesitated a couple seconds, then raised his hands—now holding his inhaler and sidearm overhead.

The weapon in Dooley's hand was plucked away by the old man, whose face remained neutral rather than gloating. Dooley watched as the man checked the handgun's cartridges, then held the weapon on its owner.

"Back yard, now," the old man ordered.

The gun barrel in Dooley's back eased off. He turned enough to see a woman in her seventies backing into the hallway. The barrel didn't waver.

"I have friends," Dooley threatened.

"Not here, you don't." The old man scoffed. "I saw you following me home. You're alone."

"Look, I just want an inhaler canister."

"It doesn't matter," the woman chirped in a high voice. "Jacko, he's already seen too much."

Dooley swallowed. So, that's what they meant by the back yard. These two weren't amateurs.

"Outside!" the man shouted and cocked Dooley's sidearm.

Turning to face the hallway, Dooley moved slowly, mentally scrambling for any advantage. How could so much in his life go so terribly wrong so quickly? He couldn't die like this, not after finding such a stash of provisions with only two elderly folks guarding it! Forget ELM. This was the treasure he now wanted!

He reached the hallway, fully aware that the shotgun in the woman's hand was aimed steadily at his torso.

The hallway was narrow without room to maneuver, but he rapidly approached the back door. Hopefully, his injuries from that morning didn't hinder his movements when it came time.

At the door, he gripped the handle and drew it slowly inward. *This was it—move or die.* What a fool he'd been to risk his life by sneaking alone into a house! But the payoff could be tremendous if he could only get away.

Halfway out the door, he lunged left at unkempt rose bushes and simultaneously flung the door closed. The shotgun blasted through the door frame, sending searing heat past his hip before he landed in the thorny rose bushes and rolled away.

What was left of the door crashed open behind Dooley, but he only glanced back as he scrambled for the corner of the house. Once rounding it, he smiled triumphantly as he sprinted toward the street. *He'd gotten away!*

A block later, he slowed, wheezing heavily. Much to his surprise, he still held his inhaler! Upon shaking it, he found it was empty. With difficulty, he tried to manage his breathing, sucking air as if through a straw.

Continuing to scurry along, he was intent on turning west at the next available street and returning to Pepper Park. But his return was pointless if he had no inhaler. Someone out here had to have something! If he had to, he'd burn down another neighborhood in his search for a single inhaler canister. Now with no firearm, he'd have to be extra careful. Two narrow escapes from death in one day was already testing fate. A third wasn't worth the risk.

Suddenly, he saw movement ahead. Dooley crouched behind a rancid mountain of trash bags to spy on three travelers. No day packs burdened their backs. Two men with only sidearms and one slight, red-headed woman. They were walking south rather quickly, but so freely without a heavily-armed escort? He'd thought people's fear of the Dooley Gang was more prominent in this area.

He was only a couple of miles from Pepper Park, but finding out where these new strangers were heading was too tempting to ignore. Since they wore no packs, they must have come from somewhere nearby.

Wheezing as he went, Dooley hustled from vehicle to vehicle behind the southbound trio. Less than a mile later, Dooley watched the three approach a wall around a gated community. Even the air smelled different there. Hints of greenery could be seen over the high wall.

The gate was opened for the three. Dooley found himself in the street seconds later, his hands open at his sides. An armed sentry inside the property stepped into the open gate after the trio had entered.

"I'm unarmed," Dooley said breathlessly to the guard. Through the opening, he spied fruit trees and gardens and endless flower beds. *Paradise.* "Please, I need help. My asthma . . . My last inhaler ran out. You must have something in a place like this?"

Dooley didn't mind playing the vulnerable one to get what he wanted. And what a find!

"It's just you?" The guard, a beret on his head, studied the avenue behind and beyond Dooley. "You're alone?"

"Yeah." Dooley panted like he'd run miles. He could feel his chest tightening. "Please, my family died in the Pan-Day looting downtown. It's just me now."

"And you're sick?"

"Asthma. Since I was a kid."

The guard hesitated still, studying Dooley's appearance. Then he looked back into the property where others were working among the plants and trees. Only this guard was visibly armed. Dooley was already mapping out an assault on the place for his gang, but first he needed their help.

Chapter Seven

Oliver hopped onto the roof of a four-door car parked on the street. From his new elevation, he could see farther down the street that he and Levi had chosen to travel to get to the Garden.

"They'll see this a mile away!" yelled Levi as he climbed up the side of a nearby building. The young man laughed like he was playing on a jungle gym rather than in a war zone, then turned and leapt onto a fire escape ladder to climb higher.

Though Oliver was five years older, it was difficult for him to view the Caspertein soldier as anything but his superior. After talking to others at ELM, Oliver now knew that Levi was already seasoned from numerous gun battles and high-octane moments, even at his age. His family had trusted him to make decisions that affected them all, so Oliver was confident to be in his company. After all, Levi had been the one who'd helped Oliver discover Jesus and feed his family months earlier.

The young father hefted the light-weight battle rifle clipped to the harness over his long-sleeved thermal. The short ELM rifle had a stronger kick than his old hunting rifle, but after a few practice shots, he'd learned to hold the weapon snuggly against his shoulder. And the non-lethal rounds loaded into the thirty-round clip gave him a sense of moral authority. He was with ELM now. They'd accepted him and Rory. And in his back pocket was a new Bible—that he no longer needed to keep hidden from anyone. These were his people, people who lived for Jesus.

"How's this?" Levi called from the platform of a water tower mounted on top of a six-story building. "Visible enough?"

"Should be good!" Oliver gave a thumbs up.

Oliver smiled as Levi shook a can of white spray paint, then sprayed the outline of a stout trunk of an elm tree on the side of the water tank. On top of the trunk, he sprayed the foliage of the shade tree. The image was as large as a man this time, but similar to other ELM trees Levi had sprayed along their route south. Anyone who knew about the Christians downtown would know that their reach extended into the city suburbs. If ELM could help it, no one would escape the reminder that every life mattered to God and His people.

A couple of dogs crossed the street a block away, but Oliver didn't bother to raise his rifle. A couple of weeks earlier, canine meat could've kept his small family fed for days. But now, he and Rory were part of ELM, eating fresh fish and garden vegetables. If Oliver had his way, Milli would join them soon, too.

"Hey, I think there's water in this thing!"

Levi thumped on the side of the water tank. It was still early morning so they weren't in a hurry to reach the Garden property, but Oliver still felt anxious. He had to try one last time to convince Milli that her new companions were murderers dressed as humanitarians. That morning, while it was still dark at ELM, Titus had prayed for God's hand of protection and His will to be done on their trip. Now a few hours later, Oliver realigned his faith in the God of the Bible that the Casperteins were teaching him to follow.

Suddenly, a gunshot blasted from high overhead. Levi grunted and fell from the water tank platform. Oliver pivoted and raised the short rifle, gazing through its scope at a nearby elevated window. A man filled his sights. Oliver fired so quickly that he surprised himself. Hunting stray dogs had apparently sharpened his marksmanship skills.

The man slumped unconsciously against the windowsill. His assault rifle dropped from his hands and clattered several stories below on the pavement. A woman screamed from the open window, then the man's form was tugged inside the room and out of sight.

Sliding off the car roof, Oliver stooped behind the hood, only his head and rifle exposed. He knew there could be other shooters.

"Hey, Levi!" Oliver tried to slow his breathing. If he'd gotten his partner shot on their first journey together, how would he ever look the ELM people in the face again? "You there?"

"It ain't easy lacking cat-like skills!" Levi chuckled and stood upright on the rooftop. He carefully rotated his arm, perhaps having fallen on his shoulder. "You get him?"

"Yeah." Oliver pointed at the window four stories up in an adjacent apartment building. "There's still someone up there."

"Cover me."

Licking his lips, Oliver was relieved that Levi wasn't seriously injured. He wouldn't be caught off-guard ever again while watching out for the young soldier.

Levi investigated the edge of the roof on which he stood.

"There's a water hose here that leads from the tank to that apartment," Levi said. "It's quite a setup."

"What do you want to do?" Oliver hoped Levi wanted to leave, but he'd already learned something about the Casperteins. They were all about meeting their neighbors. "We don't need the water."

Climbing down the fire escape, Levi crossed another roof, then leaped down to the street. He joined Oliver at the car, then Levi stood in the open rather than finding cover.

"You weren't hit?" Oliver asked.

"Not even close." Levi gestured to the water tank above. "The bullet punctured the tank, but no water came out. They're low on water and it's summertime. There won't be much rain for a couple more months. We should let them know they're welcome downtown."

"But they're killers." Oliver studied the other windows. "There could be more shooters up there, too. We're probably outnumbered."

"Maybe." Levi slapped Oliver on the shoulder. "It ain't easy making friends out of foes, but that's the job."

Oliver lowered his rifle and stood upright as Levi skirted a trash pile to reach the door of the apartment building. He should've known that traveling with Levi was never a simple out-and-back trek. This was how Jesus-followers lived, Oliver was quickly learning. They saw God's purpose and direction in every situation, especially when something didn't go according to their plans. This was how he wanted to live and how he wanted to teach Rory to live as well!

Following Levi, Oliver saw that the front door of the apartment building was roughly disguised as being boarded up, but Levi pried it open with his knife. A few rotting boards had been haphazardly nailed to a plywood cover, but the door remained on its hinges.

Stepping cautiously inside, they found a narrow walkway between trash and clutter against the wall that led to a stairwell. Levi aimed his rifle up the stairs, vigilant regardless of his hoping to make friendly contact.

They started up. Oliver trailed behind a few steps to offer cover from another angle like Oleg Saratov had instructed him to do. He'd called it cover formation, which was new to Oliver since he'd only hunted dogs alone for months prior to joining ELM.

On every stair landing, garbage was heaped, often blocking the way up unless they moved the debris out of the way. The familiar odor of backed-up sewage reached

Oliver's nostrils. He'd discovered survivors in hiding in his old neighborhood simply from the stench of their challenging existence. During the months, he'd avoided those he'd discovered, but that was no longer his motto.

Finally on the fourth floor, they edged down a dim corridor of closed apartment doors. A dusty glass window at the end of the hall offered just enough light.

"That's the door," Oliver whispered after counting the apartments from the stairs. "What now?"

"Stand aside." Levi waved him away from the door so that they stood on either side. Then he knocked lightly on the door. The sound wasn't hollow as expected, but like it was firmly reinforced on the inside. "Hello in the apartment. Open up. No one's going to hurt you. We just want to talk to you. Until you hear what we have to say, we can't move on."

Silence.

"They aren't going to open," Oliver said.

"Open up!" Levi ordered and knocked louder. "I know you're afraid, but we're not leaving until we talk this out. You can't be shooting travelers who are just passing through. We know your water supply is already really low, so you need to hear about where we came from and where you're welcome to go, and where there's lots of water."

Silence.

"I think it's just one woman still in there," Oliver said. "She won't open to a couple of men."

"Listen, lady," Levi continued, "your man shot at me, but he missed. No harm was done. Check your man's pulse. He's not dead. He's just unconscious. My partner shot him with a tranquilizer. We're from downtown with a group of believers in Jesus Christ. We're called ELM. You're safe with us. Let us tell you how to get safely downtown where we have plenty of water and food."

Something moved in the apartment. Oliver shifted his rifle, still edgy from the gunfire they'd received a few minutes earlier. He could've died if the shooter had aimed at him instead of Levi.

The sound of a chain rattled free, then they heard a beam dragged or slid aside.

"It's open," a woman stated.

"Hold your fire," Levi urged. "We're coming in, but just to talk. Oliver has a family and my name is Levi. I live with my parents downtown. Will you hold your fire?"

"Yes, unless you do something."

Levi turned the door knob and pushed the door wide open. Oliver restrained himself from recoiling. With the door open, the odor of unwashed bodies was even stronger.

"Okay, I'm coming in." Levi raised his gloved hands and stepped into the doorway. He didn't seem bothered by the choking smells. "These are scary times for many. My partner and I are just here to help you get over your fear."

Oliver eased into the doorway behind Levi. A middle-aged woman with greasy hair awkwardly held a hunting rifle aimed at Levi. The window across the untidy living room remained open.

A man in his fifties wearing tattered clothing lay on the floor, his head turned to the side against a propane tank. The apartment was littered with hundreds of empty water bottles and food containers. Oliver had seen this before. In fact, he'd lived it. When people were too afraid to leave their residence, garbage gathered like termite mounds.

"You saw that your man is still alive, right?" Levi asked.

"He's my husband." The woman didn't lower the rifle. "We've been married for twenty-six years. But he's not waking up. I tried."

"In about forty-five minutes he will." Levi lowered his hands. "My people believe that every life matters to God, so we don't kill anyone, not even our enemies. If you recall, ma'am, your husband fired a shot at me first."

Stepping to his right, Oliver nearly upset a stack of newspapers. He guessed they used them for toilet paper like many others had. The woman's husband lay awkwardly. A sick feeling welled in Oliver's stomach. *He'd actually shot a man!* If the stranger didn't wake up for some reason, he wasn't sure how he'd live with himself.

"Looks like a funeral bed." Levi nodded at a garland of grass and a few dandelions encircling a bare mattress on the floor. "Did someone die?"

The woman looked away, and Oliver understood why. He'd scavenged through enough houses to know how an arranged suicide appeared.

"We weren't just low on water," the woman admitted. "We've been eating, well, things humans shouldn't eat. There's not a crumb of food for blocks around us. I know because we've searched as far as we dared to."

"How providential that your husband alerted us to your presence." Levi unzipped a pocket on his vest and drew out one of his mother's homemade protein bars. Oliver knew they tasted slightly like flavored cardboard since they were composed mostly of cooked plants and goat's milk, but it was food. "We're here for you."

She licked her lips, then slowly lowered her rifle until finally she let it clatter to the floor.

Oliver saw her sway on her feet an instant before Levi rushed forward to catch her. She didn't lose consciousness since her eyes remained open even as Levi held her in his arms, but Oliver guessed her nerves and malnutrition had overwhelmed her. Or maybe it was just both sheer exhaustion and relief.

Stepping over to her husband, Oliver shifted the man's limbs around so he could lay more comfortably on the floor. Levi broke off a bit of the bar and fed it to the woman, then offered her water from his own canteen.

For a few minutes, Oliver scouted around the rest of the apartment. The first of two bedrooms had been turned into a bathroom or outhouse, complete with a hole cut in the floor above the apartment below. He'd seen this before as well: residents attempted to distance themselves from their refuse. The consequences of living in a bathroom usually backfired by the spread of disease and an odor that alerted everyone nearby that survivors were present.

The second bedroom wasn't a bathroom, but it smelled no better. Three human bodies had been wrapped in plastic and leaned against the wall. Perhaps the man and woman had been too fearful to leave the apartment to bury or hide the bodies outside. Or they were loved ones whom the survivors simply couldn't part with. Under such desperate circumstances, Oliver had found that common sense sometimes seemed to be lacking. In survival mode, the unequipped mind fractured, and what was unthinkable one moment seemed completely normal the next.

When Oliver returned to the living room, the woman was sitting on her own on the edge of the mattress, and Levi was kneeling in front of her. She spoke softly, explaining that she was Hilda Marly, and her husband's name was Veck. They'd been on a cruise ship offshore when Meridia had struck. Quarantine rules had forced them to jump overboard at night and swim a mile to reach Imperial Beach. They'd trudged inland to find people they knew. The apartment had become both a refuge and a prison for five adults.

"We set up the water hose months ago," Hilda said. "But we knew it wouldn't last forever. We've lived every minute afraid it would be discovered. And here you are."

"The water tank on the roof is pretty visible," Levi said, "but the hose was disguised by the way you weaved it with the phone lines over to here. It was Veck's shot that alerted us to your whereabouts. Most people wouldn't hope to find water still in a tank that visible, and most wouldn't climb a building just to see if it had any water."

"This could've been a lot worse," Oliver said to Levi, "if you'd been wounded."

They visited for a few more minutes until Veck began to stir. Oliver went to the man's side and helped him sit upright as consciousness returned fully and his eyes focused.

"What happened?" Veck asked.

"They're friendly," Hilda said.

"It seems that God wanted us to meet you." Levi handed Veck half of the bar that Hilda hadn't eaten. "Oliver and I are on our way to a place in Stillwater, so we can't stay long, but we can get you pointed toward downtown. We have a community by the shore with most of the comforts of a modern home."

"You have room?" Veck sat up straighter as he munched awkwardly on the bar, revealing his dentures. "Everyone around must be trying to move in there."

"Oh, it's not like that. Not yet, anyway," Levi said. "It's not too safe to travel except under armed escort. Besides, people are suspicious of others who're offering sanctuary for free. We also have the military living across the bay, and they haven't exactly been hospitable to civilians."

"But you're offering us sanctuary and safety?" Veck asked. "For free? You're right—that's a little suspect, I'd say."

"We can't change people's paranoia. All we can do is remain available to them. Dozens have already arrived, making us all more stable since everyone's willing to work and contribute somehow."

Veck's gaze went to his wife, then to the bed surrounded by the garland. Oliver saw defeat on his face, or shame. Suicide had been the answer only hours earlier, but now it must've seemed preposterous. There was no question in Oliver's mind that God had led them there. If only the same Miracle Worker could reach Milli's confused heart.

Oliver and Levi rationed out a little more food and made arrangements with the couple to pick them up on their way back downtown, hopefully that night or the next morning. Hilda wept, and her husband's emotions followed as Levi and Oliver embraced them each in turn.

Before the two men left, Levi knelt and prayed for the couple's future, their safekeeping, and more importantly, their receptivity to the truth of God's love and forgiveness.

"That cost us two hours," Levi said as the two reached the street outside, then continued southeast. "Sorry about that."

"Well, I'm not sorry," Oliver said, his rifle cradled in his arm as they walked side by side. "They were trying to kill us, but now they may as well be our best friends! I'm glad we didn't run away from meeting them. Most people would leave someone like that behind."

"Grace has a way of breaking down barriers. Chevy taught me that."

"We'll need some of that grace in the Garden." Oliver eyed Levi as the younger man marched on steadily. He was hard to read sometimes. "I think we'll need a lot of grace this afternoon."

"Amen to that."

Oliver couldn't imagine raising Rory without his mother, who'd chosen another lover, another people, besides her family. Yes, God's grace would need to be present—and hopefully that grace wouldn't be rejected by the people who thrived on killing each other.

✝

Sazon had pain in his shoulders like he'd never known in his life. The night had been spent in sleepless misery, his arms pulled wide by the ropes tied to the two orange trees. Though he could kneel on the green grass, he couldn't relax his arms lest they pop out of his shoulder sockets. His hands were numb from the cuffs on his wrists which were in turn attached to the ropes.

He'd begged more in the night—some of it audible and some of it silently from his soul. All of the begging was aimed toward whatever God there was since no one else came into the orchard area to offer him water or food. His throat was parched. His lips were cracked. His muscled body ached for nutrients. But both Caspertein men had spoken of a loving God, so Sazon reached out to Him.

His pleading in the night had been for mercy from God. To his surprise, his mind had been flooded with memories of all the merciless things he'd done. Instead of comfort, he'd been plagued with guilt. Was God trying to tell him that he deserved everything he now suffered? What misery! What agony of the soul!

From sweat and tears now dried, his long hair clung to his forehead and across his large nose. It obscured his vision a little, but he could still see across the property and between the nearest villas. The residents moved amongst the rows of plants and flowers around the chapel—watering, weeding, and harvesting. He resisted the urge to scream obscenities or to plead for mercy. They wouldn't listen to him any more than he had listened to the pleadings of others who'd been designated by Malden to die.

Even if he were offered water or food—or freedom—he was still a dead man. *Two injections?* No human could survive even one of Ferguson's toxic shots, not even a strong man like himself.

The next hours had been filled with wonder as his thoughts made sense of what had been revealed about himself. Maybe having his many evils revealed to him was a form of penance or atonement. Since he faced certain death, having his wickedness wiped clean definitely seemed worth these final hours of suffering. But what good could God offer him if Sazon's own suffering washed away his many evils?

Now, he gave up on the idea of making penance. There was no way a few hours of discomfort or even agony could pay for months of killing people. And during his years prior, he'd lived a life of rebellion towards his parents, cheating on his taxes as an adult, and indulging in weekend drunkenness and relationships. No, he decided, this was merely torture during life before he faced whatever punishment the afterlife might exact. Maybe there was no merciful God after all . . .

During moments of fury, he'd stood and tried to yank the ropes free from the trees. But all he received were deeper cuts from the cuffs on his wrists. The poison and exhaustion were sapping his strength.

He'd been like a god, even worshipped as one, in the Garden for months, doing Malden and Ferguson's bidding. And now, he cried out to God, whoever He was, however He worked. If only he knew more about the One he was certain could deliver him from his dread of death!

Levi used his fingers to dig into the soil at the base of an orchard tree inside the Garden wall. He brushed a snail aside and scooped up recently irrigated dirt to smear on his face. Next to him, Oliver rung his socks out and changed into a fresh pair from his pack. The poor father had slipped knee-deep into the Stillwater River when the two men had hopped the stream on the east side of the Garden.

It was noon. Levi had left all his food with Veck and Hilda as they recovered, but he was too excited to be hungry. They were inside the Garden! The plan was to fetch Milli as quietly as possible, but Levi was aching for a crack at the Garden residents who'd murdered so many. He recalled that his father hadn't merely helped Emily retrieve her chair, but that he'd also confronted the Garden's leadership. Though revenge wasn't his motive, he wouldn't mind tranquilizing a few of the residents just to humble them from their superior positions.

"Get down!" Oliver alerted.

The two hugged the grass behind the fruit tree, their packs beside them.

"Where?" Levi mouthed to Oliver a few inches away. He slowly unclipped his rifle under him to shift it into firing position.

But Oliver didn't answer. Instead, he breathlessly stared beyond the tree. Levi watched his eyes follow someone moving through the orchard.

A few seconds later, Oliver relaxed and they both stood.

"That's two patrols in five minutes," Oliver whispered. "I didn't even recognize that last guy."

"It's understandable." Levi licked his lips, then spit, having forgotten he'd rubbed wet dirt across his face. "They've stepped up security and probably taken in a few more residents since they've been reaching out to other communities."

"People just want the food here." Oliver remained wary of another patrol that might come upon them. "Death comes later."

"We'll never get you to Milli with all these patrols," Levi said, "even if they're just single man patrols. Let me go ahead and find a hiding place to cover you. I'll call you on the radio when I'm situated. Radio check."

"Yeah, I hear you."

Levi pulled on his pack and drew his silenced sidearm instead of raising the rifle.

"Courage, Oliver."

Oliver took a deep breath and held up his gloved hand to show his shaking fingers, proving he was nervous.

"We could die right now. They could shoot us or inject us or—"

"It's okay." Levi offered a grin. "We wouldn't be the first to die on a mission of mercy, but you're a believer now. Death really has no sting for us any longer."

"But you're not a father. I'm thinking of Rory."

"Sure, I'm no father," Levi agreed, "but we left Rory in my family's protection. He's in good hands. Now, let's go get Milli, huh?"

Edging around the tree, Levi saw the way was clear then darted to the next tree deeper inside the Garden. In the distance, he could see the villas his father and Oliver had described—eight villas shaped like horseshoes, four apartments in each, and the chapel at one end of the main path.

He understood Oliver's sense of fatherhood more than he admitted, even though he had no kids of his own. There were many people back at ELM for whom he felt responsible. At only twenty years old, he had no offspring, but he felt like he had many children. The way his father and Annette talked, they thought the same sentimental way about those who'd joined them in the downtown apartments. Everyone was family and potential children of God.

Movement! Levi crouched and steadied his shoulder against a fruit tree, his arms leveled as he held the handgun. His sights were trained on another patrolling man, this one on a track directly toward Oliver!

Holding deathly still, Levi took in the sentry's attire as he moved clumsily through the orchard. Dress slacks and a white collared shirt under a shoulder holster? The man's sidearm wasn't even drawn. It was still clipped in his holster.

The man was twenty feet away from Levi when he tranqed him. The man's eyes had been trained on the grass and leaves on the ground. Without a shout or a noise, the sentry crumpled to the grass. Levi swept the area for more movement, then went to the fallen Garden resident.

After disarming the thirty-something, clean-shaven sentry, Levi disassembled his sidearm to toss its components left and right. But there was nowhere to hide the unconscious man. The orchard was too manicured, too flat, absent even of a burn pile or raked leaves. Leaving the man there was out of the question. He'd be discovered in minutes if the patrols continued so regularly.

The trees! Levi spotted a few thick branches up an orange tree that would hold a man's weight. It was the best he could manage for now. In one hour, the tranquilized man would wake up, so he had no time to waste.

Since Levi was larger and stronger than most grown men, he flopped the man over his shoulder and climbed the tree with the unconscious sentry's feet and arms dangling. Huffing ten feet up, Levi draped the man over a thick bough.

Back on the ground, Levi studied the hiding place with skepticism, but it was still better than leaving him on the ground.

He prowled from tree to tree, avoided another sentry, and reached the back wall of one villa. With his back to the wall, dark apartment windows peered out on his left and right. Someone inside might've already seen him approach, but he heard no shouts or alarms. If the other residents all wore the same nice clothes during their daily chores and duties, he would definitely stand out in his jeans, black ammo vest, and mud-smeared face.

Someone on foot was walking through the orchard almost directly at him. The rose bushes nearby weren't thick or tall enough to hide Levi's bulk, so he moved to the window on his left and pushed and nudged the glass until it slid aside. He stepped on the windowsill and leapt into the dim room. When he landed with a thud, he paused only long enough to realize he stood on thick carpet. Then he pivoted and slid the window closed.

"I think I heard someone knock on the door," said a woman in another room. "Give me a minute."

Levi's eyes adjusted to the dimness of a living room as a patrolman walked by the apartment window outside.

The woman who spoke appeared in bare feet in the foyer and was about to open the front door. Levi tranqed her in the back, then turned toward a side room while she collapsed noisily to the floor. A man in a t-shirt and trousers rose from a desk as Levi stalked into the room and fired into his chest.

The apartment was quiet.

"Oliver," he called on the radio, "you good? Over."

"For now. Just hurry. Over."

Going to the front window, Levi observed the villa's courtyard, garden designs, and fountain. The path from the north to south separated the property in half. He could see a lot, but not as much as he'd need to cover Oliver in his search for Milli.

Relocating was risky, but Levi didn't have a choice. He needed a better vantage point, especially of the chapel front and maybe more of the main path or bridge farther north.

A door closed nearby. From another apartment to his right, a woman in a pantsuit and gardening gloves walked past the fountain, then turned right toward the bridge. If she'd looked to her left, she would've seen Levi in the window. But she had no reason to expect anyone contrary inside the Garden perimeter, so no alarm had sounded yet.

Levi opened the front door. A half-dozen gardeners were bent to their tasks near the path—weeding, harvesting, or watering. He eased out the door and closed it softly behind him. Casually, he walked to the apartment door on his left. Without stopping, he turned the doorknob, entered, then closed the door.

No one shouted outside and no one screamed inside. He remained undetected so far. As he searched the apartment for occupants, he found it empty and came upon a back bedroom window. As intended, he'd arrived at the very heart of the Garden. The chapel with its stained-glass windows and flowers stood not ten yards away from the back window.

"Oliver, I'm in position. Do your best to find Milli. Over."

"Not yet," Oliver whispered back. "I had to hide in the riverbank. Too many patrols. It'll take me ten minutes to get back to where we were. Over."

"We've got time." Levi checked his watch. It wasn't even noon yet. "Take your time. Lots of guns around here now, way more than you and Dad thought were here, so be careful. Over."

"Any sign of Milli? Over."

Leaving the bedroom, Levi peeked out the front window.

"There are a few women her age, but I see no one in the gardens with short, red hair. I'm in the second villa to the south and on the east side of the path. Over."

"Okay, I can get there if I'm careful. My old apartment was on the other side of the chapel from you. If everyone is outside working, I might be able to go through the chapel to get to the farthest villa. Over."

Returning to the bedroom, Levi slid open the window a few inches, enough to push his muzzle through if need be. The air that rushed through the opening smelled so sweet, much fresher than any scents downtown where fishing was the main food industry and the odor of rotting garbage still blew on the breeze. No wonder people were attracted to the Garden . . . until they were discovered with an infirmity.

Then Levi saw it. Above the door of the chapel were two stained glass windows. Between the windows was empty, gray wall space, about four feet wide and four feet high. He clenched his left fist. *No!* As inviting as it was, he couldn't risk it—not just to leave an ELM mark! It wasn't necessary. *Not here. Not now.*

"Oliver?" Levi called. "You on your way? Over."

"Nope. I'm still waiting for a clear run. Now there's a guy on top of the bridge. He might spot me if I run south. Over."

Levi was about to tell him they had all day, but that wasn't the case. The first man he'd tranquilized would wake up in forty minutes.

"Be careful," he said, "but at first opportunity, get down here. Over."

After taking off his pack, Levi checked the garden and path to the left and right, but his eyes kept returning to the space on the chapel wall. It would take him only thirty seconds. Those in the gardens and flower beds weren't even paying attention. If there were no sentries on the path between the chapel and the bridge, anyone farther away probably wouldn't identify him as a stranger. *Probably*. If he left his rifle behind.

Unclipping the rifle, he laid it next to his pack. Titus' words of warning weeks earlier still rang in his ears. Taking unnecessary risks put others' lives in danger. It had been juvenile to go for a joyride down the zipline, and it would be an amateur move to risk everything now just for a little ELM attention. But Levi couldn't resist. Mischief was in his blood. This would make for a great story someday—like his dad's legendary stunts for COIL.

From his pack, Levi drew the can of white paint, then slid the window wide. The chapel was so close! He studied the flower bed on either side of the door. The stained-glass windowsill would make for a good step to reach high on the right side.

After climbing through the villa window, he knelt for only a couple seconds. No one was looking. No voices nearby or residents approaching.

He walked briskly out of the plants and reached the path. His heart pounded as he approached the front doors of the chapel, then veered right into the flowers. A few flowers were flattened under foot, but he reached the stained-glass window two seconds later. With a lunge, he vaulted onto the sill and steadied himself with one hand near the glass to lean left and reach high. His left hand shook the can of paint, then he sprayed. The trunk. The foliage. A perfect elm tree. With a little added flourish, he scrolled the letters E-L-M inside the outline of the foliage.

The emblem would remind the residents that the Garden was vulnerable. They weren't as elite as they thought they were. Titus had said their chapel was their place of meeting and worship, and Levi had just left their mark—as if God Himself had inspired him to declare the powerful Gospel on their sacred building.

Levi hopped off the sill and landed directly in front of a green-eyed, middle-aged man with a freckled face. He glanced up at the white elm and letters above the door from which he'd just emerged. This had to be Mayor Ridley Malden, Levi decided from the descriptions given from Oliver and Titus. The only thing better than leaving his mark on the chapel wall would be to humble the mayor of this death cult.

With a flash of his hand, Levi drew and fired his silenced sidearm. As Malden collapsed, a syringe dropped from his fingers. Levi crushed the syringe under his boot, holstered his weapon, then grabbed Malden's hand to drag him into the chapel sanctuary to hide him.

But a second person was standing in the chapel doorway. It was a woman in her mid-twenties, her red hair cropped short. This had to be Milli, Malden's latest lover—deduced from Oliver's description.

She thrust her hand forward. Levi gasped as he watched the needle pierce the heavy fabric of his ammo vest. He felt the sharp spire plunge into his belly. But he swung an instant later and knocked her wrist sideways. The syringe snapped off, leaving the needle inside him. The vial fell into the flowers. Milli backed away, holding her wrist and glaring hatefully at him. Kicking at the flowers where the syringe had fallen, Levi saw that it lay there in the dark soil, the fluid still in its glass vial. *Thanks be to God!*

His hesitation and fear that he'd been injected gave Milli a moment to gather her own wits. Her scream was inhuman just feet away from Levi. She took a breath to scream again, but Levi silenced her with a tranq in the torso.

More people than Levi expected seemed to materialize from villa courtyards, rows of vegetables, and the orchard beyond. Some held spades and gardening shovels. Others carried drawn firearms. They all appeared armed with syringes.

And all that Levi had was a silenced twenty-two pistol, accurate up to only twenty or so paces.

Men shouted and approached at a run. Women converged, standing shoulder to shoulder to rush him. Levi imagined all of them had become expert killers by now. If even a drop of toxin reached his bloodstream, he guessed he'd be dead within twenty-four hours, but right now, he needed to escape!

He dashed to the villa and reached through the window for his pack and rifle. Since he'd already blown the mission, he wasn't about to make it worse by leaving behind one of their powerful battle rifles!

A bullet zipped past his head as he scrambled over flowers to return to the chapel. He hurdled Malden's sleeping form and dove into the open door of the chapel. His rifle slid across the floor and his pack tumbled free. More bullets smacked the side of the chapel before he dragged Milli completely inside so he could kick the door closed.

"Hold your fire!" ordered a man outside. "Hold your fire!"

"What's going on?" Oliver asked on the comm. "Levi, you there? Over."

"Um, just a little mishap. I'm in the chapel and I have Milli. You'll need to—"

"You have Milli? Does she want to come with us? Does she want to talk things out? Over."

"Oliver, we're blown. They're surrounding the chapel as we speak. I messed up and broke cover. Now I need you to cover my exit with Milli. Get to the back of the chapel. I probably drew everyone to me, so you should be in the clear. Can you get here in sixty seconds or less? Over."

"I'm coming!"

"Hurry. Shoot anyone on sight. It's a mob out there. Over."

Levi touched his stomach but he couldn't feel the needle. Maybe he'd been mistaken and it hadn't really broken off inside him. There was no way he could step outside and study the dropped syringe closer. Annette had taught him first aid, but never what might happen if a syringe needle broke off inside the body's soft tissue!

He couldn't worry about the needle now. It was his fault they were in this scramble. Getting Milli out of the Garden for her own sake and for Oliver's peace of mind was a priority.

Kneeling, he clipped on his rifle and tugged his pack onto his back. Somewhere, he'd dropped the can of white paint, but that was a loss he wasn't about to recover. Though he couldn't see out of the stained-glass windows, the shadows across the glass and voices outside indicated he was about to be overrun by several dozen people.

"I'm almost to the chapel!" Oliver huffed over the radio.

"Okay, I'm going out the back with Milli. I can't wait. Catch up to us if you can!"

Milli was so light, he guessed he could run with her over his left shoulder. In his right hand, he held the battle rifle ready to aim and fire, but reloading with only one arm would be difficult. The thirty-round magazine in his rifle would have to last.

At the back of the chapel, he kicked open the rear exit door and charged out like a bull across a narrow, paved path to the grass beyond. The two southern-most villas stood on either side of him and the orchard lay ahead.

Men's shouts behind and to his left forced Levi to angle westward. Several handguns fired ineffectively. They were immediately answered by the booming cannon of Oliver's battle rifle. Those in the Garden shrieked so loudly that Levi stopped to look back.

Oliver was firing from his shoulder as he sidestepped after Levi. If he was aiming at only those residents with firearms, Levi couldn't tell. Men and women with various gardening tools or firearms seemed to fall indiscriminately. The rest scattered in appropriate fashion in the sights of the barking large caliber rifle.

Continuing on, Levi wove through orchard trees, expecting the rear wall to come into view at any second.

The firing ceased behind him and Levi smiled. It was just like his father's stories. Even outnumbered, he and Oliver had defeated the Garden murderers because of superior tactics and weapons. God had provided and He was sustaining them!

Suddenly, Levi swerved and stopped. He heard Oliver reload his rifle as he ran at a trot with his jostling pack to catch up. But Levi's attention was on a figure not twenty yards away—a man tied or chained between two fruit trees.

Cautious of an ambush, Levi approached who he realized was Sazon! The man's right eye was still bandaged, and his wrists were cuffed and connected to nylon ropes on either side. The muscled, long-haired man appeared dead or unconscious, his skin pale.

"Levi!" Oliver slipped on the grass and breathlessly fell to one knee. *"It's Sazon!"*

"I know!" Levi laid Milli gently on the ground and checked Sazon's pulse. "I crossed him yesterday outside ELM. He's alive."

"What are they doing to him?"

"Nothing good. It's probably because he lost his eye. Can you carry Milli?"

"Yeah." Oliver knelt next to her. "Did you shoot her?"

"I had to." Levi drew a blade from his hip and cut the ropes to free Sazon from the trees, though the cuffs remained on his wrists. "She stabbed me with a syringe."

"What?" Oliver stuttered. *"What?"*

"It's nothing," Levi said, though he heard the uncertainty in his voice. "Sazon, you awake? Come on, big guy."

Sazon's head rolled aside and his eyelids fluttered. His lips were cracked, so Levi helped him to his canteen.

"What're you doing?" Oliver asked, lifting Milli over his left shoulder. "Come on! Let's go. They'll catch us!"

"Not without him. They'll kill him if we leave him. Sazon, you with me? He's coming around."

"He's the worst one, Levi! We can't take him. We have to get out of here!"

"Caspertein . . ." Sazon's voice was hoarse, his breathing ragged. "I'm . . . dying."

"I've got you. It's okay. Can you stand?"

"They're coming!" Oliver warned. "I count . . . three guys. We leave now or we die!"

"Can you get over the wall with Milli?" Levi asked. "Go! Get her out of here!"

"But what're you gonna do?"

Levi studied Sazon as he trembled while trying to stand.

"Go!" Levi nodded resolutely at Oliver. "We're right behind you. Don't stop until you reach Hilda and Veck's building."

"You're really taking him? But he's a killer!"

"He's a killer who's been thrown away." Levi checked his rifle and aimed at the approaching gunmen. At least one of the three had returned to get a rifle, so the enemy wasn't firing only pistols now. "I have to believe he's seeing things differently, finally."

Oliver backed away with Milli, then turned and hustled toward the back wall.

Firing, Levi dropped the first Garden man with a rifle. The other two dove for cover.

"You ready for this?" He put his left arm around Sazon and supported his heavy frame to get him standing. "I don't think we're gonna outrun them, but at least they'll follow us instead of Oliver."

Sazon swayed on his feet.

"Leave me. I'm . . . dead already. They . . . injected me . . . twice."

Though he heard his words, Levi focused on gauging the route north—exactly where he'd come from.

"Hang onto me. I might need both arms for this. Come on."

Levi led them to the left through the orchard while keeping an eye out for the two men with handguns. It was likely one of them would retrieve the fallen man's rifle to continue after them.

"I'm afraid . . . to die," Sazon gasped a few steps later.

"That makes sense. If they injected you twice, you're definitely in trouble. When did they get you?"

"Yesterday, after you and I talked."

"Yeah, I told you this was a possibility." Levi spotted a prowler angling toward them. "Hold that thought."

He let go of Sazon to aim carefully with both hands while standing. Eighty yards away, a man skulked through the orchard. Levi fired twice, finally striking the man's thigh while his head and upper body were concealed by a tree.

"We have to cross the bridge." Sazon pointed to the right. "Get back to the path by following the river."

Levi saw the shallow gorge and stream ahead and turned east, supporting Sazon's weight more and more by the minute. A villa lay on their right as they approached the path through rows of vegetables.

"What if I die now?" Sazon's feet dragged, barely keeping up with Levi's haste. "I don't know anything about the God you spoke of."

A sentry who stood on top of the bridge shouted for others and pointed at the two men. Levi aimed and fired first, dropping the sentry.

"You need to know that God loves you, even though you've sinned against Him and others." Levi reached the path and faced the chapel. There, a dozen residents were gathered, facing them. Some were armed, but it seemed the most aggressive in the Garden had already been tranquilized. "God sent His Son to die the eternal death you deserve. He took your place to give you the opportunity to live eternally. It's time to trust in Him."

"I know about the cross." Sazon pointed east. "Watch him."

Swiveling, Levi fired three times at a patroller approaching from around a villa.

"God gives eternal life to the one who believes that His Son died for him." Levi drew Sazon with him to the top of the bridge arch. One sentry remained at the iron gate. The rest of the residents approached in a huddle up the path, lacking courage. "Jesus rose from the dead after three days in the tomb. That proves He can give us new life, eternal life, by the Spirit of God. When we believe this is true, He forgives us completely. He wants us to become reborn."

They neared the front gate. The lone sentry shifted nervously on his feet, then retreated by jogging to the east into the orchard. The gate was unmanned, but still closed.

"Can God keep me from dying?" Sazon gasped. "The poison, it could take me any minute. I feel it. It's trying to . . . stop my heart."

"Yes, God could heal you right now." Levi fell against the gate, Sazon with him. "But if He chooses not to, then you face death as a brief transition. You understand now that you've done wrong against your Creator and Lord?"

"Well, I don't know all of it from my youth, but I know what I've done the past year. As soon as Dr. Ferguson tried to kill me, I understood what I'd done. I thought what I did made sense to stay alive. This is . . . where it got me."

Levi threw off the bar with one hand and pushed one side of the gate wide open. Together, the two men turned to acknowledge the small mob behind them. They now stood on top of the narrow bridge. Those with firearms were shoved to the front by others.

"Then trust God to take you into His arms. You only qualify to be made new in His eyes if you know you don't rightly qualify for anything but His anger. That's when He'll show you mercy."

"What're we waiting for?"

"This is your past, I think." Levi surveyed the faces and posture of those on the bridge. Those with firearms didn't fire their weapons, despite the urging from others. "That's your old life there. You see it in all its ugliness now. After you pass, my dad and I will still have to deal with them. I'm seeing their faces, memorizing them so I can recognize and see them coming."

"You won't see them coming." Sazon's head wagged. "Sorry, but Malden and I trained the first ones. They'll find their way into every neighborhood by offering food no one can resist. Who can resist food when they're starving? Then they kill anyone who isn't perfectly healthy in mind or body."

"I guess we'd better get on down the road then, huh?" Levi turned him around to leave through the open gate. "We've got a long walk back to ELM."

"No, I won't make it." Sazon tossed his head to gesture behind them. "And they'll come after us."

"They will?"

"Yeah, they have to. They can't let me leave— especially me—to tell others what they do here."

"I don't think they have a choice but to let you leave."

"Why do you say that?"

"Because they'll have to take me out first." Levi chuckled. "They may be committed, but I'm infinitely more stubborn. Besides, it looks like everyone who was an actual threat was put to sleep for a while."

"Then just bury me somewhere in the sunshine."

"Not until we finish our talk about eternal life."

They crossed the street outside the Garden and continued northwest up the avenue.

"Eternal life." Sazon's words slurred and slowed. "I like the sound of that."

"It ain't easy watching you slip away, big guy, knowing you're going to paradise and I'm staying in this garbage heap to clean up your mess."

"You'll live." Sazon coughed. "I met your dad. You Casperteins seem to be survivors . . ."

Milli woke with a spasm, instantly alert but confused about where she was since she was leaning against a brick wall. Her memory was spotty, but she knew she'd been in the Garden that morning, so what was she doing out here in one of the neighborhoods?

An expensive, nylon backpack lay on the pavement nearby. She couldn't remember anyone in the Garden having that kind of gear. Then she understood: someone had brought her here and left the pack beside her. Was she supposed to carry it?

Using the wall, she rose to her feet and studied her surroundings—a laundry, a bowling alley, and a café. Other establishments had been burned down. Nothing was familiar. She didn't know how to navigate outside the Garden, not in this upset world. Even when she'd lived with Oliver, she'd remained indoors most of the time, never scouting around the community. And before Pan-Day, she'd always used the navigation system in her car to find unfamiliar destinations.

Around the corner of the brick wall, she heard gravel crunch underfoot as someone approached. She reached down and picked up a large segment of broken asphalt to use as a weapon if needed. Mayor Malden had been teaching her and the others in the Garden how to use friendliness to convince strangers that they were harmless, but she had no problem using a weapon to kill at that moment. Of course, she'd been trained to manipulate her way to get close to a target where she could use a syringe. But she had no syringe now, so she'd need to defend herself like any other—

"Oliver!" She lowered her urban weapon, then raised it again as her surprise waned. *"You kidnapped me!"*

"Keep your voice down." He held out his empty, gloved hands. Over his shoulder was a rifle type Milli had seen only in the hands of Malden's enemies. "There are scavengers at the end of the alley. We need to let them pass."

"Where are you taking me?" She measured her chances at running across the street and finding her way back to the Garden. Scavengers might capture her. That would be worse than being with Oliver. "Where's Rory? What have you done with my son? He's not even yours!"

"So, you do remember being his mother." Oliver shrugged on his pack. The confidence and authority in his voice was completely foreign to Milli. He'd always seemed so inexperienced, so worried. "Rory is safe downtown with good friends. Remember Levi Caspertein? We can go live with his family. It's amazing, Milli. They have shown me so much, and they have food and water and—"

"No one has what the Garden has!" Milli felt her fury rise. What he said sounded like blasphemy. "I don't remember how you got me here, but I'm going no farther. Shoot me if you want, but I'm married to Ridley Malden now. We had a ceremony and everything!"

"Married?"

She watched the injury she'd caused develop on his face. Yes, she was back in control of this weak man.

"He's a real man. We're starting a new family. And we don't have to starve in the Garden. You never did know what you were doing out here. Why would I go back to all that with you and Rory?"

"But Rory's your son. Don't you . . . want *him* anymore?"

"Of course I want him, but my happiness comes first. I'm learning to love myself again. Can't you see that? I have to live my best life. Don't you get it, Oliver? I'm done with you. I'm the mayor's wife now. I'm *somebody*. They respect me. You never did that for me."

"I . . ." Oliver mumbled words through his obvious pain, but Milli couldn't make them out since he was on the verge of tears.

"Tell me which way to the Garden. I'll return there myself."

"Rory's that way." He pointed. "But I won't bring him back to the Garden."

"I don't care." Milli raised her head. "Keep him if you want him. Malden says he's a weak runt, anyway. He doesn't resemble what the Garden wants to project—our image of perfect health, breeding, and honor."

"Milli, you have health problems, too, like everyone else. You're not perfect. For months, all you did was cry and hide."

"That's because you wouldn't take care of me! Malden takes care of me. I have a purpose now. I'm a Garden advocate, a Sympathy Agent."

"A murderer."

"You would never understand." She cursed him. "We have a vision for humanity that requires making sacrifices."

"Sacrifices like Sazon? We found him in the orchard. Milli, you guys tied him up to die like an animal!"

"It's humane and natural to die when you can't function any longer for your community. Malden says—"

"No!" He held up his hand. "I've heard it myself. All he's told you are lies. I don't want to hear them again. You're confused, Milli. Levi and I risked our lives to get you away from there, to take you to live with normal people. Doesn't that mean anything to you?"

"Normal people?" She cackled. "You mean people overwhelmed with disease and weakness? People who overwhelm their resources because they breed like rats? No, I'm part of the new system. I believe in the quality of life. *My* quality of life! You can't force me to go back to the old way. I'll fight you!"

She regripped her asphalt weapon. Syringe or not, she could still kill him. He was an enemy of the Garden's protocols. There was no reason he should live. Malden had told her that people who resisted the Garden's sympathy were mentally ill. And the mentally ill couldn't enjoy any kind of quality of life. They needed to die, for everyone's good.

Certain he wouldn't harm her in return, Milli attacked, swinging her weapon left and right, then in a stabbing motion as he backed up. When he stumbled and fell over backwards, she was immediately on top of him.

But Oliver caught her wrists as she snarled and spit at him. He was stronger than she'd imagined. So much so that she fought to get away now rather than trying to kill him.

With a burst of energy, she kneed him and pushed away. Though she'd lost her weapon in the scuffle, she backed away on her feet, finally free. She rubbed her wrists as he rolled over and stood upright. He didn't seem to be injured by her assault, but the look in his eyes seemed to show pity.

"I don't ever want to see you again!" She detested that tears were streaming from her eyes, but they weren't tears of fear as during previous months. They were tears of hatred. *"Leave me alone!"*

He stared open-mouthed as she backed away, then she turned and ran. Since he'd pointed out the direction of downtown, she now had an idea of where the Garden was. All she had to do was follow the Stillwater River to the compound, and she'd be back with her own kind.

Sure enough, ten minutes later, the gates of the Garden came into sight. But that wasn't all. Milli stopped walking in the middle of the street when she noticed Sazon collapsed in the arms of a young, blond man on the curb. The stranger seemed familiar, as if she'd seen him somewhere recently, even interacted with him, but her memory was spotty. The place they'd chosen to rest was filthy, where garbage had been washed in a recent rain and piled against a broken grocery cart. The more she peered at the stranger caring for Sazon, the more she realized who he was from Oliver's description. It had to be Levi Caspertein, who looked like his father, Titus, the outsider who'd visited the chapel with Emily.

Creeping closer, Milli stood directly in front of where the two men sat. Sazon's breath came in gasps. Levi held the man's head in one hand, his other rested on the dying man's chest. He was definitely dying. Milli remembered the moment the day before when she'd injected him. The loss of Sazon's eye made him unfit to live among healthy people.

"Rest in the arms of your Shepherd," Levi said softly to Sazon. "Trust in Him to take you safely home to eternity. You're His child now. Enjoy His peace in these last moments. You are not alone . . ."

Milli felt embarrassed to witness such an intimate moment. Sazon had taught her to kill, and now, he was this . . . big child in this other man's arms.

Levi's words were so full of something profound that Milli was comforted deep inside. But she resisted such a sentiment. The Garden held the answers, not God or

Jesus. Sazon would die now, and when Malden and his new army of Sympathy Agents reached downtown—the Casperteins would die as well. The Garden meant life. Everything else meant death.

Sazon's chest rose twice sharply, then he exhaled a long breath and was still. Levi's bowed head slowly lifted to acknowledge her presence where she stood before him.

"You're going back in there?" he asked.

"Yes." Milli clenched her teeth. "Don't try to stop me."

"No, you've chosen what you want right now." Levi sighed, his eyes dry but so sad, too sad for a man so young and strong. "When you're ready, you can come downtown. My family will receive you and help you. But don't bother coming with your syringes. We know who you people are."

Though Milli didn't respond, in her heart she wanted to prove him wrong—that she would find a way with Malden to get downtown and kill those unworthy to live.

She continued to the Garden gate, and someone inside must've been watching, because it opened for her to enter. When she looked back, Levi was carrying muscled Sazon down the street.

Cursing, Milli entered the Garden—her home, her family, her heart. Nothing and no one outside mattered to her any longer.

Chapter Eight

As soon as the radio crackled with Levi's voice, Titus knew his son was back in speaking range.

"Come again, Levi." Titus adjusted a couple knobs on the radio console in the back room of the top floor apartment at ELM. "Come in, Levi. Say again. Over."

"We're coming home," Levi said more clearly. "It's me, Oliver, and two others. Over."

Titus heard the tone of his son's voice. Weariness, but maybe disappointment as well. He hadn't named Milli, just two others. Apparently, Oliver hadn't been able to convince his girlfriend to return with him. Young chess prodigy Rory would grow up without his mother, it seemed, but there were plenty of caring mothers in the ELM building to keep the youngster loved and guided.

"Understood. See you at the gate. Out."

He left the radio room wherein he still monitored several frequencies an hour or two each day. Annette was in the kitchen, where she spent most of her evenings organizing the following day's cooking or baking needs for families in the Hopefuls' and Overcomers' buildings.

"Already done for the night?" Annette turned only halfway from the counter to acknowledge him, then frowned at a wrinkled page of recipes. "I think I figured out what to do with all those zucchinis. Here's a recipe for apple pie—made from zucchini! Serious! It says you won't know the difference! And I'm going to call it Zapple Pie."

"Zapple Pie." Titus chuckled. "It ain't easy reinventing America's favorite dessert."

Standing against the fridge for a few seconds, he watched her work tirelessly to care for others day after day. Finally, she turned from the counter.

"So? What's on your mind?" She crossed her arms and smiled knowingly. "I thought it was your tradition, after checking the radio, to fall asleep while pretending to read in the living room soft chair."

"It ain't easy being so predictable. But not tonight." He stepped close and took her by the shoulders. "Tonight, we'll be debriefing Levi. He's minutes away."

"Levi?" Her eyes opened wider. "He's back in range? Why didn't you say? Is he okay? Is he injured? Should we—"

"Why don't we just go downstairs and welcome him home. He didn't say anything was wrong except that he's returning with Oliver and two others. No Milli, it seems."

"That's it?" She groaned. "Oliver's probably heartbroken. Well, wake everyone up! Let's go!"

"It's almost eleven at night, Annette." Titus picked up his rifle as they left the apartment and knocked on Carla's door. "She's the only one I think who won't want to miss this."

"True," Annette considered. "Wynter needs her rest with the baby on the way. And Oleg and Chevy worked all day getting those dollies working next door."

Carla opened the door in sweats and a ponytail, her facial scars on full display, but Titus had noticed she'd become less conscious of her appearance.

"Levi's back," Annette told her.

"I'll get my jacket." Carla grabbed an ammo vest and her rifle beside the door. "Is he okay?"

"No reason to think otherwise." Titus pulled on gloves to man the dolly cable. "His voice sounded strong on the radio. Probably just tired."

When the three reached the courtyard, they hustled with flashlights to the east entrance, manned by two volunteers from the Hopefuls. Everyone was taking the threats of the Garden and the Dooley Gang seriously. Titus visited with the two sentries for a few minutes until he noticed Carla run beyond the gate and into the street beyond. Annette followed her as four weary figures drew closer in the starlit darkness.

Although Oliver was new to their number, he was a professing believer now, so he was equally smothered by both women's attention. Titus was next, shaking each man's hand in turn, first Oliver and then Levi's. He freed Oliver of his pack to carry it into the perimeter for him, and Carla took Levi's. Finally, Levi introduced two newcomers, Veck and Hilda Marly.

"No problems here?" Levi asked Titus as Annette immediately took charge of the two new arrivals. "Dooley didn't come back?"

"Not yet." Titus sensed a change in his son's demeanor. "No strangers, either. We've got pairs of men at all the gates now, armed with whistles and bells. Word will get out. We're willing to help anyone, but we won't stop guarding those under our protection."

"Was it a long walk back?" Carla asked Oliver. "We didn't expect you guys back until tomorrow."

"I just want to sleep for a week," Oliver said, "even though we were only gone a day. Rory's okay?"

"Yep, I put him to bed myself," Annette said, "in Levi's bed. We can go get him, unless you want to let him sleep. I'd like to get Veck and Hilda moved into the Overcomers' building."

"Nah, let him sleep." Oliver took his pack from Titus as he parted ways with Annette and the new couple for the other building. "I'll come get him in the morning if that's okay."

"Good night, Oliver." Titus waved. "We'll talk things over tomorrow."

Oliver waved back and trudged away, his head down as he followed Annette and the other two.

Titus and Carla waited until they were walking together into the ELM building before they insisted at the dolly that Levi tell them what had happened with Milli, their mission objective.

"She just wouldn't come with us." Levi rested his hands on his hips. "We took on a lot of gunfire and fought for our lives to get out of the Garden with her. But in the end, she battled with Oliver and returned. That place has a serious hold on her."

"It's all the food they grow, probably," Carla said.

"No, it's more than the veggies and fruit," Levi said. "It's their beliefs that have enslaved them.

"Like Chevy said happened before Pan-Day—people convince themselves that they're choosing life even as they're murdering people."

"A shootout, huh?" Titus clucked his tongue. "Will they retaliate?"

"I think so—in their own way." Levi pressed his fingers on his stomach. Titus noticed and wondered if he'd been wounded, but he had no visible injury or blood on his vest. "They're assassins, and they're already stronger now than when you were there, Dad. Everyone has a syringe. They're recruiting and training. And I saw more firearms than you told me to expect."

"They're getting more organized." Titus rubbed his jaw. "We should probably warn Coronado Island. About Dooley, too. Even if we don't see eye-to-eye with General Brogdon on most things, they're the local authorities here, so they should be notified of a dangerous death cult a few hours' walk from the bay."

"But I do have some good news." Levi's eyes brightened in the light of the flashlights. "Remember our old friend, Sazon? He went back to the Garden yesterday with only one eye. They couldn't accept that, so they injected him and tied him out in the orchard to die."

"How sick!" Carla gasped. "Did you help him?"

"Yeah, I got him out." Levi smiled sadly and nodded. "But God had already done the work on that guy's heart. He trusted in the Gospel before he died around noon today. I buried him in a sunny lot where a school had burned down."

"Praise God," Titus said. "All the destruction of life and property around us, and big ol' Sazon comes to Christ. Good work, Levi. We might suffer a lot of loss in this world, but when a soul is won to Jesus, the losses become insignificant."

"It was tough holding him in my arms as he died." Levi shook his head. "And with Milli leaving Oliver? I guess it was a hard day all around."

Embracing his son, Titus had never been prouder of him than in that moment—seeing things from God's perspective even though everything in the mission seemed to have gone wrong.

Carla clung to Levi as the three rose together in the dolly. Titus knew that Annette still didn't like the way Carla was so close to her son, but he knew Levi had drawn the line for the older woman. She was like a relative to him, nothing more. Besides, Carla had clearly set her sights on their resident Russian, Oleg, who was closer to her age.

The next morning, Levi was up early and off to the bay to join the morning's fishing fleet before Titus even left his apartment. Now without Dusty, Titus guessed his son was feeling the weight of his recent losses. He knew God would both comfort and counsel him through this time. Levi would become a better leader by learning how to deal with death and loss God's way, rather than becoming bitter and growing old with resentment.

Titus made his rounds, checking on the three perimeter sentry shifts and encouraging the men in their new posts. Oleg and Chevy were adjusting the dolly in the Overcomers' building, or Building Three, as it was also called. Carla offered an armed escort for a goat foraging party of women and two goats on leashes, and Annette had invited newcomer Fran Quill to join her in the kitchen to prepare food items for the newcomers, Veck and Hilda.

In the courtyard, Gabby was incoherently ordering Conrad to sweep up the sand that had overflowed the children's sandbox, and Wes was teaching a discipleship class in front of the Hopefuls' building, filling in for Chevy while the mechanic was installing another dolly.

As Titus was returning to the ELM building for lunch and a stint with the radio upstairs, he noticed Levi approaching early from the fishing crew. Normally, Levi stayed with the crew until the fish were cleaned and they returned all together. But Levi was alone.

Crossing the courtyard, Levi stumbled and dropped his rifle, yet continued forward. Titus knew something was wrong and ran to his son. He caught him as Levi collapsed.

"What's wrong?" Titus peripherally checked Levi's body for a gunshot or other serious injury. "Levi, talk to me! *Annette!* Someone get Annette!"

Levi's mouth moved as he tried to speak, but Titus could make out no words.

"I don't understand, Levi. Something happened on the boat? Were you attacked?"

Levi strained, then exhaled. His eyes closed and he went limp in Titus' arms.

Titus glanced toward the bay. He'd heard no gunshots. No one had called him on the handheld radio. From what he could see of the north shore, everyone was still working on processing the day's catch. Maybe Levi had excused himself early if he wasn't feeling well.

Meridia! But no, Titus thought. This couldn't be the virus. He had no symptoms. Meridia was a slow killer, not suddenly striking a person like this. This was something else . . .

His stomach! Titus remembered Levi had been rubbing his stomach the night before. He unzipped Levi's vest and lifted his shirt. For several seconds, he stared at a tiny, red spot surrounded by pinkish skin. Levi had said nothing about being injected, or even being close enough to anyone at the Garden to be injected by them. However, the needle injection site in his belly was unmistakable.

"Please, Lord, not my son . . ." Titus bowed his head. He heard Annette coming—with many others. Levi was beloved by everyone. ELM had no greater hero.

Levi Caspertein had been poisoned by the Garden assassins!

✝

Inside the Garden, Neil Dooley wiped his nose as he stood on the path next to the iron gate. His nose always ran when his asthma was heightened. At the moment, he was breathing less raspy, but half the night, he'd been doubled over with tears in his eyes as he'd tried to manage his breathing.

The Garden was now quiet, but Dooley had arrived the day before only minutes prior to an intense gun battle that had broken out across the gardens and throughout the orchard trees. The residents of the Garden, in their suits and summer dresses, had run frantically this way and that to find weapons to fight some invader. Minutes into the ruckus, during which Dooley had harbored inside a villa apartment recently offered to him to clean up—he'd heard the name Caspertein. The Casperteins had a presence even here?

The gunfire had ceased the evening before, and the tranquilized residents had woken, streaming in from where they'd fallen all over the Garden property. Dooley knew all about the Caspertein threat, but he said nothing to those who now hosted him. He'd been promised an appointment with the community doctor as soon as she was free from checking the many patients who'd been assaulted by the Casperteins the day before.

Still standing at the gate, Dooley understood why both doors were closed and barred. The Garden's resources needed to be protected. Food, water, and medicine seemed to overflow within the walls, but outside, survivors had nothing. Yet he'd found his way inside! They had to have an inhaler, just one. That's all he wanted!

He placed his palm against the cold metal of the gate. The sweet smells of citrus and flowers in the air were still polluted by the smell of gunpowder. Spent gun shells still littered the path. Those in the Garden were willing to fight for what they had, so bringing the Dooley Gang over the wall or through the gate would be met with resistance. But to his advantage, these people didn't know about his past, the dozens he'd killed. No, it was in the hundreds now. The fires they'd set to the north had killed many in hiding. And ambushes? Travelers burdened with luggage had been his bread and butter for months. That's how he'd come across the Casperteins and the rumors of someone named Maddix Striber.

Cursing, Dooley turned from the gate and faced the Garden property. His losses and defeats due to the Casperteins were behind him now. They'd pay for everything they'd taken from him. He'd even make Fran pay. What had he seen in her, anyway? *Traitor!*

"They're calling for you," said a dark-haired man who stood on a platform on the wall. He pointed up the path at the bridge. The sentry held a rifle and turned his gaze back to the terrain outside the Garden. "They'll take care of you now."

Dooley walked away from the gate, but slowly, his hand on his chest, hoping his asthma didn't hinder him until he found another inhaler. At the bridge, a young man in a suit was waiting for him. Strangely, no one inside the compound was smiling or expressed joy, even though they had rows of vegetables and fruit trees surrounding their buildings. And before him sat compact villas, each with a fountain and flower garden. Nothing had been scorched by fires here, nor drought or even starvation.

Residents in straw hats looked up as he crossed the bridge. Their eyes followed the young man who'd been sent to escort him somewhere. But then the workers looked away, not making eye contact with Dooley or introducing themselves. Maybe they'd experienced more difficult times than Dooley realized to maintain such a place, but by their fashionable clothing, they seemed to be living in absolute luxury. Even the apartment he'd been shown to the evening before had been beautifully furnished—and offered running water!

After Dooley was shown to the chapel, he was left to stand alone in front of the doors. A woman stood high on a ladder as a man held the ladder so she could scrub with a brush at white paint above the door. The paint was fresh, so it was coming off easily, but Dooley recognized what someone had sprayed above the door. It was a tree—surely an elm tree. At least he had something in common with these people—they knew the Casperteins to be an enemy and invader.

A kind-faced man with green eyes emerged from the front doors and carefully walked around the ladder. A young woman joined him and took his arm. She wore a summer dress that seemed to highlight her washed red hair.

"Hi there. I'm Mayor Malden. Ridley Malden. Welcome to the Garden. We apologize for the chaos you witnessed yesterday. That's really uncharacteristic of us here at the Garden."

"It's the way of the world now." Dooley shook the man's hand and nodded politely to the woman who seemed a little withdrawn. "I'm Patrick. Patrick Roland. Wow, I'm overwhelmed by everything I see. Everything's so beautiful. The room you gave me, even these clean clothes—made me cry. We've all lost so much this year, but offering charity to strangers who need help—I'm in your debt."

"Oh, we don't believe in charity here, Patrick." Malden's continued smile showed his amusement. "We believe everyone should contribute to their own wellbeing. That way you owe me nothing and I owe you nothing. Whether you stay here in the Garden or go your own way, we're both square. Have you eaten?"

"I was given a plate of fruit when I arrived yesterday. Thank you." Dooley patted his belly. "Before that, I hadn't eaten in days. But you really have enough for me to stay? Is that an option?"

"We'll find you a responsibility that is your own. You'll earn your citizenship here and adopt our way of life. A couple people have left us recently, so we actually need someone who can maintain our composting piles. They need to be watered a little and aerated each day. It's not hard work, but you'll get to know the landscape by moving from pile to pile, preparing loamy soil for more plants."

"Uh, wow!" Dooley laughed. "You guys don't waste any time, do you? But maybe before I get too busy . . . I could really use a new inhaler."

He drew his old inhaler from his pocket.

"An inhaler?" Malden and the redhead exchanged looks.

"Do you have any new canisters? Asthma has me struggling to breathe, like I'm breathing through a straw. Once I'm breathing better, I'll do any job you want me to do."

"Asthma?" Malden's smile was replaced by a concerned and sympathetic frown. "Of course. With all the activity yesterday, we didn't get a chance to even check your health. Here at the Garden, we give everyone just what's necessary for everyone's best life. None of us wants to be a burden to the whole. Am I right?"

"Right." Dooley chuckled nervously at the strange wording. "I appreciate it."

"In that case, Milli?" Malden turned to the redhead on his arm. "Could you please take Patrick here to see Dr. Ferguson? Let her know he has asthma and make sure he receives his shot."

"A shot?" Dooley bit the inside of his cheek. "I don't need a shot."

"It's for your best," Malden said, his smile returning, "and everyone else's best. Milli?"

"Come along, Patrick." Milli's previous shyness evaporated. She took his arm instead of the mayor's and grinned up at him. "I'll be with you the whole time. Come on. Everything's going to be okay now. We're all about restoration here in the Garden. I can tell you're going to be a part of our efforts here."

Dooley submitted to her gentle lead and walked along a side path toward a villa beyond the chapel. He couldn't believe they'd accepted him. *What gullibility!* So what if they wanted to give him a shot? Unlike ELM, the food and water in this place was obvious and available. No secrets. Yes, given a week or two here, he'd figure out the mayor's weaknesses, exploit them, and maybe become mayor himself! Of course, he'd need the gang for all that. Kid would love this place! They could arrive in ones and twos, slowly invading this haven of luxury until they controlled it all.

"You're sure this doctor has asthma meds?" Dooley asked as they stopped in front of a villa door. "You'd be saving my life!"

"Dr. Ferguson will be able to take good care of you." Milli patted his arm. "Don't worry. We'll all be better off by making sure you're cared for."

✝

Sergeant Dom Lesage walked to the ferry landing that overlooked the bay. The evening sun was setting at his back, which cast the last rays on the tall buildings across the water. He wondered how the Casperteins were faring.

There'd been patrol reports of a couple different gun battles southeast of downtown. The Casperteins were most likely pushing against criminal threats. General Brogdon's orders were clear: wherever the Casperteins were involved, the PSDF was to avoid. ELM was simply too well-armed and organized to bother with.

Though Dom had returned the day before from his recon mission into the South Bay area, he'd told Brogdon he needed another day to recover before he returned to active duty. It was another lie. Like the lie that he'd told Brand Windfield and the O'Sheas. He wasn't really a Caspertein, but he wished he were. Maybe God had destined him to be like this—a vicious soldier, both despised and feared by his own troops.

The few days he'd pretended to be Dom Caspertein had been the best days of his life. He'd actually rescued three kidnapped kids! But he couldn't tell anyone, at least no one on the island. Levi would appreciate the recounting of his experience, but he hadn't seen the young Caspertein soldier for over two months.

Somehow, Dom needed to find a way out of his life—and join ELM and the Casperteins. He was certain God was calling him to somehow be separate from his old life.

"It ain't easy, Levi," Dom mumbled while admiring the cityscape, "but I'll join you guys someday. Someday, I'll really be Dom Caspertein . . ."

I pray you were blessed by reading Book Two of *The ELM Series, EVE of DESPAIR!* If you enjoyed it, please leave a review wherever you bought this book. It would help me to know if I hit the mark with this new series. Thank you! *~David Telbat*

WHAT'S NEXT?

Book Three of *The ELM Series* is next! On the next page, find an excerpt of *EVE of FEAR*. Enjoy!

EVE of FEAR

Book Three of *The ELM Series*
Excerpt

Sergeant Dom Lesage stood in the dark. Lights were on farther up Orange Avenue and beyond at Hotel Del Coronado, the Pacific States Defense Force's head-quarters. But near the ferry landing overlooking San Diego Bay, the island was shadowed and quiet.

"So close!" Dom felt his gut ache with emotion as he gazed at the buildings across the water. There were lights on over there as well, at the Caspertein's ELM compound. His heart was there, with all that Titus Caspertein was offering the survivors left in the city. But Dom was here, committed to the military by his own doing, weighed down by its policies he himself had strengthened, and burdened by his past of bloodshed and other atrocities.

He turned to his right. The Coronado Bay Bridge wasn't lit up, but he could see its length spanning toward the mainland. That bridge was his route to start a new life with the Casperteins, but crossing the bridge wouldn't eliminate his connection to General Brogdon. The man dominated the PSDF, and President Criswell was forced to go along with his general's ambitions. Or maybe Criswell was unaware that Brogdon undermined his authority at every turn.

But Dom wanted to leave behind the politics of the PSDF for good. The community of faith that the Casperteins had built the last eight months appealed to Dom much more. Once, he'd been in conflict with the powerful family, but that had changed when he'd snuck into a neighborhood to the south, feigning to be a Caspertein relative. He'd been accepted by the locals, but they'd even depended on him to live up to the Caspertein code of honor and self-sacrificial zeal. In just a few days, he'd realized what life was really about, which meant his days in the PSDF were numbered. True joy and living courageously was right over there across the bridge, but first, he needed to leave the island.

Starting a new life downtown wouldn't be possible unless he ended his life here.

Turning his back on Seaport Village across the bay, Dom started walking up Orange Avenue. If everything went right in the next hour, he could be knocking on the Casperteins' door by dawn. Every life mattered to God, so every life mattered to the Casperteins.

His sense of urgency to get over there was heightened by the news he'd heard that morning: Levi Caspertein had been in a coma for a month! The son of the infamous Titus Caspertein had already become a force to be reckoned with in the area, so the PSDF was all abuzz with what it could mean for taking back influence from the Casperteins. General Brogdon was always thinking about expanding his control, especially over the area so close to his headquarters.

Dom felt convinced that if he were at ELM, Levi would be revived from his coma. The two had shared a great adventure, and Levi had saved Dom's life from a northern enemy. It was only right, Dom felt, that he should return the favor by saving Levi.

The Coronado neighborhood was quiet that night, now near midnight. Much to the satisfaction of the residents, Brogdon had started up the brewery next to the veterinary hospital. The steady flow of alcohol had made the evenings quite lively, but Dom and other leaders had been drilling the soldiers hard out on the airfield grass. The combatants had learned that if they stayed up too late drinking their miseries away, they'd be even more miserable during readiness drills the next morning.

The majority of the shops, stores, and markets along Orange Avenue had been renovated and were now occupied by military families. There was such fear of the virus and other threats inland that people tried to live as close to the military headquarters as possible. There was no curfew at the time, but Dom had kept sentries on watch on some streets, by Brogdon's orders, to maintain a semblance of security. Dom knew there were flaws in the layout of the island. The shores were vulnerable. An enemy could come ashore by boat in several areas. But he hoped no one knew that. Even though he was leaving the island that night, he didn't want to think of a world without at least some government presence, even if it was a dominating authority like the PSDF.

He stopped suddenly on the street where a Humvee was parked outside a salon transformed into a residence. A uniformed soldier was snoring in the driver's seat of the Humvee. He was supposed to be on watch. Six months earlier, Dom would've publicly whipped the man, then cut his rations for sleeping on watch. But he hadn't struck anyone in weeks. The Casperteins had proven that there were other ways to motivate people to do a job well.

Moving beyond the pub, Dom reached Hotel Del Coronado where his own room was located. But instead of going to his room, he went to the northwest corner where two guards on either side of a door saluted him. He knocked lightly. The general was probably asleep, but an ambitious corporal from Iceland, Rawin Morhaine, had led a patrol inland. Brogdon was always willing to be woken by news of supplies or resources being discovered.

Dom heard movement inside, then the door opened a crack. General Galt Brogdon had kept himself fit, even though he spent most of his time indoors. He wasn't as tall as Dom, but Brogdon had a commanding presence—even while sleepy-eyed.

"Sergeant?" Brogdon straightened and opened the door wider. The general had never promoted anyone over sergeant, possibly to protect his own rank. "Did Corporal Morhaine radio in?"

"I wasn't in the comm-room." Dom had rehearsed the coming conversation, but it needed to be spoken in private—so the general could save face. "I didn't see the patrol return yet. May I speak with you? It's important."

"That Morhaine reminds me of you. He's an up-and-comer!" Brogdon left the door open as he turned away and poured himself a drink from a bottle. "Every day, he's in here asking about PSDF structure. We're lucky we got such a wolverine from Riverside after we crushed them, huh?"

"Yes, lucky."

Dom closed the door and stood with his hands folded. He was used to the general embellishing his military exploits. The PSDF hadn't crushed the Riverside military. They'd been decimated by the Meridia Virus, then the Casperteins had encouraged the PSDF to recruit from their survivors to join them at Coronado.

"What's on your mind?" Brogdon didn't offer him a drink. "You look different. You trying to pull off a casual look?"

"Oh." Dom touched his windbreaker. "This is what I wore last month when I went undercover in the South Bay."

"Right. Impersonating a Caspertein. Ingenious."

"Thank you, sir." Dom cleared his throat. "The thing is, I was doing more than an impersonation. It stuck. We need to talk about my resignation. I can just go quietly and—"

"Wait. *Your resignation?*" Brogdon calmly set down his glass, but his voice was full of guarded force. "Sergeant, is this a joke?"

"It's not a joke. I'm . . . no good to you now. I'm not the person I was. I never will be again."

"Where else would you go?" Brogdon chuckled, maybe nervously. "You're a savage, Lesage. No one wrestled this country into submission better than you did. If the troops knew even half the things I've asked you to do to maintain order—"

"I know." Dom nodded. "That's one reason why I need to leave. Those things I did are, well, you could say they're on my conscience."

"*Your conscience?*" Brogdon scoffed. "A jackal doesn't have a conscience, Sergeant! You do what you do because you have to. It's your nature. This country needs a hand of brutal control to be rebuilt. We can make it better, Lesage, you and I. Now, why don't you get some sleep? We'll talk about this in a day or two. You'll see it my way."

Dom stood uncomfortably before the general for a few seconds. He'd heard Brogdon's speech a hundred times since Pan-Day. Perhaps it had meant something to him months earlier, but his heart had been different back then.

"You asked where I'd go if I left," Dom said. "I wouldn't be going far. I'd hope to remain in good contact with you, if you so desire. I want to go downtown. To join the Casperteins."

"*The Casperteins!*" The general's neck seemed to swell.

A knock on the door delayed any further response Brogdon may have had. He shoved Dom aside to reach the door and open it.

"Hello, General!" Corporal Rawin Morhaine was a giant of a man who'd received special permission for his long, Icelandic hair to not be cut. "Sorry to bother you so late, sir, but you said you wanted an update as soon as our patrol returned."

"Yes, yes, come in." Brogdon closed the door after Morhaine, scowled at Dom, then crossed his arms. "Well, let's hear it."

"We received heavy resistance from a number of solitary community outposts between here and Indian Springs."

"Define heavy." Brogdon ordered. "Be specific."

"A mile east of the interstate, we ran into a barricade," Morhaine explained. "They had snipers on the wall. When we used an armored truck to force their gate open, they fired an RPG at us. We lost the truck and four men."

"That's unacceptable, Corporal. That barricade must be destroyed and everyone with it. We can't have pockets of resistance in our own back yard, not if we plan to push to Seattle and the Mississippi Valley."

"Yes, sir. But we can't kill an idea by killing the enemy. The locals who we questioned along the way thought the Casperteins were running things here."

"*What?*" Brogdon frowned at Dom, then looked back at Morhaine. "An example needs to be made, Corporal. Do whatever you must! Let people know the Casperteins are not in charge. We are!"

"Then let me tear down the ELM compound, sir. Let me go downtown."

"Hmm, I don't know." Brogdon turned away, scratched his jaw, and sat on the edge of his desk. "We have an agreement with the Casperteins. And we have a history, even if I do want them brought down. When dealing with them, we've not escaped unscathed. Titus Caspertein was a predator before Pan-Day, and now he's thriving like never before."

"But Levi, the son, is said to be out of the picture now. In a coma or something. Morale is low at ELM. Uh, sir?" Morhaine stepped closer. "This could be our moment. They're weakened. I could use mortars. We could clear ELM out in a single night."

"I wouldn't mind that den of cougars being dispersed." Brogdon's eyes narrowed. "They have only a few riflemen—and most of them are women. But we have to avoid a massacre. Mortars would kill indiscriminately.

President Criswell wouldn't stand for a pile of civilian bodies this close to our capital."

"We could use psychological warfare," Morhaine proposed. "Like we used against you guys when we were trying to move south. And we could impersonate someone else during an attack on ELM."

"Yes, that's what you did to us, I remember," Brogdon said with a sly smile. "I've been meaning to tell you that crimson jacket looks a lot better than the rags Riverside gave you to wear."

"Thank you, sir."

"So, psychological warfare, huh?"

"Harassment measures and fear tactics. The anticipation of war can be as destructive as the collapse of infrastructure, if you don't want me to attack them outright."

"Fear tactics? I don't know . . ." Brogdon shook his head. "The Casperteins are a special breed. They're not like the Christians before Pan-Day, who were easily manipulated and worldly. These are fearless, as far as I can tell."

"Give me a week, sir." Morhaine smirked. "I'll bring them down without firing a shot. Threats and intimidation will break up that Jesus-rabble."

"If you can get us some of their .308 rifles, even better." The general held up his hand. "And if you get a clean shot at Titus Caspertein, take it."

"Yes, sir."

"And Annette Caspertein—I want her here."

"No problem." Morhaine smiled.

"But wait." The general scowled, then glanced at Dom. "This one can no longer be trusted. Especially after what he just heard us say. He was talking about defecting to the Casperteins."

Dom blinked, too slowly realizing Brogdon was exposing him then and there. Morhaine drew his sidearm and held it on Dom.

"What do you want done with him?"

"No, wait, sir," Dom said. "After everything we've been through together?"

"Exactly!" Brogdon sneered. "Put him in isolation until I decide what to do with him. My own sergeant turned by the Casperteins! A total humiliation."

"I promise I'll put them in their place, General." Morhaine opened the door and waved in the guards. "Take this man into custody. Isolation. No one is to talk to him."

Dom submitted his wrists as he was cuffed behind his back. Why had he returned to speak to Brogdon at all? He could've been downtown by now if he'd just packed up and left. Now he knew Morhaine's disdainful plans for ELM, but he wouldn't be able to warn them of what tactics were coming.

The guards led him from the room. Behind him, Dom heard the general speak.

"Corporal, I believe you'll make sergeant if you can follow through downtown."

"I won't let you down, sir," Morhaine promised. "That's a guarantee."

Dom didn't fight his escorts as they led him from the hotel and marched him north to the airfield, where the makeshift brig had been set up—metal containers on the runway asphalt.

Far to the east, the lights at ELM's tall apartment buildings reflected off the bay's water. If only he were over there with them. If only he could be counted among the fearless and uncompromising—those whom Brogdon despised so much!

The End

EVE of FEAR, Excerpt

Character Sketch

Annette Caspertein – Titus' wife and Levi's step-mother; selfless and giving toward all who come to rely on her husband's network

Avery "Chevy" Hewit – A mechanic and evangelist within ELM

Brand Windfield – A lone survivor outside San Diego; handler of search-and-rescue canine named Dizzy

Dom Lesage – Sergeant in the PSDF; strict and brutal with troops and civilians

Dustin "Dusty" Howard – Levi's roommate who recently came to Christ

Emily Pickford – Paraplegic from the Garden; determined to survive at all costs, until her eyes are opened to those costs

Fran Garrick – Neil Dooley's girlfriend; bitter and sharp-tongued, eager for bloodshed and dominance

Jaimie Ferguson – Doctor within the Garden; kind and generous toward her victims as she determines protocols for Mayor Malden

Kid Irling – Dooley gang member; willing and vicious, looking to Dooley's leadership to cause chaos

Levi Caspertein – Son of Titus and Annette; twenty-year-old who's finding his own way for Jesus under his father's leadership of ELM

Neil Dooley – Leader of the Dooley Gang; headquartered in Pepper Park, his methods are wild and deadly

Oleg Saratov – Titus' oldest partner and friend; once an Interpol agent from Russia

Oliver Gleason – Father of Rory and boyfriend of Milli; cautious and hesitant, this survivor yearns for answers about the Bible

Ridley Malden – Mayor of the Garden; sinister and manipulative

Sazon – Head Sympathy Agent in the Garden; muscled, aggressive, logical, lethal

Titus Caspertein – Husband of Annette and father of Levi; leads ELM from the San Diego complex with nearly 100 people

Wes Trimble – Husband of Wynter; one-eyed ex-CIA agent within ELM

Wynter Trimble – Wife of Wes; fussy aunt of Levi and sister of Titus

Glossary

CARE – The Garden's Protocol: <u>C</u>leansing <u>A</u>ll, <u>R</u>estoring <u>E</u>verything

ELM – <u>E</u>very <u>L</u>ive <u>M</u>atters; the name of the Caspertein complex in San Diego and the motto that identifies their Gospel efforts

PSDF – <u>P</u>acific <u>S</u>tates <u>D</u>efense <u>F</u>orces; headquartered on Coronado Island, San Diego

QOLs – <u>Q</u>uality-<u>o</u>f-<u>L</u>ifers; a nickname for the Garden assassins

About the Author

D.I. (David) Telbat is a Christian author best known for his **clean, Suspenseful Fiction with a Faith Focus**. This includes his bestselling and award-winning *COIL Series, Steadfast Series, Last Dawn Series, Hidden Humanity, Called To Gobi*, and other Christian Suspense and End Times novels. He wrote his first book at age 14, and he hasn't stopped since!

David studied writing in school and worked for a time in the newspaper field. Getting into serious trouble with the law as a young man became a turning point in his life. The Lord used that experience to draw David into a personal relationship with Him. Re-focusing his life for Christ, he now seeks to honor God with his life and writing by doing what he loves most—writing and Christian ministry.

Subscribe to receive David Telbat's FREE, bi-weekly **D.I. Telbat Newsletter** with one of his Christian short stories, or an Author Reflection, or his Novel News Update. Also receive **exclusive subscriber gifts**, such as his ***Three For Free—three-novels-in-one eBook***! Come join the adventure, discover D.I. Telbat books, and subscribe to his newsletter through his <u>ditelbat.com</u> site or his author pages at <u>books2read.com/ditelbat/</u>.

www.ingramcontent.com/pod-product-compliance
Lightning Source LLC
Chambersburg PA
CBHW020344120726

47904CB00002B/450